'Alex?' Luna whispered.

'Stall them,' I whispered back. 'We need ninety seconds.'

'Verus,' Cinder growled as he came into range. 'Should have kept running.'

'Who's running?' I asked lightly. I stood slightly between Cinder and Luna. Lisa was off to one side, looking nervously between us, forgotten by everyone.

'No,' Cinder said. His voice was low and dangerous. 'You won't bluff me this time.' He opened one hand, half concealed down by his side, and dark fire flared up around his fingers, a red-black aura that caused the light to dim. 'You twitch, I'll burn you to ash. Let's see you trick your way out of that.'

He wasn't kidding; in dozens of the futures unfolding before us I could see Cinder lunging forward to do exactly that. But the very fact that he was willing to try something so crude was oddly reassuring – if he had anything else up his sleeve, he wouldn't be making the threat. 'You know, Cinder,' I said, 'I hate to point it out, but there's about a hundred people watching you.'

'No one'll miss you,' Cinder growled.

'Wrong,' I said calmly. 'Or haven't you heard? I'm in demand these days.'

BY BENEDICT JACKA

*Alex Versus novels*
Fated
Cursed
Taken
Chosen

# BENEDICT JACKA

# FATED

www.orbitbooks.net

ORBIT

First published in Great Britain in 2012 by Orbit
Reprinted 2012 (four times), 2013 (twice)

A CIP catalogue record for this book
is available from the British Library.

ISBN 978-0-356-50024-9

Typeset in Garamond 3 by
Palimpsest Book Production Limited, Falkirk, Stirlingshire
Printed and bound by CPI Group (UK) Ltd, Croydon, CR0 4YY

Papers used by Orbit are from well-managed forests
and other responsible sources.

 MIX
Paper from
responsible sources
FSC® C104740
www.fsc.org

Orbit
An imprint of
Little, Brown Book Group
100 Victoria Embankment
London EC4Y 0DY

An Hachette UK Company
www.hachette.co.uk

www.orbitbooks.net

It was a slow day, so I was reading a book at my desk and seeing into the future.

There were only two customers in the shop. One was a student with scraggly hair and a nervous way of glancing over his shoulder. He was standing by the herb and powder rack and had decided what to buy ten minutes ago but was still working up the nerve to ask me about it. The other customer was a kid wearing a Linkin Park T-shirt who'd picked out a crystal ball but wasn't going to bring it to the counter until the other guy had left.

The kid had come on a bicycle, and in fifteen minutes a traffic warden was going to come by and ticket him for locking his bike to the railings. After that I was going to get a call I didn't want to be disturbed for, so I set my paperback down on my desk and looked at the student. 'Anything I can help you with?'

He started and came over, glancing back at the kid and dropping his voice slightly. 'Um, hey. Do you—?'

'No. I don't sell spellbooks.'

'Not even—?'

'No.'

'Is there, um, any way I could check?'

'The spell you're thinking of isn't going to do any harm. Just try it and then go talk to the girl and see what happens.'

The student stared at me. 'You knew that just from these?'

I hadn't even been paying attention to the herbs in his hand, but that was as good an explanation as any. 'Want a bag?'

He put verbena, myrrh and incense into the bag I gave him and paid for it while still giving me an awestruck look, then left. As soon as the door swung shut, the other kid came over and asked me the price for the second biggest crystal ball, trying to sound casual. I didn't bother checking to see what he was going to use it for – about the only way you can hurt yourself with a crystal ball is by hitting yourself over the head with it, which is more than I can say for some of the things I sell. Once the kid had let himself out, hefting his paper bag, I got up, walked over and flipped the sign on the door from OPEN to CLOSED. Through the window, I saw the kid unlock his bike and ride off. About thirty seconds later a traffic warden walked by.

My shop is in a district in the north centre of London called Camden Town. There's a spot where the canal, three bridges and two railway lines all meet and tangle together in a kind of urban reef-knot, and my street is right in the middle. The bridges and the canal do a good job of fencing the area in, making it into a kind of oasis in the middle of the city. Apart from the trains, it's surprisingly quiet. I like to go up onto the roof sometimes and look around over the canal and the funny-shaped rooftops. Sometimes in the evenings and early mornings, when the traffic's muted and the light's faded, it feels almost like a gateway to another world.

The sign above my door says 'Arcana Emporium'. Underneath is a smaller sign with some of the things I sell – implements, reagents, focus items, that sort of thing.

You'd think it would be easier just to say 'magic shop', but I got sick of the endless stream of people asking for break-away hoops and marked cards. Finally I worked out a deal with a stage magic store half a mile away, and now I keep a box of their business cards on the counter to hand out to anyone who comes in asking for the latest book by David Blaine. The kids go away happy, and I get some peace and quiet.

My name is Alex Verus. It's not the name I was born with, but that's another story. I'm a mage; a diviner. Some people call mages like me oracles, or seers, or probability mages if they want to be really wordy, and that's fine too, just as long as they don't call me a 'fortune teller'. I'm not the only mage in the country, but as far as I know I'm the only one who runs a shop.

Mages like me aren't common, but we aren't as rare as you might think either. We look the same as anyone else, and if you passed one of us on the street odds are you'd never know it. Only if you were very observant would you notice something a little off, a little strange, and by the time you took another look, we'd be gone. It's another world, hidden within your own, and most of those who live in it don't like visitors.

Those of us who *do* like visitors have to advertise, and it's tricky to find a way of doing it that doesn't make you sound crazy. The majority rely on word of mouth, though younger mages use the internet. I've even heard of one guy in Chicago who advertises in the phone book under 'Wizard', though that's probably an urban legend. Me, I have my shop. Wiccans and pagans and New-Agers are common enough nowadays that people accept the idea of a magic shop, or at least they understand that the weirdos have to buy their stuff from somewhere. Of course, they take for granted that it's all a con and that the stuff in my shop is no more magical than an old pair of socks, and for the most part they're right. But the stuff in my shop that isn't magical is good camouflage for the stuff that is, like the thing sitting upstairs in a little blue lacquered cylinder that can grant any five wishes you ask. If *that* ever got out, I'd have much worse problems than the occasional snigger.

The futures had settled and the phone was going to ring in about thirty seconds. I settled down comfortably and, when the phone rang, let it go twice before picking up. 'Hey.'

'Hi, Alex,' Luna's voice said into my ear. 'Are you busy?'

'Not even a little. How's it going?'

'Can I ask a favour? I was going through a place in Clapham and found something. Can I bring it over?'

'Right now?'

'That's not a problem, is it?'

'Not really. Is there a rush?'

'No. Well . . .' Luna hesitated. 'This thing makes me a bit nervous. I'd feel better if it was with you.'

I didn't even have to think about it. Like I said, it was a slow day. 'You remember the way to the park?'

'The one near your shop?'

'I'll meet you there. Where are you?'

'Still in Clapham. I'm just about to get on my bike.'

'So one and a half hours. You can make it before sunset if you hurry.'

'I think I *am* going to hurry. I'm not sure . . .' Luna's voice trailed off, then firmed. 'Okay. See you soon.'

She broke the connection. I held the phone in my hand, looking at the display. Luna works for me on a part-time basis, finding items for me to sell, though I don't think she does it for the money. Either way, I couldn't remember her being this nervous about one. It made me wonder exactly what she was carrying.

You can think of magical talent as a pyramid. Making up the lowest and biggest layer are the normals. If magic is colours, these are the people born colour-blind: they don't know anything about magic and they don't want to, thank you very much. They've got plenty of things to deal with already, and if they *do* see anything that might shake the way they look at things, they convince themselves they didn't see it double-quick. This is maybe ninety per cent of the adult civilised world.

Next up on the pyramid are the sensitives, the ones who aren't colour-blind. Sensitives are blessed (or cursed, depending how you look at it) with a wider spectrum of vision than normals. They can feel the presence of magic, the distant power in the sun and the earth and the stars, the warmth and stability of an old family home, the lingering wisps of death and horror at a Dark ritual site. Most often they don't have the words to describe what they feel, but two sensitives can recognise each other by a kind of empathy, and it makes a powerful bond. Have you ever felt a connection to someone, as though you shared some-thing even though you didn't know what it was? It's like that.

Above the sensitives on the magical pecking order are the adepts. These guys are only one per cent or so, but unlike sensitives they can actually channel magic in a subtle way. Often it's so subtle they don't even know they're doing it; they might be 'lucky' at cards, or very good at 'guessing' what's on another person's mind, but it's mild enough that they just think they're born lucky or perceptive. But sometimes they figure out what they're doing and start developing it, and some of these guys can get pretty impressive within their specific field.

And then there are the mages.

Luna's somewhere between sensitive and adept. It's hard even for me to know which, as she has some . . . unique characteristics that make her difficult to categorise, not to mention dangerous. But she's also one of my very few friends, and I was looking forward to seeing her. Her tone of voice had left me concerned so I looked into the future and was glad to see she was going to arrive in an hour and a half, right on time.

In the process, though, I noticed something that annoyed me: someone else was going to come through the door in a couple of minutes, despite the fact I'd just flipped my sign to say CLOSED. Camden gets a lot of tourists, and there's always the one guy who figures opening hours don't apply to him. I didn't want to walk all the way over and lock the door, so I just sat watching the street grumpily until a figure appeared outside the door and pushed it open. It was a man wearing pressed trousers and a shirt with a tie. The bell above the door rang musically as he stepped inside and raised his eyebrows. 'Hello, Alex.'

As soon as he spoke I recognised who it was. A rush of adrenaline went through me as I spread my senses out to cover the shop and the street outside. My right hand shifted down a few inches to rest on the shelf under my desk. I couldn't sense any attack but that didn't necessarily mean anything.

Lyle just stood there, looking at me. 'Well?' he said. 'Aren't you going to invite me in?'

It had been more than four years since I'd seen Lyle but he looked the same as I remembered. He was about as old as me, with a slim build, short black hair and a slight olive tint to his skin that hinted at a Mediterranean ancestor somewhere in his family tree. His clothes were expensive and he wore them with a sort of casual elegance I knew I'd never be able to match. Lyle had always known how to look good.

'Who else is here?' I said.

Lyle sighed. 'No one. Good grief, Alex, have you really gotten this paranoid?'

I checked and rechecked and confirmed what he was saying. As far as I could tell, Lyle was the only other mage nearby. Besides, as my heartbeat began to slow, I realised that if the Council was planning an attack, Lyle was the last person they'd send. Suddenly I *did* feel paranoid.

Of course, that didn't mean I was happy to see him or anything. Lyle began walking forward and I spoke sharply. 'Stay there.'

Lyle stopped and looked quizzically at me. 'So?' he said when I didn't react. He was standing in the middle of my shop in between the reagents and the shelves full of candles and bells. 'Are we going to stand and stare at each other?'

'How about you tell me why you're here?'

'I was hoping for a more comfortable place to talk.' Lyle tilted his head. 'What about upstairs?'

'No.'

'Were you about to eat?'

I pushed my chair back and rose to my feet. 'Let's go for a walk.'

Once we were outside I breathed a little easier. There's a roped-off section to one side of my shop that contains actual magic items: focuses, residuals, and one-shots. They'd been out of sight from where Lyle had been standing, but a few more steps and he couldn't have missed them. None were powerful enough to make him think twice, but it wouldn't take him long to put two and two together and figure out that if I had that many minor items, then I ought to have some major ones too. And I'd just as soon that particular bit of information didn't get back to the Council.

It was late spring and the London weather was mild enough to make walking a pleasure rather than a chore. Camden's always busy, even when the market's closed, but the buildings and bridges here have a dampening effect on stray sounds. I led Lyle down an alley to the canalside walk, and then stopped, leaning against the balustrade. As I walked I scanned the area thoroughly, both present and future, but came up empty. As far as I could tell, Lyle was on his own.

I've known Lyle for more than ten years. He was an apprentice when we first met, awkward and eager, hurrying along in the footsteps of his Council master. Even then there was never any question but that he'd try for the Council, but we were friends, if not close. At least for a little while. Then I had my falling out with Richard Drakh.

I don't really like to think about what happened in the year after that. There are some things so horrible you never really get over them; they make a kind of burnt-out waste-land in your memory, and all you can do is try to move on. Lyle wasn't directly responsible for the things that happened to me and the others in Richard's mansion, but he had a pretty good idea of what was going on, just like the rest of the Council. At least, they *would* have had a good idea if they'd allowed themselves to think about it.

Instead they avoided the subject and waited for me to do the convenient thing and vanish.

Lyle's not my friend any more.

Now he was standing next to me, brushing off the balustrade before leaning on it, making sure none of the dirt got on his jacket. The walkway ran alongside the canal, following the curve of the canal out of sight. The water was dark and broken by choppy waves. It was an overcast day, the sunlight shining only dimly through the grey cloud.

'Well,' Lyle said eventually, 'if you don't want to chat, shall we get down to business?'

'I don't think we've got much to chat about, do you?'

'The Council would like to employ your services.'

I blinked at that. 'You're here officially?'

'Not exactly. There was some . . . disagreement on how best to proceed. The Council couldn't come to a full agreement—'

'The Council can't come to a full agreement on when to have dinner.'

'—on the best course of action,' Lyle finished smoothly. 'Consulting a diviner was considered as an interim measure.'

'Consulting *a* diviner?' I asked, suddenly suspicious. The Council and I aren't exactly on the best of terms. 'Me specifically?'

'As you know, the Council rarely requests—'

'What about Alaundo? I thought he was their go-to guy when they wanted a seer.'

'I'm afraid I can't discuss closed Council proceedings.'

'Once you start going door to door, it isn't closed proceedings any more, is it? Come on, Lyle. I'm sure as hell not going to agree to anything unless I know why you're here.'

Lyle blew out an irritated breath. 'Master Alaundo is currently on extended research.'

'So he turned you down? What about Helikaon?'

'He's otherwise occupied.'

'And that guy from the Netherlands? Dutch Jake or whatever he was called. I'm pretty sure he did divination work for—'

'Alex,' Lyle said. 'Don't run through every diviner in the British Isles. I know the list as well as you do.'

I grinned. 'I'm the only one you can find, aren't I? That's why you're coming here.' My eyes narrowed. 'And the Council doesn't even know. They wouldn't have agreed to trust me with official business.'

'I don't appreciate threats,' Lyle said stiffly. 'And I'd appreciate it if you didn't use your abilities for these matters.'

'You think I needed magic to figure that out?' Annoying Lyle was satisfying, but I knew it was risky to push him too far. 'Okay. So what does the Council want so badly you're willing to risk coming to me?'

Lyle took a moment to straighten his tie. 'I assume you're aware of the Arrancar ruling?'

I looked at him blankly.

'It's been common knowledge for months.'

'Common knowledge to whom?'

Lyle let out an irritated breath. 'As a consequence of the Arrancar conclave, mages are required to report all significant archaeological discoveries of arcana to the Council. Recently, a new discovery was reported—'

'Reported?'

'—and subjected to a preliminary investigation. The investigation team have concluded quite definitely that it's a Precursor relic.'

I looked up at that. 'Functional?'

'Yes.'

'What kind?'

'They weren't able to determine.'

'It's sealed? I'm surprised they didn't just force it.'

Lyle hesitated.

'Oh,' I said, catching on. 'They *did* try to force it. What happened?'

'I'm afraid that's confidential.'

'A ward? Guardian?'

'In any case, a new investigation team is being formed. It was . . . considered necessary for them to have access to the abilities of a diviner.'

'And you want me on the team?'

'Not exactly.' Lyle paused. 'You'll be an independent agent, reporting to me. I'll pass on your recommendations to the investigators.'

I frowned. 'What?'

Lyle cleared his throat. 'Unfortunately it wouldn't be feasible for you to join the team directly. The Council wouldn't be able to clear you. But if you accept, I can promise I'll tell you everything you need to know.'

I turned away from Lyle, looking out over the canal. The rumble of an engine echoed around the brick walls from downstream and a barge came into view, chugging along. It was painted yellow and red. The man at the tiller didn't give us a glance as he passed. Lyle stayed quiet as the barge went by and disappeared around the bend of the canal. A breeze blew along the pathway, ruffling my hair.

I still didn't speak. Lyle coughed. A pair of seagulls flew overhead, after the barge, calling with loud, discordant voices: *arrrh, arrrh.*

'Alex?' Lyle asked.

'Sorry,' I said. 'Not interested.'

'If it's a question of money . . .'

'No, I just don't like the deal.'

'Why?'

'Because it stinks.'

'Look, you have to be realistic. There's no way the Council would give you clearance to—'

'If the Council doesn't want to give me clearance, you shouldn't be coming to me in the first place.' I turned to look at Lyle. 'What's your idea? They need the information badly enough that they won't care about where you're getting it? I think sooner or later they'd start asking questions, and you'd cut me loose to avoid the flak. I'm not interested in being your fall guy.'

Lyle blew out a breath. 'Why are you being so irrational about this? I'm giving you a chance to get back into the Council's favour.' He glanced around at the concrete and the grey skies. 'Given the alternative . . .'

'Well, since you bring it up, it just so happens that I'm not especially interested in getting back into the Council's favour.'

'That's ridiculous. The Council represents all of the mages in the country.'

'Yeah, all the mages. That's the problem.'

'This is about that business with Drakh, isn't it?' Lyle said. He rolled his eyes. 'Jesus, Alex, it was ten years ago. Get over it.'

'It doesn't matter when it was,' I said tightly. 'The Council haven't gotten better. They've gotten worse.'

'We've had ten years of peace. That's your idea of "worse"?'

'The reason you've had peace is because you and the

Council let the Dark mages do whatever they want.' I glared at Lyle. 'You know what they do to the people in their power. Why don't you ask *them* how good a deal they think it is?'

'We're not starting another war, Alex. The Council isn't going anywhere, and neither are the mages that are a part of it, Light or Dark. You're just going to have to accept that.'

I took a breath and looked out over the canal, listening to the distant cries of the seagulls. When I spoke again my voice was steady. 'The answer's no. Find someone else.'

Lyle made a disgusted noise. 'I should have known.' He stepped away and gave me a look. 'You're living in the past. Grow up.'

I watched Lyle walk off. He didn't look back. Once he'd disappeared around the corner I turned back to the canal.

So long as magic has existed, there's been a split between the two paths: the Light mages and the Dark. Sometimes they've existed in uneasy truce; sometimes there have been conflicts. The last and greatest was called the Gate Rune War, and it happened forty years before I was born. It was a faction of the Dark mages against almost all of the Light, and the prize to the winner was total dominion over Earth. The Light side won – sort of. They stopped the Dark mages and killed their leaders, but by the time it was over most of the Light battle mages were dead as well. The Light survivors didn't want to fight any more wars, and the surviving Dark mages were allowed to regroup. Years passed. The old warriors were replaced by a new generation of mages who thought that peace was the natural order of things.

By the time I arrived on the scene, Council policy was

'live and let live'. Dark mages were tolerated so long as they didn't go after Light mages, and vice versa. There was a set of rules called the Concord that governed how mages could and couldn't act towards each other. The Concord didn't draw any distinction between Light and Dark, and there was a growing feeling that the division between Light and Dark was out-of-date. At the time, I thought it made a lot of sense. My own master, Richard Drakh, was a Dark mage, and I didn't see why Light and Dark mages couldn't get along.

I changed my mind after I had my falling-out with Richard, but by then it was too late. That was when I discovered that while the Concord had all sorts of rules for how mages were allowed to treat each other, it didn't have any rules at all for how they were allowed to treat their *apprentices*. After I escaped, I went to Lyle and the Council. They didn't want to know. I was left alone, with an angry Dark mage after me.

Even now if I close my eyes I can still remember that time, the horrible paralysing fear. It's impossible to understand unless you've experienced it – the terror of being hunted by something crueller and stronger than you. I was barely out of my teens, hardly able to look after myself, much less go face to face with someone like Richard. Now I look back on it I can see the Council was really just waiting for Richard to get rid of me and remove the whole embarrassing mess. Instead I survived.

So you can see why I'm not the Council's favourite person. And why I've no desire to get into their good books, either.

I knew that Lyle was gone and wasn't coming back, but I stayed where I was for another twenty minutes, watching the reflections in the dark water and waiting for the ugly memories to settle. When I was calm again, I put Lyle and everything he stood for out of my mind and went home. I didn't feel like doing any more work that day, so I left for the park, locking the shop behind me.

London is an old city. Even visitors can feel it – the sense of history, the weight of thousands of years. To a sensitive it's even stronger, like a physical presence embedded into the earth and stone. Over the centuries pockets have developed, little enclaves in the jungle of buildings, and the place I was going to is one of them.

The park is about ten minutes' walk from my shop, tucked down a twisting backstreet that nobody ever uses. It's overgrown to the point of being nearly invisible behind the fence and trees. There are construction vehicles parked outside – officially the park's supposed to be closed for redevelopment, but somehow the work never seems to get done. There are buildings all around, but leaves and branches shelter you from watching eyes.

I was sitting on a blanket with my back against a beech tree when I heard the faint rattle of a bicycle on the road outside. A moment later a girl appeared through the trees, ducking under the branches. I waved and she changed direction, walking across the grass towards me.

A glance at Luna would show you a girl in her early twenties, with blue eyes, fair skin and wavy light brown hair worn up in two bunches. She moves very carefully, always looking where she places her hands and feet, and often she seems as though her body's there while her mind's somewhere far away. She hardly ever smiles and I've never seen her laugh, but apart from that you could talk to her without noticing anything strange . . . at least to begin with.

Luna's one of those people who was born into the world of magic without ever really getting a choice. Adepts and even mages can choose to abandon their power if they want to, bury their talents in the sand and walk away, but for Luna it's different. A few hundred years ago in Sicily, one of Luna's ancestors made the mistake of upsetting a powerful *strega*. Back country witches have a reputation for being vicious, but this one was mean even by witch standards. Instead of just killing the man, she put a curse on him that would strike his youngest daughter, and his daughter's daughter, and her daughter after that, following his children down and down through the generations until his descendants died out or the world ended, whichever came first.

I don't know how that long-dead witch managed to bind the curse so tightly to the family line, but she did a hell of a thorough job. She's been dust and bones for centuries but the curse is just as strong as ever, and Luna's the one in this generation who inherited it. Part of the reason the curse is so nasty is that it's almost impossible to tell it's there. Even a mage wouldn't notice it unless he knew exactly what to look for. If I concentrate I can see it around Luna as a kind of silvery-grey mist, but I only have the vaguest idea how it does what it does.

'Hey,' Luna said as she reached me, slinging her backpack off her shoulder. Instead of sitting on the blanket she picked a spot on the grass, a few yards away from me. 'Are you all right?'

'Sure. Why?'

'You look as if something's bothering you.'

I shook my head in annoyance. I'd thought I'd concealed it better than that, but I always have trouble hiding things from Luna. 'Unwelcome visitor. How's things?'

Luna hesitated. 'Can you . . .?'

'Let's have a look at it.'

Luna had been only waiting for me to ask; she unzipped her backpack and took out something wrapped in a cotton scarf. She leant forward to place it onto the edge of the blanket and unwrapped it, staying as far away as possible. The scarf fell away, Luna scooted back, and I leant forward in interest. Sitting in the folds of the scarf was what looked like a cube of red crystal.

The thing was about three inches square and deep crimson, the colour of red stained glass. As I looked more closely, though, I saw it wasn't transparent enough to be glass; I should have been able to see through it, but I couldn't. Instead, if I looked closely, I could see what looked like tiny white sparks held in the cube's depths. 'Huh,' I said, sitting up. 'Where'd you find it?'

'It was in the attic of a house in Clapham West. But . . .' Luna paused. 'There's something strange. I went to the same house three weeks ago and didn't find anything. But this time it was sitting on a shelf, right out in the open. And when I went to the owner, he couldn't remember owning it. He let me have it for free.' Luna frowned. 'I've been wondering if I just missed it, but I don't see how. You can feel it, can't you?'

I nodded. The cube radiated the distinct sense of otherness that all magic items do. This one wasn't flashy, but it was strong; someone sensitive like Luna couldn't have walked by without noticing. 'Did you touch it?'

Luna nodded.

'What happened?'

'It glowed,' Luna said. 'Just for a second, and—' She

hesitated. 'Well, I put it down, and it stopped. Then I wrapped it up and brought it here.'

The cube wasn't glowing now so I focused on it and concentrated. All mages can see into the magical spectrum to some degree, but as a diviner I'm a lot better at it than most. A mage's sight isn't really sight – it's more like a sixth sense – but the easiest way to interpret it is visually. It gives a sense of what the magic is, where it came from, and what it can do. If you're skilled enough you can pick up the thoughts the magic was shaped out of and the kind of personality that created it. On a good day I can read an item's whole history just from looking at it.

Today wasn't one of those days. Not only could I not read the item's aura, I couldn't read any aura on it at all. Which made no sense, because there should have been at least *one* aura, namely Luna's. To my eyes Luna glowed a clear silver, wisps of mist constantly drifting away and being renewed. A residue of it clung to everything she touched: her pack glowed silver, the scarf glowed silver, even the grass she was sitting on glowed silver. But the cube itself radiated nothing at all. The thing was like a black hole.

Left to their own devices magic items give off an aura, and the more powerful the item, the more powerful that aura is. This was why I'd had Luna bring the thing out here; if I'd tried to examine the cube in my shop I'd have had a hundred other auras distracting me. The park is a natural oasis, a kind of grounding circle which keeps other energies out, allowing me to concentrate on just one thing at a time. It's possible to design an item so as to minimise its signature, but no matter how carefully you design a one-shot or a focus, something's going to be visible. The only way to mask a magical aura completely is to do it actively, which left only one thing this could be. I dropped my concentration and looked up at Luna. 'You've found something special, all right.'

'Do you know what it is?' Luna asked.

I shook my head and thought for a moment. 'What happened when you touched it?'

'The sparks inside lit up and it glowed. Just for a second. Then it went dark again.' Luna seemed about to say something else, then stopped.

'After that? Did it do anything else?'

'Well . . .' Luna hesitated. 'It might be nothing.'

'Tell me.'

'It felt like it was looking at me. Even after I put it away. I know that sounds weird.'

I sat back against the tree, looking down at the cube. I didn't like this at all. 'Alex?' Luna asked. 'What's wrong?'

'This is going to be trouble.'

'Why?'

I hesitated. I'd been teaching Luna about magic for a few months, but so far I'd avoided telling her much about the people who use it. I know Luna wants to be accepted into the magical world, and I also know there's not much chance of it happening. Mage society is based on a hierarchy of power: the stronger your magic, the more status you have. Sensitives like Luna are second-class citizens at best.

'Look, there's a reason not many mages run shops,' I said at last. 'They've never bought in to the whole idea of yours and mine. A mage sees a magic item, his first reaction is to take it. Now, a minor item you can keep out of sight, but something really *powerful* . . . that's different. Any mage who finds out about this thing is going to be willing to take time off his schedule and track you down to take it, and he might not be gentle about how. Just owning a major item is dangerous.'

Luna was quiet. 'But you don't do that,' she said at last. I sighed. 'No.'

Luna looked at me, then turned away. We sat for a little while in silence.

Luna's curse is a spell of chance magic. Chance magic affects luck, bending probability so that something that might happen one time in a thousand, or a million, happens at just the right time – or the wrong one. The spell around Luna does both. It pulls bad luck away from her, and brings it to everyone nearby.

The really twisted thing is that from what I've learned the spell was originally invented by Dark mages as a *protection*, not a curse, because it makes you as safe from accidents as a person can possibly be. You can run across a motorway in rush hour, climb a tree in a lightning storm, walk through a battlefield with bombs going off all around you, all without taking a scratch.

But the accidents don't go away; they just get redirected to everyone nearby, and when the spell is laid permanently, the results are horrible. The closer Luna gets to another person, the more the curse affects them. She can't live in the same house as anyone else, because something terrible would happen within a month. She can't keep pets, or they die. Even having friends is dangerous. The closer other people are to her, and the longer they stay near, the worse the result. Whenever Luna comes to care about any other human being, she knows that the more time she spends with them, the more they're going to be hurt. She told me once that the first boy she kissed ended up in a coma.

I've spent some time researching Luna's curse, trying to find a way to break it, but haven't gotten anywhere. I might be able to get somewhere if I studied her intensively, but Luna's life is hard enough without being treated like some kind of science project. Still . . . 'Luna?'

'Hm?'

'There's something I was . . .' Something brushed against my senses, and I stopped. I looked into the future and my stomach suddenly went cold.

Luna was watching in puzzlement. She could tell from my expression that something was going on, but she didn't know what. 'Alex?'

I jumped to my feet. 'Get away!'

Luna started to rise, confused. 'What's going on?'

'There's no time!' I was desperate; we had only seconds. 'Behind the tree, hide! *Hurry!*'

Luna hesitated an instant longer, then moved quickly behind the beech. 'Stay there,' I said, my voice low and urgent. 'Don't make a sound.' I turned back just as a man stepped from the trees in front of me.

He was powerfully built, with a thick neck and wide hands, and muscles that bulged through the lines of his black coat. He might have looked like a bouncer or a bodyguard, maybe even a friendly one, if you didn't look too closely at his eyes. 'Verus, right?' the Dark mage said, regarding me steadily. 'Don't think we've met.'

## 2

The two of us stood facing each other across the grass. The wind had dropped, and the birds around had gone silent, sensing danger. I stood still, keeping my face blank and not letting myself show any sign of the sickening sensation you get when you've made a really bad mistake. I'd left my house without weapons or defences. Once upon a time I never would have dreamt of stepping outside without them, but months of safety had lulled me into dropping my guard.

Now I was paying for it. I was standing in front of a Dark mage, and if he decided to come at me, I was toast – literally. The silence stretched out while I looked frantically into the future, trying to see what would happen. 'I guess we haven't been introduced,' I said at last, keeping my voice steady.

'You can call me Cinder.'

I raised my eyebrows. 'Subtle.'

'Trying to be funny?'

'I don't know, are you laughing?'

He grinned then. 'Smart mouth.'

I didn't answer, but as I looked at the futures branching out from ahead of us, I felt a chill. This conversation could unfold in a thousand ways, and most of them led to Cinder attacking me, brutally and without warning. And the cause of the fight was . . .

I stopped, trying to keep the confusion off my face. It

was the red cube, the same one that had been left on the blanket just two feet behind where I was standing. The instant Cinder saw it he would do his absolute best to kill me, and I had no idea why.

Right now Cinder was focused on me, but in only a few seconds he would notice. I made a snap decision and deliberately turned my back on Cinder, crouching down to fold up the blanket. 'I reckon . . .' Cinder began to say, then stopped. 'Hey.'

I didn't turn around. 'What?'

'I'm talking to you.'

I wrapped the blanket around the cube, keeping the thick cloth around the thing. 'And?' I took out my bag and started packing the blanket inside. From behind, I could feel Cinder's confusion. No one turns his back on a Dark mage unless he's crazy or planning something. I felt a surge of magic starting to build up behind me, and I glanced over my shoulder, feeling an itch in my back. 'Stop that,' I said, keeping my voice cool.

A trace of anger was showing on Cinder's face. 'I think maybe you don't know who I am.'

I slung the pack over my shoulder, and turned to face Cinder. I'd learnt to hide my fear while still young, and it served me well now. Instead of slowing me down the fear sharpened me, focusing my senses. I could feel the slight tension in Cinder's body as he squinted at me, angry and puzzled. Turning my back on him had been an insult, and now he was focused on me, trying to decide if I was powerful or just stupid. Behind, I could sense Luna pressed flat against the beech tree, a mouse menaced by a hawk. 'I don't much care,' I said. 'You're here because you want something. Get to the point.'

Cinder looked at me through narrowed eyes, his anger simmering before coming under control. 'You met Lyle,' he said at last.

'And?'

'He try to hire you?' Cinder's tone made it clear that he already knew the answer.

'What if he did?'

'You helping him?'

I hesitated. Looking into the future wasn't helping now – too many branches. I didn't want to answer, but if I didn't, Cinder would assume the answer was yes. That could be bad. 'I don't work for Lyle,' I said finally.

Cinder grunted and suddenly looked less threatening. 'Smart.' He paused. 'We pay better.'

It took me a second to take that in. When I did, I blinked. 'You're offering me a job?'

'Need a seer. Could get others. Better we get you.'

'What's in it for me?'

'Same as the rest. Share of the value.'

'What's that?'

'Huh?'

'What's the value? How are you going to share it?'

Cinder smirked. 'You're the seer. Find out.'

'Funny.'

Cinder's smirk faded. He looked steadily at me. 'Wasn't joking.'

If I agreed, Cinder would expect me to go with him, and if I stalled, he'd take it as weakness. 'No thanks. I don't work on credit.'

'There'll be a share.'

'You *think* there'll be a share.' I shook my head. 'Come back when you've got something more solid.'

Cinder's face darkened, and I felt the futures shift. Suddenly, the possibilities were looking a lot worse. 'That your last word?'

I kept my voice very calm. 'Don't try and threaten me, Cinder.'

Cinder looked me up and down, slowly and deliberately. He wasn't calling his magic up but I could sense he was ready to. 'Seems to me,' he said, 'I could take you any time I want.'

'You could try,' I said lightly. Inside, I was panicking. I had no weapons, the cube was in the backpack over my shoulder, and Luna was hiding not fifteen feet away. If a fight started, it would be a disaster. I could see the futures forking ahead of me, depending on whether Cinder decided I was bluffing or not.

For a moment Cinder hesitated, then he grinned again and the futures shifted decisively. 'I reckon you got nothing.'

Shit, shit, shit. Every future I could see now led to an all-out battle. I searched through them frantically, trying not to let it show in my voice. 'Bad idea.'

'Oh yeah?' He spread his arms invitingly. 'Take your best shot.'

Twenty seconds. Suddenly I found a cluster of futures free and clear of danger. I scanned them desperately. What was the difference, what did I have to do? Ten seconds. The air started to darken around Cinder, the sunlight going from yellow to blood-red.

A name. I rehearsed it, spoke. 'Morden.'

Cinder stopped dead. His magic faded away and the evening sunlight flooded back. 'What?'

I stood there, not answering. 'You working for him?' Cinder asked at last.

I raised my eyebrows. 'What do you think?'

Cinder hesitated, and the seconds stretched out. It looked almost as if he were afraid. 'Why didn't you—?'

'You didn't ask.'

Cinder's expression firmed up again. 'You tell the old man we meant it. He's not our master.' Cinder was still trying to sound threatening, but he wasn't going to attack, not any more. 'He's smart, he'll stay out of this. You too.'

'What am I? Your postman? Tell him yourself.'

Cinder stared at me, then took a step back, disappearing into the trees. I felt a surge of magic and he was gone.

I stayed standing for another ten seconds, scanning the future to see if Cinder would be back. Once I was absolutely, positively sure he wouldn't be, the strength went out of my legs and I flopped to the ground. My heart was hammering. 'Jesus,' I muttered.

'Alex?' Luna finally said from behind the tree.

'He's gone,' I managed. I tried to get up and found I couldn't. My hands were shaking. All I could do was sit there as Luna emerged, looking around at the normal, everyday shapes around her. The birds that had fallen silent at Cinder's approach had started to sing again, and there was no sign he'd ever come. Luna knelt down, closer than normal. 'Are you okay?'

'I'm fine.' I brushed my hair back, then gripped it to stop my hands shaking.

Luna made as if to reach out to me, then checked herself and pulled back, drawing away to a safe distance. There was concern in her blue eyes, though, and strangely that made me feel better. 'What happened?'

I took a deep breath, remembering that Luna couldn't look into the future. I'd seen all the ways the meeting could end with the grass burnt black with flame, but Luna had heard only voices. 'That was your first Dark mage.'

'They're dangerous?'

'Understatement of the year.' My breathing was steadying down. I pulled myself to my feet and patted the backpack to make sure the cube was still there. 'I don't understand,' Luna said. 'Who's Morden?'

'Southbound terminus on the Northern line.'

Luna looked at me blankly.

I sighed. 'No clue. All I know is that it was the only thing that would have got Cinder off my back.'

'But why?'

'Because it made Cinder think I'm working for this Morden guy, and he didn't want to pick that big a fight. But now Cinder's going to go hunt up some people to ask, and once he finds out it was a bluff, he'll be back. I just bought myself a whole lot of trouble.'

'You were bluffing?'

I started for the edge of the park. 'Let's get out of here before he figures that out.'

My flat is just above the shop, up on the first floor. It's got what passes for my kitchen as well as a sofa, a table and a couple of chairs for my rare-to-nonexistent visitors. There are three watercolours on the walls, inherited from the previous owner, and the windows look out over a low roof onto a view of the London skyline. The sun was dipping low in the sky, and the lights had started to come on across the city, outlining the buildings in yellow and orange. Across the canal and visible over the bridges are blocks of flats, their sides turned towards me, and I like sometimes in the evenings to lie on the sofa and watch the shifting patterns of the lights in the windows, wondering what they mean.

Luna was curled up on one corner of the sofa, while I was sprawled in my favourite chair. 'So,' I said, setting my glass down with a sigh. 'Now you know one of the reasons I don't hang around with other mages.'

Luna gave me a questioning look and I shook my head, more to reassure myself than her. 'Well, it's done and we got away safely. Could have been a lot worse. You were a good girl to run and hide when I told you.'

'Don't call me a good girl. You're not *that* much older.'

'Don't argue. Be a good girl.'

Luna gave me one of her rare smiles. It faded quickly though. 'Alex . . . You were scary. Your voice was so cold. I thought you were going to . . .'

'Going to what?'

Luna was silent. 'You were really bluffing?'

'He was looking for weakness.'

'I thought you didn't know him?'

'I know people like him.' I fell silent, lost in old memories.

'He talked like he knew you,' Luna said after a pause.

I didn't answer.

'How *do* you know people like him?' When I still didn't answer, Luna went on. 'Is it about what you did before you got this shop?'

'Luna . . .' There was a warning note in my voice.

Luna fell silent. When I looked up, though, she met my eyes, not backing down. 'You're better off staying away from this,' I said at last. 'Just knowing about these people can get you in trouble.'

Luna tilted her head. 'I thought you said I was already in trouble?'

I hesitated. Mages have a policy of not discussing their business with outsiders. The Council wouldn't be happy if they found I was telling this to Luna. On the other hand, the Council doesn't like me anyway.

And besides, I've never really bought into the idea of keeping people ignorant for their own good. What you know can hurt you, but what you don't know can hurt you a lot worse. 'All right,' I said. 'What do you know about Dark mages?'

Luna curled her legs under her on the sofa. Her white fingers were clasped around a mug of tea, a faint wisp of steam drifting upwards. 'I thought they were mages who went bad.'

'No.' I tried to figure out how to explain it. 'Well . . . maybe. Dark mages follow a philosophy called the True Way. The True Way says that good and bad as we see it are conventions. Our ideas about good and evil come from customs and religions designed to benefit the people in power. Dark mages think that obeying them makes you a sheep. Like when you asked for that cube from that man today? A Dark mage would say you should have just taken it.'

'You mean stealing it?'

'A Dark mage would tell you that you only feel stealing is wrong because your parents brought you up that way. Right and wrong are just conventions, like which side of the road you drive on.'

Luna thought about it for a few seconds, then shook her head. 'But he'd have called the police.'

I nodded. 'That's the bit they think matters. What stops people breaking the law is the threat of punishment, and the threat only means anything if there's the power to enforce it. To a Dark mage, power is reality. The more power you have, the more you can shape the reality around you. Strength, cunning, influence, whatever, but the one thing they don't tolerate is weakness. Dark mages believe weakness is a sin, something shameful. If you're not strong enough to take what you want, it's *your* fault.'

Luna frowned. 'Oh.'

'Do you understand?'

'I suppose.' Luna thought for a second. 'I've heard people say stuff like that. I suppose they've got a point.'

I shook my head. 'It's not about having a point. Dark mages don't *say* these things. They *live* them.'

Luna looked at me, and I knew she didn't understand. 'That man, Cinder,' I said. 'What do you think he would have done if he'd found you?'

Luna looked suddenly uneasy. 'I don't know.'

'Whatever he wanted,' I said. 'He might have ignored you. He might have laughed and walked off. He might have raped you and left you bleeding on the ground. He might have taken you back to his mansion as a slave. And he wouldn't think twice about doing any of those things.'

Luna stared. 'And something else,' I went on. 'No *other* Dark mage would think twice about him doing any of those things either. If you can't stop him, it's *your* fault. Understand now?'

Luna's eyes were wide, and I could tell I'd finally gotten through. 'You know these people?'

'Yes.' Luna began to say something else but I shook my head. 'Don't ask me about it. Not now.'

Luna fell silent. The pause dragged out and became uncomfortable. 'I should go home,' Luna said at last. I nodded and rose.

I walked Luna out. She kept at arm's length just like always, but there was a distance that hadn't been there before. Over the past months, Luna had started to open up to me a little. Now all of a sudden she was drawing back.

Once she was gone, I locked the door with a sigh. I'd been trying to scare her, and I had. I didn't like showing Luna that side of me but I knew the safest thing would be for her to stay away for a few days, at least until this business with Cinder was settled. But I had the feeling that it would be a lot longer than a few days before Luna called me again for advice.

Somehow that depressed me. I shook it off. No one likes guys who get sentimental.

I took the red crystal cube and put it somewhere very hard to find. Then I headed for my room. I'd been planning to make inquiries about the cube but Cinder's reaction had changed all that. If just the sight of it was enough to make him try to kill me, I didn't want to spread it around that I had it. Instead I'd keep it secret until the fuss had died down, and in the meantime I'd arrange for it to be thoroughly investigated by an expert in magical items . . . namely, me.

But first I needed to find out more about this Precursor relic that Lyle and Cinder were so interested in. And this time, I wasn't going out empty-handed.

Being a diviner is all about being prepared; that was why I'd been so scared when Cinder had caught me napping. Diviners can't do the flashy things that elemental mages can. We can't fly or throw fire or disintegrate things. We aren't any tougher or stronger than other men, and our magic gives us no power over the physical world. But what we do have is knowledge, and applied in the right way that can be some pretty impressive leverage.

I set about making sure I'd have something to apply that leverage to. I dressed in a warm shirt and jeans, then put on a pair of black running shoes before turning to the items scattered around my desk. My first choice was a crystal sphere the size of a marble with a fingernail's worth of mist swirling inside – I dropped it into my right-hand coat pocket, checked to see that I could reach it quickly, then did the same with a small glass rod in the matching pocket on my left. Next was a packet of trail dust – my last one; I'd have to get some more. A tapering crystal wand about eight inches long clipped into my coat, then I filled the rest of my pockets with a general selection of odds and ends: a jar of healing salve, a handful of tiny pieces of silver jewellery and two vials containing a pale blue liquid.

Next I went on to my mundane items. Most mages aren't fond of technology but I prefer to take every advantage I can get. A small, powerful torch went on my belt along with a few tools and a slender-bladed knife held securely in its sheath. I reached for the drawer which held my gun, paused, then decided to leave it behind. It would probably be more trouble than it was worth.

Finally, I went to my wardrobe and took out my mist cloak. It's not the most powerful item I own, but it's the one I most trust. To casual eyes it looks like a length of some kind of grey-black cloth, thin and light and soft to the touch. If you keep looking, the colours seem to shift and flow at the edge of your vision, subtly enough that you might think you'd imagined it. Mist cloaks are woven from moonbeams and the webs of snowspiders, and they're rare and little known items. They're imbued items, not simple focuses, and as I put it on the colours rippled quickly before going still. I patted it affectionately, then turned to look at myself in the mirror.

I saw a tall figure, angular lines blurred by the shadows of the mist cloak. From beneath the hood a pale, quizzical face looked back at me, guarded and watchful, spiky black hair framing a pair of dark eyes. I studied myself for a moment, then turned to the door.

Time to get to work.


The sun had long set by the time I stepped off the ladder onto the roof of my flat. A few muted stars shone down from above, their faint glow almost drowned out by the yellow blaze of the London lights. Rooftops, chimneys and TV aerials were all around me, shadowed in the darkness, and from below came the sounds of the city. The air carried the scent of car exhausts and old brickwork.

Mages like to think their magic sets them above everyone else, and I guess in some ways that's true. But when you get right down to it, mages are still people and, just like other people, they gossip. Lyle might think his Precursor relic was a secret, but I was willing to bet it wasn't anywhere near as secret as he thought it was. And if the news was out, I knew someone who'd have heard all about it.

The roof of my flat's maybe twenty feet square, peeling white paint bordered by a small parapet with a dusty chimney sticking up to one side. If you're a good climber you can cross to other houses, and often I do. I stood in the centre, took the glass rod from my pocket and wove a tiny thread of magic through it, whispering as I did. 'Starbreeze. Dancer of the air, friend to the clouds, you who know the secrets of the mountain peaks and all between earth and sky. I am Alexander Verus and I call to you. Come to me, lady of the wind.' A faint breeze sprung up, as the whispering wind swept my words away and into the north. I repeated it again for south, west and east, then looked into the future.

The good news was that Starbreeze would be here soon. The bad news was that the assassin stalking me would be here sooner.

It's nearly impossible to surprise an alert diviner. It's how we survive in a world of things bigger and nastier than we are. I'd detected the man hunting me even before I'd stepped outside my door. The only question was what to do about it.

I don't usually let people pick fights with me. It's not hard to give someone the slip when you can see the future, and the kind of people who like picking fights tend to have lots of other enemies. It's easier just to keep your head down and wait for someone else to deal with them. In this case, though, if I shook this mage off, the first thing he'd do would be to try and break into my shop, and that would risk him finding the cube. I was better off dealing with him directly.

Of course, that didn't mean I was going to fight *fair*. I hopped down to the roof of the house next to me and kept going until I reached the roof of a small block of flats to my south, five buildings down. The building had been renovated ten years back, and the roof now held a couple of ventilators, but it still had the old chimney stacks near the edge. The combination of old and new made the roof cluttered, giving plenty of cover. I checked the roof to make sure the layout was as I remembered, then leant against one of the ventilators, closed my eyes, and waited.

Not much light from the streets below reached up to the city rooftops, but there was plenty of sound. From all around I could hear the muted chatter of people on the streets below, mixing with the rumble of cars carrying their passengers home for the last time before the weekend. The breeze carried the scent of Indian and Italian food – the restaurants were just starting on the dinnertime rush. All around was noise and bustle, but the roof itself was quiet. The only sound from nearby was the rustle of wings from roosting pigeons across the street. As I listened, the rustle suddenly went quiet.

I spoke into the darkness without opening my eyes. 'You'll miss.'

Black lightning cut the night air, slashing through the space I'd been in as I twisted away. The bolts were jet black, visible only as a greater darkness against the night sky, and they made no sound but a low hiss. I completed my spin with my back pressed against the ventilator, and as suddenly as it had begun, everything was still.

I leant just slightly around the ventilator's edge. 'Told you.'

The mage who'd attacked me was on the next roof over, a dark shape crouched behind a chimney. Looking into the futures in which I approached, I could see he was a small man, spindly and thin, wearing dark clothes and a mask that hid his face. He was squinting in my direction, one hand lifted to shield or strike. 'Come out, little seer,' the man said when I didn't move. His voice was harsh, with a trace of an accent.

'Why don't you come over so I can see you better?'

I sensed the man's lips curl in a smile. 'Because I can see you . . . right *now*.' As he said the last word another stream of black lightning flashed from his hand.

The black lightning was death magic, a kind of negative energy that kills by shutting down a body's systems, especially the brain and heart. Death magic is incredibly fast, as quick as the lightning it resembles. As if that wasn't enough, this particular attack was augmented with kinetic energy, giving it a physical punch as well. It'd be a real bitch to shield against, even if I could make shields, which I can't.

But all the speed in the world doesn't matter if the target's not there. I'd ducked back out of sight as the man had cast his spell and the bolt struck the edge of the ventilator where my head had been, the lightning grounding as the impact made the metal shudder. I heard the man swear. 'You know, I was expecting Cinder,' I said conversationally. 'Was he busy?'

'Cinder's a fool,' the man snarled. I could sense he was off balance; he wasn't used to missing.

'He didn't try to pick a fight with me,' I said, then smiled into the darkness. 'I'd say that makes him brighter than you . . . Khazad.'

The man – Khazad – stopped dead. 'How do you know my name?'

'What's the matter, Khazad?' I asked. 'Bitten off more than you can chew?'

There was a moment's silence, then from behind the chimney, Khazad stood up. Darkness flickered around him as he wove a shield. 'I don't scare as easily as Cinder,' he said quietly, and began walking towards me.

So much for ending it the easy way. 'So is this your way of asking me to join your team?' I asked as Khazad closed in. 'Because I've got to say, your sales pitch sucks.'

'You can help us or you can die,' Khazad said, and I could tell he was smiling. 'I don't mind which.'

Khazad had reached the parapet separating one roof from the next. He began to climb over it, slowly and carefully, keeping one hand free and his eyes on the ventilator. I took the opportunity to move back into the shadow of the chimney stacks, keeping the ventilator between him and me. Khazad's feet came down onto the flat's roof and he straightened. 'Running already?' he said mockingly.

'You know, I can see why you make enemies like Morden,' I said. 'Your group really isn't great on social skills.'

'You're not working for Morden,' Khazad said calmly. 'You don't work for anybody. No one will care if you die here.'

Khazad had cleared the ventilator, but I'd been moving as well and now there was a chimney stack between us. There was a reason I'd chosen to fight Khazad up here. Death magic is deadly, but it needs a direct line of sight to its target. A fire mage like Cinder could have just burned the whole rooftop, but Khazad needed a clear shot. I changed direction, moving towards the drop to my left. 'Just out of curiosity, how do you think killing me is going to help you get this relic?'

'Who says I have to kill you?' Khazad said. His voice was confident: he thought he was backing me up against the edge of the roof. Good. 'All you have to do is do what I say.'

I'd backed into a dead end. The chimney stack I'd been hiding behind ended at the roof's edge. Glancing down, I could see balconies and a cluttered alleyway with a dumpster. Khazad was fewer than thirty feet away, heading straight towards my hiding place.

Most mages have some way to use their magic to find people: fire mages can pick up a man's body heat; air mages can feel his breath; life and mind mages can directly sense the presence and thoughts of a human being the same way that you can touch or taste. For death mages like Khazad, it works a little differently: they sense living creatures as an absence, a concentration of life where their magic can't go. That was how Khazad had been able to sense me in the darkness, and it was how he was following me now.

I drew the crystal wand from my pocket and concentrated, channelling my magic through it. There was no effect to normal eyes, but to my mage's sight the thing brightened, glowing. The wand is the simplest of all magic items, a battery. All it does is hold the magic and essence of the person who uses it. It doesn't really *do* anything, but it's very noticeable. There was a gutter on the edge of the roof, and I laid the wand in it. 'You'll have to find me first,' I said over my shoulder, and flipped the hood of the mist cloak over my head. I took three quick steps backwards and pressed myself up against the chimney stack, going very still.

Let me tell you a bit about mist cloaks. They're imbued items, with permanent magic of their own, and their basic function is to sense their surroundings and shift colour to match, camouflaging the bearer no matter where he is. Right now, I knew the mist cloak had shifted to match the bricks behind me, blending my shape with the chimney's like a chameleon. As long as I didn't move, the illusion would be perfect.

But mist cloaks have a second function which very few people know about: they also block detection spells. To magical senses, a human wearing a mist cloak gives off no reading, as though they aren't there. From Khazad's point of view, first he was sensing me, then he was sensing a source of magic coming from the exact same place that I'd been in a second ago. If he'd been paying close attention he might have noticed the flicker as the sources had switched, but he didn't have any reason to think I'd moved. In fact, he didn't even slow down. 'Find you?' he said, and I could tell he was smiling. 'I already have—'

Khazad came around the corner and stopped. A few steps ahead of him was the edge of the roof, streetlights glowing dimly from below. I was just two steps to his right, pressed motionless against the chimney. This close, I could see the side of Khazad's face behind the mask. His skin was light brown, and he was shorter than I was, small and lightly built. He was staring down at where the wand was hidden, just in front of him.

Mages have a tendency to over-rely on their magic. It's human nature; if you have something that works ninety-nine per cent of the time, you tend to forget about the hundredth. Khazad's eyes were telling him that there was nothing there, but his magic was telling him that there was something just over the edge, and it was his magic he trusted. He moved forward, his movements quick and jerky like a bird, his shield flickering as it dimmed the light behind him. He reached the very edge of the roof and stared down at the wand lying in the gutter.

I came up behind Khazad and shoved him hard in the

small of the back. His shield stung my hands as it took the blow, but while kinetic shields can spread out an impact, they don't do much to stop it. Khazad went flying over the edge with a shout. There was a crash as he hit the balcony, followed by a satisfying crunch.

I picked up the wand and dropped it back in my pocket, then turned and walked away, humming to myself. I didn't bother checking to see how badly Khazad was hurt; he wasn't going to be chasing me any more, which was all I cared about. I walked back to my roof, sat down and waited.

A couple of minutes later, something tickled my ear. I turned to see a semi-solid face made of swirling air just a few inches away, looking at me with wide eyes. 'Boo!'

To ordinary eyes Starbreeze looks like air – that's to say, invisible. To a mage's sight she looks like an artist's sketch done in lines of glowing vapour. Swirls of air magic make up her body, her shape changing from day to day depending on her mood. Today she was in one of her favourite forms: an elfin girl with short hair, big eyes and pointed ears. 'Scared you!'

Starbreeze's full name is about half a page long and lovely to hear, the sense of a rising wind over a snowy hillside, carrying with it the hint of spring, with the first stars of night appearing in the sky above. When I first met her I tried to remember it, until I found that she changes it every time she's asked. Now I just call her Starbreeze like everyone else. Starbreeze is an air elemental, a spirit of wind. She can fly or shift her form with no more effort than it takes you or I to walk. She can feel the movement of a butterfly from across a field, hear a whisper from halfway across the world. She's ancient and timeless. I don't know how old she is, but I think she might have been born at the time the world was made.

She's also dumb as a sack of rocks.

'Hi, Starbreeze.'

'You're different,' Starbreeze chirped. Then she brightened. 'Pretty cloak!' She dived right into me, turning into a swirl of wind around my clothes, sending my cloak billowing out, then starting to tug it over my head. 'No!' I said, pulling it down.

'Give me,' Starbreeze called, her voice coming from somewhere around my back.

I took a firmer grip on the mist cloak. 'No. You'll lose it.'

Starbreeze reformed behind me, and I turned to face her. She was pouting. 'Won't.'

'Yes, you will. You'll forget all about it.'

'Won't.'

'What happened to the last thing I gave you?'

Starbreeze looked vague. 'I forgot.' She brightened. 'Air stone!'

I sighed inwardly. Starbreeze has seen my cloak a dozen times, and it goes clean out of her head every time I'm gone. I suppose I'm lucky she can remember 'Alex'. Actually, I'm lucky she remembers 'Starbreeze'. I reached into my pocket and took out one of the tiny pieces of silver jewellery: a brooch, shaped like a butterfly with wings spread. Starbreeze hopped forward, eyes wide. 'Ooh!'

'Do you like it?'

Starbreeze floated up into the air and spun around so that her head was pointing down at the roof. She hung upside down with her chin cupped in her hands a few inches from the brooch, stared at it with rapt eyes for a few seconds, then nodded eagerly.

I closed my hand over the brooch and lowered it. Starbreeze's face clouded over. 'Bring it back!'

'I'll give it to you,' I promised. 'But I need you to tell me something first.'

'Okay!'

Starbreeze doesn't rest, doesn't sleep and can hear anything carried on moving air. It'd make her the perfect spy, except that most of what she hears goes in one ear and out the other. 'I'm looking for a Precursor relic, a new one.'

'What's a relic?' Starbreeze said curiously.

'A powerful magical thing. It would have been found a week or two ago.'

'What's a week?'

'The Council would have been looking into it. They'd have been guarding it, maybe setting up some kind of research team.'

'What's the Council?'

I sighed. 'Anything interesting in this city? Anything with magic?'

'Oh!' Starbreeze brightened. 'Men came to the place with the old thing. Tried to open it up.' Starbreeze giggled. 'Lightning man came. It was funny!'

I frowned. 'Which men?'

Starbreeze shrugged. 'Men.'

'Where did they come to?'

'Blue round place.'

'Is there anywhere else in this city where men have been doing something magical with an old thing?'

'No, no, no.' Starbreeze swirled around my head, rolling over in the air. 'Go there?'

I thought for a second. If Starbreeze took me to the 'blue round place', I'd be able to find out whether it was what I was looking for. The only risk was she might get halfway, forget where she was going and drop me somewhere random. Last time that happened I ended up in Puerto Rico. If you're wondering why I bring so much stuff with me on these trips, now you know.

On the other hand, I was pressed for time and this was the best lead I had. I nodded. 'Let's do it.'

Instantly Starbreeze swept in around me. For a moment a whirlwind clouded my vision, then there was a tingling through my body and I could see again. Looking down, I saw my body fade away, becoming mist and air. Then we were in the sky, flying at incredible speed into the darkness.

There's no feeling as amazing as being carried by an air elemental. Imagine flying in a hang-glider, soaring over the city by night. Now imagine that you're going ten times as fast, so that the streets and lights and crowds below roll by like an unfolding blanket. Now add the feeling that there isn't a breath of wind, and that you're lying in mid-air watching the land zoom past below. When an air elemental carries you in its body, the rushing wind doesn't touch you; it's like swimming through the sky.

Tonight, though, I didn't have much time to enjoy it. I had one brief glimpse of a huge curving roof, a pale green dome forming a bubble out of the centre, before Starbreeze turned me back from air and dropped me to the ground so fast that I was standing on flagstones almost before I knew what was happening. I was standing under the night sky in a massive dark courtyard in the shadow of a vast building. Opposite the building was a high fence with a pair of tall gates, and through the closed gates I could see lights and passing cars. The courtyard itself was almost pitch-black and for a moment I was disorientated, then I saw the massive columns to my left and suddenly I knew exactly where I was.

Starbreeze swirled upwards. 'Starbreeze, wait,' I whispered up to her. 'Don't you want the brooch?'

Starbreeze paused in mid-air and stared blankly down at me. 'Brooch?'

I sighed inwardly. 'Here.' I held out the silver butterfly. 'This is for you.'

'Ooh!' Starbreeze said raptly. A puff of wind whisked the butterfly out of my hand and Starbreeze leapt up and away out of the courtyard and into the night sky, spiralling higher and higher, tossing the brooch from breeze to breeze until she disappeared into the air and vanished.

I was left alone. I took a quick glance around me and got to work.

3

The spot Starbreeze had dropped me was just outside the British Museum. The courtyard was bordered to the north by the museum itself, to the east and west by outbuildings and to the south by stone walls, tall gates and a high iron fence with spikes. Beyond the fence, buses and cars tracked steadily from left to right to left along Great Russell Street, casting light and sound through the railings, but the courtyard itself was silent.

As I waited for my eyes to adjust, I looked through the futures and saw that if I moved forward I'd run into a line of massive columns, behind which was the museum's main entrance. Starbreeze had said something about mages trying to open something. It might be Lyle's relic, in which case this place would be under Council guard. Otherwise, it might be someone's secret project. Either way, it was a safe bet nobody inside would be happy to see me.

If there's one thing all diviners share, it's curiosity. We really can't help it; it's just part of who we are. If you dug out a tunnel somewhere in the wilderness a thousand miles from anywhere and hung a sign on it saying, 'Warning, this leads to the Temple of Horrendous Doom. Do not enter, ever. No, not even then', you'd get back from lunch to find a diviner already inside and two more about to go in.

Come to think about it, that might explain why there are so few of us.

In any case, even if this wasn't what I was after, I couldn't resist having a closer look. I flipped the hood of my mist cloak up over my head and walked into the shadows of the huge columns. In the wall beyond were double doors of metal and glass. Through the glass I could see an open area with two men at a security station, one sitting, one standing. The only way through into the museum proper was to cross in clear line of sight of both men. I stood watching for two full minutes, then opened the door and walked inside.

Everyone knows diviners can see the future. But what does seeing the future mean?

Most people think it's like reading a book. You skip a few pages ahead, see what's going to happen. That's impossible, of course. You reach a fork in the road: do you go left or right? You might go one way; you might go the other. It's your choice, no one else's.

What a diviner sees is probability. In one future you go left; in another you go right; in a third, you stop and ask for directions. A hundred branches, each branching again and again to create thousands, for every one of the millions of people living on this earth. Billions and trillions of futures, branching in every way through four dimensions like a river delta the size of a galaxy.

You can't look at all that at once. If you opened your sight to all the possible futures of everything around you, even for an instant, the knowledge would destroy you, wipe away your mind like an ocean wave rolling over a drop of water. Seeing into the future is a constant discipline, always keeping your guard up, always focused. The real reason there are so few diviners is that most of them either go crazy or block their power off so that they don't have to deal with it any more.

The diviners who *don't* go crazy learn to see futures in terms of strength. Everyone develops their own code, a way of interpreting the information. To me, futures appear as lines of light in the darkness. The stronger and more likely the future, the brighter the glow. The next thing you learn is how to *sort* futures, search for groupings of events in which things happen a certain way. And once you've done that, all you have to do is look back along the strands and find out which actions lead to them.

In ninety-nine out of a hundred futures, opening the door and walking in led to me being spotted by the security guards. I searched for the future in which I *wasn't* spotted, looked back to see what I had to do to make it happen, and did it. I didn't have the faintest idea why I had to move that way. I just knew it would work.

To anyone watching, it looks like pure fluke. One guard points at something, and the other turns just as I open the door and close it behind me. They carry on talking and I stand quietly in the shadow of the doorway. One looks away briefly and I walk out across the floor as the second bends down to fumble in a drawer. I walk past, staying behind the first one as he turns back, and pass through the exit at the other side just before the second one looks up again.

Afterwards, when the balloon goes up, both guards will swear they never took their eyes off the door.

The Great Court of the British Museum is massive, more than fifty feet high with the huge cylinder of the Reading Room running from floor to ceiling at the centre. Floor

and walls are painted white, reflecting the light and empha-
sising the empty space, and the ceiling is slightly domed.
An equestrian statue stood to the right; to the left, a stone
lion snarled down upon an information desk covered with
pamphlets. I crossed the floor, half my mind on keeping
my footsteps silent and the other half searching the possible
futures for more guards, noting as I did that a patrol was
due in about three minutes. I picked a map off the desk
and glanced at it. The bulk of the ground floor was taken
up by the west wing, mostly filled with permanent exhibits
from Ancient Greece and Rome. Somehow I couldn't see
Lyle's relic being one of those; if the Rosetta Stone or the
Elgin Marbles were magical, I was pretty sure someone
would have noticed by now. At the back, around the third
floor, were some rooms marked in brown as 'exhibitions
and changing displays'. That sounded hopeful. I slipped
the map into my pocket and started for the stairs.

As I climbed the curving staircase around the Reading
Room and mapped out my path through the museum, the
back of my mind was puzzling about why any kind of
magical item would be here. Mages, as a whole, are not
the most public-spirited of people. If they find something
they want, they take it. They don't leave it on display.

Unless in this case they *couldn't* take it. If the Council
couldn't move it to a safe location, that might explain why
Lyle was desperate enough to try contacting me.

I'd just reached Ethiopia and Coptic Egypt when something pinged on my precognition. Two guards were ahead.
I paused until I knew neither was looking in my direction,
then peeked my head around the corner. The men were
about thirty feet away, standing in front of a staircase
leading up, and they were carrying . . .

*Bingo.* The security guards at the door had worn the black uniforms and pullovers of British Museum security, with a silver 'BM' on their epaulettes. These two wore plain clothes. They carried no obvious tools or weapons, but I could sense the auras of magical items, and from the way one had moved I'd spotted a gun in a shoulder holster and *that* made them Council security. Mages don't do sentry duty, not unless it's literally a matter of life or death; they're too important for that. Instead they have private soldiers, equipped with modern weapons and magical aids.

These two weren't mages, or even adepts, but they were alert and competent. As well as that, I could tell from here that the top of the stairwell behind them was warded with a barrier. The barrier would contain a well-hidden alarm; anyone entering the fourth floor without the magical key, whether by foot or by spell, would set off a silent warning signal. Knowing the Council, the guards wouldn't be trusted with the password key. An elemental mage could blast through the guards and the barrier, but would set off the alarm. A more subtle mage would be able to avoid raising the alarm, but they wouldn't be able to get through the barrier.

It was a typical Council defence: cost-effective and ruthless. The job of those two guards was to be, basically, cannon fodder. If a mage attacked them, their chances of survival were nil. Their only purpose was to raise the alarm and give advance warning to Council reinforcements gating in. But no matter what I thought of the methods, I had to admit it was a fairly good setup. For a normal mage, getting past both the guards and the barrier without raising the alarm would take hours of preparation, if not days.

It took me slightly over five minutes. When you know

exactly what *will* set off an alarm, then you know exactly what *won't*. Think about it.

The fourth floor was sealed off from the rest of the museum with boards and screens. Worn red carpet covered the floor and a scattered handful of lights cast the room in a dim glow. Standing in the centre of the room was a statue.

I should probably mention at this point that what I was doing was, under mage law, illegal as hell. The Council might turn a blind eye to torture and murder, but trespassing, well, *that's* serious. With my reputation, I'd be in serious trouble if I was caught. However, I was pretty sure by this point that I'd be in *more* serious trouble if I stayed home. I had no particular desire to sit around waiting for the next guy in line to take a shot at me.

I scanned the room. A few other exhibits had been pushed into the corners: a vase, a standing lamp, something that looked like a totem pole. None radiated magic. A lift was at the far end, but it was dark and unpowered. There were no windows. Apart from the stairs I'd climbed to enter this room, there was no way in and no way out, which meant I was standing in a dead end if anything went wrong. I would have to work fast.

The statue was of a man, life-size, wearing robes that looked like ancient ancestors of the ceremonial gear Light mages wear to formal occasions. He looked in his fifties or sixties, with a flowing beard. His right hand grasped a wand, while his left hand was held out in front of him, palm up and slightly cupped as though asking for something. The face was superbly detailed, right down to the age lines and the set of the eyes; the sculptor had obviously used magic to preserve his work. The expression and pose of the man was commanding, proud. I circled the statue once more then, after a moment's hesitation, reached out and touched it.

Nothing happened, as I'd known it would. The statue looked and felt like stone, though slightly cooler to the touch than stone should be. This was Lyle's relic, all right. Even without my mage's sight, I could feel power radiating from the thing. I looked around the room, putting together what must have happened. The museum had gotten hold of the statue and brought it here. The Council had found it, sent agents. Their orders would have been to study the item, determine its power. First they would have tried to activate the statue, then if that didn't work they would have tried to move it.

What had happened then?

I turned back to the statue, studying the face. The expression was calm, but with a hint of something else – arrogance? Danger? Looking closely, I could see traces of old scars. A battle mage, then, and a good one, if he'd lived to that age. The more I looked, the more I felt there was something expectant about the statue, as though it were waiting for something.

The outstretched hand lay there, open and inviting. I looked into the future to see what would happen if I put something into it.

I watched the scene unfolding ahead of me for just a second, then broke off the vision and stepped back hastily until my back fetched up against the wall. Suddenly I understood exactly why Lyle and Cinder needed a diviner, and what had happened the last time someone had tried to activate this thing. The statue had been perfectly preserved – and its defence system had been perfectly preserved, too.

I'd learned all I needed to know. It was time to get out of here.

I'd taken two steps towards the door when I heard the sound from downstairs. It was a quiet sound, the sound of something soft and heavy falling, and it made me stop dead.

Remember what I said about diviners learning to focus on the futures that tell you what you need to know? Well, it comes with a drawback. If you're focusing on one set of futures, you aren't paying attention to the others. So if you're about to be cornered by some people you really don't want to meet, you won't notice it until something draws your attention – something like the sound of a body hitting the floor.

It was not turning out to be a good day.

Most people's first response to danger is to run away. It's a survival instinct which natural selection has done a good job of encouraging. It's an old saying that if you're being chased, you only have to outrun one person. If everyone else runs away and you don't, by default that makes you the one person. Hence people whose first response to danger *isn't* to run away tend to get weeded out of the gene pool by teeth, or bullets, or fireballs, as the case may be.

Personally, my first response to danger is to take a closer look and see what's going on. Refer back to what I said about diviners being curious. Also refer back to what I said about there not being many of us. I looked into the future of what I would see if I ran downstairs, following the gaze of my future self.

The first thing I saw were the two guards who'd been stationed on the landing. Both were now lying on the floor, quite dead. Standing over them were three figures. As my future self saw the figures, they saw me, and I got one glimpse of what they'd do before I cut the vision off abruptly. Just that look was all I needed to know that I did *not* want to be found here.

Footsteps sounded on the stairs, and I knew I had fewer than thirty seconds. Running was out, fighting was out. The only choice left was to hide. I moved into one of the corners, sliding in behind the totem pole so its irregular shape would break up my outline, then pulled the hood of my mist cloak over my head. The footsteps below stopped, and I knew they'd reached the barrier. There was a flicker of green light and the barrier was gone. Figures strode in.

There were three of them, two men and a woman, quick and quiet, their heads turning as they checked the corners. All three were masked and wore dark clothes, but even with the masks I recognised the hulking shape of the nearest. It was Cinder. He looked straight at the corner in which I was hiding, but his eyes swept past without seeing. 'Empty.'

'Find some more,' snarled the second man. It was Khazad. Apparently going after me hadn't been the only item on his to-do list for tonight. He was limping and smelt of rotting vegetables. Maybe he'd hit the dumpster on his way down. 'I'm not done.'

'Enough,' the woman said sharply, and the sound of her voice made me forget all about Khazad. The clothes hid her shape and all I could see was a pair of blue eyes, but even a glance at them made me go still. I couldn't place her voice, but somehow I felt as though I'd met her before. 'Cinder, do your tests.'

Cinder made a gesture and dark red lights sprang up around the room, small red flames smouldering in mid-air. In the red glow, he studied the statue, turning his back to me. 'How long we got?'

'They'll still be getting out of bed,' Khazad said, his voice simmering with anger. 'They get in our way, too bad for them.'

'We aren't here for you to play,' the woman said. She checked a watch. 'Two minutes. Cinder?'

The woman's voice was sending chills through me. Something about it kept nagging at my memory, but I couldn't quite match it. If I could just see her face . . . but in the red light, all I could make out were her eyes as she stood with arms folded, staring at the statue. She was average height and moved with a smooth grace.

'Trying,' Cinder muttered. He was holding up his hands, weaving glowing red threads around the statue. I could recognise it as a divining spell of some kind, but a crude one. He wasn't going to learn anything useful. Cinder must have realised it the same time I did, because he lowered his hands and let the light die. 'Need a diviner.'

Khazad looked at Cinder angrily. 'You say something?'

Cinder returned Khazad's gaze. 'Said you'd bring Verus. Said you didn't need any help.'

Khazad showed his teeth in a snarl. I could feel the hate radiating off him, and I made a mental note to make sure I stayed out of Khazad's way for a while. I was getting the impression he wasn't the forgive-and-forget type.

'Cinder,' the woman said again, and Cinder looked away from Khazad, breaking the stand-off. I couldn't help but grin. *Hey, don't sell yourself short, guys. You did manage to bring along a diviner, you just can't see him.* Destroying the barrier had triggered an alarm, and Council reinforcements were on the way. I already knew that Khazad's guess had been accurate. The reinforcements were going to be too late to do me any good.

But the three Dark mages didn't know that. The woman took a final glance at her watch and shook her head. 'We're out of time.'

Reluctantly, Cinder held out his left hand. The woman handed him something the size of a tennis ball, covered in a dark cloth. Cinder turned to the statue and hesitated.

Khazad gave an ugly laugh. 'Losing your nerve?'

'Shut up, Khazad,' The woman's voice had a snap of authority to it. Khazad fell silent mid-laugh and glowered. The woman's eyes swept past him and suddenly locked on the corner in which I was hiding.

I caught my breath. Blue eyes stared into mine. In the dim light, I knew that I would be only a shadow in the corner. But if she came forward even a little . . . I closed my fingers around the glass marble in my pocket.

'Fine,' Cinder growled. The woman dragged her eyes away to look at him, and I let out my breath silently. 'Let's do this.'

Cinder stepped forward towards the statue, unwrapping the whatever-it-was. His back was to me, and I wanted to find out what he was holding in his hands, but self-preservation made me look into the future instead. Cinder was going to place the thing into the statue's hand, the statue was going to activate, and—

Oh, *crap*.

I'd been hoping these three knew what they were doing. Judging by what they were about to set off, it was obvious they didn't.

As Cinder wove a protection spell around the statue, I knew I didn't have much time. My current location was about to become very unhealthy. I could try stepping out to give the three Dark mages a warning, but I didn't even bother checking what the consequences of *that* would be. Pretty much every future in which I stayed in this room led to me being burnt to a crisp within the next thirty seconds.

It was time to go back to Plan A: run away very quickly.

Cinder finished his spell, placed something in the statue's hand, then stepped back. With his bulk between me and the statue, I couldn't see what was happening, and all my attention was going towards calculating at exactly which point I should run. There was a faint white glow from the statue, dim in the red light, then a red flicker. Then the light died away and there was silence.

Khazad spoke into the vacuum. 'Is that it?'

*Never* ask questions like that around active magic.

The room brightened with pale light, swallowing the red glow of Cinder's magic in a white aura. Something large appeared in the room, just above the statue, and right in the middle of the three very surprised Dark mages.

And in the moment's pause where the three of them were staring open-mouthed at the creature in front of them, I sprinted past and down the stairs as fast as my legs could carry me.

I've been involved in a good few combats over the course of my life, and pretty much all of them have either started or ended with me running away. There is a reason for this. Mages can inconvenience, immobilise, hurt, injure, stab, slice, burn, bend, fold, spindle and mutilate you in a variety of creative ways, but pretty much all of them require that they know where you are. If you can stay out of sight it's hard for them to know where you are, and if you can move faster than they can it's hard for them to keep you in sight. So if you lead a lifestyle that brings you into frequent contact with unfriendly mages, and you have plans for your life that don't involve getting turned into a small pile of charcoal, it's a good idea to learn to run fast. To run fast you need training, fitness and, most of all, motivation.

I had three Dark mages and an angry guardian elemental behind me. I had motivation in spades.

As I tore down the stairs, I heard a shout from the woman, followed by a hollow boom and a red-black flash as at least two of the Dark mages took a shot at the elemental. A second later the stairs flashed white and there was a crack of thunder as the elemental took a shot back. I didn't know whether I'd been spotted and I didn't hang around to find out. I made it back the way I came into the Great Court and to the top of the staircase with a speed that an Olympic sprinter would have had trouble beating.

The Great Court showed no signs of battle; the three Dark mages had probably bypassed the doors and gated in. The good news was that there were no security guards.

The bad news was that the Council reinforcements had just turned up.

There were five of them, just entering through the front doors. The battle mages of the Council are more of a police force than anything else, but you still don't want to mess with them. This group were shielded, armed and ready for trouble.

But they didn't have advance warning and I did. As I reached the top of the staircase I pulled the crystal marble from my pocket and threw it to shatter at the foot of the stairs. Silvery vapour surged out, filling the Great Court with an obscuring mist, and the mages disappeared from view in an instant. I sprinted down into the mist, relying on my magic to avoid a fall.

If I'd been lucky, that would have been it. I could have passed them in the mist and left them to fight it out behind me. But their leader was fast, already throwing up shields, shouting orders, and I knew I'd never make it through the door. I made a snap decision, jinked right, ran across the Great Court into the West Wing and just made it into the doorway before one of the other mages evaporated the mist to nothingness with a surge of air magic.

I'd been forewarned in time to freeze in the shadow of the door, my mist cloak gathered around me. The mages were clustered around the main entrance, defensive spells glowing around them. 'Where'd he go?' the leader snapped. He was a tough-looking man in his middle years with iron-grey hair.

'Can't see him,' another mage said, scanning the court. 'Didn't feel a gate.'

'He couldn't have made one that fast . . .'

'We don't know that,' the leader said. 'Ward the door; we need to push up.'

With care and persistence, you can track down even someone in a mist cloak. I knew the mages of the response team would be able to find me given enough time. I also knew they weren't going to get it.

The air mage who'd blown away the mist heard the sound of running footsteps first and called a warning to the others. The response team swung their attention to the top of the staircase just as the three Dark mages appeared at a dead run. Even at this distance I could see that Cinder and Khazad's clothes were smoking. The leader of the Council mages started to shout something up at them, and the ensuing conversation would have been very interesting if the elemental hadn't followed them out a second later.

Elementals are living, sapient manifestations of the building blocks of our universe. They're not usually all that smart, although calling them stupid isn't quite right either – 'limited' is a better word. Either way, one thing they're not is weak. Take Starbreeze – she isn't particularly powerful as elementals go, but she could still transform you into air without breaking a sweat. She could also, should she feel like it, scatter that air across so many thousands of cubic miles of atmosphere that your body would be in every time zone at once. With that in mind, you can see why mages avoid picking fights with even lesser elementals.

The elemental hovering at the top of the stairs was definitely not a lesser one.

Standing upright it would have been maybe twelve feet tall, a rough humanoid shape with two arms, two legs, a body and what could have been a head, every part of it crackling blue-white electricity. It didn't walk so much as fly, blazing a jagged path through the air to light up the Great Court with dazzling light, staring with brilliant eyes down upon the mages facing it. Ah, I thought. 'Lightning man'. So that was what she meant.

The leader of the Light mages shouted something, but no one was listening to him any more. About five of the Light and Dark mages hit the elemental at the same time, fire and wind and earth slamming into it as one.

The elemental hit back, and a lightning storm blazed outward from the top of the stairs, bolts slamming off shields to crackle down into the floor.

By this point I was running again. For a diviner like me, a two-sided battle is more than dangerous enough. A three-sided battle isn't even worth thinking about. By my count there were now *four* sides: the Dark trio, the Council reinforcements, the elemental and me. My curiosity wanted to stick around and see who won, but it was outvoted.

The only problem was that the free-for-all I was running away from just happened to be right between me and the exit. I sprinted past the Rosetta Stone and Assyria, took a right at the Nereid Monument and ducked into a corner in the Greeks and Lycians displays. Pulling out my glass rod, I channelled a thread of magic and whispered urgently. 'Starbreeze, friend to the air and – no, wait. Lady of the wind, dancer of, friend to, um . . . oh, hell with it, Starbreeze, it's Alex Verus, and I need you *right now*. Get me out of here!'

There was a crash from the direction of the Great Court and the air lit up white. I'd picked the furthest corner I could find, but from the way the floor vibrated, it wasn't far enough. 'Starbreeze! Come on! Where are you?'

Running footsteps echoed from where I'd come. I scanned, then snapped a quick look around the corner. Running through the gallery which held the Nereid Monument were two figures in dark clothes: Cinder and the woman. I ducked back and swore under my breath. 'Why do these people keep *following* me?'

'Who?' Starbreeze said in interest.

I jumped and spun to see Starbreeze hovering right next to my face, the transparent lines of her face almost

invisible in the darkness. Starbreeze giggled. 'Scared you!'
She pointed brightly back towards the Great Court.
'Lightning man!'

'Yeah, I noticed. Let's get out of here!'

'Stay and watch?'

Around the corner, the sound of approaching footsteps
had stopped. Dimly I heard Cinder's voice, muttering,
'—someone there.'

'Khazad?' the woman's voice muttered back.

*Why can't they find their own place to hide?* 'Let's not,' I
urged. 'Look!' I rummaged through my pocket and came
up with a silvered earring. 'Here, Starbreeze. *Starbreeze!*'

Starbreeze was floating five feet up in the air, gazing
absently in the direction of the battle. She gave a look
down at the earring, then shook her head and went back
to staring at the wall happily. 'Lightning's pretty.'

'Starbreeze, come on!'

Starbreeze shook her head. 'Uh-uh.'

Over Starbreeze's voice, I could just hear Cinder talking.
'—not Khazad.'

'Burn the room he's in.'

'Can't tell which room.'

'Burn them all, then.'

As I heard those last words my precognition screamed.
I went from a standing start to a dead run in one second
flat, sprinting out through the exit on the right.

There was a *whoompf!* and a wave of heat washed over
me, followed by the wail of smoke alarms. I turned back
to see that the gallery I'd been standing in was a cloud of
ash and smoke. The edge of the blast had missed me by
maybe ten feet.

As I watched the sprinkler system came on, water hissing

as it struck the molten glass of the display case, Starbreeze came zipping out of the smoke. 'That hurt!' Her voice rippled, upset, and her form was shaky, specks of ash fluttering as she moved.

'Then let's *go*! Get us out of here!'

Starbreeze swept down and around me, turned me into air, and whisked me up and out of sight. I had one fleeting glimpse of Cinder and the woman emerging from the smoke, then we were moving at Starbreeze's full speed, and let me tell you, full speed for Starbreeze is *fast*. The museum blurred and before I had time to take a breath we were outside and soaring upwards, the dome of the British Museum turning into a speck beneath us as we vanished into the night.

I had plenty to think about on the trip back. Whatever that statue was, it was valuable enough that the three Dark mages had been willing to take heavy risks to be the first to activate it. They'd tried to pick the lock and failed. It was obvious now why they'd wanted a diviner so badly: with my help, they wouldn't have set off that trap. Now they'd botched their first attempt, the security on the museum would be doubled. That meant they'd either have to quit, or come after me again. Somehow none of them struck me as the quitting type.

Thinking about them made me think again about the woman. Something about her kept nagging at my memory. I was sure I'd met her, but I couldn't remember where.

By the time I managed to convince Starbreeze to take me home, the adrenaline rush from the battle had worn off and I was dead tired. Starbreeze dropped me off on my roof and swirled away as I climbed wearily down to my flat. I'd made some new enemies, given the Council further cause to dislike me, and nearly got killed twice. Not a great day's work.

But it hadn't been for nothing. I've always believed in the power of knowledge. Any problem can be solved if you understand it well enough, and somewhere in what I'd learnt today was the key to this whole mess. I just needed to figure it out.

Once I was back in my bedroom all I wanted was to sleep, but I had more work to do. I hung my mist cloak in the wardrobe, giving it a pat and watching as its colours rippled slightly at the touch of my hand. Then I fetched the cube from where I'd left it and set it down on my desk. Cinder had been willing to kill me for this, which meant I needed to know what it did. It was going to be a long night.

4

The caverns were cold and still, and footsteps echoed in the distance. In the centre of the room was a stone bier, and laid out upon it was a body dressed in the white gown of a sacrifice. Her red hair was the only colour in the darkness, and her eyes were closed.

I tried to run to the girl lying on the stone, but my limbs felt heavy and slow. I didn't dare call out for fear of being heard. When at last I reached her, my hands seemed shadowy. I couldn't tell if it was her skin that was cold, or my own.

Then suddenly I realised that the footsteps had stopped. I froze, listening. When the laugh came it was right behind me, and I felt a surge of terror as the flames began.

I came awake with a gasp, my heart hammering in my chest. I lifted my head and winced as pain stabbed from my neck. I opened my eyes a crack, closed them again at the gritty feeling, and as I came fully awake realised I was slumped over my desk. The grey light of an overcast morning was coming in through the window, making me squint and starting up the beginnings of a headache.

I don't sleep well. I never did, even as a child, but the things that happened in Richard's mansion made it worse. Usually the nightmares are pain and fear, but it had been a long time since I'd remembered Shireen. Seeing her again, even in a dream, made my heart clench. Watching someone die is bad, but knowing that they have to be dead yet never being sure is worse. Instead of one clean cut it allows you to keep a tiny sliver of hope that fades only gradually, bit by bit, as the years slip by. It's cruel.

I tucked my head into my hands and breathed steadily, letting my heartbeat slow. As I did, I ran through my mental exercises, pushing the memories away. I'd just finished when the phone rang. The screen read 'Caller ID Unknown'. I let the phone ring eleven times, then on the twelfth hit the 'Talk' button and put the phone to my ear. 'Lyle, you have thirty seconds to explain what's so important you needed to wake me up.'

'Alex? It's Lyle.'

'Gosh, Lyle, thanks. There's no way I could have figured that out on my own by, oh I don't know, seeing the future.'

'There's no reason to be so rude.'

'Reason number one: because I hate you. I'd add more, but you've only got fifteen seconds left.'

'There's something we need you—'

'Heard it.' I leant back.

'We'd be prepared to—'

'Heard that too. Five seconds.'

'Wait! It's urgent that you—'

'Bye, Lyle. Don't call back.'

'There was an organised attack on the Precursor relic last night,' Lyle said, his voice crisp. 'The Council met for an emergency session this morning.'

All of a sudden I was wide awake. Adrenaline will do that to you. 'Okay,' I said at last, once it was clear Lyle was waiting for a response.

'The Council has decided secrecy is no longer an issue.'

'Okay.'

'This brings us to you. You understand?'

'What do you mean?'

'Well, at least you've finally got a civil tongue in your head,' Lyle said dryly. 'I'm glad you've grasped the gravity of the situation.'

Gravity was an understatement. If the Council thought I was part of Cinder's group, I was *dead*. I waited, heart in my throat.

'So, I'm offering you the same job as before.'

I stared at the phone for five seconds. 'You're what?'

'The leader of the investigation team would like to employ your services,' Lyle said. 'We'll work out the details later.'

I closed my eyes and silently let out the breath I'd been holding. Lyle wasn't calling about last night. Well, he was, but not the way I'd been afraid of. 'Look,' I said after a moment's pause. 'I said already—'

'Your problem was that the job wasn't official, correct?'

'. . . Yeah.'

'There's a ball tonight at Canary Wharf,' Lyle said. 'You're invited. Council members will be attending, including the member directly responsible for the investigation team. He'll speak with you personally.' His voice was dry. 'Official enough for you?'

For the second time, I was left speechless. 'Um . . .' I said at last.

'Oh good. The invitation will be delivered to your door in sixty seconds. Hopefully you'll consider it important enough to get out of bed. Oh, and *do* pay attention to the dress code. It would be very embarrassing if you and your escort were turned away at the door. I'd offer to lend you something, but unlike you I don't have the luxury of sleeping all morning. See you tonight.' Lyle broke the connection before I could think of a comeback.

I listened to the dial tone, then hung up. If Council members were going to be at this ball, that made it an Event with a capital 'E'. Everybody who was anybody in the mage world would be there. Lyle was serious, and that meant the Council was too.

Out of perverse curiosity, I lifted my watch and looked at the time, watching the seconds ticking off. Lyle had finished his call at 9.38 a.m. Exactly as the display ticked over to 9.39 a.m, there was a distant banging at my front door. I hate show-offs.

I pulled myself to my feet, wincing at the stiffness in my legs, and went downstairs. A teenager was standing outside my shop window, holding a white envelope in his hand. Apprentice employed as a gofer; some things don't change. I unlocked the door, nodded at the 'Alexander Verus?' and took the envelope from him. As he disappeared up the street, I opened the envelope and took out the card inside.

It was the real thing. In flowery language and copperplate handwriting, the card stated that the High Council of the British Isles would be honoured if Alexander Verus, etc., etc., would present himself with an escort of his choosing, etc., etc. There was a footnote about the dress code in slightly pointed language that I couldn't help wonder if Lyle had put in specifically to have a dig at me. Like there's anything wrong with jeans and sweaters.

I went back upstairs and dropped into my chair, staring at the card while flipping it back and forth between my fingers. It was made of cream-coloured paper with black lettering, and embossed at the top in gold was the Council's coat of arms. As I scanned it, I could detect the magical fingerprint that marked it as a genuine invitation. The only question was what I was going to do about it.

I don't like the Council. I don't like its ideas and I don't like its people. The Council doesn't even follow its own laws, much less the spirit behind them, and as far as they're concerned, morals are whatever's convenient at the time. They have absolutely no problem with throwing people to the wolves, including people who are supposed to be working for them.

On the other hand, if I just turned Lyle down, I'd be back where I'd started. After the events of last night, I was pretty sure that the Council's plans for this Precursor relic were going to be stepped up, whatever they were. The members of the team detailed to investigate would know a lot more than I did. Maybe enough for me to figure out what Cinder and that woman were up to.

And I'd only be going to talk to them. I could still turn them down if I wanted.

Yeah, right.

The starting time on the invitation was 8 p.m GMT. That gave me about ten hours to decide what to wear, pick out my shoes, and make sure I wouldn't be killed before the doors opened. With that settled, I picked up my phone again and dialled Luna's number.

She picked up on the third ring. Luna gets up earlier than me, but then she doesn't stay up till the early hours of the morning analysing weird magical artifacts. 'Hello?'

'Hi, Luna, it's me.'

'Hey, Alex.' Luna's answer was friendly, but there had been a tiny pause before she spoke.

'Listen, can you do me a favour? Could you come around to my place some time today?'

'Um . . .'

'I know it's short notice. I've found out something

important about that cube of yours but I need you to run a test. Is that okay?'

'Well . . .' Luna hesitated, then her voice firmed. 'Okay. I can come by now. About an hour?'

'Great. See you then.' I broke the connection and turned to look at the cube. I'd been up for a good four hours last night studying the thing. I still hadn't figured out what it did, but I was starting to get a pretty good idea what it *was*.

Magic items are inherently difficult to create. By its nature, magic is tied to life, created by the exercise of a living, conscious will. Trying to make a permanent magic item out of an object is sort of like trying to make a permanent light source out of bits of wood. But mages are a persistent lot, and over the years they've worked out ways to get around the problem.

The simplest way is to use items which aren't magical at all but which guide and direct raw magic in a specific form. These are called focuses, and they're effectively tools built for a single purpose, like a hammer or a chisel. Energy channelled into them is shaped and directed in the same way that water follows the banks of a river, and given enough time they can even pick up an imprint of the personality of the user. They've no power of their own, but they're useful in the right hands.

Another approach is to make one-shot items like the fog crystal I'd used the night before. In this case a mage casts a spell, then seals it in an item; typically you break the item to cast the spell. These are usually low-power effects, and their main function is to make schools of magic available to those who can't access them normally. A skilled crafter can whip up a one-shot item in a couple of hours, and they do a brisk trade in the magical economy.

Sometimes, though, neither a focus or a one-shot will do it; you need something that'll last *and* has power of its own. But to use magic, you have to be alive. The solution that some creative (and probably slightly crazy) mage came up with a long time ago is to make an item that *is* alive. The resulting creations are known as imbued items, and they can be extremely powerful and extremely dangerous.

Luna's cube was an imbued item. It was too powerful to be a focus, and too complex to be a one-shot. It was complex enough that it even had protections against detection magic; there was a kind of null field around it that warded away active scans. I'd tried looking into the future to see what the consequences would be of forcing my way in, and decided quickly that I did not want to do it. This thing had a lot of energy, and it was quite capable of releasing it explosively if provoked. As yet, I hadn't been able to communicate with it, and I wasn't sure if there was any way to. Imbued items tend to be single-minded, and they usually don't talk, making their own decisions based on whatever sensory input they have access to. I'd discovered the cube had a network of microscopic holes in its outer shell; that was what produced the sparkling effect when you looked into the depths. I had the feeling they were access points of some kind, and that the right signal of visible light might activate the cube, but any such signal would be extremely complex. Without more information, there was no way I could guess it.

One person, though, *had* been able to produce a response from the cube: Luna. I didn't know why, but if she'd been able to get a reaction once, maybe she could do it again. At least, that was what I was hoping.

I checked my watch. Luna was due in forty-five minutes.

I washed and shaved, then looked into the future to see what time she'd arrive. I paused, then looked again.

Luna wasn't coming.

That was strange.

I looked a third time, then a fourth. As things stood, Luna wasn't going to come to my door within the next hour, or any hour for that matter. Frowning, I pulled out my phone and called, but got her voicemail. I looked into the future, trying for a clue, and couldn't see one. A thread of worry started to curl up from somewhere inside. Maybe she'd been in an accident?

No, that didn't make sense. The one good thing about Luna's curse is that it makes her near immune to accidents.

But it doesn't make her immune to things done on purpose . . .

A new, unwelcome thought intruded. Maybe Luna wasn't coming because she didn't want to. The more I thought about that, the more likely it sounded. Ockham's razor states that the simplest explanation is usually correct. The simplest explanation for Luna not showing up was because she didn't want to see me. God knows I've had enough people flake on me before. I got up and paced, tense and nervous, glancing at my watch. Twenty minutes. Did Luna need my help? Or did she want to stay away?

Give a problem like this to an engineer, and he'll give you an answer straight away: 'insufficient data'. But in life, you have to make calls on insufficient data all the time. I forgot about my magic and listened to my instincts.

My instincts told me Luna wouldn't have flaked after promising to come.

She was in trouble.

In two strides I was at my desk. I went through the drawers in a clatter, shoving handfuls of items into my pockets, snatched my cloak from the wardrobe, then ran downstairs and out the door. As I hurried down my street I pulled out my phone and dialled Luna's number. It didn't work. I swore and tried again. This time it rang. One ring, two rings, three rings . . . 'Come on, come on,' I muttered as I hurried along.

There was a click. 'Hello?'

'Luna, it's Alex. Where are you?'

'Um, five minutes away. What's wrong?'

'Luna, this is important.' I tried to keep my voice calm. 'I need to know where you are *exactly*.'

'Uh . . .' I heard Luna stop and turn around. 'I don't know the name of the street. It's the one off Camden Market with that glass building on the corner.'

Luna was only a short walk away. But if she wasn't going to arrive . . . I felt a chill. That meant that whatever was going to stop her was there with her right now. 'Turn around! Go back into the market!'

'What?'

'Back into the market, or the shops. Anywhere there's lots of people.'

'But your house is the other way.'

'I know! Luna, please, just trust me. Do it now!'

There was a moment's silence. I'd broken into a run, and I was quickly covering the distance. Then I heard Luna's voice. 'All right . . .'

'Are you in the market?'

'Yes, but Alex, there are people everywhere! I can't stay far enough—'

'I'll be there in two minutes. Just keep moving, and—
Luna? Luna!'

The line had gone dead. I swore and kept running.

Camden Market is one of the big tourist attractions of
London. It fills the blocks between Chalk Farm Road and
the Grand Union Canal, and even on off-days it's busy. On
Saturday mornings it's packed to the seams with street
sellers, tourists, arts-and-crafts types, teenagers, goths,
punks, trendies, performers, bargain-hunters, antiquists,
dealers, kids and just about everyone else, all forming a
seething mass. The shops sell antiques, knick-knacks, and
fashions of the kind that newspapers call 'alternative' and
most people just call 'weird', and everywhere is filled with
people, talking and eating, bargaining and shopping, filling
the place with noise. Finding one girl in Camden Market
is like looking for a contact lens at a football match. It's
impossible for a normal person.

For a mage, though . . .

Luna turned off Chalk Farm Road and down Camden
Lock Place. To most eyes she would have blended in with
the crowd, a girl of medium height wearing casual clothes
and backpack. Only the way she shied away from anyone
who got too close made people glance at her. From time
to time she would look nervously over her shoulder, scanning the bustling crowd.

Luna turned down a side-street where there were fewer
people. She shook her head at a man trying to give her a
leaflet, skirted a clothing stall, crossed onto the pavement.

Something appeared out of the shadows next to her.
Luna jumped, then stopped as she recognised me. 'Alex?'

'This way. Quick!'

One of the best things about Luna is that she knows when not to argue. She'll ask questions for hours without a break, but when I tell her to *move*, she moves. Luna ran down the stairs and I held the door open for her, then slammed it shut, hearing the lock click.

We were in an underground parking garage, filled with rows of cars lined neatly between support pillars. Fluorescent lights cast a weak glow over the concrete floor. The sounds from outside were muffled, a steady buzz. 'Alex?' Luna asked. 'What's wrong?'

'Two people after you,' I said. I hadn't laid eyes on them yet, but if Luna and I hadn't ducked out of sight I would have done. 'A man and a woman.'

Luna just looked at me, confused. 'They would have moved on you as soon as you got to the end of that street,' I said, and pointed. 'Find somewhere to hide. We're not out of the woods yet.'

As Luna hurried to the side wall, I pulled the packet of trail dust from my pocket and tore it open. I ran to the other side of the garage and opened the door at the other end, leaving it ajar so that a sliver of light crept through. Then I paced the distance back, sprinkling the trail dust left and right. The brown powder sparked briefly as it touched the floor, vanishing. Once I'd covered all the floor we'd stepped on, I walked quickly to where Luna was waiting. 'What are you doing?' she asked.

I threw the last handful of the trail dust back where we'd gone, then crumpled up the wrapper and stuffed it into my pocket. 'Covering our trail. Are you okay?'

Luna's face clouded. 'I touched someone. I was trying to get away, but he bumped into me, and . . . Alex? What's wrong?'

I'd been looking into the future; now my heart skipped a beat. 'Get down. Behind the car!'

Luna's eyes went wide and she obeyed, kneeling down next to the wheel of a big 4 x 4. I yanked my mist cloak out of my bag and pulled it around my shoulders, then stepped back into the shadows and flipped the hood up over my head, feeling the cloak blend with the wall. Luna had looked away for a second, and now as she turned back, her eyes passed over me without seeing me. 'Alex?' she whispered.

'I'm here,' I whispered, and Luna started. 'Stay down, stay quiet.' I shut up and an instant later I heard the door rattle. Luna heard it too, and went very still. I stood upright in the corner, just another shadow in the dark.

The handle of the door we'd entered by was rattling. There was a moment's pause, then a flicker of sea-green light. Dust puffed into the air, and suddenly there was a hole where the handle had been. The door swung open with a creak.

The two people who stepped through wore different clothes from last night, but I still recognised them. One was Khazad, spindly and stick-thin, his movements bird-like and quick. Now that I could see his face I could see he looked vaguely Middle Eastern, his eyes darting from side to side. The second was the woman who'd been ordering him around. Unlike Khazad, she still wore her mask, and as I saw that I leant slightly forward. Khazad came down the steps and turned from left to right. He was holding something in one hand, frowning.

'Well?' the masked woman said after a moment. She was still above, scanning the area. I saw her eyes pass over me, but she gave no reaction. I knew she shouldn't be able to see through my mist cloak at this range, but it wasn't me I was worried about.

'Wait,' Khazad said.

'Is she here or not?'

'This thing's screwing up,' Khazad said in frustration. 'Stupid piece of crap.' He raised a hand, and something dark gathered in his palm.

As it did, I felt something from Luna. I glanced down and stared. The silver mist of Luna's curse was moving. A strand of it slipped invisibly outward, reaching ten, twenty times further than normal, curving over the cars to brush against the object in Khazad's hand. 'Shit!' Khazad snarled.

'Well?'

'I don't fucking believe this! It's dead!'

'Is it,' the woman said absently. She was still scanning from left to right, her eyes passing over where Luna and I were hidden, and I didn't dare move.

'Screw it,' Khazad said angrily. He stuffed the whatever-it-was into his pocket. 'What about a trail?'

'Wiped.'

Khazad glanced up, his eyes narrowed. 'Thought she was a norm?'

'She isn't a mage.' The woman's eyes traced the wall from behind her mask. 'But there's something . . .'

I held my breath. The woman's eyes had come to rest on me, and she was staring right at where I was hidden. *Again. How does she know?* Five seconds passed, ten.

'Well?' Khazad demanded.

The woman looked away, and I let out a soft breath. 'That door,' she said, her voice suddenly sharp again. She started walking towards the door I'd left ajar, disappearing behind the pillars. I strained my ears to listen. Khazad said something I couldn't hear, finishing with '—not there?'

'We've got her address,' the woman said. 'One thing at

a time.' The door creaked open and their footsteps receded up the stairs.

Luna started to move, but I signalled for her to stay down and she did. I counted off a full minute, looking through the futures, then walked forward, pulling the mist cloak from my shoulders. 'Let's go.'

'Who were they?' Luna asked, scrambling to her feet. She looked anxious rather than scared, which probably meant she didn't understand what we'd just heard.

'The man's called Khazad. I don't know the woman's name. You don't want to meet them.'

As we hurried back the way we'd came and emerged out into the street, Luna spoke up hesitantly. 'They kept saying "she". Did they mean—?'

'Yes.'

Luna shut her mouth and we walked the rest of the way back in silence.

We were back in my flat, above the shop. Luna was curled up on my sofa in the same spot she'd been lying in last night, watching me. Her white hands were curled around a coffee mug. She'd been sitting listening for the last ten minutes, only speaking to ask questions.

'So that's how it is,' I finished. 'Cinder, Khazad and that woman tried for the relic last night. Now it looks like they're going for something else instead.'

'The cube?'

'Cinder was looking for it yesterday, and those two are working with Cinder. Now they're looking for you.'

Luna was quiet for a second. 'Why?'

'Probably traced the cube to the same place you got it. They don't know you gave it to me or they'd have been trying to break in here. Right now, you're their lead. They're not going to give up easily.' I hesitated. 'I'm sorry for getting you into this.'

Luna only shook her head. 'How were they tracking me?'

'Khazad had a focus. There are lots of ways, he was using one of the simple ones. Luna—'

'It was my curse, wasn't it? That was what stopped him finding me.'

I blinked. 'You can tell?'

Luna nodded. 'Sometimes. When there's something I'm really afraid of. It's like a part of me reaches out and touches it, and it's gone.'

'Huh.' I sat back. I'd always thought Luna's curse was a passive thing, but what Luna had just said made me wonder. Being able to feel it that clearly . . .

'She said she had my address, didn't she?'

I'd been reaching for the glass of water on my desk. As Luna spoke I went still, then picked up the glass and took a drink, hoping she hadn't noticed the pause. This wasn't something I wanted to tell her. 'Yes.'

Luna was silent for a second. 'The man I got the cube from doesn't know where I live,' she said at last. 'He knows my number, but . . . Oh, of course. My name. They could have looked my address up with that.' She shook her head and looked up. 'Well, I suppose it doesn't matter much. I can't go home, can I?'

I let out a breath. 'No. They'll be at your flat by now.'

'They won't hurt anyone else in my building, will they?'

'It's not your neighbours you should be worried about! These people are *dangerous*!'

Luna nodded. 'I know.'

I put a hand to my head and sighed. 'I'm sorry. I should

never have gotten you into this. If I'd known you'd turn up something that would get you involved in this stuff—'

'No. This is what I want.'

I stared. 'Luna,' I said carefully. 'If those three catch you, they'll quite likely kill you. You understand that, right?'

Luna looked back at me steadily, her clear eyes looking into mine, then she dropped her gaze and traced her finger around the rim of her mug. 'When you called me this morning, you were afraid I wasn't going to come, weren't you?'

'I—' I checked myself. 'How did you know that?'

'You always tell me how dangerous your world is,' Luna said. 'It's like you think you need to warn me off.' She dipped the tip of her finger into the tea and looked at it. 'It doesn't bother me, you know.'

'Luna—'

Luna looked up to meet my gaze. 'If those three are going to be chasing someone, it's better that it should be me, isn't it? I mean, if I was a normal girl, they'd have caught me back there.'

I stared at her.

'So,' Luna said at last. 'You said you needed me to run a test? I mean, before we got distracted.'

'I—' I let out a breath. 'All right.' The cube was sitting on the coffee table in between us, looking ordinary and dull in the morning light. 'Try picking that up.'

Luna nodded and obeyed. The cube swung between her fingers as she looked at it, then gave me a glance.

I grabbed a pencil and paper and scribbled a word, then pushed it across the coffee table, taking care to keep my distance. 'This is a general-purpose command word. Hold up the cube and say it.'

Luna waited for me to sit back, then reached forward and picked up the paper. To my eyes the silvery mist of her curse engulfed the paper as she studied it, frowning slightly. The cube hung silent in her other hand, the silver mist sliding off it without sinking in. Imbued items have a will of their own. Until they decide to use their power, they're nothing but blunt objects. One way to get an imbued item to obey you is to find the item's special purpose and bring it to bear somehow. If you don't know the item's purpose, you're out of luck; the item won't obey anyone except its master.

But if you can guess who its master might be . . .

'*Annath*,' Luna said.

Light flowed from the cube and in an instant the gloomy room was lit up in red and white. The crystal surrounding the core glowed with energy and thin lines of light sprang outwards, playing over the sofa, the table, the walls. For one instant, Luna was backlit in the glow, holding the cube aloft, her eyes lifted up in wonder.

Then the light snapped out, and the room was back to normal. Luna dropped the cube and it bounced, came to rest on the sofa cushions, and sat quietly. Luna twisted around and stared down at it. There was a moment of silence.

I let out a breath. 'Okay then.'

'What was that?'

I got to my feet. 'Luna, it's going to be better if you're somewhere very hard to find for a while. I'll explain along the way.'

## 5

I explained along the way, and carried on explaining. Luna kept asking questions and didn't stop, long after I expected her to go quiet. It was as though now she'd finally gotten me to open up, she wanted to learn everything she possibly could.

Learning about magic's dark side is a major tipping point for newcomers, and the way they react tells you a lot about who they are. Some freak out completely – once they realise that messing with this stuff can get them killed, they run and never come back. Others just get a bad case of the shakes and adjust bit by bit. I've seen the whole range – or at least I thought I had. But Luna had been near-missed by Dark mages twice in as many days, she'd just learned that they weren't going to stop until they found her, yet she hadn't turned a hair. Why was she so calm?

I think it was at that point I first realised just how little I really knew about Luna. I'd always focused on her curse – how it worked, whether I could do anything to fix it. I'd never learnt what really made her tick.

'So there are lots of those spells?' Luna was asking. 'Could they find me another way?'

'Easily,' I said. We were walking up a grassy hill, avoiding the path to keep clear of people. A pair of students were throwing a frisbee off to our left, and dogs ran across the meadow. 'But most of the powerful ways to track someone take time. If they're smart they'll stake out your flat while they put something together.'

'Will my curse help?'

'Chance magic needs some randomness to work with. If they get something that can find you reliably enough, there's not much it can do.'

Up ahead, a family was laughing and tramping downhill on the path. We fell silent briefly as we waited for them to go by, letting Luna give them a wide berth. 'I still don't see why this thing with the cube makes a difference, though,' Luna said once they were gone. We crossed over and headed for the woods on the other side. 'Why does it matter whether I can use it?'

'It's more than that. I spent three hours last night playing with that thing and didn't even get a flicker. You touched it and it obeyed you straightaway. Imbued items *choose* their wielder. I'm pretty sure that for anyone but you, that cube's nothing but a piece of glass.' I left unsaid the question of why it had picked her, mainly because I didn't have any idea myself.

'You said they wouldn't know that—'

'They *probably* don't know that. But they obviously know more about that thing than we do. Maybe they know it'll only bond with one person.'

'Why does that make a difference, though?' Luna asked. We'd entered the woods and were away now from the bulk of the crowds. The trees were just starting to come into bloom, and birds sang cheerfully from the branches. 'I mean, either they're hunting me because they think I've got the cube, or because they think I can use it. Either way . . .'

'It means that no matter what happens, this isn't going to be over quickly. One way or another, they're going to keep looking for you until something makes them stop.'

Luna paused and we walked a little way in silence. 'Okay,' she said at last. 'So what are we doing *here*?'

The two of us were standing on Hampstead Heath, the biggest park in inner London – and the most beautiful, at least in my opinion. Regent's Park is probably more famous, but it's a bit too cultivated for me. The Heath's just wild enough to be interesting. On a Saturday afternoon like today, it's swarming with men, women, children and dogs, doing everything from eating picnics to flying kites. At first glance it's not the place you'd expect to find anything magical but, as I said, it's wild while still being in the city. For some people, that's a useful combination. 'I need some clothes for a party,' I said. 'You need somewhere to hide. This is the only place I know we can get both.'

Even with all the people who use the Heath, it has its secrets, and we'd come to one of them. A dried-up stream had carved a ravine out of the earth, the sides rough and uneven. An oak tree grew on the top of the bank, its roots reaching down the slope. Although we could still hear the sounds of people around us, the banks and the growing trees hid us from them. Of course, the other reason no one was here was because there wasn't anything to see.

Luna looked around at the earth and trees. 'Here?'

I smiled. 'Watch.'

The roots of the oak tree made a tangle in front of us. I studied them for a second, then reached out and placed two fingers on one of them. 'Arachne?' I said to the tree. 'It's Alex. Can we come in?'

There was a brief pause, then Luna jumped as a voice

came out of thin air. 'Alex, dear! Come right inside. Find a seat in the dressing room while I finish up.'

There was a rumble of moving earth, and both of us stepped quickly back. The hillside seemed to shudder as the roots of the oak tree began to move, twisting aside and up, dripping dirt and bits of dry earth across the ravine, revealing a gaping space beyond. As the rumbling quietened, the roots wove themselves into the shape of an archway. Within was only darkness.

I gestured to Luna. 'After you.'

Luna hesitated for only a second before walking in. I followed, ducking my head, and with another rumble the roots closed behind us.

Like I said, one of the tipping points for newcomers is learning about the dark side of magic. Another is when they start meeting creatures out of myths and legends. The issue is learning not to judge by appearances.

Human beings tend to react better to good-looking people. It's called the halo effect – someone's attractive, so you trust them more. It's natural, which makes it a hard habit to break, but once you start dealing with magical creatures you'd better learn to break it, and fast, because some of the most vicious things out there can make themselves look like absolute angels. Like unicorns. Don't get me started on unicorns. For some reason everyone has this idealised image of them as beautiful innocent snowflakes. Beautiful, yes. Innocent, no. After you've had one of the little bastards try and kebab you, you wise up quick.

But it goes the other way, too. There are things in the dark corners of the world that look like the nightmare children of Stephen King and H. P. Lovecraft. Just looking at them is enough to make any sane person run screaming, but if you're brave or stupid or savvy enough to stop and talk to one, you'll find to your surprise that you can get along okay. They're not *safe*, of course; nothing in the magical world is really *safe*. But you can talk with them and trust them as well as the humans you meet here, and often better.

I tried to explain this in a halting sort of way to Luna as we walked towards Arachne's cave. 'She sells clothes?' Luna asked.

'The best. Most mages won't use them, though.'

'Are they too expensive?'

'It's . . . how she looks.'

'She's ugly?'

'Not exactly. Just brace yourself for when you meet her.'

The tunnel we were walking down felt dark after the sunlit heath. Now my eyes had adjusted, I could see the blue glowing spheres mounted in the corners of the tunnel that marked the path. The floor had been packed dirt at the tunnel mouth, but now it was stone, worn smooth by running water and polished to a sheen by generations of footsteps. The grey tunnel sloped downwards, twisted and opened into an oval chamber blazing with colours.

The room was filled with couches and chairs, and every flat surface was covered with lengths of cloth, from finger-length ribbons to bolts the size of rolled carpets. Dummies and hangers were mounted on the walls, and every single one held clothes of some kind, from suits to tops to full-length dresses, in every colour from red to yellow to green to blue to violet. I've been to Arachne's cave dozens of times and every time I practically have to shield my eyes as I walk in. It's like watching a flock of birds of paradise holding a fashion parade on a rainbow. Across the far end of the room, practically invisible in the riot of colour, was a translucent curtain. Rustling sounds came from within.

'Alex, dear!' The voice came from behind the curtain. Up closer you can just hear the clicking sound under Arachne's voice, though it's faint enough that you wouldn't notice unless you knew what to listen for. 'Where have you been? Clear off a couch and sit down . . . Is that a guest?'

'This is Luna,' I called back. I heaved an armload of clothes off the nearest couch to give Luna space. Luna was so busy staring that she didn't notice.

'What a pretty name. Hello, Luna, can you hear me?'

'Um, it's nice to meet you,' Luna called. She moved to a chair and traced a finger down a pale green ribbon, then tested it between her fingers, looking at it curiously.

'Are you wondering what they're made of?' Arachne called, and Luna dropped the cloth with a start. 'Everyone does, you know.'

'Um, yes.' Luna touched the ribbon again, fascinated. 'Is it silk? I've never seen anything like it.'

Arachne laughed, and again there was that odd clicking noise. 'Almost. Not the kind you're thinking, though . . . Well, then, Alex, if you're here, I expect you want something, hmm?'

'Yup. The ball at Canary Wharf.'

'My, my. That's tonight.'

'Invitation was late. Got anything lying around?'

'Oh, good heavens, Alex,' Arachne said, and I could hear the exasperation in her voice. 'Well, at least you've got the sense to come here. Let's have a look.' There was a shadow of movement behind the curtain, then Arachne emerged, and for the first time Luna got a good look at her.

Arachne is about the size of a minivan, and weighs maybe half a ton. Her body is black, with a cobalt-blue sheen that glimmers slightly when she moves, and she has eight eyes in two rows of four at the front of her head. Each one of her eight legs has seven hairy segments, ending in tips where the hairs are finer and can act almost like fingers. Two mandibles hide her fangs and rustle slightly as she talks, making the clicking sound.

In other words, she's a gigantic spider. Arachne is quite safe – well, more or less – but she's every arachnophobe's worst nightmare, and even people who aren't scared of spiders are likely to scream the house down the first time they meet a tarantula bigger than their car.

Luna didn't scream, but the blood drained from her face, and her eyes went as big as dinner plates. 'Alex?' she said, her voice very high.

'It's all right,' I said reassuringly. 'She won't hurt you.'

'Alex, she's a giant spider.'

'She won't hurt you.'

'Alex, *she's a giant spider.*'

'I know,' I said patiently. 'She won't hurt you.'

'Well?' Arachne said expectantly. 'Aren't you going to introduce us?'

Keeping a careful eye on Luna, I stepped forward. 'Right. Arachne, this is Luna. She's still pretty new to all this. Have you got somewhere she could sit down for a while?'

'Oh, of course.' Arachne scuttled sideways, and Luna jumped. Arachne beckoned down a side tunnel. 'You look exhausted, dear. Why don't you have a rest? Help yourself to something to eat. Don't worry, it's human food.'

'Alex?' Luna said again, keeping very still.

'It's okay,' I said quietly. 'Luna, trust me. You're as safe here as anywhere.'

Luna gave me a look with very big eyes, then took a deep breath and edged across the room. She managed to make it past Arachne without flinching or screaming, and Arachne's eight eyes followed her as she stepped sideways into the tunnel. She gave me one last nervous look and backed away.

'Well,' Arachne said brightly once Luna had gone. 'She seems nice.'

'Sorry about that,' I said. 'Like I said, she's—'

Arachne waved a foreleg. 'Oh, I'm used to it. Now let me have a proper look at you.'

For something so big and heavy, Arachne is a lot faster than she has any right to be. She was looming over me almost before I knew she was moving, one leg on either side of me and eight black eyes looking down from above. This was why I'd wanted Luna out of the room. No matter how well she'd managed to control herself, I thought it would be best if Luna had a little time to calm down before she saw Arachne's way of having a chat. It's really not as threatening as it looks; Arachne just wanted to see me properly. She's very short-sighted, and she's most comfortable when she can use her sense of touch, which means her favourite way to talk to someone is to have them right between her front legs, under her fangs. I sat down on one of the couches and patted one of Arachne's hairy legs. 'Good to see you again.'

'And it's nice to meet your friend at last. I'd wondered why you'd been so busy the last few months.'

Despite her looks Arachne smells nice, kind of like

incense. Sitting next to her feels almost like being in a
herbalist's. 'Well, that's part of the reason we're here.'

'That's a nasty little weaving she has. You've been trying
to unravel it, haven't you?'

'You can see it?' I said in surprise, then shook my head.
'Of course you would. Yeah, I've had a few tries. Didn't
work, though.'

'Of course not; it's grown up with her. The spell's woven
into her pattern.'

'Any way to take it off?'

'Not without killing her.'

I sighed. 'Kind of what I figured. Listen, you have to
be careful not to get too close to her. The width of a room
is fine, but any closer than that—'

Arachne gave a gentle hissing sound and her mandibles
vibrated – her equivalent of laughing. 'Silly child. A little
weaving like that won't hurt me.'

I looked up in surprise. 'You can avoid it?'

'Now, before she gets back, why don't you tell me why
you're going to the ball? I don't remember you being one
of the Council's favourites.'

I explained to Arachne then, telling her all about Lyle
and his offer, leaving very little out. 'And Lyle's not the
only one,' I finished. 'Some Dark mages want my help too,
and they're tracking Luna. I wanted to ask you a favour
and see if she could stay here until I get the chance to talk
to some people at the ball. If I'm lucky I'll be able to clear
things up there.'

Arachne sat in silence for a moment. Her opaque eyes
looked down at me, showing nothing. 'You're in dangerous
waters, Alex.'

I shrugged. 'Mages always want to use diviners for what

we know. It's just my bad luck they're desperate enough to come to me.'

'Luck? Really?'

I looked up curiously. One problem with talking with Arachne is that it's really hard to read her facial expressions. 'What do you mean?'

'It's not luck that's made every other diviner in these islands vanish.' Arachne settled herself down slightly. 'My customers have been running thin the past few weeks. Something is going on, and the careful mages don't want to be involved.'

I had to grimace at that. 'And I'm already involved. Great. I don't suppose you know what it is?'

Arachne rustled a no. 'I think you should find out. I'll watch your apprentice.'

I laughed. 'She's not my apprentice. But thanks.'

Arachne tilted her head, and a moment later I heard Luna's footsteps approaching. I got up off the couch and ducked between Arachne's legs to see Luna enter. Her eyes flickered to Arachne, but the colour had come back to her face. 'Um. Hi. Uh, it's nice to meet you, um, Miss Arachne. I'm sorry about before.'

Arachne waved one of her legs. 'Don't worry about it, dear. You're doing very well. Now, Alex, what sort of outfit were you thinking of?'

'Uh . . .' I said. 'You know what, you decide.'

'Well, at least you're showing some sense.'

I rolled my eyes and turned to Luna. 'I need to look up some contacts. Arachne's agreed to let you stay here for a little while.'

Luna's eyes widened just slightly. 'Stay here?'

'I won't be long. These tunnels are warded; no one's

going to be able to find you. Right now it's probably the safest place you can be.'

Luna looked from me to Arachne, then took a breath and nodded. 'Okay.'

'Wonderful,' Arachne said cheerfully. 'And while you're here, why don't we have you fitted?'

Luna looked at Arachne doubtfully. 'Fitted?'

'For a dress, of course. I have something I think would match perfectly with a little work. Why don't you come over to the fitting room so I can have a proper look at you?'

Luna gave me one last anxious look, then turned to Arachne and smiled bravely. 'Um, sure. Thank you.' As I turned to leave, I saw Luna following Arachne through the curtain into the chamber beyond.

I came out of Arachne's cave into the sunlight, and blinked for a while as the roots closed behind me. Now that Luna was inside, a weight had been taken off my shoulders. It might not look it, but Arachne's cave is one of the best-protected places in London. Hidden behind the webs and wards, Luna was safe – at least for a little while. I turned and climbed uphill, coming out into the open again, then found a bench to sit on.

Most people's idea of seeing into the future is someone in funny clothes staring into a crystal ball and reading tea leaves. They'd be pretty disappointed if they saw me. I'm not a fan of crystal balls, and I absolutely hate the tea leaf method. Tarot cards I do use, but only in very specific situations and not often. No, what real diviners do when they want to get some work done is find a quiet, secluded spot, get comfortable, then lie back and close their eyes. To the layman, this looks remarkably like slacking off, but the best diviners can find out pretty much anything you care to name without ever leaving their armchair.

Arachne's suggestion to find out more had clicked with a stray memory from my conversation yesterday with Lyle. When I'd asked Lyle about the other diviners, he'd told me they were all busy, and mentioned Alaundo and Helikaon. Alaundo I only know by reputation, but Helikaon I knew very well indeed. And something Lyle had said didn't fit. I'd never known Helikaon to turn down work from the Council. Why was he doing it now?

It wasn't much, but I had the feeling it might be important. I wanted to talk to Helikaon, and I didn't have time to waste looking him up. I was going to have to do this the quick way.

The technique is called path-walking. You pick out a strand of your own future, and follow it, guiding the choices and seeing what happens. My first destination was Helikaon's flat in Kensington. I looked into the future, tracing out the path where I went searching for him, taking a taxi to his flat, walking up the stairs, knocking at his front door. No matter how I did it, there was no response. The place was empty. As I watched, the future thinned and faded to nothingness, never to exist.

Next up was Helikaon's house in the country, where he conducts most of his business. Helikaon's house is a modest one by mage standards, a single-storey building on the South Downs. I looked into the future and saw myself walking up the dirt path to the house at the top of the hill. The building was silent and still, the windows shuttered. There was a note of some kind on the door, something that would turn me away. The vision flickered as I circled the house, searching, finding nothing.

I could always break in. I looked into the future that had me bypassing the lock on the front door, walking inside. My future self stepped in, and—

*Ouch.* Okay, that I did not expect. Now I knew something was going on. Helikaon didn't normally leave booby traps in his front hall, especially not ones as nasty as that. Maybe the back door? Around the ash trees, round to the small door on the other side, onto the porch, inside—

Jesus! That was just *vicious.* I didn't know it was even possible for a body to dissolve so fast. What the hell had that been, some kind of acid?

I definitely wasn't snooping around Helikaon's property any time soon. As I made that resolution, the future of me going there faded completely. Shaken, I took a moment to steady myself. Watching yourself die is a creepy experience, especially if you're not prepared for it.

Once I'd calmed down, I forced myself to try again. I was running out of places to look, but there was one more spot that Helikaon and I had used a long time ago. Not many knew about it. But if he'd wanted a place where no one could find him . . .

And there it was. I couldn't tell at this distance what we were saying, but I knew Helikaon was there. I opened my eyes and sat up. I needed something from my flat, then I had a journey to make.

The fastest way to travel by magic is by gating. Gate magic creates a portal between two places, usually by bringing about a similarity between points in space. It's one of the more difficult magical arts, and generally requires you to know both the place you're leaving and the place you're going to very well. Unfortunately, I'm one of the minority of mages who can't use gate magic. Divination can't affect physical correspondence, only perception.

The next option is to use a mount, like a pegasus or an air elemental or a *taia*. It's a lot slower than gating, but has the advantage that it can get you to a lot of places that gate magic can't. Using a mount allows you to travel to warded locations, gives you the ability to explore places you don't know, and also lets you show off your rare and expensive status symbol, if you're into that sort of thing. The main downside is that mythical animals have a tendency to attract a lot of unwanted attention when you fly them through London in broad daylight.

For those who can't gate and don't have the luxury of a mount on call, there's a third way. Crafters make items called gate stones that give someone with magical skill a limited access to gate magic. They only work for one location each, and they're inferior in every way to a true gate spell, but for someone like me, they're often the only way to get around.

Despite their name, gate stones don't have to be stones. This one was though; a jagged shard of granite with runes cut into both sides. Standing in my bedroom, I made some preparations, then focused my will, said a sentence in the old tongue and pushed. For a long moment nothing happened, then with a shimmer a jagged-edged shape appeared in the air. Its edges were flickering, and I stepped through quickly before it could fade away. As soon as I was through it dissolved, leaving no trace behind me.

The first thing I noticed was the cold; the air was a good twenty degrees cooler than in my flat, and a chill breeze was blowing. The air was thinner too, and I shivered. I was on a mountaintop, hundreds of feet above sea level. The view to the left was just as spectacular as I remembered, and I turned to get a proper look. The mountain dropped off in a steepening slope into valleys and hills, descending steadily, clearly visible in the afternoon sunlight. Grassy slopes and granite peaks were spread out before me, and in the far east, just visible over the hilltops, I could make out the glitter of the sea. The sky above was cloudless and blue.

From behind came the *clop, clop* of hooves on rock. I turned, and smiled. 'Hey, Thermopylae. How you doing?'

Thermopylae gave a pleased whinny as he trotted towards me. He was pure white but for his hooves and nose – a powerfully built horse with a scraggly tail that swished behind him as he walked. Two huge feathered wings stretched from his shoulders, each big enough for me to hide behind. They were half furled at the moment, swaying slightly as he balanced himself on the uneven stones. He came trotting up, his nose twitching, as I took some sugar out of my pocket and gave it to him, laughing as he butted me with his huge head in his eagerness to get to it.

'Oi!' a voice called from the north. 'Stop spoiling my horse and come if you're coming.'

I grinned and gave Thermopylae the last few lumps, then patted the pegasus on the neck and started walking. As I came around the rocks I saw an old, ramshackle hut made of planks of wood. A man who looked older than the hut was sitting on a stone in front of it, brewing tea over an open fire.

Helikaon looks about sixty, strong and spry despite his age. His hair was yellow-gold once, but now it's a bleached white. Even in this weather he wore only a shirt, its sleeves rolled up and its neck open. A short sword, a *xiphos*, hung at his side, but he wore it so casually you wouldn't notice unless you were looking. 'Worst thing about living this high is getting the water to boil,' he grumbled. 'Least you're on time.'

I sat down. 'At least you haven't lost your touch.'

'None of your lip! I've forgotten more divination than you'll ever know.'

'It's how much you remember I was wondering about.'

'Oh, very funny.' Helikaon glared at me. 'You know the trouble with you lot nowadays? No respect for your elders. Thinking you know everything . . .'

I took a look at the water, ignoring his mutters. 'It'll boil in ninety-five seconds.'

'That's not boiling. *Bubbling* isn't boiling. And who do you think you're trying to impress, giving me a number? Have a little patience for once and wait.'

I grinned. 'Good to see you again.'

'Sure, sure. Make yourself useful and get some cups.'

I did, and waited for the tea to be ready. There was something comforting about the old ritual of waiting for Helikaon to make sure it was prepared to his satisfaction, listening to his grumbling when it wasn't exactly right. It was a beautiful view, looking down through the clear air onto the wilds of Scotland, and the fire held back the worst of the mountain chill.

'I'm surprised it's still standing,' I said at last, looking at the weather-beaten hut.

'It'll last.' Helikaon gave me a glance. 'Longer than you, maybe.'

'So I guess you know why I'm here.'

Helikaon snorted. 'Please. You're *loud* when you walk through the future, know that? I haven't been able to get any peace all day.'

'Okay.' I laid the cup of tea carefully down upon the ground. 'Why did you turn Lyle down?'

'Why d'you think?' Helikaon pointed at me. 'I don't want to do what you're doing, and if you're smart you won't either. Go back to Arachne and find a hole to hide in.'

'It's not as simple as that.'

'You get in the middle of this, could end up dead. Council can't pay enough to be worth that.' Helikaon glared at me from under his bushy white eyebrows. 'Used to be I had to twist your arm to go near those old men.'

'There's someone else.'

'Ditch 'em.'

'What's with turning your house into a deathtrap?'

Helikaon grinned. 'Caught you out, heh? Shouldn't have been snooping.' His grin vanished. 'These boys play rough. You want to convince them to leave you alone, you have to talk their language.'

I looked away.

Helikaon studied me. 'Time was you'd be happy as a pig in shit to see a Dark mage get eaten by a trap like that. Change of heart?'

'It's not that.' I turned back to Helikaon. 'Look, I've been out of the loop. I know you've still got your contacts. What's going on?'

Helikaon sipped his tea, then shrugged. 'Been building a few years. Dark mages pushing for status. I know,' he held up his hand to forestall me, 'they've got it. But they want more. Seats on the Council.'

I stared at him. 'The *Council?*'

'Old news, boy.' Helikaon gestured out towards the vista below us. 'Council are split as usual. Some want to give in, some want to stall. Darks'll probably get their way in the end. Weight of numbers.'

'Numbers?'

'They've been recruiting. Pretty aggressive. Some mages, they can turn. The ones they can't . . .'

'I know what happens to the ones they can't,' I said flatly.

'But not united. That's what it's about.' Helikaon pointed south. 'That relic's got a Precursor artifact, big one. Dark mage who got hold of it could set himself up as their leader. More power than any faction in the Council. Council wants it too, use as a bargaining chip. All of 'em need a seer to get inside.' Helikaon pointed at me. 'All'd rather see you dead than helping the others. 'S'why I'm up here. You should be too.'

The two of us sat silently for a minute. 'What does this thing do?' I asked.

'Don't know. Wards too heavy. Council knows more. Not getting close enough to ask.'

'So that's what Cinder and Khazad are after.'

Helikaon shook his head. 'Muscle. Someone's giving 'em orders.'

I remembered the masked woman I'd seen just a few hours ago, and somehow I was sure it was her. 'So now you know,' Helikaon said, interrupting my thoughts. 'What'll you do?'

'I don't know,' I said after a pause.

Helikaon snorted. 'Bull. You're going to that ball no matter what. I'll tell you what's going to happen with that relic. Light and Dark are going to fight and kill for it.

Use their fancy magic to blow holes in each other till one side wins, then everything'll go on just the same.' Helikaon paused. 'What's up with you, Alex?'

I sat silently. 'When you came to me I told you,' Helikaon said. '"Forget about revenge. Keep your distance." You listened then. Now you're getting involved. You're smarter than this.'

'Maybe I'm tired of not getting involved,' I said. I looked up. 'What about friends, family? Don't you have anything you'd stand and fight for?'

'You ever listen to a word I say?' Helikaon looked at me, his eyes hard. 'Remember what I told you first time we met? Anything you take into your life, you have to be able to walk away from ten seconds flat, never see it again. Anything else, *anything* else, it's dragging you down. You're asking if I've got anything I'd stand and fight for? No, Alex, you fucking idiot, I don't. That's why I'm eighty-three and still alive. You think you'd have found me if I didn't want you to? Soon as you leave, I'm moving on. You won't see me till this is over.'

The silence stretched out. 'Hard way to live,' I said at last.

'You think life's supposed to be easy?'

I finished my drink and set the cup down with a click. 'Thanks for the tea.'

Helikaon didn't say anything and I walked away. The pegasus came trotting over to me as I passed out of sight, and I gave him a final pat. 'Bye, Thermopylae.' Then I reached into my pocket for the gate stone that would take me home.

I had a lot to think about on the journey back.

When I'd first met Helikaon, it had been right after the final showdown with Tobruk. Even back then Helikaon was a master, able to do things with divination magic I didn't even know were possible. I'd learned more about the art from him than anyone else – path-walking, precognition, future sight – but more important had been *how* he'd taught me to use my powers. At the time I met him, I was burning with fear and anger from the nightmares I'd been through in Richard's mansion. I had fantasies about taking revenge, going back and killing them all. Helikaon taught me to shut away the fear and the fury, detach myself and find a measure of peace. It saved my life, I know that now. I would have died if I'd gone back. Getting away and staying away, letting everyone forget about me, had been the only way to survive, and that's what I'd done.

But despite all he'd done for me, Helikaon and I never became master and apprentice, and now I remembered why. There was a coldness to him, a distance, which I was repulsed by and yet envied him for. I knew that the way Helikaon shut out others gave him a clarity of vision I couldn't match, but I still couldn't bring myself to share it. I'd fled to my shop in Camden, stayed away from other mages, but I hadn't stayed detached. I'd made friends: Arachne, Starbreeze, Luna. Did that make me a worse diviner than him, or had I gained something as well?

By the time I made it back to Hampstead Heath, the sun was a red glow in the western sky. I leant against the tree, thinking, looking at the branches above me. Their tips were glowing red in the sunset, the contrast vivid against the blue sky. The earth was still warm from the day's sunlight, the Heath gradually becoming quieter as more and more people turned their footsteps towards home.

For the first time I seriously considered taking Helikaon's

advice. What if I did as he said and walked away? I'd be safe again, just as I had been since I escaped from Richard's mansion . . .

*Did you?*

The thought startled me. I came to a stop, wondering where that had come from. I *was* safe, always had been, since then. I'd kept away from other mages, kept to myself. I wasn't in danger any more. If I left I could stay that way.

But even as I imagined leaving, I realised I wasn't going to do it. When I'd been in greatest need, Lyle and everyone else from the Council had abandoned me. If I ran now, I'd be doing the same thing to Luna that they'd done to me. I shook off my doubts and reached up to open the tree.

It's always risky introducing two people who've never met. You can never be quite sure how they'll get on, especially when one's human and the other looks like the star of a high-budget horror movie. So I was pretty nervous as I returned to Arachne's chamber. I couldn't help thinking of all the things that could have gone wrong: Luna panicking and running off alone, Arachne losing her temper with Luna and kicking her out. So far Luna had been bearing up well, but it was a lot to absorb in a very short time. What if being left alone with Arachne had been one shock too many?

Lost in thought, I didn't recognise the sound I was hearing at first. When I did, I slowed, puzzled, then turned the last corner and walked in.

Luna was laughing, though her voice was distant. I couldn't see her, but from the sound she was in one of the small side chambers to the far left of the room. Arachne was in the centre, working at a table. 'There, you see?'

Arachne said. She was working on a dress in white and green, altering something in its design. She worked with all four front legs at once, needles and scissors moving so fast I couldn't follow what she was doing. 'Now, I think your instincts were right the first time. Pale colours look much better on you. I've taken out the green, so why don't you give it another try?'

'Okay!' Luna said from across the room. 'I really like the pink one as well though.'

'It does set off your skin . . . I'll keep it out just in case. Oh, hello, Alex.'

'Hey.' There was a pile of dresses on the sofa nearest to the changing rooms. 'Been busy?'

'Hi, Alex!' Luna called from behind the curtain. Her voice was muffled, as though she was pulling something over her head. 'Have you seen these clothes? They're amazing!'

I grinned at Arachne. 'Arachnophobia's no match for shopping, huh?'

'Don't be graceless,' Arachne said, and glided across the room to pass the dress over the top of the curtain. Luna's bare arms reached over to take it. 'Here you go, dear. Have a look at both while I see to Alex.' Arachne drew the curtain back from another side chamber. 'Now, Alex, before you put these on, I want you to promise you'll take *care* of them.'

'Sure.'

'I mean it. You hang them up properly, have them washed in that funny way, what's it called—?'

'Dry-cleaned.'

'—and don't get them slashed or dissolved or chewed up or burned.'

'It hasn't happened *that* many times.'

'Oh really? What about the first set I made for you?'

'That was *ten years ago*! Would you have even noticed if it had been me that didn't come back instead of the clothes?'

'It was a full wardrobe. Some of my best work, too. With a little work they'd still fit . . .'

'Look, you know what happened there. I couldn't exactly have gone and asked for them back.'

'And the outfit I made you for Unicorn's Run. Have you any idea how hard it is to get blood out of silk? Then there were the ceremonial robes for the investment ceremony. You said to make it fire-resistant, and I did. I even told you exactly what temperature it would tolerate. And then—'

'I didn't say fire-*resistant*, I said fire *proof*. Besides, that thing with the inferno elemental was *not* my fault.'

'What are you two talking about?' Luna called from behind the curtain.

'Nothing,' Arachne and I said at exactly the same moment, then looked at each other.

'I think it'd be a good idea if she went with you to the ball,' Arachne said.

I blinked. I'd been trying to decide the same thing but . . . 'A mage's ball isn't exactly the safest place for a newbie.'

'She has to learn sometime. Besides, Alex, I think you should have a talk with the girl. You aren't doing her any favours by sheltering her.'

Before I could ask Arachne what she meant she'd scuttled away into her private chambers. I shrugged, then went into the changing room and took a look at the outfit laid out on the table. I probably should have asked for something specific instead of leaving it all up to Arachne. Oh well.

'What was that about?' Luna asked curiously, her voice muffled from the wall and the curtains between us.

I started to undress. 'Arachne gets upset about the state I leave my clothes in.'

'It doesn't happen often, does it?'

'No.' I hesitated, mentally counting. 'Not really.' I counted again. 'Okay, maybe. But I only get clothes from her when I'm going to meet a lot of other mages.'

'You mean like now?'

'Yeah, like—'

I stopped and turned my attention to my new outfit. Laid out on the table it looked like a dinner jacket, although there was something a little different about it. I picked up the shirt.

'Alex?'

'Uh-huh?'

'Is it okay if I come to the ball with you? I won't get in your way.'

The shirt was causing me problems. I didn't answer straightaway, and Luna took my silence as a sign that I needed more persuading. 'I mean, if those people are going to be looking for me, a crowded ball would be a good place to be, right? It'd be harder for them to try anything with lots of other mages around. And some of the people might have information. I could help you find things out.'

I finished with the trousers and held up the tie, running it through my fingers. 'Arachne told you to say that, didn't she?'

Luna went quiet. I shook my head and started putting the tie on. 'She's really taken a shine to you.'

'So, um—'

'You can come.'

'Really?' I could hear the excitement in Luna's voice. 'Great!'

I shook my head, but I didn't smile. What I really wanted to ask was why she was so excited to be going. Luna wasn't stupid; she had to realise that a gathering of mages would make for a dangerous night out. But it wasn't the right time to ask.

A faint scuttling sound alerted me that Arachne was back. 'All ready?' she called, and brushed the curtain aside to come in. Arachne's always been a little hazy on human ideas of privacy. She looked me up and down approvingly. 'Good.'

I turned to take a look at myself in the mirror. Putting it on, the outfit had looked like a dinner jacket. Wearing it, it still looked like a dinner jacket, but it was . . . different, somehow. The figure looking back at me looked smart, elegant. It was hard to put your finger on it, but if I'd seen a picture of myself I might not have recognised who it was.

'Well?'

I took a last look, then nodded. 'I like it.'

'Well, at least you have some taste.' Arachne handed me a white ribbon. 'Tie this on the lapel.'

I looked at the thing curiously. It was more than just an accessory; I could feel magic radiating from it, with the subtle weave of Arachne's signature, but it seemed passive, rather than active. 'What does it do?'

'Oh, I think you should be able to work that out.' She moved round to where Luna was changing, and I heard her asking Luna which one she liked best.

I walked out into the central chamber, studying the ribbon with a frown, searching through futures. There was something about the weave that I recognised, something that made me think of chance magic, inverted. But it wasn't a spell I'd ever seen, unless . . . My eyes widened suddenly. *Oh . . .*

'All ready?' Arachne's voice called. 'Come on, Alex, are you watching?' I looked up in surprise just as a girl stepped out from behind the curtain.

It was Luna, but for a moment I didn't recognise her. She was wearing a dress of white and green that left her arms and shoulders bare, spiralling down in layers to cover her feet. The cloth shimmered slightly as she moved, the pale green and the snow-white reflecting the light around her. A gauzy shawl was wrapped around her arms, and she'd tied her hair up with a pair of white ribbons, leaving her neck bare.

'What do you think?' Luna asked. She sounded a little nervous, but she was smiling.

I stared at her for a few seconds before answering. 'Not bad.'

Arachne snorted. 'Don't listen to him, dear. You look perfect. A few more touches and you'll be all ready to go.'

The sun had set by the time we finally said goodbye, and as we walked out of Arachne's lair I could see the first stars shining in the sky above. The air had cooled, and around us, Hampstead Heath was quiet. 'Had a good time?' I said as we walked out into the gully.

'I had a great time.' Luna was smiling; you would never have thought that only a few hours ago she'd been scared of being left with Arachne. 'Is she named after the weaver? The one from the Greek myth?'

'If I had to guess, I'd say it was the myth that was named after her.'

Luna looked at me for a second before her eyes went wide as she got it. 'But that was – how long ago?'

'Two, three thousand years?' I shrugged. 'I've never asked.'

The Heath was fast emptying of people, and here in the densest part, it was all but deserted. As the light faded from the evening sky we walked to a ridge and into a grove of trees. I took the glass rod and recited the incantation. 'What are you doing?' Luna asked curiously.

'Calling us a ride.' I grinned. 'An air elemental called Starbreeze. Be nice to her.'

Starbreeze must have been close; I'd hardly finished speaking before she sprang up in front of me in an invisible rush of wind. 'Hi, Alex!'

Luna jumped as the voice came out of mid-air, and Starbreeze pointed at her. 'Ooh! Who's that?'

'This is Luna,' I said. 'Could you go visible for a second?'

'Okay!' Luna jumped again as, to her eyes, Starbreeze seemed to materialise out of thin air right in front of her. Today Starbreeze had decided to look like a woman in her thirties, with long hair and clothes woven of mist. She floated closer and stared at Luna in interest, studying her clothes. 'Pretty.'

'Um, pleased to meet you,' Luna said, recovering. She stepped back and Starbreeze floated closer, then whirled in a circle around her, faster than Luna could turn.

'Starbreeze, we need to go to the tower at Canary Wharf,' I said. 'Can you take us there?'

Starbreeze stopped whirling and brightened. 'Oh, the ball! I want to go there!' She vanished in a puff of wind, leaving us alone in the grove. 'Starbreeze!' I yelled after her. '*Starbreeze!*'

Starbreeze reappeared in the blink of an eye, visible again. 'Hi, Alex! Ooh!' She pointed at Luna. 'Who's that?'

I sighed. 'Could you take us to Canary Wharf? *Us.*'

'Okay!' Starbreeze swept forward over us, and I felt my body start to transform. Then suddenly it stopped, and I was standing on the grass again.

I looked around in surprise; that had never happened before. Starbreeze had zipped away, and was floating at a safe distance, pointing at Luna. She looked upset. 'Don't want to take her.'

'What's wrong?' I asked.

'*She's* wrong.' Starbreeze shivered slightly. 'Hurts.'

Luna sighed. She'd been keyed up, excited, but now the animation faded from her body. 'It's me. I know.'

'It's all right.'

Luna shook her head. 'It's okay, I should have known.' She gave me a half-smile. 'You go ahead. I'll meet you there.'

'Oh, I think we can do better than that.' I held out my arm. 'Take my hand.'

Luna looked down, then up at me. 'Um, what are you doing?'

'Arachne's very old and very wise,' I said. 'Your curse can't hurt her. And right now it can't hurt me either.' I took the ribbon hanging from my lapel, held it up so she could see. 'As long as this is still white, I'm safe. So,' I smiled, 'ready to go?'

Luna looked at me for a long moment, very still. When she spoke, her voice was suddenly cold. 'Are you making fun of me?'

I stared at her. 'What?'

'I can't touch anyone. You know that. If this is a joke—'

'Luna!' I touched my fingers to the ribbon. 'Arachne made this specially for you. It's the same spell as your curse, but inverted; it absorbs it. As long as you're near it, Starbreeze'll be fine, and so will I.'

Luna's mask wavered, and I saw she was uncertain. She looked from me to Starbreeze, still floating off to one side. I held out my hand and she took one hesitant step forward, almost within arm's length. Then she gave a shiver and backed away, shaking her head. 'No.'

I dropped my hand. 'Luna, it'll be fine.'

'You don't know that! How can you tell?'

'I don't know, maybe because I can see the future?' I stopped and took a deep breath. Being snarky wasn't going to help. 'I know you can't see how this thing works. But trust me, it does.'

Luna shook her head.

'Look, I thought you were getting on with Arachne? She obviously likes you; she wouldn't go to this much trouble for anyone. Take her word for it.'

'No.'

'Goddamn it! What are you planning to do, sit here all night?'

Luna shook her head again. Her face had firmed, and her voice was steady. 'I'll get there on my own. It was at Canary Wharf, right? I can find my way.'

'No you *can't*. You won't make it halfway across London before Cinder and Khazad and that woman find you, and your curse can't protect you from *one* Dark mage, much less three!'

'I guess I'll have to take the chance.'

'It's not a chance! You're as good as dead if you go out there!'

'And *you're* as good as dead if I touch you!'

I stopped, staring. Luna glared at me, then caught her breath as she realised what she'd just said. She closed her eyes, inhaled, and straightened her back. When she opened her eyes, she looked calm again. 'Thank you for trying, really. But it's fine.'

'That's it, isn't it?' I said slowly. 'You're afraid.'

Luna went still, then shook herself. 'It's okay,' she said levelly. 'You go with Starbreeze.'

'You're scared of what'll happen.' I gave a short laugh. 'Look, you don't need to worry. It'll be fine.'

Luna stared at me. 'You think it's funny?'

'No.' I caught myself. 'Look, there's nothing to be scared of—'

'You don't know that.' There was an edge in Luna's voice.

'Yes, I do.'

'You don't know everything.'

'I know enough about this—'

'*Shut up!*'

I rocked back, and Luna took a pace forward, glaring at me. 'You always think you know everything. You don't! You don't know what it's like, you've never *felt* what it's like. Stop acting like you do!'

I stared. I'd never seen Luna like this. She'd never before even raised her voice. 'Luna—'

'*Stop it!* Stop telling me what to do! I don't want your— I don't want—' Luna's voice wobbled and she swallowed. I took a step forward, but she jumped back, glaring at me. 'No! Stay away from me!'

I took a deep breath. Luna stared at me, fighting back tears, and I tried to figure out what I needed to say. 'Look,' I said at last. 'You've always trusted me so far. Trust me now.'

'No! I haven't— I mean—' Luna turned away, running a hand through her hair, breathing fast. 'I can't, I— You don't know what you're asking. I can't get close, I—'

'If Arachne says something works, it works. You won't hurt me.'

Luna drew in a shaky breath. 'Alex, you don't know what it's like. The only way I can live is if I tell myself it has to be this way. If I let myself—' She realised what she was saying and put a hand to her mouth, fright in her eyes.

I looked at Luna, standing alone and frightened on the hillside, and finally understood. All I could feel now was pity. I held out my hand to her. 'Luna—'

But as Luna recognised the expression in my eyes, she finally snapped. 'Stop looking at me like that! *Stop feeling sorry for me!*' She took a step back. 'I'm not going to the ball. I don't want to be with you. Get away from me!'

I tried to keep my voice calm. 'It's okay—'

'*Shut up!*' Luna shouted. 'I'm sick of you and I'm sick of your *stupid* magic and I'm sick of you pretending you know everything. I don't want you to teach me anything any more. *Leave me alone!*'

You've probably figured out by now that I'm not the most tolerant of people. I have a really low bar for how much crap I'll take from others, and I especially hate getting pushed around by people I'm trying to help. Probably one of the reasons I can never get a girlfriend, but that's another story. The sensible part of me knew that Luna was just saying these things to try and make me lose my temper. Trouble was, it was working. I sucked in a breath and, out of sight, flexed my left hand, clenching it into a fist, then letting it relax. When I spoke, my voice even sounded calm. Mostly. 'Let's get one thing clear,' I said. 'I am not leaving you out here with a bunch of Dark mages hunting you.'

'It's not your choice!'

'Yes, it is,' I snapped. 'I don't care how stupid you're acting, I'm not going to let you kill yourself.'

'Try and stop me.' Luna's eyes were wide, and she was breathing fast. She was standing a few paces away, half turned and poised to run. It would only take one more push to make her flee, and I had the nasty feeling that in the state she was in she might just be able to outrun me. I took a breath, and went still. 'You know what?' I said as I let my leg muscles coil. 'Fine.'

I was on Luna before she had the chance for more than a yelp. She tried to spring back, but I got one hand on her wrist and the other around her shoulders. And as I did, I came into range of her curse. To my mage's sight, Luna's curse is a silver-grey mist, following her like a cloud. As soon as I started towards her, it had stretched out towards me, silvery tendrils reaching out eagerly. If I didn't trust Arachne so well, I don't think I'd have had the nerve to make the jump.

But the tendrils never reached my body. As they touched my clothes, they twisted downwards, curving away to soak into the ribbon like water into a sponge. Silver mist poured steadily from Luna, flowing off my clothes like water off a duck's back. The ribbon absorbed it all and, as I watched, its corners began to darken. Around that point, though, I stopped having any attention to spare.

I'm a head taller, fifty pounds heavier, and a good bit more skilled than Luna, so I'd been thinking I wouldn't have much trouble keeping hold. However, it was at this point I first learned that holding on to a healthy and active twenty-two-year-old girl who's seriously trying to break free is a lot like trying to give a cat a bath. The whole thing lasted about thirty seconds, and it was claws, knees and elbows the whole way.

By the time things slowed down, I was holding Luna with one arm behind her back and my right arm across her neck, just tight enough to keep her pinned without pressing into her throat. Luna's other hand was gripping my forearm, trying to drag it away, and Starbreeze was watching from a few yards away, absolutely fascinated. She was obviously having a great time.

'All right,' I managed at last. Luna had landed an elbow in my stomach and it was making it hard to catch my breath. 'Stop trying to tear my arm off and listen.'

Luna kept pulling a second longer, then she sagged suddenly, going limp. Her shoulders shook.

'Better,' I said. Luna's head was turned away from me, so I had to talk into her ear. 'First, your curse isn't touching me. You should be able to tell that since I'm holding onto you without being hit by a meteor or something. Now, we're going to the ball. Once you get there you can do whatever the hell you like. But I'm not cutting you loose until then. Understand?'

There was a long pause. 'Yes,' Luna said at last in a muffled voice.

'All right,' I said. 'Starbreeze? Take us to the ball.'

'Hurt,' Starbreeze said doubtfully.

'It'll be okay. She won't hurt you.'

'Well . . .' Starbreeze brightened. 'Okay!' She swept in around us and once again my body thinned to air. Stray wisps of the curse brushed Starbreeze, but most of it was pulled into the ribbon, and a second later we were floating.

Luna gasped, but it was done before she could react. Our bodies were air, drifting apart. I was still holding Luna's hand, but it felt like slippery glass. I couldn't have kept my grip if she'd pulled away, but *she* was holding onto *me* now, both hands latched on tight. Starbreeze took off and the ground blurred beneath us as we soared into the sky.

I don't think I'll ever forget that flight. There was something primal about it, excitement and anticipation mixed together. There was danger behind and danger ahead, but now we were free. The fight was forgotten, left behind on the distant ground. I'd flown with Starbreeze many times before, but never with someone to share it.

London is amazing by night. Instead of the grid pattern of most cities, its streets twist and turn, and from above every one of them is outlined by streetlights. The parks are patches of shadow, the main roads glowing rivers. The Thames is a dark snake winding through the centre, its banks lit up with the waterfront buildings, boats and bridges leaving dots and slashes of light across its dark waters. Above, the stars shone down out of a cloudless sky, Orion and Cassiopeia looking down on us. Starbreeze flew higher and higher, leaving the bustle and danger of the city far below.

At one point I dragged my gaze away from the lights of the city below to watch Luna. Her shape was misty and transparent, and she was gazing down at the view, drinking it in. All I could see of her was her eyes, and there was something timeless in them, like distant stars. Only the pressure of her hand reassured me that she was still there.

I felt a strange sense of loss when Starbreeze finally began to circle downwards. The skyscrapers of the Docklands appeared below us, growing larger and larger, then we were racing past them, plummeting between the towers of steel and glass. The ground rushed up to meet us, halted, and Starbreeze brought us down to the stone gently as a feather. Canary Wharf towered before us.

6

The official name for the tower at the centre of the Docklands is One Canada Square, but everyone in London calls it Canary Wharf. It's the tallest building in Britain, eight hundred feet high to the flashing double strobe at the top, and it dominates the London skyline, a symbol of wealth and power. Officially the whole tower is office space, and since it's not open to the public there's no one to say otherwise. Starbreeze had dropped us off within a small park in the shadow of some trees and, looking forward, I could see other couples on the plaza, moving towards the blaze of light that was the tower itself. I felt awake and alive, on full alert. There was work to be done.

At my side, Luna was peering up at the tower. She looked as though she might have been crying, but the journey had wiped away any tears, and her face was unreadable. I stood waiting to see if she'd speak, but instead she looked down and began to shiver, wrapping her shawl around her bare arms. Canary Wharf is right in the middle of a meander of the Thames, and a cold wind was blowing off the water. 'Let's get inside,' I said.

'I'm fine,' Luna said, still shivering.

I sighed inwardly, put my arm around Luna and started walking her towards the distant entrance. She didn't resist. 'There are anterooms,' I said. 'I'll find you somewhere safe.'

Luna shook her head mutely. I looked down at her. 'What's wrong?'

'I'm going with you.'

'What?'

Luna didn't look up and I rolled my eyes heavenwards, just barely stopping myself from saying something that I knew would make things worse. First I had to drag her here, now she was refusing to leave. I can see the freaking *future* and women still don't make sense. 'All right,' I said at last, once I'd gotten myself under control. 'You're going into a place where knowledge is power. Don't reveal anything about yourself. You shouldn't even introduce yourself as "Luna" if you don't have to, and don't for God's sake tell anyone your full name. Mages put people into two groups. There are other mages, and then there are sheep. Just by showing up here you're proving you're not a sheep. But all that's going to depend on how they see you, and they're going to be judging you every second you're there. The people in there aren't your enemies – well, mostly – but they aren't your friends, either. Don't let down your guard.'

The wind returned, ruffling my hair, and this time it wasn't cold. I looked up to see Starbreeze floating above me, back in her invisible form. 'You're staying?'

Starbreeze pointed up cheerfully at the tower. 'Make another lightning man?'

Luna looked from me to Starbreeze. She still couldn't see her but was getting used to guessing where the air elemental was floating. 'Lightning man?'

'Don't ask.'

Starbreeze swirled around our heads and Luna glanced up at her passing. 'She thinks you're going to make things fun?'

Talk about backhanded compliments. 'Given what she calls fun, I hope not.'

'Not you!' Starbreeze chipped in. She pointed at Luna. 'Her. Ooh!' Starbreeze looked upwards and her face lit up. She shot up into the night sky and out of sight before either of us could say a word. Luna and I looked at each other, then kept walking.

The ground floor lobby was huge and spacious, paved in Italian marble. A steady murmur of voices echoed around the concourse. A boy in his teens crossed the floor towards us. 'Good evening,' he said politely. 'For the ball?'

I handed him my invitation and he gave it a quick glance. 'Thank you. Far lift, top floor.'

I took the invitation back with a nod and started for the corner. Luna had been studying the boy curiously, and whispered to me once we were past. 'Who was he?'

'Apprentice,' I said quietly. 'I used to do jobs like that once.'

The buttons inside the lift went up to 45. I hit the top one and the doors hissed shut. The lift whirred upwards with a hum of powerful machinery, and I knew we'd arrive in less than a minute. 'Some of the people inside will be mages, some will be adepts or hangers-on,' I told Luna. 'Don't look surprised or shocked, no matter what you see.' I paused. 'Ready?'

Luna nodded. 'Ready.'

'Okay. Game face on.'

The doors hissed open to reveal a group of four big men in dark clothing, their eyes tracking us as we stepped out. The one at the front asked for my invitation, and this time the check was more thorough. Once he was satisfied, he nodded. 'Thank you. Enjoy the ball.' Up ahead, a pair of double doors stood open, and light and voices streamed through. We walked in.

The room we'd entered was enormous, the ceiling reaching far overhead with angled corners. A double balcony ran the circuit of the walls, recessed so that the people walking it were concealed behind the railings. At the centre was a square column stretching all the way to the roof. Walkways ran between the upper balcony to the higher levels, and scattered on the underside of the walkways and all around the walls were sets of chandeliers, glowing with hundreds of lights. Everything was made of steel and glass reflecting the light and throwing it back so that the entire vast hall was as bright as full daylight. It was dazzling, and both Luna and I blinked as we stood there, our eyes adjusting.

The hall was filled with noise; there were hundreds of people thronging the floor with more looking from above. Men and women were crossing the floor, talking, watching, dancing, standing, spread out across all of the vast room. The entry hall was set a little above floor level, and from our position Luna and I could see out across the whole crowd. To one side a band was playing upon a stage, and on the dance floor maybe fifty were dancing while others looked on. Another area had been set aside for games, with mages' chess, duelling pistes and more. Near the central column was a buffet, and on the far side, partially blocked by the column, I could see the greyish glow of a sphere arena, suspended in mid-air.

We stood there for a minute, just watching. No one seemed to be paying us any heed yet. That wouldn't last. 'Well,' I said, and took Luna's arm. She flinched and started to pull away in reflex, but I gave her a smile and she hesitated. 'Let's go attract some attention.'

We walked down the stairs to the floor, and Luna fell in by my side. As we did, I glanced down at Arachne's ribbon, making sure that Luna didn't see me do it. A quarter of its length had gone black, the darkness spreading slowly as it drew in the silvery mist.

I led Luna towards the band and the dance floor. We passed other men and women as we walked, strolling and talking, all wearing expensively tailored evening wear. In my normal clothes I would have stood out like a sore thumb, but in Arachne's outfits we fitted in perfectly. Arachne pretends not to care about fashion, but she always seems to match it. Most of the men were wearing dinner jackets like mine, while the women were wearing dresses that were . . . well, they were dresses. I have no clue what kind. Hey, I'm a guy, what do you expect? There's a reason I go to Arachne when I want to look good.

The band was a string ensemble. They were playing a waltz, quick and cheerful. 'Want to dance?' I said to Luna as we reached the dance floor.

Luna shook her head. 'No, thanks.'

'Great.' I pulled Luna out onto the floor.

'Alex!' Luna protested, her voice rising. People turned to look, and she hushed it to a whisper. 'I can't—'

'Relax,' I said as I took her right hand in my left and raised it. 'I can.'

'You know I don't know how to dance!'

'Just follow my lead. Put your other hand on my shoulder.' I moved it. 'There. Start off on your left foot. And one, and two—'

'I can't do this!'

'—and three,' I said, and led off. Luna nearly tripped over, then righted herself, clinging to me desperately as we moved through the crowd.

Although I don't look it, I'm a pretty good dancer, a legacy from my time with Richard. I haven't gotten much use out of it since then, but it's like riding a bicycle – you never forget. The nice thing about dancing as a man is that if you're good enough, you can carry a girl even if she doesn't have the first clue what she's doing. I stuck to basics, letting Luna get used to the rhythm as I scanned the crowd for familiar faces. There weren't many. I don't generally get invited to high society events, and the mages here were the elite.

Of course, not all were mages. Many would only be adepts, or maybe not even that. Some would be enspelled, and they'd be waking up tomorrow morning remembering tonight as nothing more than a dream. And some would be apprentices or even slaves, here only at the whim of their masters.

Here's the catch, though – there's no way to know just by looking whether someone is a mage or not. Some mages like to advertise, but the smart ones usually take care to avoid revealing their power until it suits them. It's easy to look at a crowd like this and notice only the ones who catch your eye – the woman wearing a white dress that seemed to be made entirely of feathers, with gaps exposing glimpses of pale skin, the man dressed entirely in red, with a snake-headed cane at one side – but usually the ones you have to watch out for are the ones you *don't* see.

The music shifted into a slower dance, and as Luna began to realise that she wasn't going to trip over, her death grip on my arms loosened. I could feel her muscles relax slightly through the hand on her back. 'Having fun?' I said into her ear. The mist still swirled around her, but the ribbon was drawing it away from the other dancers.

'I'm going to get you for this,' Luna said, breathless.

'I'll take that as a yes.'

'Is everyone watching?'

'Yup. Oh, don't stiffen up, you were just starting to relax.'

Luna's fingers dug into my arm. 'Why are they all looking at me?' she whispered into my ear.

'Probably wondering where you got your dress.'

'Alex!' Luna tried to hit me with her free hand and nearly stumbled.

'Tsk. You don't want to fall.'

Luna made a noise that sounded almost like she was laughing. 'We're new,' I said, my voice serious again. 'Everyone here is watching everyone else. Probably a hundred people have made a note of us by now. Don't be surprised if you're approached as soon as this dance ends.'

'Me? Why?'

'Curiosity. Information.'

'What should I say?'

'Whatever you like, as long as you don't give too much away. Let them come up with their own ideas and don't correct them.'

We did another circuit of the dance floor, passing close to the band. All four were women. They looked natural at first glance; only if you looked closely would you see the slightly glazed look in their eyes. We turned back towards the crowd, and I saw who I'd been waiting for. 'Look over my shoulder,' I said as I turned. 'Greek-looking guy in a dark blue suit with fancy trim. Talking to the man in red.'

'Mm . . . okay, I see him. Who is he?'

'Name's Lyle. Major league asshole. Tied in with the Council.'

'He's the one who invited you?'

'Yup.'

We did another revolution. 'Are you going to talk to him?' Luna asked eventually.

'He can wait.' Lyle was starting to send irritated glances in our direction. The music came to a halt, and I came apart from Luna with a smile and gave her a small bow. There was scattered clapping.

'That was . . .' Luna hesitated. She looked different somehow – flushed and wondering, alive in a way I'd never seen before. 'I've never . . .'

'I know.' I took her arm and led her off the floor as a new dance started. I didn't bother to hurry; I knew Lyle would come to us.

He materialised out of the crowd before we'd even reached it. 'Ah, Alex,' Lyle said with a good imitation of surprise. 'I'm glad I bumped into you.'

'Hey, Lyle. Thanks for the invitation.'

'Don't mention it.' Lyle looked at Luna. 'I don't believe we've met?'

'I hope you're not trying to steal her from me, Lyle,' I said with an easy smile, then glanced at Luna. 'This is Lyle, an acquaintance of mine. We know each other very well.'

Lyle bowed to her. 'An honour to meet you.' He straightened. 'If it's convenient, Alex, I've some things to discuss with you in private. Barrayar, perhaps you could show the lady around.'

A man who'd been waiting at Lyle's side stepped forward. He looked like a functionary. 'You'll have to excuse me,' I said to Luna. 'I'll be right back.'

'That's fine,' Luna said, and gave Lyle a smile. 'Pleased to meet you.' Lyle gave another bow, then turned and started walking. I followed. Behind, I heard Barrayar starting to introduce himself.

'"I'll be right back"?' Lyle murmured once we were out of earshot. 'Seems you still haven't learned not to make promises you can't keep.'

'I wouldn't get too cocky, Lyle.' Other men and couples glanced at us as we passed, first at Lyle, then with more curiosity at me. Lyle was a known quantity here; I was something new. 'I only agreed to listen.'

'And you think you'll be getting a better offer?'

I grinned lazily. 'Oh, you'd be surprised just how many people are taking an interest in your relic lately.'

Lyle gave me a sharp look, then turned away.

Servants were moving through the crowd, white-clothed figures with their faces hidden behind opaque masks offering food and drinks. We passed a crowd around the buffet table and climbed a small flight of stairs up to one of the exits from the hall. The exit led to a staircase, leading upwards and then doubling back. We went up two levels and came out into a smaller corridor, this one plain and undecorated. Windows on the left side looked down into the main hall, but the sounds were quieter up here, the music and conversation from below muffled. The corridor ended in a door, leading into an antechamber. As we walked in, I checked, staring at the figures ahead.

In front of the opposite door, facing us, were two creatures sculpted from silver and gold. They stood seven feet tall on triple-jointed legs, and had two pairs of segmented arms carrying eight-foot-tall ceremonial glaives and devices of tapering metal the size of heavy guns. Their heads were turned towards us, and faceted golden eyes watched us silently as we entered. These were *gythka*, mantis golems, and their presence meant a Council member was here. Lyle hadn't been kidding.

'Lyle Trahelis,' Lyle said as he walked up; he hadn't stopped. He gestured in my direction. 'He's with me.' He approached the door and paused, looking back at me. 'Hurry up, Alex. We haven't got all day.'

The mantis golems hadn't moved an inch since we entered, and their eyes watched us, opaque and unreadable. Lyle stood negligently in the shadow of two of them. I knew he was showing off, and I couldn't sense any danger, but I've lived on my wits too long to ever be comfortable about exposing myself. Even though I knew the guards weren't going to touch me, the thought of passing beneath those shining blades made my skin crawl.

I took a breath and walked forward. One of the guards swivelled its head to watch. Up close it smelt of sweet oil and polished metal. I couldn't see any joints in its body; it looked like an insect crafted in silver. Its future held no choices, a solid line instead of branching forks. *Gythka* are constructs with no will of their own, programmed to obey Council members absolutely. According to rumour, they're almost indestructible. I've never seen the rumour tested. Lyle pushed open the door and we stepped inside.

The room within was dimly lit, with a high ceiling and a dozen widely spaced chairs. The entire left wall was a giant window, a transparent panel looking down onto the great hall. Below was the arena and the buffet table, and to one side I could see the dance floor and the band. It was an impressive view, perfectly placed to see and be seen by the people below . . . except that when I'd looked up from floor level, this spot had looked like a blank wall. The window was one-way glass. We could see the people below, but they couldn't see us.

Five people were sitting in the room, but it was the

man at the centre who caught my attention. He was in his fifties, with thinning white hair and eyes that faded into the shadows. I'd seen his picture before, but never in person, and it took me a moment to put a name to the face. This was Vaal Levistus, one of the members of the Council. He glanced up as we entered. 'Mr Verus. I'm glad you could come.' He gestured to the others. 'Leave us.'

They obeyed in silence, giving me sidelong looks as they filed out. Lyle hesitated in the doorway. 'Councillor?'

'Thank you, Lyle.'

Lyle shot a glance at me and closed the door. There was a smooth click and Levistus and I were alone. Although I could see down through the window into the main hall, with the door closed the room was suddenly silent. Soundproofed. People outside could neither see nor hear.

I'd been scanning ahead ever since I landed outside, looking into the future of what was going to happen to Luna and to me, and I'd found no sign of danger – at least, no immediate danger. But beyond that door, the future had broken up, forking into too many different paths, and now I knew why.

Divination can only predict what can be predicted. Some things are truly random, or so close that it makes no difference. You can't predict the roll of a dice, because there are so many thousands of things that can nudge it one way or another that by the time you could pick out a future it would have stopped rolling. Any really complex system has too much chaos to be easily predictable; it follows patterns, but not ones that can be reliably foreseen. But there's another thing that can't be predetermined – thought. Free will is one of the points at which divination magic breaks down. If a person hasn't made a choice, then no magic can see beyond it. You can see probabilities, but they're no more than guesses, wisps that fade as fast as they appear.

Looking into the future of what Levistus was going to do, I came up with so many answers I couldn't begin to pick one, dozens of futures branching in every direction, ever-shifting. Some looked peaceful; others didn't. This was a dangerous man.

When I didn't move, Levistus gestured to the chair on his right. 'Sit.'

'What about her?'

Levistus looked up at me. 'Who?'

I cleared my throat. 'You asked for everyone to leave.' I nodded at an empty space about six feet behind where Levistus was sitting. 'What about her?'

Levistus watched me for a long moment, his face showing nothing, and for the second time in two minutes my skin crawled briefly. 'Thirteen,' he said at last. 'Visible.'

The air in the spot I'd looked at shimmered and took form. One moment it was empty, the next a wispy, transparent figure of a woman was standing there, its shape visible as thin lines in the gloom. It was an air elemental – but it wasn't. Normal elementals have a primal feel to them, something timeless and alien. Except for her body of air, this one looked like a real woman. She was tall, with long legs and hair falling around her shoulders, and she was naked, her body clearly visible. She looked sensual, eerily beautiful, and I felt my body responding until I saw her eyes. They glowed a faint white, and they were utterly empty. She watched me blankly, like a statue, completely still.

'Interesting,' Levistus said. 'How did you detect her?'

I *hadn't* detected her. 'Trade secrets.'

'Hm.' Levistus looked away. 'Take a seat. Thirteen, to the corner.'

Silently, the air elemental glided to the corner of the room. I noticed that the place she had been standing would have put her right behind the chair Levistus had indicated for me, and felt a slight chill. Whatever she was, that creature scared me. She had been *totally* invisible, both to my eyes and to my mage's sight. The only way I'd known she was there had been through the common elements in the futures ahead of us and, from my brief look, they hadn't been pleasant ones.

I took the chair to the other side of Levistus, the one he hadn't nodded to. As I did, I searched my memory for everything I knew about the man sitting next to me. Though not yet a senior member, Levistus was talked about as one of the more powerful members of the Council, and that put him in the political top ten of the entire country. If Lyle was one of his agents, he'd progressed even faster than I'd thought. Like most Council masters, Levistus was believed to use mind magic, but that could just as easily be rumour. Beyond that, his nature and goals were a mystery . . . but nothing I'd heard suggested he was in the habit of employing out-of-favour diviners.

The view below us was directly onto the sphere arena. Spheres is an old, old game among mages, and two players had just started a bout, their faces locked in concentration as their globes of light formed, moving inwards into the sphere, one set white, one set black. A crowd had gathered to watch, standing on the raised steps around the arena, talking to each other as they followed the movements. Both the lights in the sphere and the crowd moved in eerie silence, inaudible through the layer of glass.

'I believe you may be able to help me with a problem,'

Levistus said. His voice was educated, detached, with no trace of emotion. His eyes didn't rest on me as he spoke but looked down at the hall below, passing over the crowd. 'I expect Lyle has told you the details.'

'Some of them,' I said. I could see the air elemental, Thirteen, out of the corner of my eye; she was still watching me.

'The relic contains a Precursor artifact. I want you to retrieve it.'

'Contains?' I managed to keep my voice only mildly curious.

'The relic is a storage device. The artifact is within.'

In the sphere below, the globes of light clashed, manoeu-vring for position. One spun away, winking out as it left the sphere, and the crowd applauded silently. 'I think,' I said, 'if I'm going to be retrieving this item, I'd like to know a little more about it.'

'That is not your concern.'

'I'm sorry, Councillor,' I said. 'I'm not going to take this job unless I know exactly what this thing does.'

Levistus turned to look at me. Up close, I could see that his eyes were colourless, a pale grey, revealing nothing. I held my breath, feeling my muscles tingling. The futures ahead of me flickered and changed.

Levistus opened his mouth and one future eclipsed the others, becoming real. 'The artifact is an item known as a fateweaver,' he said. 'It has the ability to alter chance and outcomes. In appearance it is a wand of ivory, unmarked, approximately twelve inches long.'

'I'm sure you could lay hands on a dozen chance mages who could alter outcomes, Councillor.'

Levistus made an irritated brushing motion, as if to say he didn't have time for flattery. It had been a long time since

I'd spoken with a Council mage, but the conversation wasn't going how I'd expected. High-level mages tend to be full of their own importance, expecting compliments and ceremony. Levistus was all business. It made him easier to talk to, but also more dangerous. 'Fateweavers are spoken of in the histories. Commanders in the Dark Wars carried them, and there are references to them changing the course of entire battles. This is the first opportunity to see one recovered intact. It is essential it does not fall into the hands of a Dark mage.'

I nodded slowly, remembering. The Dark Wars had ended the Precursor civilisation. Records of that time were fragmentary, but it was well known that the weapons employed had been devastating. If this artifact was one of them, it was clear why everyone wanted it so badly.

Another burst of silent applause came from the crowd below. The globes were interlinked, now, both mages manoeuvring for position. 'I believe that answers your question,' Levistus said.

It didn't, but it was clear that was all he was going to tell me. I didn't want to push further so I switched to a safer subject. 'What about payment?'

'You will have the favour of a member of the High Council.' Levistus turned to look at me with his grey eyes. 'I would consider that payment enough.'

'I appreciate the offer, Councillor, but I'd prefer something more tangible.'

'The prospect of keeping this item out of Dark hands doesn't appeal to you?'

Damn, this guy was good. He knew about my past, and he was using it. And he was right: if this thing really was a weapon from the Dark Wars, there was no way I'd want someone like Cinder in control of it.

But that didn't mean I trusted the Council with it, either. And I had the sudden feeling that Levistus was testing me. He obviously knew I had no love for Dark mages or the Council. But he probably didn't know whether I was an idealist or a cynic. Depending on how I answered . . . Seconds ticked away.

'I don't think it's my business whose hands it ends up in,' I said at last.

Levistus was watching me with those blank, colourless eyes. 'A mercenary, then?'

I looked back at him. 'Yes.'

There was a moment's silence, then Levistus nodded slightly, and I felt the futures ahead of us shift as something fell into place. 'The service I require from you is a simple one. You will assist the investigation team in gaining entry to the relic, and you will make your way through the relic's defences to retrieve the fateweaver. In return, you will have your pick of the other items within.'

'How do I know there *will* be any other items?'

'I can arrange payment in other terms if you wish. But –' Levistus tilted his head slightly, '– the chance for first pick of an undisturbed Precursor relic? I doubt you truly intend to pass that up.'

A beat, then I nodded. Down below at the arena, the crowd had thickened, and all of them now seemed to be watching intently. A group of globes arced around, and another round of applause broke out, the men in their suits and the women in their elaborate dresses clapping silently behind the crystal.

'And once you have the fateweaver, you will bring it to me.'

'Wouldn't the leader of the team be responsible for that?'

'The leader is not your concern,' Levistus said. 'I am employing you to retrieve the item. That is what you are being rewarded for.'

'Doesn't the Arrancar ruling . . .?'

'The Arrancar ruling states that archaeological finds must be submitted to the Council.' Levistus spoke without heat or emphasis. 'I am a member of the Council; therefore, you will submit it to me. The item's destination is a Council secret. You will reveal the terms of your employment to no one, not even authorised Council representatives. Should any of the mages on site attempt to take the artifact for themselves, they are to be considered Dark agents and neutralised in any manner necessary.'

My heart stopped beating for an instant, then sped up. What Levistus was asking me to do was just one step away from treason. And keeping it secret . . . 'Does the team know about this?'

'As I said, you are to reveal the terms of your employment to no one.' Levistus' eyes rested on me, steady and incurious. 'I believe it is time you gave me your answer, Mr Verus. Do you agree to the terms of this contract? Yes or no?'

I needed time to think. 'You're asking for a lot.'

'Which is why you are being paid so handsomely. As I said: yes or no?'

I suddenly realised that the future before me had split into two paths. Levistus wasn't kidding. He was only going to accept a yes or no answer. And if I said no . . .

I looked into the future of what would happen, and it was all I could do not to jump. If I said no, Levistus' air elemental, Thirteen, was going to kill me, right here, right now. She would send her body down my throat and suffocate me as I thrashed helplessly while Levistus watched with his fingers steepled and half an eye on the people below. Then she would transmute my body to air and remove any trace that I had ever walked into this room. I snapped back to the present and took a deep breath. The room was silent, still but for the movements of the crowd behind the crystal. They were fewer than fifty yards away but might as well have been on the moon. Trying not to show anything on my face, I looked sideways to see that Thirteen was still standing there, her face blank, and it was all I could do not to shudder.

I'd walked into something out of my league. Levistus wanted this artifact for himself, not for the Council, and he was willing to kill to keep it. Information wasn't my priority any more. Walking out of this room alive was.

'You realise it may not be possible to gain access to the artifact,' I said at last.

'And if so, you will be compensated for your time,' Levistus replied. 'However, should the artifact be accessible, I will expect that it be delivered to my hands, rather than anyone else's. Quickly and discreetly.'

The bout below had reached its climax. The crowd all watched intently as the black and white spheres swirled with dizzying speed. 'Will I have any . . . assistance with this?'

For the first time Levistus smiled, a thin, dry smile that did not touch his eyes. 'Oh, I have many agents, Mr Verus. Rest assured, they will be there, making sure everything goes to plan.'

The silence in the room stretched out, second passing upon second. 'Well, Councillor,' I said at last, my mouth dry. 'You make an offer that's difficult to refuse.'

'Excellent,' Levistus said. 'I believe our business is concluded.'

## 7

I barely noticed the blades of the mantis golems as I walked out. My heart was still pounding and, as I came back onto the balcony ring, the chatter of the crowd below was like soothing music. I kept moving, dimly aware of people to either side of me, only caring about gaining as much distance as I could from Levistus and his personal killer.

Someone was calling my name. I didn't pay attention. A hand came down on my shoulder and I turned to see Lyle's face frowning at me. 'Are you deaf? I need you to—'

Most mages don't study hand-to-hand fighting; they rely on their magic for everything. I'm not most mages. I've been studying martial arts for a long time and, while I'm nowhere near a master, I'm a *lot* faster than I look. After you study long enough, the basic moves become reflex. I was on edge, and Lyle grabbing my shoulder was all it took to make me snap.

Lyle's back slammed against the wall hard enough to knock the wind out of him. I leant into him, one arm against his throat, and this time I didn't go to any effort to avoid causing pain. 'You asshole,' I hissed into his face from a few inches away. 'Were you in on this? If I hadn't walked out of that room, what would you have done?'

'What are you talking about?' Lyle choked. His eyes were shocked, frightened.

*'How much do you know?'*

'You're crazy! Get off me!'

'How much did you know, Lyle?! What did Levistus tell you?'

'I don't know!' There was panic on Lyle's face; he was sweating. 'He just needed a diviner! That's all he said!'

*'Do you think I'm that fucking stupid?* Levistus' pet was about to *kill me*! What were you going to say, that I'd just *gone for a walk?*'

'What? There wasn't anyone there!'

I glared into Lyle's eyes for a long moment and saw only terror. He was more scared than he should be, and it was with only mild surprise that I realised that deep down, Lyle was a coward. He could act strong when he was in control, but put him in real danger and he crumbled. It's funny how you can know someone for half your life, and then some trivial thing opens your eyes. I'd always known safety was Lyle's religion, yet for some reason I'd never made the connection.

I let go, and Lyle fell back, shrinking into the corner of the alcove. 'You're a fool,' I said quietly. 'You're telling me you didn't know what sort of man you were working for? I don't buy it, Lyle. You knew; you just didn't want to think about it. Just like always.' I shook my head. 'You haven't changed at all.'

'I don't know what you're talking about.' But Lyle's eyes were scared. I knew he was lying, and so did he.

I walked away. There were a handful of others up on this section of the balcony, and they'd all stopped to watch. They eyed me as I passed. News of this would spread quickly, but right now, I didn't care.

The second-floor balcony ran the entire circuit of the hall, and its side was open to the floor below. Arched pillars supported the level above my head and a steel handrail gave protection against falling. After a moment my thoughts steadied enough for me to realise that I was walking back around towards the dance floor, where I'd last seen Luna. I kept going, hoping to spot her from above, and before long I was within earshot of the band again. The music was captivating, and I felt my pulse starting to slow. I settled into the shadow of one of the pillars and leant on the railing, looking down over the crowd.

As I looked from side to side my mind flitted back over my encounter with Levistus. I finally understood what Helikaon had been trying to tell me. I'd never liked the Council, but I realised now that I'd been blind to the threat it could be. I'd walked into that room without understanding just how dangerous the competition for this artifact was, and I'd nearly paid for it with my life. Well, now I *did* understand. *Everyone* after this artifact was willing to kill to get it, and if things kept going as they were, I was going to end up in the middle. That was not a safe place to be.

I felt a presence to one side and turned. A man was standing on the balcony a few steps away. 'Mr Verus?' His voice was cultured, polite. 'Might I have a word?'

'Depends on the word.' I studied the man. His clothes looked high quality but nondescript. He had no visible escort or companion, which could mean something, or nothing at all.

The man smiled slightly. 'I believe you've just had a meeting with Councillor Levistus. I'd like to offer my assistance, should you be willing to accept it.'

'Yeah?' A scan of the future told me the man was no immediate threat. I turned back to the railing and went back to searching the crowd for Luna. 'I think I've had all the assistance I can handle for a little while, thanks.'

'I can understand how you'd feel that way. However, I think you'd benefit from taking the time to listen to what I have to say.'

The last thing I needed was yet another mage trying to take advantage of me. But for the moment at least, this guy was harmless, and I didn't have time to shoo him off. 'Okay, shoot.'

*There.* Luna was a little to the side of the dance floor, in the centre of a small crowd. Everyone was smiling, and from a quick glance at the body language the mood looked pleasant. Luna was talking to a woman in a shimmering pink dress who was watching her with her head tilted in interest. She seemed to be holding her own, and I felt myself relax slightly.

I realised the man next to me was speaking. '. . . be interested?'

'Sorry. Could you say that again?'

'As I said,' he repeated patiently. 'Levistus is not the only mage on the Council, and his ambitions are far from being a secret. If you're worried about the terms of your employment with him, I might be able to offer some assistance.'

I sighed. 'Let me take a wild guess. As part of the terms of this assistance, you or whoever you're representing would get the items inside the relic, right?'

'We would prefer to see any Precursor artifacts in our hands rather than his, yes.'

'I'm sure you would.' I turned to face him. 'Look, Mr . . .?'

'Talisid.'

'Mr Talisid. I'm rapidly losing count of the number of factions out to grab this artifact. What exactly makes you different from the others?'

'For one thing,' Talisid said calmly, 'we aren't threatening to kill you if you don't cooperate. Or even if you do. I'm sure it's already occurred to you that being a loose end in one of Levistus' plans might not be the safest of positions?'

For the first time I turned my full attention to the man. He was a hair under medium height, in his forties, dressed in dark clothes with a receding hairline. He looked like a blackbird against the peacocks on the dance floor, but there was a steadiness to his gaze that suggested he might be someone to take seriously.

'You seem to know a lot about what was supposed to be a private conversation,' I said at last.

'Diviners don't have a monopoly on knowledge, Mr Verus. Deduction can work just as well.'

'You're with the Council?'

'I represent a faction of the Council. At the moment, I believe our interests coincide with yours.' Talisid moved past me to rest his arms upon the railing, his clothes dark against the metal. 'Not everyone on the Council is happy with the Dark mages' growth in power. And even those sympathetic to their proposals would prefer not to see one of them gain control of such a powerful relic. In this case, the majority is with us.'

'If you've got the majority on your side, why do you need me?'

'Unfortunately, while a majority of the Council have a preference for the artifact not falling into the hands of a Dark mage, they have an even greater preference for the artifact falling into the hands of themselves.'

I let out an exasperated breath. 'This is ridiculous. Do you guys even know what this thing does? You're all going to look really stupid if it ends up being a dud, you know that?'

'We've got more important concerns than looking stupid, Mr Verus,' Talisid said patiently. 'And as I was saying, we may be able to assist you.'

Something pinged on my danger sense and I looked down. Luna was still talking in the middle of her crowd, but that wasn't where the thread of trouble was coming from. I scanned up and down, looking through the crowd for movement. Three figures caught my eye. They were spread through the crowd, but linked somehow, and—

Oh *crap*. It was the three Dark mages, Cinder, Khazad and the masked woman, and they were after Luna. They were surrounding her, closing in steadily from three sides. She was talking, oblivious, as they moved closer and closer.

I spun and headed for the nearest staircase. 'Mr Verus!' Talisid called sharply.

'Sorry!' I called over my shoulder. 'It'll have to wait!' I broke into a run, sprinting along the balcony and down the wide staircase. A couple talking close to one another on the landing broke off and pressed themselves to one side as I came flying down. I reached ground level in twenty seconds flat and slowed to a fast walk as I came out into the Great Hall. I knew where Luna was going to be, and I needed to get there first.

I didn't. As I came within sight of Luna, I saw the three Dark mages surrounding her. The others she had been talking to were nowhere in sight. I caught a glimpse of one disappearing behind a knot of people, throwing a nervous glance back at Cinder. The floor was still crowded and the buzz of conversation drowned out what they were saying, but I didn't need to use my magic to know that

Luna was in danger. I scanned quickly through the futures and found a way to approach without being seen.

The woman talking to Luna was the same one I'd seen at the excavation site and Camden Market, though I still didn't know her name. She was wearing a dress of royal blue that sparkled in the light, along with a mask over her upper face, and she stood looking down at Luna, one hand resting on her hip. Cinder was to her side, dressed in black with highlights of flaring red. 'Luna,' the woman was saying. Her voice was clear, musical; again, as I heard it the sound set off a chime of memory. 'You have something that belongs to me.'

Luna looked from the woman to Cinder. If she recognised her from the episode this morning, she didn't let it show. 'Do I know you?' she said at last.

'No.' The woman took a step forward. She was taller than Luna, with short blonde hair. 'If you know what's good for you you'll keep it that way. Where's the cube?'

'Sorry?'

'Don't play games with me.' The woman's voice was cold and dangerous. 'A crowd won't protect you. Give me what I want or I'll take it from you.'

Luna stood very still. The sounds of chatter around seemed to fade away. When Luna finally spoke, there was a note in her voice I'd never heard before. 'I don't think I like your attitude very much.' All of a sudden Luna sounded much older. 'If you want something, ask without the threats.'

Even with danger close at hand, I felt a sudden surge of pride. Even under pressure, Luna had recognised the woman for what she was, and done exactly the right thing: stood up to her without showing fear. All the time that

I'd been talking to her she *had* been listening, and she'd shown she could do it under pressure. In that instant I realised that, despite everything that had happened, and even though she wasn't a diviner or even a mage, I *did* think of Luna as my apprentice, and I was proud of her.

Of course, it wasn't going to stop her from being abducted in exactly fifteen seconds. But that was where I came in.

'You, little girl, just made a big mistake,' the woman said after a long pause. She made a signal with two fingers. 'Let's see exactly what you —'

As she spoke, Khazad glided behind Luna. I'd thought the small man looked like a bird the first three times I'd seen him, but he moved now with a sinuous grace, more like a snake. A needle gleamed in one hand, catching the light as he brought it towards the bare skin of Luna's shoulder.

It never got there. As Khazad moved, so did I, and as he came up behind Luna I stepped in beside him. My right hand closed on his wrist, and as he made his move I spun him around, redirecting his momentum so that the needle sunk into his own arm. There was a faint spark as the spell discharged and Khazad's head jerked in shock. Luna, Cinder and the woman all turned in the same instant to stare at me. Luna's eyes lit up; Cinder's darkened. 'You!'

'Hey, Cinder. Nice to see you again.' I turned my gaze to the woman with a smile. 'She did warn you.'

The woman stared, speechless. I turned to Luna, offering my hand. 'Sorry, I got held up. Shall we go?'

Luna took a glance back at Cinder and the woman, then took my hand with barely a pause. The other two stared after us as we walked away, Khazad in tow.

'That was *awesome*,' Luna said once we were away. All traces of how she'd been outside were gone; she looked alert and glowing.

'Are they following us?'

'No – yes. Through the crowd.'

'Okay. Break left . . . *now*.' We slipped behind a group of people. From the other side I could just hear hurrying footsteps as Cinder and the woman came walking quickly after us, fading away as we doubled back.

Khazad was still walking aimlessly by my side, guided by my arm around his waist. Luna tilted her head to look into his eyes, then waved her fingers in front of his face. He didn't respond. 'What happened to him?'

'Same thing he was about to do to you.' I lifted his right hand and pointed to the needle clutched in his fingers. It was about eight inches long, made of some kind of silvery metal, tipped with a dot of blood where it had driven into Khazad's arm. 'Enchantment effect, kind of like magical Rohypnol. They were going to use it on you, then walk you out the front door.'

Khazad's eyes were vacant; without me to guide him, he just stood there. Relaxed, his face was harsh and cruel. Luna peered over to look at him while I went through Khazad's pockets. He was carrying another of the needles along with a few other things that looked like weapons, but no written instructions or anything that would give me a hint as to which spell they'd been using to track Luna. Damn.

'Can he hear us?' Luna asked.

'Probably.' I glanced back over my shoulder. We'd swerved away from the dance floor towards the other side of the hall and had ended up next to a fountain of steel and stone that bubbled with clear water. A minor illusory effect played over the water causing it to flicker through the colours of the rainbow: red to yellow to green to blue and back again. 'We'd better dump him before he slows us down.'

I sat Khazad down on the edge of the fountain and slapped him in the face twice, hard. A few people gave me curious looks but you can get away with a lot if you're blatant enough. I'd just gone through his pockets in full view of all the guests and gotten nothing more than a few funny looks. 'Khazad,' I said clearly. 'Can you hear me?'

Khazad's eyes were still vague, but I could sense a presence behind them this time, something looking at me with a distant hatred. This was the second time I'd gotten the better of him and, even with the magic scrambling his thoughts, I could feel how much he wanted to kill me. 'That's twice you've tried,' I said. I looked into his eyes as I spoke, keeping contact. 'This is your last chance to walk away. You understand? One chance. Pull anything like this again, on either of us, and I'll see you dead.'

Khazad glared at me, unable to speak. I could sense the two Dark mages approaching from behind. I straightened and walked away, and the two of us disappeared into the crowd, the noise and bustle swallowing us. The music of the band faded as we put some distance between us and the dance floor.

'Are they still coming?' Luna said once we were away. She was craning her neck, trying to look in every direction at once.

'Yeah.' Now they weren't heading straight for us I couldn't predict their movements so easily, but I knew they'd be back.

'How did they find me?'

'They spent today at your flat. Could they have found anything from your body? Hair, nail clippings, blood?'

'No – yes. Some hairs from my pillow, maybe the bathroom . . .'

I nodded. 'If you have something that was once a part of someone, you can put together a tracer spell that works through just about anything. No chance of it failing on its own. We're going to need something stronger.'

Luna nodded. 'What do we do?'

'Head for the games area. Keep going towards those pillars at the back.'

As we crossed the hall, I led Luna in a looping, swerving course. Most divination spells are directional, and if Cinder or whatshername were trying to anticipate Luna's movements, this would slow them down. We passed knots of people, fountains, more of the white-masked servants, the buzz of laughter and conversation filling the air. The sphere arena had quieted down; a new match would probably start soon. My eyes tracked up to what looked like a blank stretch of crystal wall above the arena and between the balconies, and the hairs on the back of my neck stood up. Levistus was behind that wall, and somehow I knew he was watching me.

'Alex?' Luna asked as we walked.

'Hm?'

'Did you mean it?'

'What?'

'Khazad. When you said you'd kill him.'

'I meant it.'

Luna walked for a little while in silence. 'Thank you,' she said eventually.

I looked at her in surprise, then smiled slightly. 'You did well back there.'

Luna looked taken aback, then flushed. She was about to say something when a voice spoke from in front, interrupting. 'Hi!'

I looked up to see a girl smiling at me. She was young, maybe eighteen or nineteen, and beautiful enough to be a model. Long, shining gold hair hung down her back, and she wore a low-cut blue silk dress with long slits that showed off her legs. A black ribbon was tied around her neck. 'You're Alex Verus, right?'

'That's me.'

'Oh, it's great to finally meet you!' She came to a stop nearby, her smile showing a set of perfect teeth. 'I'm Lisa.'

'Hi, Lisa.' I kept walking, leaving her behind.

Lisa blinked, then hurried to catch up, struggling in her high heels. 'It's so cool to meet you,' she said, trying to catch my eye. 'Everyone's talking about you.'

'That's great.'

'I'd *really* like to talk to you.' Lisa came closer, walking right alongside, looking up at me with inviting blue eyes. 'Could you come here just a minute?'

Luna had been watching, first in puzzlement, then annoyance. 'Hey,' she said. 'I'm here as well.'

Lisa gave her a glance, then turned back to me. 'Alex? Please?'

'Sorry,' I said. 'We're busy.' I took Luna's hand and gestured to a pillar over the crowd, leaving Lisa behind. 'That way.' We turned right around a buffet table and a cluster of people holding drinks.

Luna gave me a searching look. 'Who was that?'

'Beats me.' I pointed towards the pillar. 'We're looking

for an archway. It'll be whitish, about seven feet tall. When you see it—'

'Wait!' Lisa called from behind. She was hurrying through the crowd after us, looking flustered. I rolled my eyes.

'Are you *sure* you don't know her?' Luna asked, eyebrows raised.

I sighed. 'You know, three days ago no one would have looked at me twice. This Mr Popular act is getting old.'

A gap opened in the crowd and I spotted what I was looking for: the azimuth duelling piste. Two slender pillars rose at either end, silvery and delicate, looking like a pair of tuning forks. At our end was an archway of white stone, seven feet high. A mage in ceremonial robes looked up as we approached. 'Hey. Looking to duel?'

'That's okay,' I said. 'We just need the annuller.'

The mage gave us a look, then shrugged. 'Be my guest.'

'Duel?' Luna whispered once he was gone.

'Not a duel,' I said. I put one hand on the cool stone of the archway and a faint silvery glow started to form across the opening. 'Watch my back.'

Azimuth duels are a non-lethal alternative to traditional mage combat, fought with focus weapons and intended to be non-lethal. Officially the Council frowns on traditional duels, though despite all their efforts traditional duels still carry a lot more prestige than azimuth ones. Annuller arches are focuses, designed to stop mages entering duels with spells active. Activating one isn't dangerous, but it's demanding and requires absolute concentration. Any distraction can ruin the whole process and force you to start over.

Naturally, this was the point at which Lisa showed up again.

'You're here,' she said, breathless. She was limping slightly; high heels aren't made for running. 'Um, could you—'

'Look, Lisa,' I said, not taking my eyes off the archway. 'This is really not a good time for us.'

'Trust me,' Luna said, and I could tell from her voice that she was smiling. 'You don't want to get too close to me.'

'No, I—' Lisa took a deep breath. 'I can't.'

'Why not?' Luna asked. She didn't sound sympathetic.

'My master wants to speak to him. He told me to invite him.'

'What master?'

'. . . Morden.'

The name sounded vaguely familiar, but I was concentrating on the annuller and couldn't put a finger on it. I finished the spell and took a step back to look at the archway. It was humming softly, and I nodded. It would take a couple of minutes to charge. 'Who?' Luna asked.

'You don't *know* him?'

'No, I don't. Why are you doing what he says?'

Lisa stared at her.

'It's okay,' I said to Luna. 'I already know what this guy wants.' I looked at Lisa. 'The question is whether you do.'

'Uh . . .'

'She asked the right question. Why are you running errands for him?'

'I . . .' Lisa licked her lips. 'Look, please, you have to come. He'll be . . .'

'We don't *have* to do anything,' Luna said in annoyance.

The hum from the archway stopped. I looked back and

saw that a silvery mist was hanging inside it, glowing steadily. 'Okay, we're clear,' I said to Luna. 'Step through.'

Luna gave the other girl a look, then walked to the arch. 'Please, can you just come?' Lisa said in a low voice. She wasn't trying to be seductive any more; she just looked frightened. It actually made her a lot more convincing. 'I've taken too long. He'll be angry.'

I gave Luna a glance, then for the first time turned my full attention to the girl in front of me. 'Look, Lisa. I don't know who your master is, but I've got a pretty good idea *what* he is. If you really want my help, tell me what he's planning.'

'I can't do that!'

'Then I can't help you.'

To one side, Luna stepped through the archway. There was a very brief flash, then the archway was still again. Luna looked back at it curiously, then headed towards me.

'Please, can't you come?' Lisa said. Her voice was pleading. 'I'll do anything. Just . . .'

I sighed slightly and looked her right in the eyes. 'Okay. Leave him.'

'What?'

'I've been where you are.' I held Lisa's gaze, holding her motionless, and spoke quietly. 'I know why you're doing this. I know why you think it makes sense. But trust me: you don't want to stay there.' Luna approached and I turned away from Lisa, nodding to Luna. 'Okay?'

'I think . . .' Luna said doubtfully. She looked at her hands. 'I feel strange.'

'It's a nullifier,' I said. Concentrating, I could see that the grey mist of Luna's curse had briefly vanished. Now it was returning again, flowing out again and into my ribbon.

'Grounds every magical connection on you, like earthing a power line. You'll feel a bit out of place for a couple of days.'

'It'll stop them tracking me?'

I nodded and started walking, ignoring Lisa. 'If we're quick.'

Luna took one step, then halted, looking over my shoulder. 'Um, Alex?' I felt her hand creep over and squeeze my forearm. I didn't think she was aware of it; she was staring towards the centre of the hall. 'Not quick enough.'

I knew what I was going to see before I turned to look. Cinder was striding across the floor towards us, a look of death on his face. The masked woman was at his side. They were fewer than twenty paces away.

You're probably wondering by this point why I wasn't shouting for help. Simple reason: if those three were willing to kill to get their hands on Luna, others would be too. Dealing with one team of would-be kidnappers was bad enough; I had absolutely no intention of adding to the number if I could possibly avoid it. The same went for them: I knew Cinder wouldn't want to attract any attention either.

Unfortunately, depending on how pissed off Cinder was, there were plenty of ways he could ruin my day even in a crowd of people, and looking into the future, I could see that we'd succeeded in making him angry enough to use them. In one hand he was concealing a weapon that he was getting ready to use. He'd aim it at Luna the second she turned to run. I couldn't see exactly what it would do, but I knew it would be bad . . . except that as I looked, I saw something else as well, something approaching steadily from the other side of the room. I straightened to face them. 'Alex?' Luna whispered.

'Stall them,' I whispered back. 'We need ninety seconds.'

'Verus,' Cinder growled as he came into range. 'Should have kept running.'

'Who's running?' I asked lightly. I stood slightly between Cinder and Luna. Lisa was off to one side, looking nervously between us, forgotten by everyone.

'No,' Cinder said. His voice was low and dangerous. 'You won't bluff me this time.' He opened one hand, half concealed down by his side, and dark fire flared up around his fingers, a red-black aura that caused the light to dim. 'You twitch, I'll burn you to ash. Let's see you trick your way out of that.'

He wasn't kidding; in dozens of the futures unfolding before us I could see Cinder lunging forward to do exactly that. But the very fact that he was willing to try something so crude was oddly reassuring – if he had anything else up his sleeve, he wouldn't be making the threat. 'You know, Cinder,' I said, 'I hate to point it out, but there's about a hundred people watching you.'

'No one'll miss you,' Cinder growled.

'Wrong,' I said calmly. 'Or haven't you heard? I'm in demand these days.'

Uncertainty flickered in Cinder's eyes, and he glanced quickly from side to side. People were watching; a *lot* of people. As Cinder saw that he was being watched, the future of him attacking faded. 'You don't want me as an enemy,' Cinder said, recovering.

'As a matter of fact, no, I don't.' I crossed my arms, watching Cinder casually. 'So make me an offer.'

The woman in the mask hadn't spoken. She was standing

a half-step behind Cinder, letting him do the talking. But she was watching me and, through the eyeholes of the mask, her eyes were boring into me like needles. I had the uneasy feeling that she recognised me, and not in a good way. It felt as though she hated me and I didn't know why. 'Fine,' Cinder said, his voice dangerous. 'I'll buy the girl.'

I felt Luna stiffen. 'Really?' I asked.

'Don't,' Cinder growled. 'You sell her. Usual price. Or we take her. And you.'

I looked at Cinder. Luna was still gripping my arm, and I could sense her nerves. I stood there, without answering, counting off the seconds. 'Well?' Cinder said.

'She's not for sale,' I said. 'And actually, I'm not interested in any offer you could make.'

Cinder stared at me. 'You said—'

'Oh, I was just wasting your time.'

Cinder just stood there for two seconds, then his eyes flashed with insane fury as he finally lost his temper. Hellfire flared up inside his eyes, and his irises actually turned red. He took one step forward, his hand coming up.

A voice spoke from one side. 'Good evening. Your attention, please.'

The man approaching was dressed in a black suit and an open-necked shirt. He had dark hair and was good-looking in a smooth, polished sort of way, like a politician. At first glance he looked young, no older than thirty or so, but there was an assurance to his walk that made him seem older. A brunette in a red dress was following him two paces behind, her eyes lowered submissively.

As soon as Cinder saw him, the flame around him vanished as though it had been plunged into water. He and the woman stood a little straighter. 'Master Morden,' the woman said. Again her voice sounded familiar, but I was taken aback by the sudden caution in it. Cinder even dipped his head in reflex before catching himself.

Ever since Lisa had mentioned the name Morden, it had been nagging at the back of my mind. As I saw Cinder's reaction, I suddenly remembered. It was the name I'd come up with to scare him off yesterday. Just the suggestion that I might have been working for Morden had made Cinder back off, and that set off warning bells. The only people to whom Dark mages show that kind of respect are Dark mages of higher rank. Much higher.

'Cinder, Deleo,' Morden said. His voice was cultured, pleasant. 'I see Khazad isn't with you. Is there a problem?'

'No,' the woman he'd addressed as Deleo said carefully. She stood quite still. 'No problem.'

'Good. I was just speaking to Councillor Travis about the membership proposal. Negotiations are advancing. It would be . . . inconvenient for there to be any public disruptions at this time.' His eyes rested on the two Dark mages.

After a long pause, Cinder nodded. 'Got it,' he said, unable to quite keep the growl out of his voice.

'Excellent. I have some things to discuss with Verus. You may go.'

Cinder shot me and Luna a venomous glance, and then – amazingly – he obeyed, turning and disappearing with Deleo into the crowd. I felt Luna's hand tighten slightly on my arm, then she seemed to realise what she was doing and let go.

Lisa had been hovering nearby; now Morden looked at her. 'Lisa. I think I told you to extend Verus an invitation?'

Lisa licked her lips. 'Um . . .'

Morden nodded once. 'We'll discuss this later.' Lisa's face actually went white, the blood draining from it completely. She stared at Morden with terrified eyes, but he'd already turned to us. 'Verus, I believe? My name is Morden. If you can spare the time, there are some things we should discuss.' He glanced over my shoulder at Luna. 'In private.'

I still didn't know who this man was, but every sign was pointing to him being *really* bad news. 'While I . . . appreciate it, Mr Morden, I don't think that would be advisable for me just now.'

'And why is that?'

*Because I've already had one private interview with a mage willing to kill me, and that's enough for one night.* 'Given the circumstances, I don't think it would be a good idea for me to be seen leaving with you at present.'

'Really.' Morden studied me with his head tilted slightly. Behind his back, Lisa and the other girl were watching him nervously. I could feel the futures shifting and spinning.

Then suddenly they settled. 'Then we'll save our discussion for a later time.' Morden smiled. 'I'm sure we'll meet again.' He gave me a nod, then turned and left, the brunette in tow. Lisa gave me a single frightened glance and scuttled after. I was left standing on my own, staring after him.

'Um . . .' Luna whispered. 'What just happened?'

'I have no idea.' I shook myself awake. 'Cinder and that woman are still out there. Let's move.'

'*Now* where?' Luna asked as we set off again through the crowd.

'Out.'

'We're leaving?'

'I think we've pushed our luck far enough.' I checked and looked down at Luna. 'Wait, are you *disappointed*?'

'Um . . .' Luna looked away and I shook my head.

The ball was in full swing, and the hall was filled with the chatter of voices. A match was being fought in the duelling arenas behind us, and I could hear shouts and cheers. I could sense that Cinder and Deleo were still looking for us, and I shifted direction towards the angle where it was least likely they'd spot us. Beyond was a short flight of stairs leading up to an exit directly opposite to the one by which we'd entered. I took Luna's hand and led her up the stairs. 'Quick,' I said. 'If we can get out without them spotting us—'

I felt the futures shift and looked over my shoulder. Deleo had climbed up onto the sill of one of the fountains and was scanning the floor, her masked face lifted above the crowd. We spotted each other at exactly the same time and our eyes made contact with a jolt before she spun and started shouting something, her voice lost in the noise.

'Oh, for crying out loud,' I muttered. 'Can't they just leave us alone?'

'Let me guess.' Luna sounded resigned. 'They're chasing us again.'

'Change of plans.' I led Luna at a run up the stairs and into the foyer beyond. I scanned ahead quickly. The corridors to the right led to a bank of lifts that would take us down to the lower floors, but looking ahead I could see that Cinder was already moving to block that direction off. He and Deleo had split up and were trying to pincer us. It might have worked if I hadn't seen it coming. 'This way.'

'Are your nights out always like this?' Luna asked as we hurried down the corridor.

'Later, all right?' The corridor opened up into a wide corner room. Ahead and to the left, windows looked down over the night city, and in the corner was a lift made of glass. I walked inside and hit the button. The doors hissed shut and the lift began to climb. Below, I could sense Cinder and Deleo, but they were going the wrong way. By the time they realised we were going up instead of down it would be too late. I leant against the corner with a sigh. 'All right. We're safe for a while.'

'Oh, that reminds me,' Luna said. 'There was someone near the dance floor called Talisid. He seemed like he really wanted to speak to you.'

'Yeah, I met him. Those guys interrupted us.'

'Well, maybe we can find him later.'

I looked at Luna in disbelief. She had turned away to watch the view, and I had to admit it was worth watching. The top set of lifts in Canary Wharf run along the edge of the tower and, unlike the ones that serve the office complex below, they're designed for sightseeing rather than speed. The lift was drifting upwards at a lazy pace, and from our position we could look down on all of London. The landmarks of the city glowed in the distance: the square shape of Centre Point, the double red lights of the BT tower, the shifting wheel of coloured light that marked the London Eye. The other skyscrapers of the Docklands were falling away below us. The sounds of the ball had faded away, and we were alone in a silent world.

'Luna?' I said at last. 'Why do you want to be here?'

I felt Luna go still. 'Don't get me wrong,' I said. 'You're handling this well. Maybe a bit *too* well. Why aren't you scared?'

Luna stayed as she was for a long moment, looking out over

the city. 'What would I be scared of?' she said at last. Her voice was light, and there was something strange about it.

'From these people? You want a list?'

'Do you know why I came looking for your shop that first time?'

I frowned. Luna was turned away, her fingers resting lightly against the transparent wall. 'Why?'

'It was a few weeks before.' Luna didn't turn to face me. I could just make out the outline of her face in the reflection off the glass. 'On a Saturday. I woke up late. I'd been sleeping longer and longer, then. I lay there and I listened to the birds singing and I couldn't think of any reason to get up. There wasn't anything I was looking forward to. That day, that month, ever.' Luna fell silent a moment, then went on, her voice absent. 'That was when I realised that if I didn't do something I was going to die. Just from not caring.'

Luna looked down at the floor, not meeting my gaze. 'I don't have anything else,' she said quietly. 'Your world is all I have. If that doesn't work, nothing else matters.'

I looked at Luna, and for once I couldn't think of a single thing to say.

The silence dragged out for a long minute, then Luna seemed to shake herself, and when she looked at me her face was normal. 'What was going on back there? With that girl?'

'I— What do you mean?'

'Was she a mage?'

I threw off the weight of what Luna had just told me, stored it away for another time. Somehow I knew that right now, sympathy was the last thing she needed. 'No. Probably not.'

'But you knew who she was?'

'I didn't know *her*.'

'But you knew something,' Luna persisted.

I looked away. 'You don't want to tell me?' Luna asked.

'It's not that.'

'Then what is it?'

'It's— Okay, it *is* that.' I looked away. 'It's something I haven't had to think about for a long time.'

'That bad?' Luna asked in surprise. I didn't answer, and she carried on. 'Why was she acting like that? That girl, Lisa. She was acting like she was his . . .'

I was silent for a moment, looking out over London. We were above the highest skyscrapers now, but I didn't see any of it. I was remembering a time long ago, the darkness in Richard's mansion, Shireen and Tobruk, Rachel . . .

'Alex?'

'Remember how I said mages split everyone into other mages, and sheep?' I stared out over the lights of the city. 'Well, there's a thing about that. If everyone who isn't a mage is a sheep, then the only kind of power worth having is over other mages.'

Luna was looking at me, and I could tell she didn't understand. 'Any mage can set himself up in the normal world. But he doesn't get any respect. Status here is how much influence you have over other mages. Favours, position, contacts . . . other things.'

'Okay . . .' Luna said slowly. 'That man, Cinder. Why was he talking about buying me?'

I knew Luna wasn't going to stop until she got an answer or a flat no. I took a breath, then let it out, calming myself. 'Dark mages like taking slaves,' I said at last. It was my turn not to meet Luna's eyes now. I didn't want to risk her seeing something in my face. 'It's like a currency for them. Even the ones who don't use slaves keep them to sell to the ones who do. Any novice or adept without connections, anyone who isn't powerful enough to look after herself . . . she's got a good chance of ending up like that. Sometimes it's even a choice. They serve one mage because if they don't they'll be taken by another. There are Dark mages who have dozens, like a business. They keep them in their mansions and bring one or two out for display.'

I fell silent. Luna had been staring at me. 'What do they do with them?' she finally asked.

I met Luna's eyes then. 'Whatever they want.'

We were almost to the top of the tower, and the stars were bright in the sky above us. It was dark and quiet, and everything else was still.

'Alex?' Luna said. 'Maybe it wouldn't be such a bad idea to go home after all.'

I nodded. The lift rose into a cage of steel and glass, and the door slid open. We stepped out into the night air.

We were standing on the corner of the tower, just at the point at which it angled in to form a pyramid. A small walkway with a transparent railing ran along the edge in both directions, stretching to the other two corners that we could see. Beyond the railing was a vertical drop, seven hundred feet straight down to the concrete below. Not the place to be if you were scared of heights. The double strobe of the aircraft warning light flashed from the pyramid right above us, dazzlingly bright. We were alone.

Luna watched as I took out the glass rod I used to call Starbreeze and whispered my summoning charm over it.

'Alexander Verus calls you; answer my prayer, queen of the sky.' I finished and tucked it away. Then I stared off into the distance, working out how long Starbreeze would be.

'Alex,' Luna said, pointing.

I followed her finger to see that she was pointing over the edge, towards the south-west corner. A dim light was moving upwards along the edge of the building, its glow just barely visible from our angle. It was already a third of the way up.

I sighed. 'Deleo. Goddamn it, doesn't that woman ever give up?' I scanned through the futures quickly. 'Cinder's still below. Probably in . . . yeah, he's at the base of the lift. Waiting for us to double back.'

Luna looked out at the night sky, then down at the rising sphere, and I knew what she was thinking. 'Deleo.'

'Hm?'

'You were wondering who'll get here first, Starbreeze or Deleo. It'll be Deleo.'

'Oh.' Luna thought briefly. 'Do we run again?'

'Good plan, but no. Running from these guys too long is a bad idea. It gets them into the habit of chasing you.' I handed Luna the glass rod. 'Stay out of sight. When Starbreeze comes, shout.'

'What about you?'

'Be a good girl and do what I say.'

'I'm not a good girl,' Luna said, but I could tell she was holding back a smile. She obeyed, backing off so that the tower pyramid was between her and Deleo's lift.

Once she was gone, I went a little way out along the walkway. Despite how high we were, the air was quite still; the Council like to keep everything scenic in case some of their guests feel like enjoying the view. Once I'd gotten far enough, I took a pair of gold-coloured discs from my pocket and laid them on either side of the walkway, one by the railing and one at the edge of the pyramid. Then I took a step back and waited.

It was a spectacular view. From the height I was standing, I could see virtually all of London. The air was cold and bracing, and I realised suddenly as I looked out into the night sky that I'd missed this. There'd been something missing from my life in Camden, something I'd discovered again in the past two days.

The glow of the lift vanished from the side of the tower, then appeared on my level, visible though the glass of the pyramid. As I watched, Deleo stepped out into the night air. She saw me, paused, then started across the walkway towards me.

I let her get within thirty feet before speaking the command word. The gold discs flared to life and a wall of force appeared, stretching from the discs on the walkway floor out past the railings, along the slope of the pyramid, and up into the air. It was invisible to the naked eye, but there was now no physical force in this world or the next that could cross that barrier.

Deleo came to a halt. Her hands had snapped up as I'd spoken, and now I watched her stare at me through the transparent wall, her eyes hidden behind the mask. As she came to a decision, green-blue light welled up about her hands.

'Don't bother,' I said. 'You could break it if you were on your own, but not with me boosting it from the other side.'

'It won't last for ever,' Deleo said. Her voice was soft and deadly, and again I felt the venom in her words.

'So let's talk.' I folded my arms, watching her casually. 'There's some stuff I've been wanting to ask you.'

Deleo didn't answer. 'For a start, I'd like to know what your plans were for Luna,' I went on. 'But I know you wouldn't tell me the truth. So I thought I'd ask about something you seem to have more of a personal interest in.' I cocked my head. 'Why do you hate me so much?'

Deleo stared back at me from the other side of the wall. The silence stretched out and I'd just opened my mouth to go on when she finally spoke. 'You couldn't stay away, could you?' Her voice was low, vibrating with some intense emotion: hate, pain, anger. 'I knew you'd be back. It was always you.'

'Uh,' I said. 'Okay, let's try this again. Why—?'

'Shut up.' Deleo's voice was raw. 'Don't talk to me. It was your fault, all of it. Now you're trying to do it again.' The light around her hands flared, brightened. 'It's people like you that always screw things up, always make it worse. If you were gone I could fix things. The ones who really matter.' Suddenly, she turned. 'Stop it!'

I stared, following her gaze. Deleo was looking at empty air, out over the railings. I searched the area and saw nothing. 'Um,' I said. 'Look, if—'

'You've had the dreams, haven't you?' Deleo asked. She sounded distracted, like she was carrying on two conversations at once. 'I can see them. You haven't escaped, no one does. It always comes back. I'm the only one who can break it.' She cocked her head, seeming to listen, then snarled. 'Shut up!'

'Okay,' I said. 'You know what, I don't want to know any more. You're nuttier than a bowl of Alpen. Just stay away from me.'

'You don't understand.' Deleo's eyes stared through me for a second, then all of a sudden they cleared and she was focused on me again. 'Give me the girl.'

'Uh, how about no?'

'You think you can protect her? You can't. The only way she'll be safe is with me.'

I actually laughed. 'Oh, that's different. I'll just hand her over, shall I?'

In a quick movement Deleo stepped up against the barrier. Her left hand pulsed against the wall of force, sending ripples through it. 'I won't let anyone get in my way,' she said. All of a sudden, her voice was deadly calm. 'You were always weaker than me. I know how to hurt you, Alex.'

Deleo and I stared into each other's eyes from fewer than ten feet away. The barrier was starting to tremble; the amount of destructive force she was pouring into it was staggering. From behind I heard Luna's voice, calling. 'Alex! *Alex!*'

I stepped back. 'Don't come after me.'

'This isn't over,' Deleo said. It sounded like a promise.

I turned and ran. Behind, I could hear the force wall whining under the strain. As I got around the corner of the pyramid, I saw Luna leaning over the railing and Starbreeze floating just beyond it. 'Time to go!' I called.

'Go where?' Starbreeze asked curiously.

'Home!' I grabbed Luna's hand. 'Fast!'

'Okay!' Starbreeze engulfed us. In a flash we were turned to air and whisked away. Looking back, I had one glimpse of the barrier breaking in a blue-green flash before the tower was shrinking behind us. 'No fun,' Starbreeze complained, her voice muffled by the wind.

'What's wrong?' Luna asked.

'Nothing happened,' Starbreeze said, sounding disappointed.

The Docklands vanished behind us, their lights merging
with the rest of London as Starbreeze lifted us higher and
higher into the sky. Already we were far enough away to
be invisible to anyone watching. 'Trust me, Starbreeze,' I
said as we banked and turned north, heading home. 'It
was exciting enough down on our end.'

Starbreeze dropped us on my roof and I gave her something
or other and watched her soar away. My shop was dark and
quiet. All around, I could hear the sounds of the city again,
distant and reassuring. All of a sudden, I didn't want to
deal with magic and mages any more; I just wanted to be
home and safe. 'Want a drink?' I said, smothering a yawn
as we walked through the hall.

Luna shook her head. Her dress was a little disarrayed,
but it made her look better if anything. She seemed to be
slowly coming down from a high. 'Stay here for tonight,
then?' I asked. 'I think there's a camp bed somewhere.'

'I think I should go.'

I looked at her, puzzled. Luna nodded down at my chest.
'Look.'

I stared for a moment before realising. In the excitement,
I'd forgotten about Arachne's ribbon. I looked down to see
that almost all of the white ribbon had turned black. Only
an inch or so was left.

'I think my coach is turning back into a pumpkin,' Luna
said, and I looked up in surprise to see one of her rare
smiles. Somehow, though, this one seemed sad. 'It's okay.
You said they can't find me now, right? I'll find a place
to stay.' She moved to the door.

'Luna, wait!' I followed. 'They can't find you with magic, but they can still look. It's not going to be—'

Luna turned and stepped into my arms, laying her head against my chest, one hand holding gently onto my coat. I stopped in surprise, looking down at her. 'Thank you for tonight,' Luna said. Her body was cool, and she smelt of clouds and wind. 'It was worth it.'

I started to put an arm around her. 'Luna—'

'It's midnight,' Luna said softly, and slipped away, hiding her face. Before I could react the door opened and closed, and I was alone. I heard her footsteps fading outside.

I stood there for a long time, then walked back to my desk and sat down. I untied the ribbon from my belt and held it up in front of me. Almost all of it had turned to black and, as I watched, the very last corner faded and darkened. The ribbon flickered once, then crumbled to dust between my fingers. In a second there was nothing left but a trace of black powder.

I sat looking at it for a long time, then went upstairs to bed.

## 8

I came awake into darkness. My chest hurt, everything was black and the screams were still ringing in my ears. As I lay tense, my heart pounding, I realised it had been a dream. My flat was silent. I lay there for a few minutes, letting my breathing slow until my eyes had adjusted to the darkness, then I rose and walked on bare feet to the window. Same old nightmares.

Once I was leaning out the window, taking deep breaths of the night air, I felt better. Being enclosed always reminds me of that time and I've learnt that an open sky is the best way to throw it off. I've always liked looking out of my window at night; something about the density, all those thousands of pinpoints and every one a person or a family. I could tell from the murmur that it was about four o'clock in the morning. Camden is never silent, but this is the quietest it gets. I could hear the sounds of distant music filtering through the bridges and over the canal, but my street was still.

I don't have many scars. Dark mages are quite skilled with methods of torture that don't cause permanent physical damage. My chest still hurt though – a phantom pain. I rubbed at it until it faded and leant on the window-sill, looking out into the night. A three-quarter moon was high in the sky, casting London in a pale light that reflected off the rooftops.

For some reason, instead of Luna, I found myself thinking

of the woman we'd left behind, Deleo. I was sure she was someone from my past – probably from my time with Richard. It's hard to remember someone just from the sound of their voice, but I've got access to ways of looking that normal people don't. I was pretty sure I could figure out who she was if I wanted to.

Except I didn't. Yes, Deleo was after me. Yes, I could probably protect myself better if I knew who she was. But even that wasn't enough to make me willingly take myself back to that place in my memory. My time with Richard is a place I've locked up in my mind; I don't think about it and I don't go back to it. Instead I ran through a brief exercise to clear my head then, when I was calm again, returned to bed and fell asleep quickly.

When I woke again, morning sunlight was streaming through the window. It took me a moment to recognise the noise that had pulled me awake – it had been the sound of my letterbox. I went downstairs in my underwear and discovered a small package had been dropped through the front door. I took it upstairs, scanning and opening it as I went, and unwrapped a roll of tissue to reveal a stylised stone key – a gate stone. It didn't come with a note, but I already knew where it would lead.

I went back upstairs and checked the news. A footnote on the news sites mentioned that the British Museum was closed due to a fire. The Council has excellent connections with the British government. I went to make my preparations.

Choosing your equipment for a meeting with other mages is a tricky business. It's a fine line between being prepared for trouble and being seen *as* the trouble. Visible weapons were obviously out. I really wanted to take my mist cloak, but given I'd been wearing it when I'd run from the Council reinforcements on Friday night, that wasn't an option either. I was fairly sure that between my cloak and the confusion, none of the Council mages had managed to get a good look at my face. If they had, this trip was going to be eventful. In the end, I picked out a nondescript set of casual clothes with relatively few tools or weapons, hoping to appear as low-key as possible.

Once I was done, I hung the CLOSED notice on the door, checked my wards, checked to see if my phone had any messages from Luna (it didn't), then went into the back room and activated the gate stone. A shimmering portal opened in the air and I stepped through. I could have walked to the museum in twenty minutes, but if I did that I'd have to explain how I knew where the gate stone was going to lead. Right now I was in the Council's good books, if only because they needed me, but I didn't think it would take much to change that.

I came down onto a polished white floor, my feet echoing around a wide room. I was back in the British Museum's Great Court. The area I'd stepped off into was marked off by ropes, and a chime rang in the air as I emerged.

The Great Court was mostly empty. The information desks and shops were deserted and most of the people I could see looked like Council security. A man dressed in brown and grey had been talking to two guards stationed at the entrance; now he finished up and walked over to me.

'Morning,' the man said once he was close enough. He was in his middle years, with iron-grey hair and a tough, competent manner. Although I'd only seen him for a few seconds, I recognised him. He'd been the one in command of the reinforcements, the one who'd shouted at Cinder to

stop. I kept my expression relaxed, and was relieved to see
no recognition in his eyes.

'Alexander Verus,' I said. 'I'm looking for the leader of
the investigation team.'

As I said my name, the man nodded. 'You've found him.
Griff Blackstone.' He offered his hand and I shook it. 'Good
to see you. Been asking for a diviner for weeks.'

Griff led me towards the Reading Room and the curving
staircase up. Now that I had a chance to count, I could
see there were at least a dozen Council guards around the
Great Court, stationed at the doors and corners. There were
no traces of Friday's battle; the floor and stairs were neat
and flawless. Earth and matter mages can repair stone so
well you'd never know it had been damaged. 'Tight security,' I said as we ascended the stairs.

'Need it. You heard about the attack?'

I looked at Griff inquiringly, which he seemed to take
as a no. 'Some team, Friday night. Broke through the
barrier and set off the relic guardian. Hell of a mess.'

'How many were there?'

'Three, maybe four. Wish we'd gotten a good look at
them.'

*Glad you didn't.* 'Are we clear for civilians?'

Griff nodded as we reached the top of the stairs.
'Museum's closed until further notice. Everyone you
meet's been cleared.' The restaurant at the top of the
stairs had been converted into a temporary headquarters,
and a dozen or so mages were gathered there: the investigation team. They all stopped to watch as we walked
in and I could tell they knew who I was even before
Griff introduced me.

Other mages have an odd attitude towards diviners. By

the standards of, say, elemental mages, diviners are complete wimps. We can't gate, we can't attack, we can't shield and when it comes to physical action our magic is about as useful as a bicycle in a trampolining contest. But we can see anywhere and learn anything and there's no secret we can't uncover if we try hard enough. So when an elemental mage looks at a diviner, the elemental mage knows he could take him in a straight fight with no more effort than it would take to tie his shoes. On the other hand, the elemental mage also knows that the diviner could find out every one of his most dirty and embarrassing secrets and, should he feel like it, post copies of them to everyone the elemental mage has ever met. It creates a mixture of uneasiness and contempt that doesn't encourage warm feelings. There's a reason most of my friends aren't mages.

So as I was introduced to the team I wasn't expecting a big welcome, and I didn't get one; polite neutrality was the order of the day. But just because I wasn't making friends didn't mean I wasn't paying attention. It was the defences I was interested in, and from what I could see they'd been beefed up heavily. There were overlapping wards over the entire museum, both alarms and transportation locks. The roped-off area I'd gated into was probably one of only two or three spots still accessible.

Once the investigation team and I had finished pretending to be friendly, Griff led me into the museum, passing more guards on the way. The landing above now held four guards instead of two, and the barrier had been strengthened – now it was an opaque wall blocking the top of the stairs. 'Barrier's pass-coded,' Griff said as we walked up the stairs. 'Pretty much the only thing that went right for us.

The mages who mounted the raid couldn't get round the alarm. Had to set it off as they went in.'

'Uh-huh,' I said, studying the ward. The password had been changed and I made a mental note to spend sixty seconds or so and re-crack it before I left. It's funny, really. Even when people go specifically looking for a diviner, they still never seem to grasp what we can do.

The room inside was the same. The statue was still at the centre, the stone man looking forward imperiously with his hand extended, and I gave it a narrow look. If you're going to build something that sets a lightning elemental on anyone who touches it wrong, you could at least have the decency to put up a warning sign or something. This time, though, there was company.

Another mage was examining the statue on his knees, a teenager in scuffed brown clothes. He had a mop of untidy black hair and a pair of glasses that he kept pushing up the bridge of his nose, only for them to fall back down again a second later.

'Sonder,' Griff said, and the young man jumped to his feet, startled. 'Diviner's here. Show him around.' He turned to me. 'You good?'

I nodded. 'I'll get to work.'

'Sonder'll get you whatever you need. Tell me if you get anywhere. We could use a break.' Griff turned and walked back down the stairs, vanishing through the black wall of the barrier without a ripple.

Sonder scrambled to his feet. 'Um, hi. Oh, you're the diviner?'

'That's me,' I said, looking around.

'I'm David. Everyone calls me Sonder, though.' Sonder started to extend his hand, then hesitated and stopped.

'You're here to look at it too? Oh!' I had walked up to the statue and Sonder hovered anxiously, not quite willing to pull me away. 'Don't put anything in the left hand!'

'Relax,' I said as I examined the statue. 'I wasn't planning to.'

'Oh good. The defence systems are really heavy. I mean, I haven't actually seen them personally, but still.'

I gave a brief glance through the futures of me interacting with the statue and found that nothing had changed. Every future in which I put something in the statue's hand led to the lightning elemental materialising in the middle of the room and trying to kill us. I took a look at the statue's hands. While the left one was empty, the right one clasped an unmarked wand. I pointed to it. 'This is what everyone's here for?'

Sonder nodded. 'That's the fateweaver. It's just a representation, though, the real thing is inside.'

'Uh-huh. Sonder? Maybe you could help me with something.'

'Really?' Sonder sounded surprised, but pulled himself together quickly. 'Well, okay. I mean, yes. If I can.'

'Everyone keeps talking about getting inside this thing,' I said. 'How?'

'Oh, right.' Sonder seemed to relax. 'Well, you see, the statue is the focal point for a Mobius spell. It's one of the techniques that was lost during the post-war period, but one of the Alicaern manuscripts has a good description. A Mobius spell takes the section of space it enchants and gives it a half-twist to bring it out of phase with reality. The ends of the enclosed space collapse inwards and join with each other to form a spatial bubble. Now, obviously, the natural result of that would be that the bubble would drift away, and of course once that happens there's no way to reestablish a link, so you need a focus to anchor it to our physical universe. Once it's been set up, there's no way to find the bubble from anywhere in the universe except via the focus. We've actually discovered Mobius focuses before, but this is the first time . . .'

As Sonder kept talking, I watched him out of the corner of my eye. Now I took a closer look I could see he was actually twenty or so; he just looked younger. He didn't look like an apprentice, though – I pegged him as a new journeyman, still fresh out from under a master's supervision. The ones outside had been less green. But were they tough enough?

There's a reason Dark mages are feared. It's not because their magic is any more powerful than its less evil counterpart, it's because of the people who use it. Life as a Dark mage is savage and brutal, an endless war for status and power with shifting alliances and betrayals. The infighting is the reason Dark mages can't unite; they're actually far more dangerous to each other than anyone else, though it's hard to remember that when one of them's after you.

But the same infighting that weakens Dark mages as a group is also what makes them so deadly as individuals. Dark mages who survive to adulthood are the toughest and most ruthless people in the world. Light mages, on the other hand, live in a society where getting places is mostly about political skill, and most of the mages I'd met in the restaurant would have gotten on the team through having the right connections. Don't get me wrong, politics among Light mages can be rough, but they play by rules. Dark mages don't.

If Deleo, Cinder and Khazad decided they really wanted to get in here, I knew who I'd put my money on.

'. . . so while there's no way to test it, in theory there's no actual reason why the gateway aspect of the focus would decay over time,' Sonder was saying. He paused, seeming to realise that I'd been quiet. 'Um, Mr Verus?'

'Just Alex is fine,' I said. 'So what you're saying is that this statue is the only door in, and it's locked.'

Sonder hesitated. 'Well, I suppose you could put it like that.'

'If it's locked, what's the key?'

'Well, that's what the team's been working on. The senior members are pretty sure it just needs the right type of key item placed into the statue's hand. Unfortunately, um, there have been a few issues fabricating one.'

'Hm.' I gave Sonder a look. 'Exactly how many times have they tried?'

'Uh . . .' Sonder scratched his head. 'I'm not actually sure. I wasn't allowed here until a few days ago.'

'And how come there isn't anyone else around?'

'Ah, well . . . there were more when I arrived, but after they told me to try to figure out a way to get it open, they left. They told me to keep them up to date.'

'Ah,' I said. In other words, no one had the faintest clue how to open the thing. That was why Lyle had approached me on Friday – it was because the investigation team had tried literally *everything* else. I wondered how many times they'd set the lightning elemental off, and how many people had been killed or wounded before the mages had wised up and started keeping their distance. That was why everyone else was on the other side of the museum: they didn't want to be in range if we became the next ones to trip the switch.

'You studied under an academic mage, right?' I asked Sonder. 'What did you specialise in? Magical theory?'

Sonder blinked. 'History, actually.'

'Do you know who this is a statue of?'

Sonder paused. 'You really want to know?'

I nodded and Sonder seemed to light up. 'Wow. That's . . . You know, you're the first one who's ever asked me that.'

'Let me guess,' I said, as I walked around the statue, studying it. 'The mages on the team just wanted to know if you could open it.'

'Yes. I mean . . . Um, well . . .' Sonder cleared his throat, a little self-conscious. 'Well, uh, the robes are in the Late Precursor style, and the design is very similar to the surviving pieces of post-war sculpture. The others think it's just a statue but,' Sonder pushed his glasses up, warming to his theme, 'the very first thing I did was look through our records. Well, there wasn't anything from the post-war period, but when I looked through our records of the Dark Wars I found it straightaway. His name was Abithriax, and he was a general in the Light armies.' Sonder pointed to the wand clasped in the statue's hand. 'You see, the fateweavers weren't just weapons, they were also symbols of rank. Now, according to the records, Abithriax was killed in the closing months of the Dark Wars, just a few years before this must have been built. So I don't think this relic was just built to store the fateweaver, I think it was built as a tomb.'

I frowned. 'A general's tomb . . .' I looked at the statue, proud and commanding. Somehow it felt right. 'So you think they buried him with his weapon?'

Sonder nodded. 'I think so. There aren't any records I can find to confirm it though.'

'No, I think you might be right.' I stood thinking for

a little while. 'Sonder, can you do me a favour? Keep researching this. I'm not sure if it'll help us get in, but it might be important once we do.'

'Oh. Um, yes, okay.' Sonder paused. 'You think you're going to get inside?'

'Yup.'

'How?'

'No idea.'

Sonder paused. 'Then why are you so sure?'

I smiled. 'Because so many people are after me. Give me some space – this might take a while.'

Sonder stepped well back and watched as I stood in front of the statue and closed my eyes. I stood quietly for a minute to clear my mind, then began methodically to look into the future.

The statue was the focal point of the room. I looked into the futures of my interacting with it and found it very easy. Every future in which I did anything to the statue, or placed anything in its hands, led to exactly the same result: the huge lightning elemental appearing in the middle of the room and attacking us. I was slightly reassured to notice that in none of the probable futures did the elemental get me. I was also reassured to notice that the future Sonder did a pretty good job of making himself scarce, too. He was obviously faster than he looked.

I settled down to the job of scanning through the futures one by one, looking for the future in which I activated the statue *without* triggering the elemental. It was slow, laborious work, and time dragged by as I stood there searching through the futures as they flickered and changed, looking for the one in which I did the right thing. I went through a thousand futures, two thousand, three thousand, trying every object, every action, every combination of spells. Nothing changed.

I was so absorbed that I actually jumped when my phone rang, snapping me out of my trance. I checked my watch to see that I'd been at it for two hours. Sonder was on the other side of the room, going through a stack of books. I shook myself awake and looked at my phone. The number was unknown. I picked up. 'Talisid.'

'Hello, Mr Verus,' Talisid's voice said. 'I'm glad you made it home safely.'

'I'd ask how you got my number, but I think I can guess.'

'And I'd ask how you knew it was me, but I think I can guess that too. Have you given any thought to our offer?'

I glanced to check that Sonder wasn't within hearing distance, did a brief scan for eavesdropping spells, then turned away and lowered my voice just to be on the safe side. 'What exactly *are* you offering?'

'Assistance. Starting from tomorrow, I'll be present at the museum as official Council liaison. I'll be able to help with any resources you require.'

'And what would you want in exchange for this generosity?'

Talisid sighed. 'Let's stop fencing, Verus. We want to stop any ambitious individuals taking the fateweaver for themselves. If you can retrieve it and deliver it to the Council, that's fine. If you can't retrieve it, that's fine too. Mostly, we'd like to resolve this with as few people killed as possible. Are you interested, or not?'

I was silent for a long time. 'All right,' I said. 'I'm not promising anything, but I'll meet you to talk things over. Six o'clock at Centre Point?'

'That'll be fine. See you then.' Talisid hung up.

Talisid's call had broken my concentration. I turned back to the statue and started to slip back into my trance, then shook my head and stopped. This wasn't working. If there was any remotely possible way I could activate this thing, I would have found it by now. I hadn't, and that meant that with what I had here, it wasn't possible.

I looked at the statue. Abithriax's stone eyes stared back at me. The longer I looked at him, the more expression I seemed to notice in his face. He *did* look like a general – confident, as if he already knew he was going to win. I wondered if he'd been wearing that same expression when he died.

I remembered what Sonder had told me. The mages who'd built this thing had known what they were doing; tricking it wasn't going to work. Maybe I was going about this the wrong way. Instead of trying to work it out by myself, I should take my cue from the people who knew more than I did. Levistus obviously thought I had a good chance of opening this door, or he wouldn't have revealed so much, but he didn't know for sure. Deleo, Cinder and Khazad had made their own attempt on Friday night using a fake key, but it hadn't worked. Then what?

Then they'd gone after Luna.

*Luna . . .*

And suddenly I got it. Maybe you've already guessed by now, and you're sitting there wondering how I could take so long to figure it out. If you are, all I can say is that it's a hell of a lot harder to step back and look at the big picture when you have to keep watching your feet for landmines. The relic key was Luna's red crystal cube. And since Luna was the cube's mistress, she'd have to be the one to place the cube in the statue's hand.

It all fit. That was why Cinder had been willing to kill me when he'd come searching for me on Friday. He and Deleo hadn't been able to find the cube so he'd intended to use my divination magic as a backup, never knowing that the cube was lying on the ground right in front of him. Khazad hadn't known about the cube either and so he'd come after me, intending to press-gang me into service or kill me so that I wouldn't help anyone else. After the failed break-in, Deleo and Khazad had followed the cube's trail to Luna and tried to hunt her down in Camden, and when *that* had failed, all three had tracked her to the ball last night. I remembered Deleo's words to Luna: *'You have something that belongs to me'*. They'd known Luna had been the one to take the cube . . . but they *didn't* know that Luna had to be the one to open it or they'd have just snatched her without asking questions. And that meant that right now, I was the only person who knew the secret to opening this door.

For a moment I felt a rush of excitement. But then, as I made the connection, my heart went cold. They knew the cube was the way in, and they thought Luna had the cube. They'd be doubling their efforts to find her. 'I have to go,' I said, and started moving. Sonder said something, but I wasn't listening any more.

I passed Griff at the restaurant talking with another mage. He frowned, then followed me, catching me up as I hurried down the stairs. 'Well?'

'I need something from home,' I said.

'What, right now?'

'Right now.'

Griff looked irritated, and was about to argue, then stopped. 'Fine. Just hurry up.'

As I left the museum, I was already working on plans. The annuller effect should keep Luna safe from magical detection, at least for now. But Deleo and Cinder had seen us by the arch so they'd know that too. I walked along the street, ticking off other possibilities. A really powerful spell could theoretically find Luna even through the annuller. Unlikely, but possible. A more serious threat would be if they switched away from using magic. There are plenty of mundane ways to find someone. Would Deleo be the type to think of that?

I reached a corner. A black cab was passing and I hailed it and jumped in. 'Cla—' I started, then changed my mind. 'Camden.' I'd need to get equipped first. The driver nodded and pulled away.

As the driver wound his way northwards through the London streets, I pulled out my phone and dialled Luna's number. The first call rang and rang before going to a dial tone. I swore, hung up and tried again. The taxi turned into Royal College Street; we were only a few minutes away from my home. I could tell that there was a chance of Luna picking up and I focused on the futures of her speaking to me, ignoring everything else, and so when the attack came I was caught completely by surprise. There was a surge of fire magic, a double *bang* as two tyres burst, and the taxi slewed left and hit a parked car at thirty miles an hour.

The next thing I remember is lying across the back seat at an awkward angle, my head spinning. There was blood in my mouth and my eyes felt fuzzy. I struggled to a sitting position to see the driver slumped over his steering wheel. My phone was gone somewhere, I could hear a hissing noise, and through the cracked windows I could see white smoke. Shaking my head, I leaned clumsily towards one of the doors, trying to get it open.

Before my fingers could find the handle, the door was yanked open from the other side. A pair of big hands reached in, grabbed me by my shirt, and dragged me out. I could hear voices and shouting in the distance, but all I could see through the smoke was the oval shimmer of a gate. Someone snapped out an order, and I was shoved towards the gate and through.

I came down on concrete with a painful thump. Twisting around, I saw other people following me through the gate. Three people. The gate shimmered and vanished, and I could see we were in some sort of warehouse. The man with the big hands bent down and hauled me to my feet again and, as my head cleared, I found myself staring into Cinder's face.

'Not so smart now, you bastard,' Cinder growled.

I remember reading a book where some pretentious writer claimed there's no moment of enlightenment more terrible than when you realise your parents are simple human beings. Personally, if you've grown up listening to your parents having screaming matches, realising that they're simple human beings isn't much of a revelation. In my opinion, the most terrible moment of enlightenment is the one where you realise you're outflanked, outgunned and a sitting duck. It's a horrible sickening feeling in the pit of your stomach that can very easily be the last feeling you'll ever have.

The room we were in was square and ugly with concrete walls, narrow slit windows high above the ground and stacks of crates in the corners. It was empty but for me and the three Dark mages. Cinder was there, holding me almost off the ground, and Khazad, his small black eyes glinting. I'd been so focused on the call that I hadn't been looking into the future for danger and, looking at Cinder's face, I knew that it might just have cost me my life.

Cinder shook me hard enough to make my teeth rattle. 'I'm gonna burn you to ash, Verus. I'll make it slow, so you can feel it. I'm gonna make you tell me which part to burn off next.'

'No.' Khazad's expression was more evil than Cinder's if anything. 'Not till I've had my turn. He's going to pay for that stunt at the ball.'

'Gonna ask you this once,' Cinder said, and pulled me close. 'Where's the girl? Where's the key?'

'You know,' I said light-headedly, 'I think you asked twice.'

Cinder hauled one massive arm back and smashed a punch into my face. If I hadn't twisted it would have broken my nose; as it was it sent me back to the floor with stars flashing in front of my eyes. By the time they'd cleared Cinder had dragged me back up again. He drew back for another go.

'Wait,' a third voice said. Deleo stepped in front of me. She was still wearing her mask, and her eyes watched me coldly. 'Give him a second.'

Cinder glowered but obeyed, and a moment later my head cleared. Cinder's grip was digging painfully into my shoulders; I didn't think I'd have much chance of breaking it even without the other mages in front of me. 'Using the annuller was very neat,' Deleo said once I'd gotten my breath back. Her voice was calm. 'It stopped us from tracking down your girlfriend. So we decided it would be simpler to track you instead. We knew you'd go back to the museum. All we had to do was wait for you to leave.' She leant in close, her blue eyes staring into mine, and there was a sudden fire burning behind them. 'I told you this wasn't over.'

I looked back at Deleo silently.

Deleo drew back, calm once again. 'You're leaving this warehouse in one of two ways. With us to where you hid that cube, or in a bag. Choose fast.'

I hesitated. Cinder grinned. Khazad was staring down at the floor. Deleo nodded. 'Go ahead, Cinder. Start with his legs.'

'Wait,' I said quickly, trying to think. I needed time.

But as I spoke, Khazad did as well. 'Something's wrong.'

Cinder and Deleo looked at him, frowning. Khazad was staring around at the walls. 'There's something . . .' His head snapped around. 'A ward. This place is warded!'

'They're ours,' Cinder grunted. He didn't relax his grip, and didn't look pleased to be interrupted.

'*Besides* ours, you idiot! Someone's been inside!'

'That's impossible,' Deleo said. 'No one could have gotten through the defences without us noticing.'

'And I'm telling you they did!' Khazad shook his head. 'It's too risky. We should kill him and go.' Black energy flared up around his hand, and I knew my time was up.

But before Khazad could strike, a voice spoke from one side. 'Your attention, please.'

Cinder dropped me to the concrete with a *thump* as he spun around. A man with dark hair and dressed in black had stepped out from behind a pile of crates. It was Morden.

\*   \*   \*

If Morden was bothered by the sight of three Dark mages a hair's breadth from attacking, he gave no sign of it. 'Good morning, all of you.' His voice was pleasant, and he held his hands clasped behind his back. 'Cinder, Khazad, I'd prefer if you attempted no attacks.'

'You said it was clear!' Cinder hissed at Khazad under his breath.

'I said we should go! If you hadn't screwed up—'

Deleo made a quick motion and Cinder and Khazad fell silent. All three seemed to have forgotten me completely, their attention locked on Morden. 'Master Morden,' Deleo said levelly. 'I don't think this is your concern.'

'Oh, don't take it personally, Deleo.' Morden sounded quite friendly. 'You've done very well. But now it's time you came with me.'

'Thank you for the offer,' Deleo said, her voice carefully controlled. 'The answer is still no.'

Morden smiled then, just slightly. 'I'm afraid you're under a misconception, Deleo. This time you're not being given a choice.'

Deleo stood quite still. Khazad took a pace forward, and his voice was soft and deadly. Black energy flared around his right hand. 'There's three of us and one of you, old man.'

I craned my neck, trying to look around, but Morden seemed to be alone. I wanted to run but knew any movement would draw everyone's attention. 'Yes, yes,' Morden said tolerantly. 'Bravado is all very well, but please realise you're in no position to argue. Now, I'm quite impressed you were able to detect the carrier ward, but if you think for a moment you should realise there must be many more, and quite frankly, at your level of ability—'

'Shut up!' Khazad said with a snarl. 'I can see your ward! It's nothing!'

Morden sighed. 'Do pay attention, Khazad. As I was saying, behind that ward are many others, and all of you are well within the blast radius. I'd prefer to do this peacefully, but—'

'Del,' Cinder rumbled.

Deleo hesitated, then made a swift motion. Cinder darted left, and energy flared up around Khazad as he drew back to strike.

The entire area vanished in a black wave. A light-eating pulse swept over all of us, nauseating and weakening and dazing me all at once. I felt my strength fade, and crumpled to the ground.

There was a moment of silence, then as if from a distance, I heard Morden speaking. His voice seemed to be fading, growing fainter and fainter. 'They always have to learn the hard way, don't they? Pack them up and make sure they're still alive.'

There was more, but I didn't hear it. Blackness swallowed me, and everything went dark.

## 9

I opened my eyes.

I was lying on a warm bed in a small, comfortable room. The walls were panelled with wood. Furniture crowded the room, neat and expensive, and a fire was burning in a fireplace. To one side was a long window; although the room was well lit, the light outside was dim and rain streaked the glass. Something told me not to move, and I didn't. Instead I lay where I was, letting my memory come back. I was wearing the same clothes as when I left. All I could hear was the faint crackle of the fire and the distant sound of the rain as it beat against the window.

I didn't have the first idea where this place was, but I knew exactly *what* it was: the mansion of a Dark mage. I don't know how I knew it was a mansion, or how I was so sure of who owned it. I just knew: memory and instinct, a feeling in the air.

When my relationship with Richard Drakh went sour – about the same time I realised how stupid I'd been agreeing to become his apprentice in the first place – I was imprisoned in his mansion. For all that time I was a slave, and I was treated like one. From time to time Richard or one of the others would spend some time with me, either to try and persuade me, or in the later months, just for amusement. Very occasionally I'd be taken out under supervision when Richard had some job he needed me for, and it had been on one of those trips that I'd finally managed to escape. But the rest of the time I'd been a prisoner.

Just like now.

It's strange. Ever since getting away from Richard's mansion, even after he was gone, the one thing that I'd been terrified of, more than anything else, was the thought of going back. Now it had finally happened, I wasn't scared at all. It was more like a relief, as though something inevitable had finally arrived. What I felt more than anything else was the old *alertness*, that animalistic sense of danger. Everything but the present fades away and there's nothing but surviving, one hour and one day at a time. I understood quite clearly that my mistake at the museum, allowing myself to be ambushed, had been the last one I could afford. This was my last chance.

I took stock. I was still wearing my clothes, and I was in a bedroom instead of a cell. I wasn't injured and I couldn't feel any bruises from the crash; I must have been healed. Adding it all up, that meant I was about to be offered some sort of deal, and that meant I had something to work with, at least for now. With that, I got up, working my arms and legs to lose the stiffness.

The room was small and cosy, the walls made of some kind of reddish wood. Outside, I could hear the wind whining, though inside the air was warm. My pockets were empty, but piled neatly on the table beside the bed was everything I'd been carrying. I went through it and found it all there, from my wallet to my weapons to even the gate stones.

Interesting. Even with my items, they didn't consider me a threat. Good faith, or overconfidence? Or both?

Old instincts took over and I checked my lines of retreat,

looking through the futures of myself trying to leave. The window was locked and warded. The door wasn't. What about my gate stones . . .?

Ouch. An interdiction spell. I concentrated and a thousand versions of myself explored the room in a thousand projected futures, looking for a way out besides the door. There wasn't one. I withdrew and nodded to myself: a gilded cage. I could probably break the window lock given time, but for now it wasn't worth the risk. I walked to the door.

It opened into a living room. Comfortable-looking sofas and chairs upholstered in red leather filled the floor, while paintings of ancient battles decorated the walls. A fire burned in a fireplace, and the room was warmly lit. Doors led deeper into the mansion.

Settled in one of the chairs, the light sinking into his black hair, was Morden. He had one leg crossed ankle to knee, and was reading from a folder. 'Ah, Verus,' he said, not raising his eyes from the page. 'I'm glad you're up. Take a seat.'

I walked to one of the sofas facing Morden. Without even looking, I knew that my future depended on the decisions of the man sitting in front of me. Pissing him off would not be a good idea. Morden kept reading for half a minute longer, then nodded to himself, closed the folder and looked up. 'Good to see you on your feet. I hope you're feeling better?'

I nodded. 'Just fine, thank you.'

'Excellent. First of all, I have to apologise for the way you were brought here. I'd hoped to resolve things peacefully, but your three pursuers seem to have more persistence than sense and, well, you were in the blast radius. I took the liberty of making sure your injuries were healed. I hope there are no hard feelings.'

I'd only gotten a short look at Morden last night. His hair and eyebrows were jet-black and he had the smooth good looks of someone who'd taken the time to develop them. Physically he could have been thirty, but his voice and eyes told a different story. If I'd had to guess I'd have said Morden was older than he looked, maybe much older. At the moment he was sitting easily, welcoming, and everything about his pose suggested hospitality. How much of that was true I'd find out soon enough.

Morden had been waiting for me to answer, and I finally spoke. 'None,' I said. 'You don't need to apologise. Given the circumstances when you showed up, I'm grateful.'

Morden waved a hand. 'As I told you last night, I had some business to discuss with you. As a matter of fact, this has worked out quite conveniently.'

I nodded, though my attention was only partly on Morden's words. Ever since stepping into the room, I'd been looking into the future. Both Morden and the mansion around us radiated power but I couldn't detect any immediate danger. It didn't seem like he was planning to hurt me. At least, not yet.

'Well, then,' Morden said. 'What do you want?'

'I'm sorry?'

'What do you want?' Morden repeated. He had a way of curving his lips up slightly as he spoke. It made it look as though he was smiling even when he wasn't. 'What are you looking to get out of this?'

'Out of what?'

'Come now, Verus. This affair over the Precursor relic and its contents. You've become involved, so obviously you must have some reason. What's motivating you?'

'Well . . . right now, staying alive would be good.'

Morden shook his head. 'Oh, I think you can do better than that.'

'Um, staying alive is a pretty big motivation for me.'

'If survival was your priority, you'd be in hiding like the other diviners. How is Helikaon, by the way? It's a pity he's decided to sit this one out. I always enjoyed working with him.'

I didn't reply. 'Let's try this another way,' Morden said. 'Who would you like to see gain possession of the fateweaver?'

'Depends what's in it for me.'

Morden shook his head again, still smiling slightly. 'That won't fly either, I'm afraid. You aren't a mercenary.'

'If you know so much about me,' I said evenly, 'why do you need to ask?'

'Oh, I know your motivations. I'm simply curious whether you do.'

I stayed silent. 'Did you know that we've met before?' Morden said. 'Before last night? I expect you don't remember; it was ten years ago. We met at a tournament. You were apprenticed to Richard at the time, but I recall you quite clearly. We spoke for a few minutes before you were called away.'

'You've got a good memory.'

'I was disappointed to hear you and your master had fallen out,' Morden said. 'Still, I wasn't surprised when you reappeared. Most of the others assumed you dead, but I had always had the feeling you'd be back. You're resourceful, Verus. It's a quality I admire.'

I didn't answer. In my time as Richard's apprentice, I'd met hundreds of Dark mages, often briefly; it was quite believable that Morden had been one of them. What bothered me was how much he seemed to know. Dark mages tend to have good intelligence networks, but there were very few who knew all the details from that time. 'We have a word for mages such as you, Verus,' Morden said. 'Rogues. Mages who reject the tradition in which they've been trained. Most look down on them, but in truth some of the most powerful mages in history have been rogues . . . on both sides. Of those, several of the most famous have been ones who ended up rejoining the tradition in which they were raised.' Morden steepled his fingers and looked at me with raised eyebrows, as if waiting for something.

It took me a moment to get it. 'Are you . . . suggesting something?'

'More of an offer, actually. Competent diviners are so rare. One of the reasons Richard went to such an effort to recruit you, and why he was so disappointed at how things turned out.'

Richard had gone to an effort to recruit me? He'd always acted as though it had been something casual. 'I thought you said rogues weren't highly thought of.'

'I believe in second chances.' Morden tilted his head. 'It can't have escaped your attention that you could use some allies. As things stand, you're friends with neither the Dark alliance nor the Council of the Light.'

'I wasn't aware there *was* a Dark alliance.'

'At present?' Morden smiled. 'If the fateweaver should be retrieved, I'm sure you can see how things might change.'

'Yes . . .' I said. 'Listen, given that you seem to know so much about me, I'm assuming you know that my last association with Dark mages didn't exactly end well. For any of us.'

Morden shrugged. 'A certain degree of conflict is expected in the apprenticeship process.'

'That's one way to put it.'

'Remember, Verus, you never completed your training. Disagreements such as yours are quite normal. Their purpose is to teach an apprentice the True Path. In your case, while events certainly didn't go well, the end result would have been considered acceptable, I think. You're a Dark mage in all but name already.'

'No, I'm not,' I said sharply. The words were out before I could think.

'It's natural you should be unhappy at the comparison,' Morden said calmly. 'You associate the name of a Dark mage with Richard's behaviour. But being a Dark mage doesn't mean being destructive or vicious. We don't believe in evil for its own sake, or any of the silly propaganda that others spread. We simply recognise the truth — that all definitions of good and evil ultimately come down to points of view. You no doubt consider Richard's behaviour evil. He would have disagreed. But think for a moment. How did you eventually survive?'

'On my own.'

'Exactly.' Morden pointed at me. 'You didn't waste time trying to convince Richard that you were right and he was wrong. You broke away with your own abilities.'

'I know what I did.' A part of me remembered that I shouldn't piss Morden off, but it was getting harder and harder. 'I was there.'

Morden simply watched. I took a deep breath, and slowly regained my cool. 'What are you trying to say?' I finally asked.

'I'm simply pointing out the obvious. You survived and

escaped because you were powerful enough, which is, of course, what this is really all about. If you hadn't, none of your beliefs would have mattered. Certainly the Council doesn't seem to share your views about, well,' Morden raised an eyebrow, 'anything, really. I'm sure you know they're never going to accept you. They didn't employ you for this job until they'd exhausted literally every other alternative, even though you were more than qualified. So, once again,' Morden looked at me pleasantly, 'you're an enemy of the Council; you live on your wits and your power. Effectively, you're a Dark mage in all but name – except for one thing.'

Morden raised his eyebrows as if inviting me to ask what it was. I didn't. 'A true Dark mage has purpose,' Morden went on once it was clear I wasn't going to speak. 'Those who lack purpose are pawns to those who do not. Which brings us back to our original question. What do *you* want?'

'What do *you* want?'

Morden smiled. 'I want the fateweaver, of course. That's hardly a secret. The question is who *you* want to get it.'

I started to answer and realised suddenly that I didn't know. I'd been so busy manoeuvring between the different factions over the last two days that I'd never stopped to think of who I actually wanted to win. And why should I have thought about it? It wasn't up to me.

Except now I *did* stop to think, I realised it *was* up to me. Enough of the pieces of the puzzle had ended up in my hands that I could make a difference. Morden was right. Until now I'd just been reacting, being pushed around by one faction or another. If I was going to get out of this in one piece, I'd have to stop reacting and start acting. And that meant figuring out exactly what I wanted.

I sat thinking for five minutes. Morden didn't rush me, waiting patiently while I worked out what I was going to say.

'What are you offering?' I said at last.

'Consider the position that of intelligence officer,' Morden said. 'I think it's a role to which you'd be well suited.'

'What's in it for me?'

'Come now, Verus. I know money doesn't motivate you.'

'I wasn't talking about money.'

'Ah.' Morden tilted his head. 'Well, for one thing, you'd get to stay alive. You listed that as your primary goal, I believe.'

'You're going to have to do better than that.'

'You are aware I could kill you at any time?'

'Very,' I said. 'But you haven't, which means at the moment you've got a reason not to. You could tell me to follow your orders or die, and I'd have to do as you said. But threatening a diviner doesn't work out very well in the long run. Not if you're planning to rely on the information he gives you.'

Morden studied me for a moment. I knew from looking into the future that he wasn't going to follow through on his threat, but something in his eyes still made my skin crawl. Suddenly he smiled. 'Very well, then. What I can offer you is safety. As long as you're working for me, neither you nor any associates you bring with you will be harmed, by *either* side. I think you'll find my security quite impressive. You'll also have whatever you can find from the site, bar the fateweaver itself. Of course, your team members will have their own shares.'

'Team members?'

'So then.' Morden leaned back in his chair. 'Tell me how to open that relic.'

I felt the futures shift into a series of forks. I took a long look at the options ahead of me, and saw the consequences of answering one way or the other. 'With a key,' I said at last.

'What does the key look like?'

'A cube of red crystal.'

'How does it open the door?'

'You place the cube in the statue's hand.'

'Do you have it?'

I paused. 'Yes.'

A beat, then Morden nodded, and I felt the flicker of a minor spell. A second later, the far door opened and a young man walked in.

He couldn't have been older than his early twenties, but no one looking at him would call him a boy. He was tall and slender, smooth-moving in a way that suggested speed, and his eyes were cold. I'd never met him, but I knew exactly what he was: a Dark Chosen, a selected apprentice. He would be fast, ruthless, a combat veteran despite his youth, deadly with his magic or without it. He was holding something in one hand, and as he came and stopped by Morden's chair I saw what it was. It was Luna's red crystal cube, the same one I'd left locked away in my shop.

'Let me introduce you to Onyx,' Morden said. 'He'll be looking after you during your stay. Do feel free to approach him if there's anything you need.'

I looked at Onyx and he looked back at me. The expression on his face suggested anyone who approached him could expect to have their throat cut. 'I'll keep that in mind,' I said.

'Excellent. Onyx?'

Onyx stepped forward and held out the cube. I lifted my hand and he placed the cube into it. Morden nodded to him and with a final glance back at me Onyx turned and left, shutting the door behind him as he went. 'A gesture of good faith,' Morden said with a smile. 'I'm afraid the defences on your shop need some work. We'll have to look into getting you some better accommodation once this is over.'

I looked at the cube, feeling its presence in my hand, patient and still. 'So as you can see,' Morden said, 'I now have everything I need – with your assistance, of course. We should be moving within a day or two; please consider yourself my guest until then.' He rose to his feet and moved to the other door. 'This way.'

I slipped the cube into my pocket, then got up and followed Morden into a long hallway. Pictures and rugs lined the walls, but I was too busy looking ahead to notice. Morden had known about the cube from the start; his questions had been traps. If I'd lied, the consequences would have been ugly. But I still had one edge, a secret that I was almost sure Morden *didn't* know. The cube would only work for Luna. If Morden tried to open the door with the cube, he was going to get a nasty surprise.

It would be a very good idea for me not to be around when that happened.

'You'll be working with Onyx on this assignment,' Morden was saying. 'Along with three others.'

'These others,' I said. 'They wouldn't be Cinder, Deleo and Khazad, would they?'

'As a matter of fact they would.'

'Ah.'

'I'm confident you'll be able to resolve your differences.'

'We're going to meet them?'

'Just Deleo.'

'And the other two?'

'Unfortunately they've proven . . . less accommodating. They should be in good condition by tomorrow.' Morden smiled. 'However, I'm sure you and Deleo will have plenty to talk about. First, though, I think a re-introduction is in order.' He opened one of the doors.

The room inside was dimly lit. It looked oddly familiar and it took me a second to realise what it reminded me of: the room in Canary Wharf where I'd met Levistus. Just like there, a handful of chairs faced a full-length window made of one-way glass. But my attention was fixed on the woman standing in the centre of the room. It was Deleo, except this time, as she turned to look at us, she wasn't wearing her mask. And this time, I knew who she was.

I stopped dead in the doorway. 'I believe the two of you know each other?' Morden said.

Both of us stared at each other in silence. 'Well,' Morden said eventually. 'I have a disciplinary matter to attend to. Let me make it clear that I will not accept any internal fighting. Both of you work for me now. If you prove unable to cooperate, one or both of you will be replaced. Understood?'

Neither of us answered. 'I said is that understood?' Morden asked, steel creeping into his voice.

'Yes,' I said. The woman facing me nodded.

'Good. Oh, and please stay here until I return. You'll understand why shortly.' The door clicked shut behind Morden and the room was silent.

'So it was you,' I said at last.

Deleo – not that that was her real name – spoke for the first time. 'You didn't even recognise me, did you?'

'If you'd called yourself Rachel, I would have.'

She looked away. 'That's not my name any more.'

Silence fell again as I went back to staring at Rachel. It's a strange feeling, seeing someone after so long. When I'd first known Rachel, she'd been a teenager, pretty and thoughtful, always changing. In her face I could still recognise the person she'd once been, but her face was immobile now, mask-like. She was striking, even beautiful in a cold way, but 'pretty' didn't describe her any more.

There had been four of us, back then. Me, Shireen, Tobruk and Rachel. Tobruk was dead. Shireen was probably dead. Rachel's fate I'd never known. After that last battle, I'd never heard from her and she'd never come looking for me. I'd forgotten her, buried her in my memory along with everything else that had happened back then. Until now.

'Why the mask?' I said at last.

'You wouldn't understand.'

'Is this how you've been keeping yourself busy? Treasure-hunting?'

'And you've been running a shop,' Rachel said contemptuously.

I shrugged. I can't say I like mages looking down on me for my day job, but I'm used to it. 'Running a shop or treasure-hunting . . . it seems to have led us to the same place.'

Rachel didn't answer. 'Just out of curiosity,' I said, 'what were you planning to do with me and Luna after you got into that relic?'

'Whatever I wanted.'

'Modelling yourself on our old teacher?'

'Fuck you,' Rachel snapped. 'We had you. You could never beat me.'

'I wasn't trying to beat you,' I said. Rachel made a disgusted noise and stalked to the end of the room, her back turned.

Despite the violence in Rachel's words I couldn't sense any danger. With her mask off she seemed a different person. I could also tell she wasn't going to answer any more questions, so I walked to the one-way glass and studied what was beyond.

The room on the other side of the glass was a torture chamber. Three small barbed cages were lined against the far wall, not quite tall enough to stand in and not quite wide enough to sit in. A rack was in one corner, and there was also a vagrant's chair and an iron maiden with its spikes just visible inside its half open doors. In pride of place, at the centre of the room, was a ten-foot-tall agoniser. Its straps and metal plates had been polished, ready for use.

Although well equipped, I couldn't help but notice that Morden's torture chamber was a little on the primitive side compared to Richard's. Richard had gone to special effort to select devices that inflicted pain without causing physical damage, so that they could be used over long periods of time without need of a healer. Maybe Morden was the old-fashioned type.

By the way, if you're getting creeped out by me discussing the pros and cons of torture chambers, I'm not surprised. Just trust me when I say you'd understand if you'd ever been there. Treating it like it's something normal helps to make it less scary. Of course, when you're treating torture chambers as something normal, that's also a sign that you should seriously re-examine your life.

'Just like old times,' I said. When Rachel didn't reply,

I looked at her. 'Did Morden put you in there? Or was it just Cinder and Khazad?'

Rachel looked at me without expression. I leant back against the wall, watching her. 'You wouldn't take orders from anyone, back then,' I said after a pause. 'You were the one in charge; that was how you sold it. Now one day and you're following Morden? What changed?'

Rachel turned her back on me again. For a moment I thought she wasn't going to answer, then she spoke. 'A lot of things changed.'

'One thing hasn't.' I smiled slightly. 'We're supposed to be working together again.'

'No.' Rachel turned to me. 'I never wanted to see you. I wouldn't have, if Cinder hadn't sniffed you out. Then you had to get involved with that girl. Why couldn't you hide like the rest? Just looking at you makes me—' Rachel clenched her fists and took a breath. 'I hate you more than I could ever hate Morden. He's just another man. You're—'

Rachel trailed off. 'I'm what?' I asked.

'You're a memory,' Rachel said, her voice low and intense. 'Every time I look at you I have to remember. Stay away from me. I'll kill you if that's what I have to do to stop seeing your face.'

The sound of an opening door made us both turn and look. From the other side of the one-way glass, three people had entered the torture chamber. As soon as I saw them I understood what was going to happen, and why Morden had told us to stay.

Morden was at the front. Behind him were the two girls who'd been accompanying him at the ball: Lisa and the brunette. The brunette's face was blank and she was pulling Lisa along by one wrist. Lisa was crying and begging, tears streaming down her face. Despite the one-way glass, we could hear everything she said clearly. 'No, master, please. I'm sorry, I'm sorry, I'll do anything. I didn't mean to. Master, please, I didn't mean to, I didn't. Don't put me in there. Master, please—'

There's a kind of horrible fascination to these things. Even when you know what's going to happen, there's something that makes you look. I'd seen what was going to happen, knew how this was going to end, yet somehow I found myself staring through the one-way glass. To one side, I was conscious of Rachel standing motionless, watching as well.

As the other girl started strapping Lisa into the agoniser, Lisa stopped pleading and just started crying. 'Lisa,' Morden said. 'Do you understand why you are here?'

Lisa mumbled something. 'Louder, please,' Morden said.

Lisa sniffed. 'Dis-disloyalty.' Her voice was shaky.

'To whom?'

'To you. Please, Master, I didn't—'

Morden raised a hand and Lisa fell silent. The other girl had finished with the straps, leaving Lisa spread-eagled. 'This is the punishment for disloyalty,' Morden said. He looked at the brunette and nodded. The other girl's face was still blank. She turned and activated the device.

I'm not going to describe what an agoniser does. You don't want to know. After the first sixty seconds I couldn't watch any more. Lisa's voice gave out somewhere around the second minute, but she still kept trying to scream.

Rachel didn't look away. She stood by the window and her face was so still it could have been carved from marble. The light of the agoniser lit up her face in reflected blue-and-white flashes. She didn't move throughout the whole thing, standing like a statue.

When it finally ended, Lisa was a weeping heap of bloody rags. Morden said something that I didn't listen to while the other girl took Lisa down and led her out of the room, supporting her to keep her from collapsing. Morden switched off the lights as they left. He hadn't looked through the window at us once. After the screams, the silence was frightening.

'Morden likes sending messages,' I said at last. My voice sounded strange in my ears. I don't think Rachel heard the tremble, but it was a near thing.

'You think that was a message?'

I looked at Rachel. 'The "punishment for disloyalty"?'

'That was half of the message,' Rachel said distantly. 'That's what he'll do if we upset him. If we *betray* him,' Rachel looked at me with cold eyes, 'he'll just kill us.'

We were shown back to our rooms and I was left alone in the small bedroom in which I'd woken up. Outside, the rain was still coming down, and night had fallen. All I could see through the darkness and the rain was the dim outlines of trees. The room was warm and cosy, keeping out the cold, but I knew the shelter was an illusion. You might freeze to death outside, but you'd still be safer than in here.

At last I had a chance to think. I walked up and down the small room, collecting my thoughts as the rain beat against the glass and the last traces of light faded from the sky.

If nothing else, at least I finally understood what had been going on. There had been two puppet-masters from the beginning: Levistus and Morden. Everything that had happened traced back to one of them. Levistus' pawns were the investigation team; Morden's were the three Dark mages. Levistus had control of the site, but Morden had the key.

And what about me? Somehow I'd managed to get myself hired by both. I was safe only as long as Levistus and Morden both thought I was on their side. That would last until Morden made his move and took control of the Precursor site. At that point, Levistus would decide I'd betrayed him as soon as I was seen with Morden's troops, and Morden would decide I'd betrayed him as soon as he tried the key in the statue and woke up the lightning elemental for another round. At which point I could expect both of them to put me on their hit list.

It comes as a bit of a shock when you stop to take a look around and realise just how badly you've managed to screw things up, especially when all your decisions seemed like good ideas at the time. Within a few days, two of the most powerful mages in England were going to want me personally and painfully dead.

So what was I going to do about it?

Staying faithful to either Levistus or Morden wasn't even worth considering. Morden's little speech had left me cold; I'd made the mistake of swearing fealty to a Dark mage once and there was no way I was doing it again. And Levistus had made it very clear that he would keep me around exactly as long as I was useful and not one second longer. Both would be happy to have me killed as soon as the fateweaver was in their hands, assuming the other didn't do it first.

Running wasn't an option either. I had no idea where I

was, nor how far this mansion's wards reached; any attempt to break out would be a roll of the dice even without the guards and defences. A better plan would be to wait until we set out and try to slip away. With my magic, I could probably pull it off . . . but all that would earn me would be assassins in my footsteps. Neither Levistus nor Morden struck me as the forgiving type.

Force was out; so was alliance. I turned it around and looked at the problem the other way. What did I have going for me?

Knowledge. I was the only person in the world who knew how to open that relic. Morden knew about the key and maybe Levistus did too, but I was the only one who knew that Luna had to be the one to turn it. But what I could learn, others could learn. Right now I was the only one who knew, but no secret this big could stay a secret for long.

So how could I use it?

Snatches of the conversations I'd heard in the last two days floated to the top of my memory. Arachne saying how seers carried great power in times of conflict. Levistus talking about fateweavers, how commanders had carried them in the Dark Wars. Morden talking about action, purpose.

It's hard to know exactly where ideas come from. Pieces of thought and memory assemble at the back of our minds, creating something more than the sum of their parts. I think it was then my plan started to come together, but only as something vague and shadowy. All I knew was that I needed to talk to Luna, but there was no way I could reach her.

At least, not in body . . .

I looked into the future: for this to work, I'd have to be sleeping at the same time that Luna was. Luck was with me and, after only an hour, I knew that now was the time. I lay down on the bed and relaxed my muscles, letting the warmth soak into my body. Night had fallen and the only light in the room was the flickering glow of the fire. My eyes drifted closed, and as I began to fall into a slumber I took my mind beyond dreams, to somewhere else. Beyond . . . beyond . . . Sleep came.

## 10

I was back home, standing on the balcony outside my bedroom window. Before me was Camden . . . or what looked like Camden. The street and the bridge and the houses were the same, but everything was brighter than it should be, the colours suffused with white. The air was still, without a breath of wind, and the canal reflected the sky like a mirror. There was no sun, but the whole sky seemed to glow. The city was so silent that you could have heard a car starting from miles away, except there weren't any cars. This wasn't London. This was Elsewhere.

Elsewhere is a world, but it's not a place. It's empty, yet you seem to meet someone no matter where you go. You can't travel to it in the flesh, only in dreams, but the things that happen can be real, and the creatures you meet play by rules you can't understand.

Even the most powerful mages are reluctant to travel to Elsewhere. *Things* live here, phantoms who can wear the faces of friends and enemies long dead, who try to trick travellers away from the paths home until they're lost to wander for ever . . . or so the stories say. Others claim that Elsewhere is an illusion, a reflection of your own mind, and all you find here is what you bring with you. Still others say that Elsewhere is the place where the world of the living meets the world of the dead, and that from here you can cross from one to the other. I don't know if any of the stories are true. What I do know is that there have been mages who've gone to sleep, intending to reach Elsewhere, and never woken up.

I turned and walked into my bedroom. The desk and wardrobe held items, glinting invitingly, but I didn't stop to take them. I took the stairs down to the ground floor of my shop. By the time I reached my front door, the world outside had changed: instead of the Camden street, the door now opened onto a courtyard of cracked white flagstones. I stepped out and heard my footsteps echo around the walls. Windows looked down from balconies on all sides and an archway led off into what looked like another courtyard. I glanced back to see that my shop had disappeared. Behind was only a blank wall.

The courtyard led into a long arcade, open on both sides to what seemed like an endless expanse of paved stone. The light from the sky shone down brightly, making it hard to see. There were white birds scattered across the flagstones – doves. They cast no shadow and were difficult to make out in the dazzling light. The nearest must have been a hundred yards away, but the place was so silent I could clearly hear the scratch of their claws on the paving stones. I kept going along the arcade until I saw a wall ahead of me, and a door. The door was made of wood and was the only colour against the white stone.

Through Elsewhere you can touch other people's minds, speak to them in their dreams and draw them into Elsewhere as well, though it's safer for them than it is for you. This door would lead into Luna's dreamscape. Whether to enter or not would be up to her.

The sound of chatter and voices washed over me as the door swung open, shockingly loud after the silence. Inside was a ballroom filled with people, mingling and talking.

The room was lit by chandeliers, but it seemed dark after the blinding light of the courtyard outside. I had to shield my eyes, squinting, as I waited for my vision to adjust. The people inside wore evening dress and feathered masks that hid their eyes. All were in couples, one man to one woman, dancing, embracing, walking, their arms interlinked, leaning together to talk.

A moment later I saw Luna. In that whole vast room, filled with couples, she was the only one walking alone. She wore no mask, only a simple white dress, and no matter where she went, the couples around her pulled away without seeming to see her. All around her was a wide empty space and, as Luna walked slowly through the crowd, the space moved with her. 'Luna,' I called, then again more loudly, 'Luna!'

Luna looked up, and all of a sudden the figures froze, falling silent. The only sound was Luna's feet on the wooden floor. She blinked. 'Alex?'

'It's me. Come here.'

Luna obeyed, wending her way through the statues. As she did the men and women seemed to fade and an instant later she was walking across an empty floor. Luna didn't seem to notice. Her wavy hair was down instead of up in bunches, and as she stepped out into the courtyard and shielded her eyes, I saw she was barefoot. It gave her a lost, vulnerable look. 'I thought this was a dream.'

'This is Elsewhere,' I said. The arcade had vanished, as had the door. We were alone in a vast, open arena. The birds had stayed, perched here and there amidst the flagstones. There was a bench of white stone nearby and I sat on it. Luna followed, looking around wonderingly.

'If it's a dream, I'm glad,' Luna said as she sat. She stared out across the dazzling stone, squinting. 'But this doesn't feel like a dream any more.' She held up a hand and stared at it, then touched it to the bench and looked at me. 'Is it real?'

'Yes,' I said. 'No. I'm real, you're real. You'll remember everything when you wake up.'

'What about . . .?' Luna made a movement towards herself.

It took me a moment to figure out what she was saying. I shook my head. 'No. You don't have to worry about hurting me, not here.'

'Really?'

I nodded, and Luna sighed. She scooted across on the bench and leant against me with a contented noise. 'Luna?' I said in surprise.

'Don't go,' Luna complained, closing her fingers drowsily on my coat. 'Dreams are the only place I can do this.' She let out a breath. 'I had a horrible day.'

I hesitated, then put an arm around Luna and leant back. What the hell, it was just a dream. 'What happened?'

'They came after me,' Luna said. 'Deleo and Khazad.'

'When?'

'This morning. They nearly caught me. Then I saw Deleo get a phone call and they vanished.'

'Was it about noon?'

Luna nodded, and I understood. That phone call had been Cinder telling them I'd left the museum. 'You ran away?'

'My phone said you'd called. I tried to call back and I couldn't get through.' Her hand tightened on my coat. 'I didn't know what had happened.'

I sighed. 'I'm sorry. I didn't mean for you to be worried.'

'It's okay,' Luna said, her voice drowsy. 'As long as you're all right.'

'What about that other man?' I asked. 'Talisid.'

'Oh, him. He was trying to get in touch.'

'Did you talk to him?'

Luna shook her head, her face still hidden against my coat. 'I didn't know if I could trust him.'

I smiled. 'Good girl.'

'I'm not a good girl,' Luna said. From the sound of her voice I could tell she was smiling, and I smiled too.

We sat in silence for a little while. 'Alex?' Luna said eventually.

'Hm?'

'Do you ever wish you were little again? That you didn't have to grow up?'

I thought of my years as a teenager, all the things I'd done wrong leading up to my fateful decision to sign up with Richard. 'No,' I said. 'Never.'

'I do,' Luna said. 'It wasn't so bad when I was young. I could be with people. It was only later . . .' Luna fell silent, leaning against me. I could feel her weight, see the wave in her hair. When she spoke again, her voice was quiet. 'I nearly let them catch me.'

'What?'

'Deleo. Khazad.'

'*What?*'

'I just wanted it to stop.' Luna let out a long, sighing breath. 'I was thinking it wouldn't be so . . . bad, being a slave. Then it wouldn't be my fault any more. I wouldn't have to worry. It made sense, then . . .'

'No! Luna, listen to me.' I took Luna's arms and turned her around to stare into her eyes. 'You don't understand what you're saying. You do *not* know the kind of things that Dark mages do to the people they get their hands on. You don't want to be held by them, ever. Do you understand?'

Luna swallowed, took a breath. 'It wouldn't be my fault. I wouldn't have to know it was because of me—'

'*No.* You don't know what you're saying.'

Luna's voice strengthened suddenly. 'Yes, I *do.*' She tilted her head up, staring at me. 'I hurt everyone near me. Everyone. Even being close . . . It won't stop, it'll *never* stop. The longer I live, the more harm I'll do. Wouldn't it—' She took a breath. 'Wouldn't it be better if I was gone? No one would miss me . . .'

I held Luna's gaze for a long moment before speaking quietly. 'I'd miss you.'

Luna kept staring at me, then her eyes filled with tears and she started to cry.

I sat there on the bench. Luna buried her face against me and kept sobbing, her shoulders shaking as she drew in shuddering breaths. I found myself stroking her hair, talking to her quietly, but that only made her cry harder. Somehow I understood that Luna needed to do this, that this must be the first time in years she'd been able to. I didn't rush her, letting her cry herself out.

At last Luna's tears ran dry. 'Better?' I asked as she sat up.

Luna nodded, sniffing. 'I'm s-sorry I'm so useless.'

'You're not useless.'

'Yes, I am. I'm not a mage like you are. I just keep myself safe and make everyone else worse.' Luna looked up at me with reddened eyes. 'Why do you even want me around?'

I let out a sigh. 'Okay, Luna? Stop it. I need you for

something. You're not useless, and if you don't *show* you're not useless, I'll be dead within the week.'

Luna stared up at me. 'What?'

I told her, then, everything that had happened and everything I'd pieced together: how it had been Levistus and Morden all along, why Deleo and the others had been after the cube, how she was the only one who could open the relic, and where I was now. 'And that's how it is,' I finished. 'Morden's going to make his move in a couple of days, and once he breaks through to that statue he's going to find that it won't open without you. If I don't have something to pull out of my sleeve by then I'm sunk.'

Luna sat for a few seconds taking it all in. 'But what are we going to do?'

'That's where you come in. You still have a way to get in touch with Talisid, right?'

'Yes, but—' Luna slumped. 'Alex, I can't do this. I can't use magic, I don't know anything. All I do is run away.'

'You wanted to get involved before.'

'I thought the one who was going to be in danger was *me*!' Luna looked up at me in distress. 'I've never done anything useful since I met you. I just get you into more trouble. What am I supposed to do against these people? I can't . . .'

'Okay,' I said. 'I'm going to tell you something important, so listen closely. It's something most mages never learn at all. The most powerful weapon you have is your mind. Magic doesn't mean anything unless you know the right way to use it. You're already involved – you don't have a choice about that any more. What you *do* have a choice about is whether you'll help me. What's it going to be?'

Luna looked back at me for a long second, then she took

a deep breath, closed her eyes and seemed to straighten. When she opened her eyes again she looked more like the girl I remembered. 'Tell me what to do,' she said, and her voice was steady again.

I explained. It didn't take long.

By the time I was done Luna's eyebrows had climbed almost into her hair. 'Are you sure this is a good plan?'

'No, it's a pretty crazy plan. But if we run they'll just chase us. Levistus and Morden will want me to get them into the relic, and once they figure out that you're the only way in – which they will, sooner or later – they'll be after you too. This is the only way I can think of that gives us a chance to get them both off our backs.'

Luna was silent, and I could see her turning it over in her head. 'What should I tell them?' she asked. 'The mages at the museum?'

'Talisid should be there,' I said. 'Talk to him. He made it pretty clear he didn't want anyone else getting hold of what's behind that door. Tell him Morden's planning an attack and you'll have his attention. But there's one thing you have to keep secret – that you're the only one who can use the cube. That's our ace in the hole. Don't let it slip to *anyone*.'

Luna sat a little while longer. 'What about you?' she asked at last.

'I've done this before. I'll be fine.'

'What if you're not?' Luna asked quietly.

'Morden needs me to get through to the fateweaver. As long as he needs me, he'll make sure I stay alive. It's what happens when he *stops* needing me I'm worried about. That's why—'

'What if you're wrong?'

I let out a breath. 'Then it's all going to come down to you after all.'

Luna met my gaze, and there was something painful in them. 'Alex—'

And suddenly we weren't alone any more. Elsewhere changes with who's in it, and the hairs on the back of my neck stood up as I felt the shift. I looked around to see that the plaza was empty and the birds were gone. 'We've stayed too long.' I got up, pulling Luna to her feet with me. 'Back through that door.'

Luna hesitated, and I dragged her along, forcing her to hurry beside me. 'Wait!' she began.

'You need to get back.' We'd reached the door, and I pulled it open; beyond was the ballroom, dark and empty. 'Remember: Talisid, the items, the plan. Don't forget.'

'Alex!' Luna tried to pull back. 'What's coming? Let me—'

I pushed Luna through the door and slammed it before she could react. Instantly the courtyard was silent. Luna was safe now, back in her own dreams. I took a breath and turned.

The girl walking across the plaza towards me was nineteen years old, and she was dressed in the same clothes she'd been wearing when I'd last seen her. That had been almost ten years ago. She'd been nineteen years old then, too. Smaller than Luna, with short, dark red hair, she looked a bit like a small furry animal, full of energy and movement. I didn't move as she approached and came to a stop a little way away. She watched me with a smile, one hand on her hip, waiting.

'Shireen,' I said at last, and let out a breath. The name sounded strange to my ears; it was the first I'd spoken it in a long time. 'So you're dead after all.'

'C'mon, Alex,' Shireen said with a grin. 'When I didn't call for nine years, that should have been a big clue.'

We stood looking at each other. When I'd known her, Shireen had so often been angry, except for that last time. She didn't look angry now; she looked at ease. 'What happens now?' I asked after a moment.

'Up to you.'

I paused, then shrugged and walked past her.

Shireen fell into step beside me. 'What, you're not going to ask me anything?'

'I'm curious,' I said. 'I'm just not sure what you are.'

'I thought diviners knew everything?' Shireen laughed. 'Okay, how about some proof? Let's see . . . How about the time we met? Wait, I know. I could tell you the time you finally turned against Richard. I remember exactly when it happened.'

'No thanks.'

Shireen sighed. 'When did you get so serious?'

'Right now, I want to leave.'

'Then where are you going?'

I started to answer, then looked around and stopped. The arcade had ended, and the building Luna had vanished into was gone. Instead, we were on a walkway running above a deserted city. On either side, stairways led down to dusty streets, stretching off into the distance. Buildings with empty windows were below, silent and still.

I turned to Shireen. 'Where's the way out?'

'Up to you.'

I hesitated. On either side, flights of stairs led down into the city, while ahead the walkway seemed to go on and on into nothingness. I didn't like the look of the streets below. I kept walking forward.

Shireen kept pace beside me. 'Why are you here?' I said once it became obvious she wasn't going to say anything.

'I need to talk to you about Rachel.'

'You've got to be kidding. She doesn't even call herself that any more.'

Shireen shook her head. 'You don't understand. She's what you could have been.'

'Yeah, well, I paid the price for that.'

'You paid the price once. She has to do it every day.'

I sighed. 'What are you trying to say, Shireen? You want me to feel sorry for her?'

'It's not about feeling sorry for her.'

'Then what *is* it?' I came to a stop and rounded on Shireen. 'In case you haven't noticed, I'm prisoner of a Dark mage who's basically Richard except not so nice. He wants me to play for his team, and my teammates are three Dark mages who each hate me for completely separate reasons. Even if I manage to keep all three of them happy – which I won't – Levistus and that invisible assassin of his are going to want me dead for switching sides. Every one of those people I just listed could kill me if they tried, and every one of them has a reason to do it. All together, there is a *really* good chance I'm going to be dead within a couple of days. So I don't have time for this, okay? I need to get out of here.'

Shireen had stood quietly. Now that I'd finished, she spoke again. 'Why are you here?'

I turned away and started walking again. Shireen followed. 'Because someone up there hates me,' I told her. 'How should I know?'

'But it was your choice.'

'What are you talking about?'

'You could have been safe,' Shireen said. 'Helikaon told you. Why did you stay?'

'Because I'm an idiot. Leave me alone.'

'You knew what you were doing.'

'If you know so much, why do you keep asking me?'

Shireen didn't answer, and I stopped and looked at her. 'Fine. I stayed because of Luna.'

As I said the last word, I felt something shift. I looked around and realised that the walkway had been steadily descending until it was level with the city rooftops. Ahead, it sloped down to street level, ending in front of a mansion. A familiar one.

Shireen spoke into the silence. 'It's in there.'

Slowly, I walked towards Richard's mansion. It was exactly as I remembered it, right down to the cracked stone at the doorway. I came to a stop in front of the double doors.

'Why are you stopping?' Shireen asked from behind me. 'Are you afraid?'

I stood silently before answering. 'Yes.'

We stood looking at the doors for a minute. The city was quiet, expectant, as though holding its breath. 'I swore I'd never come back here,' I said at last. 'When I escaped.'

'But you didn't. Not really.'

I turned in surprise to see that Shireen was looking up at me seriously. 'You never really got away. That's why you have the dreams every night. You live alone, you don't get close to anyone, the only human friend you make is a girl who can't be touched. Morden was right, you know – you *are* still living like Richard taught you.'

I looked back at Shireen in silence. 'What does that matter?' I said at last.

'Because Morden was wrong, too. You've protected yourself, but you've protected others as well. You risked your life to try and save Luna. You're not a Dark mage. You shouldn't live like one.'

'Why are you telling me this?'

Shireen sighed and looked away. 'Alex, I was nineteen when I died. I didn't live very long and I made a lot of bad choices, and by the time I figured out which choices were the bad ones it was too late. I just want something good to come from it. I've tried with Rachel, but she won't listen to me any more. There's still a bit of what we had inside her, but it's so . . . twisted now that when I try it just makes her angrier. You're all that's left. I don't want everything I touched to be evil. Please.'

I looked down at Shireen. 'What do you want me to do?' I said at last.

I saw Shireen close her eyes for a second, her shoulders going limp with relief. 'The way out is in the mansion. It's in Richard's study. Walk towards the door. Once you step into the room, don't turn aside for anything, no matter what you see. If you take even one step to the side, you'll never be able to leave. You'll be trapped there for ever.'

I nodded.

'There's one last thing. It's a message for you. I had to go to a dragon to learn it. You have to remember it word for word.'

I nodded again.

'This was the message. *"At the end, in the light of the stars, trust in your friends and forego the greater power for the lesser."*'

'"Forego the greater power for the lesser . . ."' I frowned. 'That came from a dragon?'

Shireen nodded. 'I don't know what it means, but I know it's important. It cost me a lot. Don't forget.'

'I'll make sure.' I looked at Shireen, and felt a tug of odd feelings. 'It really is you, isn't it?'

'No.'

'But you . . .' I trailed off. Shireen was shaking her head, and there was something sad in her face.

'I'm only a shadow,' Shireen said. 'I can look like her and I can feel like her and I can think like her, but she's gone. Soon I will be, too. I've only lasted this long because of her.'

I looked at Shireen a moment longer. It was a strange feeling, looking at her through an adult's eyes. I'd grown, but Shireen was still the same, frozen as she'd died. 'I'm glad I could see you,' I said at last.

Shireen smiled. 'You'll see her again. Sooner or later.'

And with that, she was gone. All of a sudden, Elsewhere felt much emptier. I was alone in the empty city but for the mansion brooding behind me.

I took a look around, then drew a breath. 'All right,' I said to no one in particular. I walked up the steps to the mansion doors and pushed. They opened at my touch. I stepped inside and they swung shut behind me.

Inside was utter blackness. Spots swam before my eyes after the brightness of the outside. I stood still for a long moment before lights started to appear, brightening ahead and above. As they grew stronger I saw I was in the entrance hall. Magelights hung from the walls and ceiling, but they seemed dimmer than they should be. Shadows clung to the corners and beneath the tables and chairs.

The mansion was silent, but it was a different silence than outside. Outside had felt empty; this was the silence of something watching and waiting. I wanted to freeze, stay still and hide. The first step was the hardest. The second was easier.

As I walked, I heard whispers at the edge of hearing. The house was the same, but different. Doors that should have been there were missing, walls were bare or blurred, tables the wrong shape or size. This was the mansion my mind had rebuilt in my dreams. One part, though, was perfect: the door at the end of the first-floor corridor, the entrance to Richard's study.

I nearly stopped then. Even though I'd been awaiting it, that simple wooden door sent a stab of fear through me that made my limbs grow heavy, and I stumbled. Only the memories of Luna and Shireen kept me going. A little bit of me screamed and ran. The rest kept walking. I pushed the door open.

The room inside was different from the rest of the mansion – it was clear and detailed, a perfect replica. A fire burned low in the fireplace, merging with the dim lights to shroud the room in gloom. The floor was covered in a thick, soft carpet, muffling sound so that it took me a second to realise that the fire made no noise. Books on shelves lined the walls. To the left was an oaken desk, covered with papers. My eyes flicked to the armchair behind the desk, but it was empty. A pen was laid upon a scattering of papers, its cap still off. Although the room was silent, it didn't feel empty. It felt as though something was waiting for me.

On the opposite wall, ten paces away, was another door. It was ajar just a crack, and a sliver of light spilled through. It was swallowed quickly in the gloom, but that patch before the door was the only light in the darkness.

The sense of something watching was stronger, but the door was right there in front of me.

I stepped forward, and—

The schoolyard was damp and cold, grey skies a reminder of the rain already fallen and a sign of more to come. Despite the damp a scattering of teenagers were in the yard, boys bragging and laughing while girls looked on and giggled. One boy was standing apart, leaning against the wall, arms folded as he stared. He was in his mid-teens, with spiky black hair . . . and he was familiar, too familiar. Looking at him made me pause, confused. I knew him, but—

Then all of a sudden it clicked into place. I was looking at myself, eleven years ago. The boy leaning against the wall was me, and the building looming into the grey sky was my last school. With a rush the memory came back. I remembered this day.

Muffled footsteps on the concrete made my younger self look up. A man was approaching, an ordinary-looking man with an ordinary, forgettable face. The kind of man your eyes flick over without ever really noticing. 'Hello, Alex.'

'What do *you* want?' my younger self said.

'What do *you* want?'

'I want to be somewhere else instead of in a school I hate with a bunch of bastards like them.' The younger me jerked his head towards the children in the yard.

'Is that all?'

'It's a start.'

'And then?' The man tilted his head slightly. 'What if you could have anything at all? What do you *really* want?'

My younger self looked up in surprise. He'd been play-acting, not expecting to be taken seriously. 'Okay,' he said, and I knew he was paying attention. 'What I really want? I want to be so powerful that I don't have to care about idiots like them. I want to be so far above them they can't even touch me. Can you get me that?'

The man looked back at him, and then suddenly smiled, an amused smile that didn't touch his eyes. 'Yes, I can.'

The younger Alex stared at him. 'Who are you?'

'My name is Richard Drakh.' He kept smiling as he looked down. 'But you can call me master.'

—my foot sank into the carpet. I looked from side to side, confused. The room was empty, quiet. But I hadn't imagined it. That had been the day I'd met Richard for the first time, as real as when I'd been there. To one side, the fire burned; to the other, the chair sat empty. Cautiously, I took another step—

The living room was warm and still. Richard was sitting in an armchair by the fire, and around him four children made a semicircle. The two girls were on the sofa, side by side. Shireen had been braiding Rachel's hair and now was watching with a frown, while Rachel was wide-eyed and curious. The younger me was in a smaller armchair to one side. It was only a few weeks after that first meeting with Richard and I looked much the same. I was sitting with my feet curled up underneath me, and the position gave me an oddly child-like look that was out of place with my sharp eyes. And leaning against the mantlepiece, slightly apart from the others, was Tobruk, the firelight catching his whimsical smile.

'The True Path is power,' Richard was saying. His voice was deep and magnetic, powerful; no one who heard him speak would ever think him ordinary again. All four of us were staring as though hypnotised, caught up in his words. 'Power to build and power to destroy. You have your magic, but true power does not come merely from being born with the gift. True power comes from one place only: your inner self. Strength, determination, force of will: these are what distinguish a Dark mage, a True mage, from a dabbler. To be willing to rise higher or sink lower than your enemy, to know that no one is above you . . . that is the True Way. Your greatest enemies are fear and compassion. Both are weakness, and weakness is death.' Richard's eyes swept slowly across the four of us, from Rachel to Shireen to Tobruk to me. 'I do not expect all of you to succeed. Some will prove weak, in body or mind or will, and if you have a weakness I will find it. But those of you who earn the right to call yourself Dark mages, who become disciples of the True Way, will be power incarnate. Lessers will speak of you in fear and envy. No one will be able to stand against you, and your words will be as the voice of God.'

The room was silent. Then Tobruk stirred. 'When do we start?'

'Now.'

I was back in the study. Looking around, I saw I'd taken only two steps across the floor. I was seeing my life as Richard's apprentice, a step at a time. I didn't know how long had passed, but I knew I needed to keep moving. I stepped forward again—

This time I was ready for the shift. I was looking at myself, Tobruk, Shireen and Rachel a few months later, back in the living room but without Richard this time, talking and planning. It was our first assignment and we were working together, but I didn't listen to the voices this time; I made my body take another step forward.

The scene blurred and steadied. Now we were outside, the setting sun painting the red rocks of a sandstone canyon. 'This was your idea,' Tobruk was saying, bored.

'But . . .' My face was uncertain, frowning. 'We don't need to do this.'

'So?'

My stomach twisted as I remembered what was about to happen. I didn't want to watch this. Another step—

The living room with the four of us again, but this time the cooperation was gone. Tobruk and I were arguing, Shireen chipping in. Tobruk's dark eyes flashed as he talked over me, and Rachel watched doubtfully, looking between us. The door opened, cutting us all off, and—

The visions came faster, blending into each other. Dissent and suspicion. Shireen and Rachel shifting step by step. Shireen angrier, Rachel desperate. My encounters with Lyle and the Council. Richard above it all, seemingly oblivious. Plots in the darkness. Deception, fear. Discovery.

And then, suddenly, everything was steady. A younger me, maybe a year older than the first time, was standing in a corridor of dry, cold stone. Next to me was a girl, thin and barely able to stand, leaning on me with bloodstains on her tattered clothes. Both of us were staring at Richard, who was standing just a little way ahead, Shireen, Rachel and Tobruk behind. 'You knew?' I was saying, and I sounded stunned.

'Oh, Alex,' Richard said. 'Don't confuse not knowing with not caring. I was willing to let you lie to me right up to the point where you disobeyed a direct order.'

I saw my younger self lick his lips. 'You don't need her. There's a way—'

'It's not about her. It's about you.' Richard held out his hand and beckoned. 'Give her to me.'

The girl looked from Richard to me, eyes wide in fright. I hesitated.

Richard sighed. 'That, unfortunately, was your last chance.' He shook his head. 'I warned you not all of you would make it. Tobruk?'

Tobruk stepped forward with a grin. 'Hey, Alex. Guess you're not top of the class any longer.' He snapped his fingers and black fire ignited, leaping forward—

I came down with a gasp. I was back in the study, but I'd crossed the floor. The door was in front of me, within touching distance. One more step and I'd be through.

A voice spoke from my left. 'Long time no see.'

I knew who it was before I looked. Tobruk was leaning back in Richard's chair, his feet propped up on the desk. He looked exactly as he'd been when I'd last seen him, a good-looking teenager with dark skin and a mobile, mischievous face. His mouth was smiling, like always. His eyes weren't.

'That's not your seat,' I said at last.

Tobruk grinned. 'Richard's through that door. Don't worry; you'll find him. All you have to do is step through.'

I looked back for a second, then nodded. 'Okay.' I started forward.

'Oh look, what have we got here?' Tobruk pulled his feet off the table and reached down to drag a girl up by her hair. It was Shireen. Her eyes were closed and she was breathing shallowly, cuts and scratches criss-crossed her face. Tobruk held her up long enough for me to see her, his fingers tangled in her hair, then he tossed her forward to slump across the desk, her head hitting the wood with a *thunk*. 'So what do you think I should do with her?'

I stood still. 'What if I burn some of her fingers off?' Tobruk asked. He shook his head. 'Nah, that'd be a waste. I think I should screw her first. She always was a good lay.'

'Stop it,' I said, my mouth dry.

Tobruk grinned. He settled back into his chair and spread his arms wide, inviting. 'Make me.'

I wanted to dive for him. Instead I took a deep breath and fought the anger, controlling it. When I spoke at last, my voice was steady. 'The only place I'm going is through this door.'

'You think I care?' Tobruk shrugged. 'You're coming back sooner or later. Matter of fact, I kind of want you to run into Richard again.' He grinned again. 'Course, if you want to speed things up . . .'

I looked down at Shireen's unconscious body. 'What did she do to you?' I asked.

'*She* didn't do anything.' The grin vanished from Tobruk's face and he leant forward over the desk at me, his eyes suddenly filled with hate. 'I was going to be Richard's Chosen. Two years of clawing to be better than the rest of you, and all for what? So you could stab me in the back like a coward. My whole life was a waste because of you! My *whole life*!' Suddenly Tobruk flashed into flame, becoming a skeleton wreathed in dark fire. It only lasted a second, then he was human again. Smoke curled from the chair. Where his hands had been splayed on the desk, charred handprints were burnt into the wood.

The two of us stared at each other. 'I did a lot of things I shouldn't have while I was here,' I said at last. 'A lot of them I don't like to think about. But you know what?' I held Tobruk's gaze, dropping my mask, letting him see I was telling the truth. 'Killing you was the only thing I ever did from that time that I don't regret at all.'

Tobruk glared at me a second longer, then snorted and dropped back into the chair. 'Yeah, whatever.'

I turned to leave.

'Oh, Alex?'

I paused for a moment, then looked back.

'Richard's going to find you,' Tobruk said. He was smiling again. 'When he wakes up he's going to go looking for you. Then he's going to find you and then he's going to hurt you and then you're going to die. And when you do, I'll be waiting for you. Make sure you stay alive till then, Alex. I'll be really disappointed if you let any of those guys kill you instead. I want to see your face when you meet him.' He gave a mocking wave. 'Be seeing you.' He turned towards Shireen.

I didn't wait to see what he was going to do with her. I stepped through the door, pushing it open. There was a moment of blinding, unbearable light, then—

My eyes snapped open into darkness. It was warm, and I was back on the bed in the room in Morden's mansion. I looked quickly through the futures just to make sure that I was really back, then I got up. The lights in the room had gone out, and the fire was cold. Outside, starlight glinted off the leaves. I stood by the window for a while, looking out into the night, before I turned and returned to bed.

## 11

A lot of people think of captivity as something glamorous, but the truth is, being a prisoner is mostly just boring. No matter how sadistic the guy in control of you, he can't focus on you twenty-four hours a day. He's got other things to do and, while he's busy, you're going to be sitting alone. After a few weeks, it can get to the point where you almost welcome a visit, just for a little human interaction. When I'd been Richard's prisoner I'd passed the time by practising divination; I couldn't reach outside the walls, but I got to know every square inch of that room. I learned some weird skills that way. Even now I can pick up anything from a pencil to a tennis ball and hit a target first time, every time, looking into the future to see exactly how I need to make the throw. If I ever give up being a diviner, I can always make a living playing darts.

So the following day as Morden's 'guest' was just like old times. The door to my room wasn't locked but I didn't go wandering; I didn't want to ruffle any feathers. Instead I sat in the chair with a book, and anyone watching would have seen me barely move all day except to turn a page.

But just because I wasn't moving didn't mean I wasn't busy. Within two hours of sitting in that chair I knew the entire layout of Morden's mansion, everything from the basement to the attic. My future selves roamed through the mansion, wandering, exploring, trying things, and everything they learned, I learned – everything from how the food was prepared in the kitchen to what would happen if you pulled the levers on the first floor. By noon I'd discovered four routes by which I could escape the mansion (with varying probabilities of success once I got outside), five places in which I could hide with little chance of detection (in the short term, anyway), two ways in which I could set off a small civil war between the mansion's various inhabitants (for the record, in all the futures I saw, Morden's side won), one way to destroy the mansion completely along with most of the people inside it (including me, unfortunately), a way to cause the mansion and most of the surrounding countryside to be overrun with intelligent giant badgers (don't ask), and one half of a process for creating crystals capable of absorbing cold- and ice-based magic (which would be very useful if I had a spare couple of weeks and if I were worried about being attacked by an ice mage, neither of which was true).

That's the thing about being a diviner. You learn a vast amount of information, of which ninety-five per cent is completely useless.

Anyway, it was the people I was interested in. It didn't take me long to confirm that Cinder and Khazad were here with Rachel, confined in the west wing. Lisa was there too, recovered enough to be able to move around. In a few of the futures, I tried to talk to Lisa; she avoided me or fled. Morden's message about disloyalty had sunk in. It left a bitter taste in my mouth. It's one thing to know why most slaves of Dark mages stay that way; it's another to watch it happen.

But despite everything, I was as focused as I'd ever been. For years I'd been trying to forget my time as Richard's apprentice, locking it up and burying it deep in my memory.

The journey through Elsewhere had shattered that, bringing it all back – but now that I'd faced it, I found to my surprise that the fear had been worse than the reality. It had hurt, yes, but it had been like cleaning out an old wound, and as I looked back I realised that it didn't scare me the way it once had. I'd gotten stronger since then.

Onyx came into my room in the late afternoon. His cold eyes rested on me as he dropped something onto the table with a *clack*. 'Put it on.'

The item on the table was a bracelet, made of some kind of black metal. I took a second to look at the consequences of saying no, then picked the thing up and locked it around my right wrist. The metal had an ugly, unpleasant feel to it, but it vanished as soon as it snapped shut.

Onyx waited a second, then flicked a finger. The bracelet flared with black energy, and a bolt of terrible agony shot up my arm, locking my muscles, like an electrical shock but worse. I lost my breath in a gasp and went down to one knee with a thud. My heart raced, and I took several deep breaths before looking up shakily at Onyx, steadying myself with one hand on the floor.

'Higher levels cripple or kill,' Onyx said. 'Want to see?'

I took a breath. 'No, thanks,' I said, my voice hoarse.

'We leave in two hours,' Onyx said. He turned and left.

I waited for his footsteps to fade away, then dropped the act, returned to the chair, and started work on the bracelet. It was the same design Richard had used, which made things simple. Once I was finished, I settled down to wait.

The sun was dipping towards the horizon when Onyx returned. He jerked his head in a command to follow, and I obeyed.

The morning room was wide, with one whole wall made

entirely out of French windows that looked out onto the flowers of the garden. The light of the setting sun streamed in, mixing with the reflection off the leaves to light the wooden floor in yellow and gold. A table stood in the middle of the room, covered with maps. Morden was behind it, and standing in front, in a sullen group, were Cinder, Rachel and Khazad. Cinder and Khazad glowered at me; Deleo/Rachel didn't. Lisa and Morden's other slave girl (whose name I'd learned was Selene) stood at opposite ends of the room, their eyes cast down submissively. Onyx walked to Morden's side and gestured for me to stand with the others. I took up a position next to the table, a carefully judged distance away from Rachel.

'Tonight at sunset, the five of you will enter the relic and recover the fateweaver,' Morden said without preamble once we were around the table. Now that the pecking order had been established, he didn't waste time on pleasantries. 'Onyx will be in command; you will obey him absolutely. Any disagreements are to be put aside as long as you work for me.' He looked between us. 'Do you have any objections? Cinder? Deleo? Verus? Khazad?'

Onyx's eyes glinted as he watched us. I shook my head slightly and saw the others do the same. Rachel was holding quite still and I noticed that she was wearing a black metal bracelet similar to mine, along with Cinder and Khazad. It was the first time I'd seen the two of them since we were captured, and both looked battered and sullen. Cinder seemed subdued and didn't react, but as Khazad caught me looking at them he shot me a hate-filled glance. I turned back to Morden, thinking as I did that it couldn't happen to a nicer pair of guys.

'We expect moderate resistance at the museum,'

Morden was saying. 'Avoid unnecessary casualties, but entering is your priority. Once you've reached the statue, Verus,' he nodded to me, 'will open it. Show them the key, please.'

Everyone's eyes were on me as I slowly reached into my pocket and produced the crystal cube. It sat quietly in the palm of my hand, the sparks glinting in its depths. Cinder's eyes were hungry, as were Khazad's. Rachel's were calculating. 'The rest of you will set up a perimeter until the door is open,' Morden continued. 'Should Verus fail, Onyx will employ a contingency plan.'

I didn't like the sound of that at all.

'Once you are inside,' Morden said, 'you will be in unknown territory. The relic interior has been sealed for at least two thousand years. However, given that the guardian elemental still functions, I doubt the traps will have stopped working.'

'Traps?' Khazad said sharply.

'Of course.' Morden raised an eyebrow. 'I assumed you knew.'

Cinder and Khazad looked at him, then as one, turned to stare at Rachel. Rachel looked between them. 'What?' she demanded.

'You didn't say anything about traps,' Khazad said.

'I'm sure she had her reasons,' Morden said smoothly. 'The fateweaver is located at the relic's centre. Once Onyx has taken possession of it, you are free to return or to stay and loot the place as you wish.' Morden smiled. 'I'll quite understand if you need some time alone. As long as you accomplish your objective, the decision of what to do afterwards is entirely up to you.' Morden looked around. 'Are there any questions?'

Khazad had been staring at Rachel; now he dragged his eyes away to look at Morden. 'When do we get paid?'

'Once Onyx and the fateweaver are in this room.' Morden looked around. 'Anything else?'

'One thing,' I said and felt everyone's eyes turn to me. 'There were quite a few guards at the museum.'

Cinder snorted with laughter, and Khazad looked at me through narrowed eyes. 'What's the matter, Verus?' Khazad's voice was ugly. 'Afraid of a fight?'

I didn't look at him. 'I'll have trouble opening the relic if I'm dead,' I said mildly to Morden.

'Onyx will explain your method of approach once you arrive.'

It wasn't what I'd wanted to hear, but I nodded. Morden looked around. 'Anything else?'

No one spoke.

'Excellent.' Morden smiled. 'Don't look so gloomy, you four. By tomorrow, you'll be free, rich and in my favour. All you have to do is bring me the fateweaver.'

My shoes swished through the wet grass as we walked out into the garden. The setting sun lit up the landscape around, showing hills and distant forests. Clouds hung overhead, glowing gold in the sunset. Morden's mansion had a powerful shroud effect, but I was pretty sure we were somewhere in Wales.

As we walked I moved to block Rachel slightly, so that the two of us fell behind. She gave me a cool look, but allowed it. 'Nice jewellery,' I said under my breath once we were far enough behind Cinder and Khazad. 'Onyx give you a demonstration?'

'I'm not afraid of Onyx,' Rachel said, turning away. She

was wearing a blue coat that looked like it might have belonged to Lisa. 'What do you want?'

Up ahead, Onyx was giving sharp orders to Khazad and Cinder, who listened sullenly. 'Did you notice something strange about that briefing?'

'Like?'

'Morden wants to use the fateweaver to become the representative of the Dark mages on the Council,' I said, keeping my voice low. 'For that to work, he can't leave any proof that he was behind the raid.'

'So?'

'Morden said we could go free or keep working for him. Either way, we might talk. The guards at the museum might recognise us. We'd be a link that could be traced.' I looked sideways at Rachel. 'That would be a problem for him, don't you think?'

Rachel started to answer, then stopped. 'Yes,' she said at last, her voice colourless. 'It would.'

I fell silent, letting Rachel work the rest of it out for herself. I knew it wouldn't take her long, and I wasn't surprised when she spoke a moment later. 'Are you still any good with locks?'

'Better.'

'How long would these bracelets take you?'

'Maybe five minutes each.'

Up ahead, Onyx turned and noticed us talking. He jerked his head. 'Move.'

We came forward and in a moment were too close to say anything more. Onyx gestured and the air in front of us rippled. A black oval eight feet tall appeared, hovering just off the ground, soaking up the light from the sunset, then it cleared and through it I could see grass and trees.

'Good luck, all of you,' Morden called, and we turned to look. He had stayed behind on the veranda, and he was smiling at us, hands clasped behind his back. 'I hope you make it back safely.'

I smiled back at Morden, my face as friendly as his. *No, you don't.*

Onyx took us by gateway to three more locations: a wood, a deserted quarry and a dense forest. Gateways can be traced if you're good enough and know what to look for; by gating to multiple locations you make it harder for anyone to backtrack to your point of origin. At each location we walked for five minutes before gating again. Cinder took the lead with Khazad on his heels, the two men forming a contrast, one heavy and lumbering, the other bird-like and quick. Rachel followed a little way behind, and I followed her a little further still. Bringing up the rear came Onyx, his cold eyes on all of us. No one spoke.

Even though I was on the receiving end, I had to admit that Morden's plan had a kind of twisted brilliance to it. The four of us had been his main competition for the fateweaver; he'd turned it around so that we were doing his work for him. He was sitting comfortably in his mansion, while we were going out to risk our necks. I'd almost admire the guy if he weren't so freaking evil.

However, the more I thought about it, the more I became sure that Morden's plan included the four of us meeting with unfortunate accidents along the way. Not only would our dead bodies tell no tales, they'd make perfect scapegoats to present to the angry Council. When Morden had offered me a job as his intelligence officer and I'd accepted, I hadn't been serious – I'd thought I'd been fooling him. I had the uneasy feeling now that *he'd* been the one fooling *me*.

Once we'd walked a short distance through the forest, Onyx stopped. 'Wait.' He opened a gateway and stepped through, letting it close behind him.

That left me with Rachel and Cinder, neither of whom I particularly wanted to be alone with. I heard Cinder growl something, and took the opportunity to slip away, putting a few clumps of trees between me and them. I couldn't afford to get too far; if I wasn't nearby when Onyx returned, he'd probably trigger my bracelet as a reminder. On the other hand, if I was quick—

I had only an instant's warning. I darted left towards cover, but something grabbed my chest and slammed me up against a tree before I could reach it. A claw of flickering black energy pinned me to the trunk, holding me up on tiptoe, unable to move.

Khazad stepped up in front of me, and there was an evil light shining in his eyes. 'Did you think I forgot?' he said softly. The claw tightened slightly, constricting my chest, and I grunted. 'You know what I did to the last man who humiliated me like you did?'

'You kill me,' I managed to say, my voice stifled, 'and Onyx kills you.'

Khazad stared at me for a long moment, then the black claw loosened and I drew in a ragged breath. 'Of course, you've got the key,' Khazad said absently.

I opened my mouth to speak and suddenly the claw tightened again, and I made a strangled sound as I lost the air in my lungs. Khazad leaned in close, his dark eyes staring into mine. 'But then, it doesn't have to be you that uses it, does it?' Khazad whispered. 'I could take it from your body. You tried to run and I was forced to kill you. I'm sure Onyx will understand.'

I was choking. My chest was crushed so that I couldn't breathe in, and my ribs were on the verge of breaking. 'Can't – open.'

'What's that, Verus?' Khazad said with a smile. 'I'm having trouble hearing.'

'Won't work – for you.'

For a long moment Khazad stared at me, head tilted as if considering. Then suddenly he smiled. 'I think you're lying.' Spots were starting to swim in front of my eyes, and I could barely see Khazad as he leaned in to breathe into my ear. 'It's a pity I can't take my time.'

A cold voice spoke from one side. 'Drop him.'

Khazad twisted to look back with a snarl. The voice spoke again. 'Now.'

For a long moment Khazad hesitated, then drew abruptly back, the claw flickering into nothingness. I sank back against the tree, using it to stop myself from falling over, and looked up as I caught my breath.

Rachel was just a little distance away, and she was wearing her mask again. If I hadn't known it was her, I wouldn't have recognised her as the same woman; she stood straighter, colder, more menacing. Blue-green light hovered at her palm, pointed towards Khazad. Khazad snarled again. 'He's mine!'

'Try it if you like,' Rachel said calmly. 'We've got time.'

For a moment the two of them stood there, Rachel with her arm outstretched, Khazad hunched and ready to spring. Then Khazad took a step back. He shot a vicious look at me and stalked away.

The light at Rachel's palm winked out and she walked

to me. 'Once we're inside, you get rid of these,' she said, tapping her bracelet. Her voice was ordinary, as if she'd already forgotten about Khazad. 'In exchange we keep you alive.'

I nodded slowly. 'Agreed.'

Rachel was studying me, her head tilted. 'You've seen her again,' she said in sudden interest.

'Um . . .'

'She comes more often when you're here.' Rachel laughed suddenly. 'You didn't know that, did you?'

I met Rachel's eyes. There was a curious distant look in them, and all of a sudden I was scared, really scared. I'd called Rachel crazy on top of Canary Wharf, then forgotten about it once I'd recognised her in the mansion, but I'd been right. Rachel really was crazy. Not all the way, but far enough. Lots of people think 'mad' means funny, but real madness isn't funny, it's terrifying. Looking into the spinning futures, I saw Rachel doing a hundred different things, and I had absolutely no way of knowing which she'd choose. 'Rachel?' I said carefully. 'Can you hear me?'

'That's not my name any more,' Rachel said absently, looking over my shoulder.

Rachel was standing just a few feet in front of me, eyes fixed attentively on something a little way past. If she struck from this distance, her beam would go right through me and the tree behind. I stood very still and didn't make any sudden movements. 'Deleo.'

Rachel suddenly turned back to me, her eyes alight. 'Yes!' She smiled happily. 'I had to do that. You see that, right?'

'Um, I think so.'

'I mean, it's not like I could just *leave*!' Rachel laughed, then frowned. 'But she won't go away.' Her frown cleared. 'She's been quiet, though. It must be because of you.' She smiled. 'She always liked you. She wouldn't say it, but I knew. Why don't you carry on?'

I had absolutely no idea what Rachel was talking about. I tried to think of what to say. 'Ra— Deleo. Onyx is going to be back.'

'Onyx?' Rachel's brow furrowed for a moment, then cleared again. 'Oh, he doesn't matter.' She smiled to herself again, then her eyes seemed to snap back into focus. 'Make sure you're ready to get rid of these.' She raised her right wrist with the bracelet. 'We have to see her again, don't we?'

An instant later Onyx emerged from the trees, and I slumped in relief. The fact that I was relieved at having *Onyx* show up was scary in itself. He beckoned to me and Rachel, and we followed, Rachel smiling as if at some private joke.


'So where the fuck are they?' Khazad demanded.

We were in London again, having returned to the city in the evening twilight. Right now we were above a tourist shop in Great Russell Street, in the living room and kitchen of a second-floor flat. The flat looked recently occupied and I tried to stop myself from thinking about what might have happened to the owners.

The flat's windows faced north, overlooking the front courtyard of the British Museum, and we'd been standing by the windows watching the museum for over two hours. Night had long since fallen, and the sky was dark, the stars drowned out by the city's glow. Buses, cars and taxis buzzed past on the street, and a steady flow of shoppers and tourists filled the pavement, but the British Museum itself was silent. Not a single person had gone in or out.

'Why's no one there?' Cinder rumbled.

*Because it's a trap*, I thought silently. Luna had delivered her message.

'Because it's a trap.' Rachel said. She glared at Onyx.

I sighed inwardly. Freaking Council. Luna had given them everything they'd needed to lay a perfect ambush and they'd managed to screw it up. There should have been guards, people coming and going, the occasional mage keeping up a pretence. Instead they'd kept their entire guard force hidden inside the museum . . . and in the process made their ambush so obvious that they might as well have stuck up a warning sign. This is what happens when politicians get put in charge of battle plans.

'I said it's a trap,' Rachel demanded when Onyx didn't answer. She was focused again, staring at Onyx. Khazad and Cinder stayed silent. 'Did you hear me?'

Onyx made a slight gesture with his fingers. Black energy wreathed the bracelet at Rachel's wrist, and she jerked, crashing to the floor as her legs spasmed and losing her breath in a strangled gasp. Rachel looked up, her eyes wild with fury, and sea-green light gathered at her hands.

Onyx gestured again and black lightning smothered Rachel, discharging into her arm, her body, the floor. Rachel writhed, helpless, spasming, trying uselessly to escape. This time the bracelet kept going and the stink of ozone filled the room. Rachel had no breath to scream, and the only sound was the scrabble of her fingers against the carpet. After five long seconds, the lightning stopped. The room was quiet again, and Rachel lay flat in the sudden silence, motionless except for the rapid rise and fall of her chest.

Onyx turned to the rest of us and raised an eyebrow. I dropped my eyes and felt Cinder and Khazad do the same. After a moment Onyx turned back to the window. Rachel took another half a minute or so to recover, then struggled to her feet, her breathing still shaky. No one spoke.

In case you're wondering, nothing Onyx had just done was particularly unusual. Discipline among Dark mages is brutal; it has to be. A Dark leader who isn't willing to hurt anyone who disrespects him doesn't stay leader for long.

That didn't change the fact that I wanted to get the hell away from this bunch of psychos as soon as I possibly could.

'Tell me what spells are up,' Onyx said.

I knew he was talking to me, and I considered lying before deciding against it. Any sign of deception now and I was done for. 'The museum's covered with a gate interdiction field,' I said. Cinder and Khazad were looking at me, and I tried not to let my voice show how nervous I was. 'It's bound to the lines of the building, and it's strong. There's . . .' I scanned. 'one section unwarded in one of the basement rooms. About a ten-foot cube.'

'Sink,' Cinder rumbled.

I managed not to let my surprise show. The arrangement was a sink ward, like a magical whirlpool. Any attempts to gate into the area would be swept down into the centre, appearing in that ten-foot space. I was starting to think Cinder might be smarter than he looked.

'So we break through the walls,' Khazad said contemptuously.

'They're warded too,' I said.

'And?'

Khazad was looking at me and there was a glitter in his

eyes. Rachel finally straightened, and Khazad turned away
as if he'd forgotten about me.

I wasn't fooled. Khazad was still waiting for the chance
to finish what he'd started in the forest. As long as I was
useful I knew Onyx would prevent any infighting. I also
knew that as soon as I stopped being useful Onyx would
have me killed without a second thought.

I wasn't intending to stick around long enough to give
him the chance. I hadn't been idle while we'd been waiting;
I'd been path-walking, and the one bit of good news was
that Luna was there, in the statue room at the back of the
museum. All I needed was a few seconds' distraction. I'd
make a break for it, Luna would open the door, we'd lock
it behind us and Onyx and the Dark mages could fight it
out with the Council to their hearts' content.

At least, that was the plan.

Onyx stirred. 'Close up.'

We obeyed, standing in a cluster. I found myself brushing
shoulders with Cinder, who gave me a single glance and
then pulled his own mask on. Khazad and Deleo were
weaving spells, black and sea-green light glowing faintly
about their hands. Onyx held out one hand, and the floor
underneath us darkened and turned black as a horizontal
gate began to form. I watched uneasily. If Onyx gated us
into that sink, we'd appear under the guns of the Council
guard force. I knew Onyx was strong, but—

Onyx tightened his hand into a fist and the gate
formed, linking us to the museum. For one moment
there was a lurch as the interdiction field tried to take,
then Onyx's spell ripped straight through it with sheer
brute force. We dropped down to the floor with a thump
– a white floor, with a staircase behind and a high ceiling

above. We'd gated into the Great Court, right at the foot of the stairs.

We weren't alone. A dozen people were scattered around the court, mages and guards. All had turned to stare at us, and as we came to our feet a mage threw out his arm. He was at the centre of a cluster of three. 'Hold it! Who are you?'

At least, that was what he would have said if he'd had the chance.

It was quite terrifying what Onyx did to those men. Normal people, when they're dropped into a hostile situation, take an instant to orientate themselves. Onyx didn't. In the time the leader took to open his mouth, Onyx slammed a bolt of force into the mage on the left, spun and did the same thing to the one on the right, then sent a blast straight at the face of the one in the middle, who was just in the middle of getting out the word 'who'. If the mage hadn't jerked back, it would have broken his neck; as it was it took him off his feet. A heartbeat later Cinder and Khazad joined in, engaging the ones remaining.

While everyone else was fighting, I was running, sprinting up the curving stairs. Behind me I heard the roar of spells as the battle kicked off. It took me five seconds to reach the top landing, and for that instant I was completely exposed to the people below. But everyone was too busy to pay attention to me, and I made it to the top in one piece.

I was getting pretty familiar with the British Museum by now, and as I ran I could pick out the sounds behind me; the roar of Cinder's fire magic, the flat slam of Onyx's force spells, the chatter of the automatic weapons of the guards. An instant later there was an explosion and the chatter cut off abruptly. I knew that Onyx's side was winning, and that I wouldn't have much time before they caught me up. I reached the staircase leading to the statue room. There were no guards and I raced up the stairs. Calling out the password and passing through the barrier without a ripple. As soon as I was through I dived and rolled.

A hammer of earth magic whistled above me, passing through the space where my head would have been if I hadn't taken the tumble. I came up from my roll and threw my hand towards the man standing by the entrance. 'Griff, you idiot, it's me! Seal the stairs!'

Griff had just started a backswing with a maul of grey-brown energy; he checked, halting his swing. 'Verus?' He stared. 'How did you get in? The guards—'

'They're getting their asses kicked, and so will we if you *don't seal the stairs*!'

'There's a barrier—'

'Which you just saw me walk through!'

'I'd have to collapse the—'

'Then *do it*!' I was getting desperate; I knew Onyx and Khazad were less than twenty seconds away. 'We're out of time!'

Griff hesitated for a heartbeat, then turned and made a fist. There was a rumble followed by a roar, and the floor shook as a section of the roof of the British Museum caved in, turning the stairwell behind the barrier into a shaft full of rubble. The barrier shivered slightly, but held. Dust flaked from the roof as I picked myself up. I couldn't hear anything from the floor below. We were sealed off – for the moment.

'*Alex!*'

I looked around and there was Luna, standing alone in the corner of the room, her eyes shining. I felt something in my chest loosen as I saw her. 'You're okay?'

'*I'm* okay?' Luna's voice wavered. 'What about *you?*'

I grinned. 'Let's catch up later.' I pulled the cube from my pocket and threw it to her; Luna caught it in reflex. Someone else peeked out their head from behind the statue; it was Sonder, his eyes suddenly alight with interest. '*Oh!* A crystal key! It must have micro-fissures that match the pattern of the light beams. Um, Mr Verus, where did you—?'

'Sonder, this isn't really the time,' I said as I got to my feet. 'And I told you to call me Alex. Luna? Do it.'

Luna shook her head with a smile as if at some joke, and slotted the cube into the statue's hand. It fit perfectly.

For a moment there was silence, then a gentle white light sprang up around the statue's hand. Needle-thin beams of light sprang out from the fingers, reaching into the cube and, as they did, the cube responded. It glowed red and more beams of light appeared, starting in the cube's centre and stretching out. The two sets of beams moved, playing up, down, left and right as if searching for something.

'Sonder?' I asked after a few seconds. 'What are we seeing?'

'It's . . .' Sonder stared at the cube, utterly fascinated. The red-and-white light sparkled and reflected off his glasses. 'Of course! *That's* why we could never get it to work!'

'What is?'

'The crystal's responding to the interrogation. Look!' Sonder pointed eagerly. One of the needle-like beams from the cube had intersected with one from the statue, and the two had merged and gone still. 'They're matching!' Sonder said. '*That's* the locking mechanism.'

'It'd better open fast,' Griff said sharply, cutting Sonder off. We turned to see that Griff had one hand pressed flat against the wall next to the barrier, and his eyes were narrowed. 'You were right. Someone out there wants in.'

Now that we were looking, I could feel it: the distant *crunch, crunch, crunch* of force effects carving through rubble, the vibrations growing steadily stronger. 'That would be Onyx,' I said with a nasty sinking feeling.

'How long is he going to be?' Griff demanded of me.

'If you strengthen that barrier . . . about eighty seconds.'

'How long till the door opens?'

'About seventy.'

Griff and Luna looked at each other, then Griff turned to the wall, his hand glowing with a pale brown light. There was a faint rumble as the stone reshaped itself, the rubble on the other side shifting and fusing into a dense blockade. Luna stood as close as she could to me, while Sonder waited on the other side.

One minute passed like an hour.

The booming sounds from behind us were clearly audible now, and they were causing the room to shake. Almost all of the lights from the cube and statue had intersected; only three had yet to fuse. I spoke quietly to Luna. 'When the door opens, grab that cube and stick close to me. Take the right exit.'

Luna nodded. 'Um,' Sonder said hesitantly from the other side. 'What should I do?'

'I'd follow Luna,' I said. 'Unless you want to meet Onyx.'

Sonder swallowed. 'I think I'll stay with you if that's okay.'

Another pair of light beams intersected, followed by another. 'Five seconds,' I said loudly. The booms from behind were like thunder now, and the floor was shaking with each one.

The last pair of beams matched. A pale light filled the room, and the statue seemed to fade, becoming something else. For one moment it was as though two things were stacked in the same location: the statue, glowing palely, and an arched doorway, leading into a wide chamber. 'Go!' I shouted, and ran. For an instant I was running *through* the statue, and there was a brief dizzying feeling as my eyes tried to process two sets of visual data at once, then I was through into an entrance hall with a domed roof, lit by dim flickering lights. Behind me Luna snatched the cube from the statue's hand and ran after me, Sonder at her heels.

From behind I heard a thunderous crash and the crack of flying stone, followed an instant later by the boom of Griff's earth magic. Suddenly the battle was in the statue room, and everything was chaos and darkness and fire. The gate was closing, fading, but too slowly, and I knew we had only seconds before the battle spilled through. I made it into the right-hand tunnel, hit something to my left, and a heavy door slammed behind us, cutting off sound and leaving us in pitch darkness.

## 12

It was pitch black.

'Luna?' I said.

'Over here.'

'You okay?'

'I'm fine; don't come too close!'

'Er, hi.'

'What's that?'

'What's what?'

'Who's there?'

'Luna.'

'Not you!'

'Sonder. Er, I mean David. I met you at—'

'I *know* who you are, Sonder.'

'You made it through?'

'Well, Mr Verus, I mean Alex, said to follow you, and—'

'Has anyone got a light?'

Silence.

'Anyone?'

Silence.

'Luna?'

'I brought the stuff you asked for.'

'So that's a yes?'

'Yes, but it's sealed. If I touch it . . .'

'Okay, okay. Sonder?'

'Yes?'

'You're a mage, right?'

'Well, yes.'

'Great, cast a light spell.'

'. . .'

'What's wrong?'

'Um, well—'

'Please don't tell me you can't make one either.'

'Well, I've never really gotten the hang of it. And there's usually someone else around who can, so . . .'

'Oh, you've got to be kidding.'

There was a fumbling sound, then there was a click and a cone of light broke the darkness, causing me to flinch. As my eyes adjusted I saw Sonder holding a torch looking apologetic. 'But I did bring one of these. Is that okay?'

As Sonder flashed the light around I saw Luna, pale but unhurt, pressed up against the wall. We were in a circular room with a doorway leading out into a corridor. I couldn't see any trace of the doorway we'd entered from, and I couldn't feel any vibration through the floor. Either the walls were really thick or we'd been transported. Either way, a quick look at the future confirmed no one was going to be following for a while.

'Where are we?' Luna asked

'Sonder?' I said.

'This is amazing,' Sonder said. He was looking around in fascination. 'We're actually inside a bubble! All of this must have been built during the Dark Wars. I've never seen an installation as well preserved—'

Luna and I looked at him, and Sonder suddenly looked flustered. 'Well, I mean— We're inside the bubble. It should be safe. I mean, it's lasted this long.'

'Can anyone else get in?' I asked.

'Oh, no. Not once the gate's closed.'

'I think it was closing at the end,' Luna said. She was still holding the red crystal cube, looking down at it. 'When I took it away I wanted it to. And it did.'

I glanced at Luna curiously. Absorbed with the cube, she didn't seem to notice. 'Um . . .' Sonder said. 'Did anyone else get inside?'

'Let's hope not. Luna? Luna!'

'Hm?' Luna shook herself. 'Oh. Right.' She stood and walked to the middle of the room. With my mage's sight I could see the silvery mist coating her and the pack, odd tendrils drifting towards me and Sonder but not quite able to reach. Luna took off her backpack, put it upside down on the ground, then lifted it quickly off, stepping away. A handful of items spilled out. 'This was everything I could find.'

'Shine the light,' I told Sonder, who obeyed. The first thing I picked up from the pile was my mist cloak, and I felt my heart lighten as I saw it. It's funny how attached you can get to an item, but then imbued items are practically living things. In any case, it's saved my life more times than I can count and, as I swung it over my shoulders and fastened it around my neck, I felt better immediately.

'Is it all there?' Luna asked.

I nodded as I went through the pile. I'd asked Luna to go to my shop using the hidden key, and bring everything I'd need. 'Good job. How did it go with Talisid?'

'He asked if I was your apprentice.'

'What did you tell him?'

'What do you think?'

I laughed, found my own torch and switched it on. 'Sonder? Go into the corridor about fifteen feet down and have a look on the right wall. There's a control set that'll turn on the lights for this area.'

Sonder hesitated. 'Are you sure it's safe?'

'As long as you don't go any further.'

'I'm not actually sure how the spells in this site work . . .'

'Yes, you are. If you study it for a couple of minutes, you'll figure it out.'

'Are you sure?'

'Yes.'

'It might be dangerous . . .'

'It won't be.'

'How do you know?'

'Because that's what I do. Look, Sonder, I've never studied places like this, and neither has Luna, but you have. The reason I'm asking you to do it is because you're the best one for the job. There'll be places further on where it *is* dangerous for you to touch anything, but when we run into those I'll warn you. Okay?'

'Oh.' Sonder hesitated, then nodded. 'Okay.' He got up and stepped out into the corridor.

I looked back to see that Luna was smiling. 'What's so funny?'

'Oh, I was telling him about you. While we were waiting in the statue room.'

I gave Luna a suspicious look. 'What did you say?'

Luna looked back at me innocently. I shook my head, then became serious. 'How did everything go?'

Luna glanced after where Sonder had gone, then sighed and leant back against the wall. 'It wasn't so bad. They didn't ask many questions. Most of them just ignored me.'

'How was Talisid?'

Luna thought for a second. 'I think he might have guessed. None of the others did. The only other one who talked to me was Sonder. You know, he seemed a bit . . .'

I laughed. 'Not all mages are the experienced type.' I'd almost finished with the contents of the backpack. She'd done a good job; I had everything that was likely to help. One item remained: a blue disc with serrated edges. I could feel that it was some sort of focus, with a fair charge of energy inside it. 'What's that?'

'Talisid said it was a communicator,' Luna said. 'He said it was synchronous?'

I'd picked the disc up and was studying it. 'Huh. I didn't know they'd managed to get these working.'

'Will it work from in here?'

I nodded. 'He must have been expecting something like this. Even for a Council rep, this wouldn't come cheap.' I looked at Luna. 'Ready?'

Luna nodded and I pressed several of the edges in sequence. They began to flash blue. I set the thing down and waited.

The lights changed from blue to green and a ghostly holographic figure appeared, standing on the disc, twelve inches tall. It was Talisid. 'Verus!' His voice was muffled but clear. 'Where are you?'

'Where do you think?'

'You're inside?'

'Inside, and likely to stay inside. What's happening out there?'

'Are you all right? Who's with you?'

'Luna and Sonder. We're fine.'

Talisid's figure seemed to relax slightly. 'That's the first good news I've heard all day.'

'What happened?'

'Cave in.' It was hard to make out fine detail on the small projection, but Talisid's clothes looked scuffed. 'I don't know who it was, but the whole room and most of the stairwell's rubble. We're starting to dig through, but—'

'Talisid?' I said. 'That wasn't really what I was asking.' I didn't raise my voice, but there was an edge to it. 'I gave you advance warning an attack was coming. I gave you the most likely day. You had twenty-four hours to prepare and a full Council security detail. Onyx had three people.'

Talisid said nothing. He didn't look happy.

'Please tell me you got at least one of them.'

'We haven't been able to confirm anything yet.'

'That's a no, isn't it?'

Talisid was silent and I put a hand over my eyes. 'I'd ask for an explanation, but hearing the full details of exactly *how* you screwed up is kind of moot at this point.'

'Look, Verus, I'm getting enough crap from the Council right now. I don't need any more from you.'

'And we're inside a sealed-off relic with anywhere between zero and four Dark mages who want to kill us. Who do you think got the better end of the deal?'

Talisid stayed silent. I took a deep breath and got myself under control. 'Where's Griff?'

'We don't know.'

'How many of the Dark mages made it inside?'

'We don't know. It's possible they were caught by the collapse—'

'Don't bet on it. Who else is there?'

'We don't know. It's *bad* out here, Verus. We've got dozens injured and at least three of the security staff are dead; Onyx went through them like a buzz-saw. Everyone we can spare is on medical detail or digging out survivors or on guard, and we still haven't linked up with everyone. Everyone was in the wrong place, it's as though—' Talisid checked and then went on. 'I was with Ilmarin – he's an air mage, one of the ones in the Great Court. He told me he felt something go after Onyx's group during the attack. Completely invisible, both to the eye and to magic. The only reason he could sense it was by the displaced air. He has no idea what it was.'

I closed my eyes again. 'Perfect,' I said once I'd got myself under control. 'Anything else while you're at it?'

'You know what it was?'

'It's called Thirteen. She works for Levistus. I don't suppose you can give us any sort of help?'

'If the portal's still open—'

Luna spoke up. 'It's not.'

Talisid looked at her, then back at me. 'We might be able to jury-rig the thing with some kind of worldgate. If we can follow the trace—'

'Can you get that done in four hours or less?' I said.

Talisid was silent. I sighed. 'I'll take that as a no. Anything else?'

'I'm sorry,' Talisid said. 'I wish I had some better news.'

'I wish you did too.'

'I'll call you as soon as we learn anything.'

'Please don't. The last thing we need is our phone going off when we're trying to avoid attention. We'll call you.'

Talisid nodded. 'Good luck.' The communicator winked off.

I didn't move. 'What did you mean about the invisible thing?' Luna asked after a moment.

'Some sort of modified air elemental Levistus uses. I'm just wondering if that's all he's got.'

'What do you mean?'

'The Council guards shouldn't have done that badly,' I

said. 'They were outclassed, but not *that* outclassed. And the way they were deployed, with no one between the Great Court and the statue . . . I think someone was trying to make sure the attack got through.'

Luna frowned. 'You mean Levistus? Why would he want to do that?'

I remembered Levistus' words from the ball, delivered with just a trace of a smile: '*I have many agents, Mr Verus. Rest assured, they will be making sure everything goes to plan.*'

My heart sank. 'Oh, crap.'

'What's wrong?'

'Luna, was there anyone who stayed near the statue all the time you were there? As in, never going away for long?'

Luna looked puzzled. 'I suppose.'

'Who?'

'Sonder and Griff.'

'No one else?'

'I don't think so. Why?'

'Because the only reason Levistus would want Morden's attack to go through would be so he could get his own people inside as well.'

Luna looked at me for a few seconds, then her face changed. 'Sonder?'

I didn't say anything. Luna looked out into the corridor after Sonder, then turned back with an uneasy look on her face. 'Wait. No. Griff was the one who was supposed to be in charge of security, right? Isn't it more likely to be him?'

'Who says it's only one of them?'

Luna started to answer then stopped.

'I don't like the idea either,' I said quietly. 'But I don't think Levistus would rely on just Thirteen. He's got agents and he'll have used them. You're right; Griff sounds more likely, but he's not here and Sonder is. Until we get out of here, watch your back.'

We sat quietly for a moment, thinking. The torches cast Luna's face in shadow, making it hard to know what she was thinking. 'We don't have many friends here, do we?' Luna said at last.

'What about Starbreeze?'

'I called her. She came the first time, but when she saw me she ran away again. I called her again when I heard you coming but . . .'

I'd been searching through the futures and as I did I felt my spirit lift. I smiled. 'Huh.'

'She's here?'

'She's here. Looks like we've got one friend after all.'

All of a sudden the lights came on. Luna and I stood up, blinking, and from out in the corridor I heard Sonder call excitedly, 'I did it!'

The room we were standing in was off-white, with a high ceiling. The edges of the walls and floor were rounded slightly so as to show no corners, making the room oddly featureless, and circular patches on the ceiling shed a bright light. I could sense that the lights were magical, which confirmed that this place was very, very old. Like I said, creating permanent magical items is a real hassle. It's far less effort to use modern technology, which means the only places that use permanent effects like this are ones that were created *before* modern technology. Luna and I walked to the exit to see a curving corridor. Up ahead, we could just see that it opened into a T-junction. 'Good job,' I told Sonder as we approached.

'I thought that would work,' Sonder said. He looked

pleased with himself. Next to him was the control panel he'd used to activate the lights. I touched my hand to the panel and focused, working out what Sonder had done. Meanwhile, Luna was looking around curiously. 'What *is* this place?'

'It was sealed up just after the end of the Dark Wars,' Sonder said. 'But there's nothing saying why. I'm starting to think the records about this place were deliberately erased. All I could find was something about the "resting place of Abithriax".'

'You said this was his tomb,' Luna said.

Sonder hesitated. 'Yes, but I'm starting to think I might have been wrong. I've been doing some reading, and it turns out the Precursors didn't actually build tombs. Not like this.'

'But if this was his resting place . . .'

'I know, but it still doesn't make sense. If you look at the studies that have been done of Precursor religion, the design—'

'Sorry, Sonder, wait a second. Um, Alex?'

I was busy with the control panel. Like most Precursor designs it was sparse; a few spheres that looked like glass, and some rods set into the wall. They were controlled with fine magical impulses. With my divination magic I could see how to make them do what I wanted, but I had no idea how they worked. Still, that was enough to—

'*Alex!*'

'Hm?' I said absently.

'What's that on your arm?'

I glanced down to see that the bracelet on my right wrist was crackling and spitting feebly. Black energy leaked from it, making my arm tingle. 'Oh,' I said. 'Looks like Onyx decided to kill me.'

Luna and Sonder stared. 'They're called death bracelets,' I said. 'Dark mages use them to keep prisoners in line.'

The bracelet was still crackling. 'Um.' Sonder said. 'Shouldn't you . . .?'

'Oh, it's fine. I dialled down the power by a factor of a hundred or so. Onyx must have fired it at maximum, otherwise you wouldn't even see it.'

'What does maximum do?'

'Kills an adult human in ten to twenty seconds, depending how strong their heart is. Anyway, we'd better get moving. Don't touch anything without checking with me first, don't go anywhere I haven't gone already, and if I tell you to do something, do it *fast*. Okay?'

Luna nodded, Sonder a little slower. Both were still staring at the bracelet. As they watched it fizzled and fell silent. We headed to the T-junction and stopped while I stood between the two paths.

'What's he doing?' I heard Sonder whisper after a minute.

'He's looking ahead to see what'll happen if we go down each corridor,' Luna said quietly.

I smiled to myself and pointed. 'Left.'

It was an hour later and the three of us were clustered in a small room. In a small alcove, set into the wall, was a single recessed crystal sphere. Before us was a closed door.

Sonder was examining the sphere while I leant against the wall next to him. Luna stood back, well out of range. 'Sonder, we're on a clock here,' I said at last.

'Sorry.' Sonder stepped back. 'Well, it's definitely a focus for some kind of mind effect—'

'I know.'

'—and I think it might be telepathy-based. Anyway, it's for communication.'

'You said you could get the door open?' Luna asked.

'Probably, but there's a trap, And after what happened last time I don't want to take the chance if we can avoid it.'

Sonder flinched slightly at that. The previous room had held an electrical trap that would have turned anyone who came close enough into a lightning rod. 'So that leaves this thing?' Luna asked.

'That leaves this thing.' I stared at the crystal sphere, frowning. 'It'll help us get past. I just don't know how.'

'What'll happen if we touch it?' Sonder asked.

'Nothing.'

Sonder and Luna looked at each other. 'If I touch it, I'll do nothing,' I said. 'I'll stand still with my hand on this thing for maybe ten minutes, and I won't move or say a word, no matter what you do. And I don't know why.'

'That would make sense if it's a telepathy focus.' Sonder volunteered.

I didn't answer. The truth was that not knowing what would happen if I touched this thing made me uneasy. Normally I always know what'll happen. You don't realise how accustomed you get to something until it's suddenly taken away from you.

When I didn't move, Sonder shifted. 'I could try it . . .'

'No,' I said, and stepped forward. 'You two watch my back. I don't think I'll be able to sense anything else while I'm using this. If you hear trouble coming, pull me off it. Kick me if you have to.'

They nodded. 'Be careful,' Luna said.

I turned to the sphere, took a deep breath, then placed my hand upon it. There was a moment of disorientation as the world seemed to flicker, then it was gone. I let my fingers rest on the sphere. Nothing happened.

I tried a command word. '*Annath.*'

Nothing.

'Open. Transmit. *Sagashiette.*'

Still nothing.

I sighed and turned away. 'Well, that was under-whelming.'

Luna and Sonder looked past me. 'Nothing,' I said. 'Weird. I'm pretty sure it should have . . .'

I trailed off. Sonder hadn't moved. Luna glanced aside anxiously, then went back to looking over my shoulder, her eyes passing over me. 'Hey,' I said. 'You guys okay?'

No reaction. 'What are you—?' I began, turning round, and stopped dead. What Luna and Sonder were staring at was me. My body was standing right in front of me, my right hand clasped on the sphere. I looked down at my hand just to convince myself it was still there, looked up, and stared. 'What the *hell*?'

I reached forward hesitantly. My hand passed through my body as though it was light, and I jumped. This was *really* weird.

I turned back to see Sonder's lips moving. He was saying something to Luna, and now Luna turned aside slightly to reply, her eyes still fixed on my body, but I couldn't hear their words. In fact, now I stopped to listen, I couldn't hear anything at all. It was dead silent.

'Good evening. Might I be of assistance?'

I only barely managed to keep myself from jumping as the voice spoke from behind me. Standing in the doorway was an old man. He had a flowing beard and long hair, both snow-white, with thin streaks of red running through them. His clothes were red as well: robes, gathered at the waist, of several shades from blood-red to crimson.

For a moment I couldn't remember where I'd seen him before, then suddenly it clicked. I'd seen his face, but it had been stone, not flesh. 'Abithriax,' I said.

Abithriax bowed. 'And whom do I have the honour of addressing?'

I stood staring at the mage in front of me. Abithriax stood looking back with an expression of mild inquiry. 'How are you alive?' I said at last. It wasn't polite, but I was shaken.

Abithriax didn't seem particularly offended. 'Well,' he said, 'that's rather an interesting question. Perhaps you'd like to walk with me? One gets so little exercise cooped up in here.'

I took a glance back at Luna and Sonder. They were talking to each other, although I still couldn't hear them. They didn't seem able to see Abithriax either. 'You'll be quite safe,' Abithriax said, as though reading my thoughts. 'No one is going to arrive for a little while.'

I hesitated a moment, then fell into step beside Abithriax and we began walking back down the corridor. Despite his age, he moved smoothly, with no trace of stiffness. 'How am I talking to you?' I said.

'The crystals on these walls form a communication network that extends throughout this facility,' Abithriax said. 'Mental projection only, I'm afraid; your body is still back in that room. The network works with your mind to translate the information.'

'If I'm here, where are you?'

'At the centre, of course.'

I stared at Abithriax for a second before it clicked. 'You're the fateweaver.'

Abithriax just smiled. I kept walking, my head spinning as everything fell into place. Of course. Something as powerful as the fateweaver would have to be an imbued item. And the more powerful it was, the stronger its own identity would be . . . I looked up at Abithriax. 'How? You were supposed to have died.'

'Oh, I did.' Abithriax looked inquiringly at me. 'Perhaps you'd like to hear the story?'

I stared back at him and finally nodded.

'Oh good. It really is so nice to have someone to talk to . . . Let's see, where to begin? People still remember the Dark Wars, I hope? I've afraid I've rather lost track of time.'

'You lived through them.'

Abithriax nodded. 'From the beginning to the end. I remember Syriathis, and its destruction. I fought through the retreats in the early campaigns, seeing my friends and allies die one by one. I was promoted, and promoted again. After our victory at the Ebon Fields I was granted my fateweaver. Years passed, the tide turned, the strongholds lost in the early years were retaken, and I was at the forefront of every battle. When the final sieges began, I was battle commander of all the Light armies.'

We'd come to a junction and Abithriax stopped. 'And then I was betrayed.' His eyes stared off into nothingness, distant. 'The Council had become afraid of me. I was too famous, too powerful. So in the last months of the war, once victory was guaranteed, they sent me to my death.'

Abithriax fell silent. I stood looking at him. 'How did you do it?' I said at last.

Abithriax blinked, looked at me, then shook his head and turned left down the junction. I followed. 'My fateweaver. All our generals carried one, but the craftsmen were never able to stabilise the design. They were always . . . unpredictable. But I learned the secret of investing myself into it, binding my identity into it a piece at a time, and as its power grew, so did mine. It was almost a part of me. Perhaps that was how I was able to make the final leap at the very end . . .'

Abithriax shook his head and suddenly his voice became brisk. 'Well then. I assume that's what you're here for? My fateweaver? Oh, there's no need to hide it,' he added as I hesitated. 'It's not as if you'd come here for any other reason. Besides, it's not as if I can carry it myself any more.'

'Yes.'

'And the others?'

'Which others?'

Abithriax raised his eyebrows. 'The other mages attempting to reach me. I may lack a physical body, but I'm not entirely blind. Half a dozen or so, I believe?'

I walked for a little while in silence. 'Can you help me against them?' I said at last.

Abithriax snorted. 'A handful of mages? I've defeated *armies*. However . . . without a wielder, I am nothing. And more to the point, there is no guarantee my wielder will be you. If one of those mages reaches me first, I'm afraid my powers will be at their disposal, not yours. In this form, I am a servant to my wielder.'

Something made me look up at that, searching Abithriax's face. He looked back at me calmly. 'And I have no control over who that wielder is. So if you have any enemies within this facility, I would suggest you make sure they do not reach me first. Because if they take possession of me and order me to use my powers to hunt you down and kill you, I am very much afraid I will have no choice but to obey.'

Abithriax and I had taken two turnings and we were almost back at the room we'd started from. The two of us stood looking at each other. 'Then I guess I'd better get moving,' I said at last.

'Of course,' Abithriax said with a nod. 'Tell that scholarly-looking apprentice with you to try a command word in the right corner. I'm not sure of the password but I'm sure you can deduce it.'

'Right. See you later.'

'Hopefully so.' Abithriax smiled slightly. 'For what it's worth, I hope you succeed.' His image seemed to dissolve into mist and he was gone.

I walked back into the room. Luna and Sonder were still there, throwing glances at my body. Somehow I knew how to break the connection. I walked into my body, layering my mental self over my physical one, placing my hand over where my real hand grasped the crystal. There was a moment of dizziness, then—

'—be in trouble.' Sonder's voice.

'He said not to do anything.' It was Luna's voice; to most people she would have sounded calm, but I could hear the trace of anxiety. 'We could— Alex!'

I turned around – *really* turned around, this time. Luna gave me a searching look, then let out a sigh of relief. 'You're okay.'

'I'm okay,' I said. 'Sonder? Take a look at the right corner. While you're doing that, I've got something to tell you both.'

As Sonder worked, I relayed what I'd learned. I briefly considered keeping it a secret between me and Luna, but there wasn't any good excuse to send Sonder out of earshot and anyway, I wanted his input. 'That's incredible,' Sonder said once I'd finished. 'I mean, just the idea of surviving that long . . . The Dark Wars were almost two thousand years ago! The things he'd be able to tell us!'

'Sonder,' I said. 'Priorities. Survive first, research afterwards. Does what he said match with what you know?'

Sonder thought for a minute. 'We've never been able to recover a fateweaver before. It was just assumed they were all destroyed, but if they were unstable, that would explain it. And there's always been a mystery about Abithriax's death. Some writers did argue for the betrayal theory, but there's never been any proof. The Old Council fell into infighting after the Dark Wars and most of the records were destroyed.'

'Do you trust him?' Luna asked.

I hesitated. 'I'm not sure,' I said at last. 'I had the feeling he was keeping something back. But I'm pretty sure he was telling the truth about what he'd do if Onyx found him first.'

'So what should we do?' Luna said.

Sonder had stopped and both he and Luna were looking at me, waiting for my decision. 'We go for the fateweaver,' I said. 'If we can take it for ourselves, we've got a chance. But I don't want either of you involved in the fighting. Onyx and the rest are going to be after me, not you. Don't do anything to draw their attention.'

I made my voice sound confident and both of them nodded, Sonder quickly, Luna a little more reluctantly. The two of them turned back to what they were doing and I bit my lip, wishing I was as sure as I was pretending to be.

The truth was that none of our options were good. I knew that trying to beat Onyx and the others to the fateweaver was likely to end in a fight, and I also knew that if it came to a battle our little group was almost certain to lose. It was tempting to run and hide. If we weren't going for the fateweaver, Levistus and Morden's agents would be too busy fighting each other to worry about us.

Except that if we did that, whoever won the battle would be free to hunt us down afterwards, with all the power of the Precursor artifact at their disposal. Whether we lived or died would be up to them. My instinct told me our best chance was to act. But it's one thing to risk your own life and another to risk someone else's. I looked at Luna withdrawn into the corner, and Sonder examining the wall, and felt suddenly afraid. For all my brave words, I didn't know if I'd be able to protect either of them.

Then I shook it off and focused, going back to watching Sonder and sifting through the futures. After a moment I knew Abithriax's advice had been good. 'There,' I told Sonder. 'Try some command words.'

'Uh . . . which ones?'

'Every one you can think of.'

Sonder looked back at the wall and hesitated. 'This feels silly.'

I sighed inwardly. For all Sonder's knowledge, it was painfully obvious how inexperienced he was. Once you've been around the block a few times you stop caring about looking silly, especially when you're dealing with magical traps. Better to be laughed at than dead, and he wouldn't have been laughed at. 'Just give it a go.'

Sonder started reciting in the old tongue. He spoke like

a scholar, each word carefully pronounced. 'Stop,' I said after a moment. 'Say that last one again and put your hand on the wall, fingers spread. Up a bit,' I said as Sonder obeyed. 'Left a bit. Hold that. Now say that word again.'

Reluctantly, Sonder did as I said. '*Etro.*'

Right in front of Sonder, a section of wall seven feet high and three feet wide glowed for an instant and simply vanished. Sonder started and jumped back. Beyond was a short corridor, bending left. 'Now I see,' I said. 'The whole room is a trap. The only safe way is to go around.'

'Is it safe?' Luna asked.

'Yes. It's—' I stopped.

'What's wrong?'

I stared for a moment before answering. 'It's not empty.'

The corridor was about five feet wide. All the way along the left side was a one-way mirror into the trap room, and as we looked in we got a perfect view of what would have happened to us if we'd stepped through that door.

Every inch of the other room – walls, floor, ceiling – was covered in mirrors. Instead of being placed evenly, they were tilted, casting images at odd angles. Reflecting from the mirrors, filling the room with a criss-cross of white light, were beams of energy, white lines that looked harmless but which I knew could cut like razors. The room was so filled with the beams that it took a moment to realise that there were in fact only three. They emerged from a single tiny panel on the back wall, then bounced around the room at every angle, multiplied a thousand times over.

In the middle of the room, trapped in a cage of beams, were Rachel and Cinder. Rachel was in a half-crouch, a beam just above her head stopping her from rising any further. Cinder was standing, leaning sideways to fit into the empty space. Beams laced the air around them, and I could see burnt patches on their clothes where they'd brushed up against the energy. Both were standing dead still.

Luna stopped as she saw them. 'Alex—'

'They can't see us,' I said. Neither Rachel nor Cinder reacted as we spoke. 'Or hear. Sonder, do you know what that is?'

'It's an energy lattice,' Sonder said. He was staring in fascination. 'I've never seen one before.'

'What does it do?'

Sonder started. 'Um, they were defence systems from the Dark Wars. They were meant to contain intruders. Once the beams are up, you have to stand there until someone comes to turn it off.'

'What happens if no one comes?'

Sonder paused. 'I don't really know.'

On the other side of the glass, Cinder said something and Rachel answered silently. Both were only inches away from beams on all sides. Sooner or later they would get tired and fall, and when they did, the beams would kill them.

It's a strange feeling, holding someone's life in your hands, and it affects people in different ways. Some hate it; they can't stand the burden and get away as quick as they can. Others revel in the power. You can think of it as a choice, and it is, but the truth is that for most of the big things, the choice was made long ago. It's only when you reach the crossroads that you discover what it was. It was nothing new to me; I'd been here before. But the others . . .

Both Luna and Sonder stared through the one-way

mirror. Neither spoke, but it was so easy to read their thoughts. Rachel and Cinder were their enemies; all they had to do was walk away. But when it came to it, they hesitated. One after another they turned to look at me, and I knew they were waiting for me to make the decision, just as I'd done a few minutes ago. I could order them to help Rachel and Cinder or to walk away and leave, and they'd obey.

'What do you think we should do?' I asked them

I saw their faces change. The seconds ticked away and, even here, I couldn't help but be curious. I looked into the future, trying to see how they'd decide, and couldn't predict either. You can't see beyond a choice that someone hasn't made. I watched as the possibilities wavered, shifting and changing.

'We have to help,' Sonder said.

'Leave them,' Luna said at the same time.

Sonder turned on Luna in shock. 'But they'll die!'

'Better them than us.'

'They're mages! You can't decide someone's life like that!'

'I decide that every day,' Luna said quietly. 'This time at least they deserve it.'

Sonder looked horrified. Luna turned to me and waited. 'You can't be going to—' Sonder said. 'I know they're dangerous, but—!'

'Stay here,' I said. 'You can watch, but don't get involved.'

A beat, then both nodded, though there was an uneasiness between them now. I left Luna and Sonder in the corridor and walked around the edge. There was another secret door at the far end, and I sealed it behind me. Ahead of me was the trap room's exit, but it wasn't an exit any more. Someone had destroyed the external controls, sealing Rachel and Cinder inside.

There were more one-way mirrors to either side, and through them I could see Rachel and Cinder, still motionless. As I studied the pattern of energy beams, I realised that if any one of us had entered the room, the changing angles of reflection from the door swinging inwards would have sent the energy beams slicing through Rachel, Cinder, and anyone in the doorway. Not only did it trap those inside, it was designed to kill anyone attempting a rescue. Nasty.

The spell that had destroyed the controls had left cracks in the wall near the door. Leaning in close, I could hear the whisper of Rachel and Cinder's voices from the other side. 'Hello?' I said. 'Can you hear me?'

The whispering stopped. 'Who's there?' Rachel demanded.

'Alex.'

'Verus?' Cinder demanded. 'What the fuck are you doing?'

'More or less the same thing as you.'

'You bastard,' Cinder said. He tried to turn around to look at the wall I was speaking from, but couldn't. 'How are you still alive? Onyx fired your bracelet!'

'Cinder, given your current situation, do you really think this is the most productive way to spend your time?'

'What do you want?' Rachel said. She was holding quite still. Behind the mask, I couldn't see her expression, but I knew she was focusing on me.

'I'm here to help you out of that room.'

'Bullshit,' Cinder snarled.

'Turn off the beams,' Rachel said.

'Can't.'

'Then open the door.'

'Can't.'

'Why not?'

'Last guy through smashed the controls.'

Rachel swore. 'Khazad,' she hissed. 'That motherfucker.'

'There's an emergency cut-off inside the room,' I said. 'It's just under where the beams are coming from.'

Cinder and Rachel flicked their eyes sideways to look. The mirrors beneath the beams looked exactly the same as the ones covering the rest of the room. 'That takes us away from the door,' Rachel said at last.

'I know.'

'I don't see any cut-off.'

'I know.'

'Fuck him,' Cinder snarled. 'You want us dead, don't you?'

I didn't answer. A few seconds ticked by with no sound other than the humming of the beams. 'How do I get there?' Rachel asked.

Cinder started and nearly got his arm burnt off for his trouble. 'What the fuck are you doing?'

'Shut up, Cinder,' Rachel said wearily. 'Alex? How do I get there?'

'There's a route through,' I said. 'Move your head forward and shift about six inches to the side and you'll see the first part.' I paused. 'It'll have to be you. Cinder's too big.'

Rachel only nodded. She moved her head and shifted. 'I see it,' she said and began to move.

'Del—' Cinder said.

'Catch me if I fall,' Rachel said, and started sliding through the beams.

If it had been Luna I'd have been terrified, barely able to look. As it was, I watched Rachel with something like indifference. Despite everything, I had to admire her body control. She didn't tremble at all as she crawled and stretched and balanced over and under and through the beams, heading for their source. I looked into the future and saw her slip and die in agony, and each time I spoke, telling her which way to move, when to stop and when to go. Rachel obeyed without question. Despite everything that had happened between us, in a weird way we still understood each other. I wondered what Luna and Sonder must be thinking, watching from the sealed corridor.

At last Rachel made it. She rested in a crouch, body angled to avoid the beams streaming from the opening just above her. 'What do I do?' she said without looking.

'Put the middle three fingers of your right hand against the mirror just below the beams,' I said. 'Up. A little to the right. Now press.'

There was a click and a small section swung open. 'There should be two crystal spheres,' I said. 'Can you see them?'

'Yes.'

'Put your finger between.'

There was a pause, then a tiny spark. All of a sudden, as if someone had thrown a switch, the beams vanished. Cinder and Rachel were standing in an empty room.

Cinder turned, looking from side to side. Rachel rose and walked towards the door. 'It won't open,' I said as she disappeared from my sight. 'You'll have to—'

At my side, the door seemed to flash green, then crumble to powder, becoming a fine dust that hung in the air. Rachel strode through, followed an instant later by Cinder. '—disintegrate it,' I finished. The room on this side of the trap was a small one, with corridors leading off right and left. Cinder and Rachel entered and stopped, facing me from only a few feet away.

Cinder looked at the smashed controls, then back at me.

There was an expression on his face I'd never seen before. 'Why?' he said at last.

I shrugged. 'We had a deal.'

Cinder looked at Rachel. She was studying me, her eyes opaque behind her mask. 'Outside,' she said at last, addressing Cinder. 'We keep him alive, he gets rid of these bracelets.'

I nodded. Rachel stepped forward and held out her right wrist, pushing back the sleeve to reveal the bracelet. 'Well?'

I pulled out a tool and set to work. Rachel waited patiently while I probed at the bracelet's inner workings, looking into the future to see the outcome of every action. From time to time my hand brushed against Rachel's skin. She didn't react, and neither did I. I might have been her dressmaker.

I finished after five minutes and moved on to Cinder, who stuck his arm out with poor grace. He was in worse shape than Rachel; I could see patches where his clothes had been burnt away, and he smelt of ash and scorched flesh. As the minutes ticked past he made a growling sound. 'Why don't you just burn 'em off?'

'Same reason you can't. I'm guessing you've tried.'

Cinder was silent. 'I can't break the locks,' I said. 'But I can shut down the receptor so it can't receive Onyx's signal. He won't be able to tell they're sabotaged until he tries to zap you.'

'That'll work?' Cinder said suspiciously.

Without looking away, I held up my right wrist, which still held Onyx's bracelet. 'It worked for me.'

Cinder shut up then, and the three of us stood there quietly. After all our history, it was a strange feeling to have them just wait there. At last, it was finished. I stepped back. 'Done.'

Cinder and Rachel looked at their bracelets. 'Doesn't look different,' Cinder said.

'It's different,' I said.

'I believe you,' Rachel said. She looked at me. 'So.'

'So,' I said.

The moment stretched out, silent, tense. I stood watching the pair of them, looking at the two possible futures, wondering which one they were going to choose.

'Don't get in our way,' Rachel said at last. She turned and walked towards the nearest exit. Cinder gave me a final scowl and followed her.

As their footsteps faded away into the distance, I let out a long breath and let my shoulders slump. I stood still for a moment, alone with my thoughts, then shook myself and looked across at the secret door. 'Guys? You can come out.'

Cautiously, Sonder and then Luna emerged. Sonder looked around. 'Where did they go?'

'Further in,' I said. Suddenly I felt very tired.

'Oh,' Sonder said, and scratched his head. 'Well . . . I guess that's better.' He walked forward, rummaging in his bag. 'You know, I think I've seen this layout before . . .'

Luna waited for Sonder to get out of earshot, then looked at me. 'We're going to run into them again,' she said at last.

I didn't answer. I led Luna and Sonder into the corridor Rachel and Cinder hadn't taken, and together we headed deeper.

## 13

The hands on my watch pointed to 2.13 a.m. As I stared, they blurred and seemed to swim until I was no longer sure what I was looking at. I forced my eyes to focus, knowing I couldn't afford to sleep.

We'd been inside the tomb for four hours. The closer we spiralled in towards the centre of the facility, the more lethal and hard to bypass the traps and security systems were. Our progress had slowed to a crawl – worse, the number of paths was steadily diminishing, forcing us closer to the others hunting the fateweaver.

Cinder and Rachel were the easiest to spot, and I stayed away from them, not wanting to find out how long our truce would last. More of a concern was Khazad. He had split from the others and was searching the corridors on his own, and in the last hour we'd been forced to hide from him three times. Each time we let him pass, he reappeared again a short while later. I was starting to worry that it wasn't a coincidence and that he was actively hunting us. I could vaguely feel his presence through the futures of our meetings, somewhere behind us and to the left. Having to stay constantly on the alert was wearing me down.

I shook off my fatigue and looked up at Sonder. 'Which way?'

Sonder had held up better under the strain than I'd expected, but was looking tired as well. He'd managed to piece together a sketch map in his notebook, extrapolating from the parts of the facility we'd seen and from the designs of other Precursor structures he'd read about. It wasn't perfect, but it was getting better. 'Left, I think. It shouldn't be trapped.'

I glanced ahead through the futures. We were standing at a T-junction. 'They're both trapped.'

'There's supposed to be a corridor. It might not be easy to open the other end, but . . . The right way is open, but I think the traps are denser.'

I sighed and slid down against the wall. 'I need to rest. Try and figure out which path will get us through.' I closed my eyes and made myself relax.

I'd been sitting only a few moments when a voice penetrated my thoughts. 'Alex?'

I opened my eyes to see Luna looking at me. She was crouching in the room's far corner, the crystal cube held absent-mindedly in her fingers, as though she'd forgotten about it. Luna had been quiet for the past two hours, her thoughts and manner more distant since the encounter with Cinder and Rachel, and I knew she'd been thinking about it.

When she spoke, though, the subject came as a surprise. 'These traps and barriers. This isn't normal, is it?'

I gave Sonder a glance and he shook his head. 'No. We've found defence systems before, but nothing like this.'

'I've been thinking about it too,' I said. 'All I can think of is what Abithriax said. Fateweavers were supposed to be very powerful. If what he said was true, his might have been the only one stable enough to be preserved.'

'Why, though?'

I frowned. 'Why the traps? To make sure no one could get it.'

Luna shook her head. 'No, I understand that. I mean, why would they seal it away and not keep it for themselves?'

I opened my mouth to answer and stopped.

'Maybe they thought it was too powerful?' Sonder said doubtfully.

'No,' I said with a frown. 'She's right. If it was that useful, there'd have to be one hell of a good reason for them to give it up.'

Sonder suddenly got a thoughtful look. 'You know . . .' he began, but as he did my precognition flashed a warning. I looked into the future and my fatigue vanished as I pulled myself to my feet. 'Damn it.'

Luna scrambled up, pocketing the cube. 'What's wrong?'

'Khazad again.' I looked through the futures, calculated. 'We've got less than five minutes. Sonder, which way?'

Sonder hesitated. 'I don't know.'

'Then we go with your first guess.' I turned left and started down the white corridor. Luna followed me without hesitation and Sonder hurried after.

We reached a crossroads. A doorway led into a long hall, while the corridor went further, bending out of sight. Behind, I could feel Khazad following in our footsteps. He was moving faster now and I wondered if he had some way of tracking us. 'Into the hall,' I said. 'We'll seal the door behind us.'

'But we'll be trapped!' Sonder protested. 'The door at the other end's sealed too!'

'We can open doors faster than Khazad can.' I glanced back; I thought I could hear footsteps. 'Out of time. Let's go.'

Luna stepped through and with only a moment's hesitation Sonder followed. I stepped inside and touched the control crystal on the wall. The area across the doorway darkened and became an opaque wall of force. The sound of distant footsteps cut off abruptly and everything was silent.

'Can he get in?' Luna asked absently. She was playing with the crystal again.

'Eventually,' I said, reaching out with my senses to search ahead. 'We just have to . . .' I trailed off. 'Someone's here.'

Luna and Sonder turned, their eyes flicking. The hallway was crowded with square pillars, providing plenty of cover. I reached into my pocket for a weapon. 'Show yourself,' I said, my voice echoing around the columns. The silence stretched out, tense.

Movement, footsteps. A man leant out from behind a pillar and stopped, staring. 'Verus?'

It was Griff. I searched the hall quickly and verified no one else was inside. 'Master Griff!' Sonder said in relief.

Griff walked closer and the four of us stood still for a moment. Only Sonder had relaxed; Griff and I were watching each other closely. Luna had hidden the cube away, and I kept my hand in my pocket.

Then Griff spoke. 'You okay?'

I nodded, and the tension eased suddenly. 'You?'

'So far.' He looked at the door. 'You closed it?'

'Khazad's outside.'

'Shit.' Griff ran a hand through his hair. 'I was hoping I'd lost him.'

Now that Griff was closer I could see that he looked on edge. There were rips in his clothing, and he had the look of a man who'd been fighting hard. 'What's at the end of the hall?' I asked.

'Locked door. I was trying to get past when I heard

you.' He looked at Luna. 'You got that cube? Maybe that'd do it.'

The four of us came together, Luna staying a little back. I took my hand from my pocket but didn't drop my guard. 'What happened at the entrance?'

Griff grimaced, his hand creeping towards a rip along the side of his coat. 'Khazad and that bastard Onyx tried to take my head off. Didn't miss by much, either. If they hadn't been in such a hurry . . .'

'No one else made it in?' I asked

Griff shook his head. 'We're all there is.'

*Which means it's either you or Sonder.* 'Let's have a look at that door.'

The hallway bent right and left and right again, ending in a sealed door. I studied the door for a second then nodded and walked up to the controls, pulling out a tool. 'I can open it. Griff, I'll need you to throw up some barriers. Khazad's going to be in the hallway before long.'

Griff gave a glance at me and Luna, then nodded. 'Will do. Sonder?'

Sonder jumped eagerly. 'I'll help!' The two of them disappeared back around the nearest corner.

Luna watched them go, then looked at me. 'You think it's one of them.'

I nodded as I began working on the controls. 'Or both.'

Luna stood there for a while. 'Can you tell which?'

'I can't see beyond a choice that hasn't been made,' I said. 'Right now we need them and they need us. Once that changes . . .'

I didn't finish, and Luna didn't ask me to. We couldn't depend on either Griff or Sonder, and our only sure ally was Starbreeze. It was tempting to call her, just for the reassurance of having her around, but Starbreeze couldn't carry Luna, and the air elemental was our one trump card. I didn't want to reveal her to Sonder and Griff until I had to.

'Alex?' Luna asked.

'Hm?'

'Why did you let them go?'

My hands went still. I didn't need to ask who Luna meant.

Why do we do what we do? I think the reasons run deeper than we can know, and often we can only guess at the truest one. 'If you can't have another ally,' I said at last, 'next best thing is to give your enemy another enemy.'

Luna was silent, but I could feel her gaze on me. She knew I was holding something back. I stopped work on the controls and sighed quietly. 'That's one reason. The other one is . . . whenever you kill someone, it becomes a little easier to do it the next time.' I turned to look at Luna. 'You've never killed.'

A shadow flickered over Luna's face. 'I've—'

I cut her off. 'Not the same. I mean deliberately.' I paused, looking at her. 'It might come to that before this night is out. If it does . . . then be very sure about what you're doing. Because either way, you're going to have to live with the consequences for ever.'

Luna stared back at me, then dropped her eyes. After a long moment, I turned back to the controls. It took me a while to get back my concentration.

When I heard Griff's footsteps again, I glanced back to see that Sonder was with him. 'I've set some wards,' Griff said. 'But the lock on the door's going screwy. You sure it's Khazad?'

'It's Khazad,' I said. 'He'll be inside in ten minutes. Your wards'll hold him another ten, maybe less.'

'Can you get this open before then?'

I nodded. 'Give me a hand.'

Griff came forward to help, and Luna stepped back. The minutes ticked by as the two of us worked together, me guiding, Griff using the power of his earth magic to manipulate the controls more quickly than I could. Griff was skilled with wards, and smart enough not to question what I told him. We worked quickly and efficiently.

There was a distant grating from far down the corridor. 'Khazad's in,' Griff said with a grunt.

'So are we.' I pointed. 'There.'

Griff aimed a surge of earth magic, and with a rumble the door slid open. Beyond was a dark corridor. I scanned quickly ahead and confirmed it was safe. 'Sonder, get the lights,' I said. 'You go in too, Luna.'

They obeyed. 'Wait,' Griff said sharply. He pointed back down the hallway, and I turned to look.

There was a scuffle of movement. I spun back just in time to see Griff dart into the corridor after Luna and throw a scattering of gold discs down at the floor where the corridor opened out into the hallway. As they struck the ground they flared to life and a wall of transparent force sprang up, blocking the entrance. Sonder had just gotten the lights working; now he spun. 'Master Griff! What—?'

Griff gestured and a hammer of earth magic smashed Sonder into the wall with stunning force. Sonder's head cracked against the stone and he hit the ground limply, his glasses bouncing away. In the same motion Griff swung back and Luna was slammed against the wall, dull brown energy pinning her arms and legs.

I hit the barrier as Griff turned back to face me. The wall didn't give and Griff watched me struggle for a few moments before giving me a nod. 'Sorry, Verus. Looks like you're staying behind.'

'You!' I snarled, straining against the invisible wall. 'It was *you*!'

Griff shook his head. 'Don't act so surprised. You were recruited by Levistus, same as me. Difference is I'm permanent and you're temporary.'

'Alex!' Luna cried.

Griff gestured and the brown energy flowed up over Luna's nose and mouth, cutting off her breath. I saw her eyes go wide with panic as she struggled to breathe. My fist tightened against the wall of force. I was fewer than five feet away but the barrier was just as unbreakable as the one I'd used on Canary Wharf. 'Griff,' I said, my voice low and deadly. 'If you hurt her—'

Griff ignored me and stood and watched Luna choke. There was nothing I could do and he knew it. After a few seconds he drew his finger down and the energy withdrew just far enough for Luna to gasp in a breath. 'Stay quiet if you want to breathe,' he told her before turning back to me. I willed myself to remain calm. 'You're making a mistake,' I said. 'If we stayed together—'

'Sorry, Verus,' Griff said. 'I'd been hoping to have you around to help with Onyx. But you see, it's *you* Khazad's after. He told me two hours ago. This way I get rid of you *and* him. That's too good a deal to pass up.'

'You want the fateweaver? Take it. Let them go.'

Griff shook his head and started working on the door controls. 'Love to cut out the deadweight, but I need her along. The fateweaver's got a lock that works the same as the front door, and she,' he nodded at Luna, 'is the only one who can open it. Well, her and that cube.'

I looked down at Sonder, lying sprawled at Griff's feet, and hoped desperately for him to get up, but as I looked into the future my heart sank. Sonder was out cold. There was nothing I could do to stop Griff from sealing the door behind him.

'Oh, one more thing,' Griff said. He snapped his fingers and I felt a surge of energy from down the hall behind me. 'I just took down the wards. Have fun with Khazad.' He took a step back towards Luna.

'Griff,' I said. I didn't speak loudly, but there must have been something in the way I said it. Griff paused and looked at me.

Griff was next to Luna, within her danger zone, and I could see the silvery mist of her curse drifting through the bonds imprisoning her. The strands flowed lazily through the air, reaching Griff, soaking into him. 'You are going to find,' I said, my voice soft, 'that Luna is very bad luck for people who try and hurt her.'

Griff looked back at me, and I had one second to remember him like that: stocky and strong, his iron-grey hair mussed slightly from the struggle. He gave me an amused smile. 'I'll take my chances.' He put out one hand and a fist of brown energy smashed the control crystals. The ones on my side flickered and went dead, and with a rumbling sound the door rolled across. I had one glimpse of Luna's eyes going wide in panic, then the door ground shut with a thud.

I was alone in the hall. And distantly, from behind me, I heard Khazad's footsteps coming closer.

\*   \*   \*

Back when I was a prisoner in Richard's mansion, Tobruk would sometimes play cat and mouse. He'd set me loose to run the dungeon, give me a head start, then come after me. Some of my memories of that time are blurred, but that feeling I remember crystal clear. Pressed against a wall, my heart in my throat and my breath coming fast, straining my ears for the sound of footsteps, feeling only dread because hiding *never* worked, Tobruk *always* found me, the only question was when.

Standing in that hallway, I felt all the old terror rush into me. Khazad was coming and he was stronger and crueller than I was, and when he found me he was going to hurt me and he was going to kill me, and there was nothing I could do. I scrabbled in my pocket, pulled out the glass rod and channelled a thread of magic into it, speaking in a rush. 'Starbreeze. Starbreeze, can you hear me? I need you. Please come. If you've ever listened to me, come now, please—'

I broke off as I felt something black and cold open up within me. Starbreeze would hear me, and she would answer . . . but too late, far too late. I turned, searching frantically for a way out, another exit. There wasn't one. All that was left was to face Khazad. Me with my tricks and toys against the full power of a Dark mage. I stood helplessly in the empty hallway, listening to the footsteps draw closer, and I was nineteen years old again, cowering in the dark, paralysed with fear.

And then something spoke inside me, something older and steadier. *You aren't a child any more. You told Luna there's always a way out. Time to prove it.*

I took a deep breath, stood up straight and waited.

\*    \*    \*

Khazad came around the corner like falling night. The Dark mage was a small man, but as he walked a cloak of shadow seemed to gather around him, turning him into something larger and more menacing. The lights dimmed slightly as he passed, and didn't brighten. Black eyes met mine.

'Hello, Khazad,' I said. My voice shook the tiniest bit.

Khazad strode forward without answering. I watched him and wondered as I did how I could have ever thought he looked like a bird. He moved with a smooth, unhurried grace, not taking his eyes off me. I knew he was probing the area, scanning for traps, making sure I couldn't trick him the same way again.

Khazad came to a stop twenty feet away, studying me. 'Where are the rest?' he said at last.

'Griff took them,' I said.

Khazad smiled. 'So he did something right.'

We stood looking for a moment more. 'I want to make a deal,' I said.

Khazad kept smiling. 'Really.'

I gestured down at the bracelet of black metal that Khazad was still wearing. 'I can switch that off.'

Khazad raised his eyebrows. 'Like you did with yours?'

'I can disable the receptor. Stop Onyx from activating it.'

'And?'

'A truce,' I said. 'You don't harm me, I don't harm you.'

Khazad stood looking at me for a moment, his eyebrows still raised, then lifted his hands and sent a bolt of black lightning straight into my chest.

The pain was so intense I didn't even feel it when I hit the ground. My lungs had frozen and I struggled to breathe. Flashing spots swum before my eyes.

'You have no idea how much I've been wanting to do that,' Khazad said thoughtfully. As my vision cleared, I saw he was crouching down in front of me, only a couple of feet away. He was looking at me. 'I told you this was coming.'

'Onyx—' I managed to say.

Khazad smiled, a flash of bared teeth. 'Oh, I'm sorry. You didn't know? I've decided to throw in with Onyx instead of Del. Wasn't hard, after what she did in the forest.' His smile widened. 'Oh, Verus, you should have heard her after I left them in that room, once she realised I wasn't coming back. I wonder if she's still alive. Hope she is. I wouldn't want it to be too quick.' Khazad blinked and looked down at me. 'But what are we going to do with you?'

I started to speak, and suddenly everything went blank.

The next thing I remember is lying against a pillar on the opposite side of the hall. I guess Khazad must have thrown me, though I don't remember it. The back of my head was wet, and my right side felt like fire. Once my head had cleared enough for me to hear, I realised Khazad was talking again. '—and then Onyx told me to go back and kill you! Amazing how things work out, right? Even promised me a reward.'

I tasted copper and spat blood. I knew this was my last chance. *Cat and mouse*, I thought dizzily. *The way to win is not to be the mouse.* 'Only one mage can use it,' I said to the floor.

'I mean, I'd have done it for free.'

I made myself look up. Khazad was strolling towards me, keeping a casual eye on me to see whether I was going to make things interesting. I drew a breath and spoke clearly, meeting his eyes. 'Only one mage can use the fateweaver. That mage is going to be Onyx. Once he has it, he won't need you. You think Onyx is planning to come back to Morden *with* anyone? You think he's going to share the credit? Why do you think you're still wearing that bracelet?'

Khazad stopped and I knew I'd gotten through. I kept pushing. 'Onyx told you he'd take it off if you killed me, didn't he? He's lying. As soon as you've done your job, he'll trigger it. Once he's got the fateweaver, there's no reason to leave you alive. Why do you think Morden didn't care about us being recognised? We were never meant to survive this. None of us were. We're just one more set of pawns—'

'Shut up,' Khazad said. He stared down at me. I held very still, and felt my life hanging in the balance. I knew Khazad was waiting for me to keep talking, but I didn't. Everything I'd said was true. My only hope was that Khazad would realise it.

Khazad stepped forward and held out his right arm. 'Take it off.'

I swallowed. 'I can't,' I said very carefully. 'But I can change it so it won't work.' I began to rise, just slightly.

'Stay on your knees,' Khazad said, and I froze. Khazad touched his left hand to the side of my neck. It felt very cold, and I could feel the tension of a spell hovering in his fingers, waiting to be let loose. 'You have five minutes.'

I swallowed. 'I do this, you let me go.'

Khazad studied me, and I knew exactly what he was thinking. 'Agreed,' he said at last. He held his right wrist in front of me, the bracelet gleaming dully. 'Do it.'

Have you ever had to work under pressure? You

probably think you have. You're wrong. Real pressure is knowing that if you make a mistake you'll be dead without ever knowing what you did wrong.

Believe me when I say I worked *very* carefully.

'It's done,' I said after a few minutes, lowering my tool. Khazad looked down at the bracelet. It looked the same as before. I'd made the same change that I'd made to Rachel's and Cinder's.

'If Onyx triggers it?' Khazad asked.

'Nothing.'

Khazad nodded. 'You said you'd let me go,' I said, my mouth dry.

Khazad looked down at me and I held my breath. His eyes were opaque, dark. Up close Khazad smelled of dust and death, the scent of old bones. I felt the thoughts running through his head, saw the futures shift. Come on, Khazad. I prayed silently. Be a typical Dark mage. Play with your food.

'Go on,' Khazad said, and stepped back.

Slowly I picked myself up. My head spun, and for a moment I thought I was going to fall. My body ached all down my right side where I'd been thrown against the pillar, and my head was pounding. When my vision cleared, Khazad was still watching. I limped away.

Khazad let me get almost to the end of the hall. 'Oh, Verus?'

I stopped and turned. Khazad was standing there, smiling. The hallway was quiet.

As Khazad lifted his arm to cast the spell that would kill me, I made a small gesture with the fingers of my right hand, the same one Onyx had made.

Black lightning surged from the bracelet on Khazad's

wrist, crackling over his body, and the spell he'd been about to throw dissolved. Shock flashed across his face, followed by agony. He hit the floor with a scream.

'Did you know death bracelets work on a signal?' I said to Khazad. The bracelet was still discharging, pouring out lethal energy as Khazad writhed and screamed. I walked back towards Khazad and stopped, my voice absent. 'They're old magic, these things. Not many people study them any more. If you understand how they work, you can change the signal. Make it respond to your command, instead of someone else's.'

Khazad's head snapped up. He glared at me, but all he could do was twist in agony as the negative energy crackled into his body, his limbs, his heart. 'You—' he managed to gasp. 'You—'

I looked down at Khazad without expression. 'I warned you. At the ball. I gave you a chance. But you could never believe it, could you? That someone like me could ever be a threat to someone like you.' I paused. 'Tobruk was the same, you know. Right to the end.'

Khazad couldn't speak any more, but he stared hate at me even as he clawed at the stone. I looked down and I watched the black lightning play over his body, and I waited for him to die.

I didn't wait long.

When Starbreeze arrived I was slumped against one of the pillars. Starbreeze whisked in and hovered over Khazad's body, looking down with wrinkled nose. She was in her elfin form, short sticking-up hair and skinny arms. 'Dead man,' she announced.

'Dead man,' I agreed. I pulled myself to my feet, wincing

at the pain in my muscles. 'Starbreeze, I need to get to the heart of this place. The centre. Can you take me there?'

'Middle?' Starbreeze said in interest.

'Middle.'

'Middle!' Starbreeze swept around me and turned my body to air. I had one last glimpse of Khazad's corpse, then Starbreeze whisked me forward, through the gaps in the stonework, carrying me the last stretch of the way.

The heart of the facility was a huge circular room. Columns rose around the edge, supporting a high-domed roof. There were inscriptions of some kind on the walls, but the light was too dim to make them out clearly. On the columns were magelights, weak and widely spaced, leaving the room just bright enough to see in, yet dark enough to cast shadows. The middle of the room was bare except for a dais at the exact centre. Upon the dais was a pedestal. Two figures stood before it.

Starbreeze set me down behind one of the columns, hidden in the darkness. As I scanned the area I felt other presences. We weren't alone.

'Alex,' Starbreeze whispered.

'I know,' I said quietly. I peered around the column. Griff and Luna were on the dais at the centre, just visible in the gloom. Luna was standing stiffly upright, as if she was being held, and Griff was close. Too close. There was a small cage of force over the pedestal's surface, and something was inside it.

'Men,' Starbreeze whispered.

'I know,' I said again. Griff and Luna weren't the only ones here. I could sense three more: two hiding in the columns to the left, and one opposite. A moment later, I

knew who they were. Cinder and Rachel to the left, and
Onyx up ahead. From where they were standing, they could
see Griff and Luna, but they couldn't see each other.

'Three more,' I whispered to Starbreeze.

Starbreeze shook her head vigorously. 'No!'

'What?'

'Another.' Starbreeze pointed towards the ceiling.

I looked up and saw nothing. I scanned the area and
again found nothing . . . and then had a sinking feeling
as I realised who it was. 'Oh. Right. Her.'

'She's wrong.'

'You can feel her?'

Starbreeze shivered. '*Wrong.*' She swept in a tight circle,
looking distressed. I looked into the futures in which I
moved forward towards the dais, getting a closer look.

The pedestal on the dais was three feet high, and resting
on it was a plain, slim, ivory-coloured wand. A cube of
unbreakable force topped the pedestal, just barely visible
against the darkness. A moment later, I saw why Griff
hadn't opened it. On the rim of the pedestal, just outside
the force barrier, were square holders exactly the right size
and shape to place Luna's cube into, just like the one at
the entrance. Three of them.

Griff was up on the dais. He was holding Luna's arm
twisted up behind her back, forcing her onto tiptoes. 'Think
harder,' he was saying.

'I don't know!'

I focused on Griff with my mage's sight and saw that
the silvery mist of Luna's curse was crammed in so brightly
around him that he looked like a searchlight, the glow so
intense that it actually made it hard to see. I'd never seen
the curse so concentrated, and more and more was pouring

in. Griff twisted Luna's arm a little higher, and she gasped; the silvery mist flowing from her into Griff seemed to intensify. 'Think harder,' Griff said again.

'I don't *know*!' Luna's voice was high, laced with pain. 'How could I know? I've never been here!'

Griff pushed Luna sprawling to the floor. He lifted a hand, and pale brown energy glowed. The stone of the dais flowed and reshaped itself into chains, locking around Luna's ankles and binding her to the foot of the pedestal. 'Well, then,' he said calmly. 'We've got a problem.'

I snapped back to the present. 'I'm going to get her.'

Starbreeze looked upset. 'No!'

I shook my head. 'Let's go,' Starbreeze urged. 'Away.'

'Griff's going to kill her.'

Starbreeze shrugged.

'You don't care. I know.' I looked at Starbreeze. 'But I do. I need you to send a message. Whispering wind.'

'Who?'

'Cinder and Rachel. The two over there.' I pointed, then leaned close and whispered into Starbreeze's ear. '*Cinder, Deleo. It's Alex Verus. Onyx is waiting in ambush behind the column at the north side of the chamber, ten pillars to the left of where you are now. He's expecting you to come from the middle.*'

There was a moment's silence as Starbreeze carried the message, then a whisper floated back. '*Verus, you bastard! How the hell are you still alive?*'

I smiled. '*Hi, Cinder. Before you ask, we've still got a common enemy.*'

'*You think we owe you anything?*'

I didn't reply. After a second, I heard Rachel's voice through the whispering wind. '*Is he moving?*'

'*No.*'

'*Tell us if he does.*'

Then silence. Starbreeze looked at me. 'Gone.'

I nodded and started to plan my course.

'Alex!'

I turned to see Starbreeze floating in the air, gazing at me imploringly. She looked miserable, and even with everything else, I felt a sudden stab of pity. Starbreeze is a creature of whim and freedom and ever-changing movement. Violence isn't in her nature. She was lost here, out of her depth, and I knew her instincts were telling her to flee. One word and she'd take me with her.

'Sorry, Starbreeze,' I told her. 'I can't run this time.' I pulled up the hood of my mist cloak and disappeared into the shadows.

As I circled the room, I reached out with all my senses, keeping tabs on the other mages. Onyx was watching and waiting, a spider in his web. Rachel and Cinder were creeping around towards him, and as far as I could tell Onyx hadn't spotted them. I knew I wouldn't see Thirteen until she struck, so I didn't waste time worrying about her. Most of my attention was focused on Luna and Griff. Once I'd circled far enough I stepped into the open, trusting to my mist cloak and my magic to keep me unseen.

I could make out the outline of the fateweaver through the barrier, and for the first time in days, I was calm. All my decisions were made. I would take the fateweaver and use it. If I succeeded, Luna and I would live. If I failed, both of us would die. As I walked softly forward, I wondered if Abithriax was watching us, pieces on the chessboard all fighting for the same prize.

My circling had taken me behind Griff, and as I crept

across the open stone I could see that he was focused on Luna. 'Put the cube in,' he ordered.

'I don't know which!'

There was the thud of a blow landing, and the hairs on the back of my neck stood up as I heard Luna gasp. 'Figure it out,' Griff said.

'I don't *know*!'

Another thud, and Luna cried out. I sped up, pushing the limits of how fast I could safely move. Griff knelt down next to Luna, giving me a clear view of her. Luna's lip was cut, drops of blood staining her skin. She looked up at Griff, afraid, but Griff's voice when he spoke was suddenly gentle. 'Luna,' he said. 'I really don't have anything against you. You're obviously in over your head here, and it looks to me like you don't have any idea what you're dealing with.' Griff looked at her, his voice steady. 'But you see, I need that barrier opened, and if you can't do it, you're no use to me. So I'm just going to keep hurting you until you try.'

'You said it'd kill me if I pick the wrong one!'

Griff raised his eyebrows. 'Then you'd better make sure you get it right.'

I'd covered half of the distance to the centre. Across the room, I could sense Rachel and Cinder closing in. Onyx hadn't moved. Luna was lying awkwardly on the stone chains that trapped her, breathing quickly.

Then Luna's head came up, and I caught my breath at the look in her eyes. 'I always hated my magic,' Luna said quietly. 'It's taken away my life. But it's what I am. It's part of me and I'm not hiding from it any more.' She stared up at Griff and spoke softly and clearly. 'Die.'

I felt something shift, and I realised that all of a sudden

I could actually feel Luna's curse radiating from Griff, an aura of doom that was almost tangible. I reached the dais, swift and silent, as Griff looked down at Luna and the futures flickered and changed.

Then the futures settled as Griff made his decision. 'You know,' he said, and his voice was quite calm, 'you don't need to be healthy to use that cube. You just need to be alive.'

I saw then what Griff was going to do. Normal people, when something bad happens, get to tell themselves that they couldn't have known. Diviners don't. I knew what Griff was about to do, and I knew that if I tried to stop him he would swat me like a fly.

I held still.

Griff broke Luna's wrist.

Luna's scream was physically painful, like knives scraping down my spine. Griff waited for it to trail away into sobbing, then spoke again. 'Try the cube.'

'I-I-I—'

'Try the cube.'

'I won't. I won't. I—'

There was the sharp *crack* of another bone and Luna screamed again, a heartbreaking sound. I clenched my fists, a fine tremor going down my arms. 'Try the cube,' Griff repeated.

Luna only sobbed.

Griff made an exasperated noise, and I felt him channelling earth magic. I couldn't see what he was doing; the pedestal was in the way. All I could see was the faint brown glow. Then Luna shrieked, and kept on shrieking. It was ear-splitting, but underneath it I could hear a grinding, *scraping* noise, like rock grating against rock. Griff spoke

again, but this time I couldn't make out his words. I dug
my hands into the stone until they bled. I knew Cinder
and Rachel were right on top of Onyx's hiding place. Come
on, I prayed, come on, come on, come on—

There was a roar and a flash of flame. The glow from
the other side of the pedestal snapped out, and Luna went
silent. Griff whirled, searching for the noise, and for an
instant his back was to me. It was long enough.

Griff felt me coming. You don't catch a battle mage
totally off guard, no matter how quick you are. He was
turning back towards me when I reached him, a shield of
energy coming up to block my attack, but I wasn't using
a weapon. I slammed into him in a bull rush, and as I did
I felt Luna's curse suddenly *take*, hard. Looking into the
future, it was as if every strand but one was extinguished.
The one strand that led to Griff's fate pulsed brightly,
becoming real.

Griff staggered backwards, off balance, on the edge of
falling but not quite going over. He kept going far further
than he should have, and was halfway across the room
before he came to a halt.

The shadows around Griff moved. Onyx strode out to
his right, Rachel to his left, Cinder behind. The three Dark
mages formed a triangle with Griff at the centre. Sea-green
light flowed at Rachel's hands; fire burned around Cinder's.
Onyx showed nothing at all. All three noticed Griff at the
same time, and turned to stare at him.

Griff looked up, and there was just enough time for his
eyes to go wide. 'Oh, shi—'

Battle mages have a frightening amount of destructive
power. Mages fighting a duel spend most of their energy
preventing the other from landing a solid hit. It's very rare

for a mage to hit an opponent with all his strength, but when it happens, it's always fatal. One spell from a battle mage can shred a human body like tissue paper.

The effect of *three* of those spells hitting at the same time doesn't bear thinking about.

I won't try and describe what it looked like. All I'll say is that it was over very fast.

Then Onyx and Rachel and Cinder turned their attention to each other, and I dived behind the pedestal as the room lit up with death and fire. 'Luna! *Luna!*'

Luna was leaning against the pedestal, her eyes fluttering. Griff's stone chains still locked her ankles to the pedestal, her right arm was twisted at a horrible angle, and her face was dead white. 'Don't touch me,' she said, her voice faltering. 'It's different, I—'

From the other side of the pedestal I could hear the roar of flame and the flat, deadly *wham* of Onyx's force magic. 'It's okay. Don't move.' I looked around, trying to figure out some way to get Luna out of here. 'We need to—'

I only had a second's warning. I dived sideways off the dais, rolling, just as something swept through the spot I'd left with a *swoosh* of air. As fast as she had struck, Thirteen was gone. I came to my feet and slipped one hand in my pocket, tense, waiting.

Fewer than a hundred feet away a furious battle was raging as Rachel and Cinder hammered Onyx with all of their power, trying to break down his shields and kill him, but I couldn't spare the time to look. I stood on the open stone, and it was Thirteen I was watching for, waiting to see how she would come at me – from the left or from the right or straight above. I couldn't see her, but I could see into the futures where she killed me, and I could see how to move to make sure that didn't happen. Not yet . . . not yet . . .

. . . *now*.

As Thirteen swept in I pivoted, and her claws missed my throat by inches. I kept turning, and as Thirteen flashed past next to me my hand flung a handful of glittering dust over her.

Thousands of the glowing grains of light fell to the floor and winked out, but hundreds more covered the air elemental and clung to her. Thirteen darted away, trying to shake the stuff off, but it had stuck. She was visible now, an outline of glittering particles in the shape of a woman. 'What's the matter, Thirteen?' I asked. 'Shy?'

Thirteen made a final effort to rid herself of the dust, then gave up. As she looked at me her invisibility faded and the lines of her body came into view beneath the dust. Pale white eyes looked at me, and she began to glide forward.

I backed away, a nasty feeling in my stomach. I could reveal Thirteen, but I had nothing that could harm her. 'Listen,' I began, 'maybe we got off on the wrong foot. The truth is, I actually really like air elementals.'

Thirteen kept advancing, and I kept backing away. Thirteen was pushing me back in a tightening spiral, coming closer and closer to the pedestal. I could feel Luna slumped against the base, fighting to stay conscious, the battle still raging behind me. 'You want the fateweaver, right?' I said. 'You need us to get it. If we're dead, you can't take it back to Levistus.'

Thirteen didn't answer, and with a sudden chill I realised that she wasn't listening to me because she couldn't. She'd been made to follow orders and nothing else, and right now her orders were to kill me. Thirteen was getting closer and closer. 'Wait—' I said urgently, and Thirteen sprang, claws reaching for my throat.

Something flashed across my field of vision and hit Thirteen in mid-leap, knocking her sideways. I caught one glimpse of Starbreeze's face, then the two air elementals were rolling away in a blur of motion and slashing claws.

I stared after them for a moment, then turned back. 'Luna!'

Luna had managed to pull herself up against the pedestal, her crippled arm cradled in her lap. Her head was right next to the three receptacles for the cube, and the force barrier holding the fateweaver glowed silently above her, casting a faint white halo around her hair. 'Go away,' she managed.

I crouched down next to her. 'Luna—'

'Go *away*,' Luna said. Her eyes were cloudy with pain, but her voice was clear. 'Not you as well.'

'Put the cube in one of the holders.'

'I don't know which, Alex, just go, I—'

'Close your eyes and guess.'

Luna stared at me. Her eyes were clear again – I think the sheer craziness of what I was saying had shocked her lucid. 'Alex?' she said carefully as the battle raged around us. 'This isn't a good time for making jokes.'

From the far side of the room, there was a hollow *boom* and Cinder came flying through the air. He slammed into one of the pillars with the *crack* of breaking bone and hit the floor. A moment later Onyx appeared. His eyes had gone pitch black and wisps of darkness trailed from his hands as he turned on Rachel. Rachel faced him, and there was no fear in her eyes; beneath her mask, her lips were curled in a silent snarl. From the other side, Starbreeze and Thirteen were a whirlwind of deadly motion.

Two mages, two elementals, two battles; as soon as Onyx or Thirteen won, we were finished. 'Don't choose,' I said to Luna, raising my voice over the sounds of battle. 'Leave it up to luck.'

'I don't—' Luna began, then stopped. Her eyes went wide as she understood.

From behind, I heard Starbreeze give a yelp of pain. 'Alex! Hurts!'

Luna took a deep breath, then pulled herself to her knees, gasping slightly as her right arm shifted. My hands itched to help her but I stood my ground. Carefully Luna drew out the crystal, closed her eyes as the sounds of battle raged all around us, then reached out blindly.

The crystal slotted neatly into the leftmost holder.

There was no fanfare this time. The crystal pulsed, and the force field over the fateweaver pulsed with it. Then the barrier was gone, and the fateweaver was clearly visible: a simple, unmarked wand of ivory. I snatched it up, and—

—silence.

I didn't hesitate. As soon as I felt the momentary dizziness I stepped back, looking around. I could see my body crouched over the pedestal, Luna slumped beneath. 'Abithriax!'

'Well, well.' I spun to see Abithriax walking towards me across the floor, picking his way through the battle in his red robes. Onyx and Rachel were duelling all around him, and a blast of force passed straight through Abithriax's image without touching him. 'Things *have* gotten lively.'

'I need to use the fateweaver!'

'Yes, you do,' Abithriax said. 'Listen carefully. To use

the fateweaver, you and I must merge. I will open my mind to you; my knowledge and skill will be yours. The link requires your willing consent.' Abithriax's eyes held mine. 'Hold back even a little, and it will fail.'

Behind Abithriax, Onyx shattered Rachel's shield into shards of sea-green light. I knew the kind of mind magic Abithriax was describing was dangerous. If I went along with this, I wasn't sure who I'd be when I returned to my body. I looked down at Luna. She was crouched down on the dais, trying to hide from the battle raging around us. 'Do it.'

Something flickered in Abithriax's eyes, then they were smooth again. He nodded and walked up to the dais. 'Then hold out your hand.'

I lifted my right arm. Abithriax reached out, then paused. 'I suggest you brace yourself.' He looked into my eyes. 'This will feel . . . a little odd.'

Abithriax grasped my hand, and everything went white.

# 14

When I came back to my body it was like waking up for the first time.

Luna was saying something, but I barely noticed. I knew exactly what was happening without needing to look. I started walking down off the dais, twirling the fateweaver absent-mindedly in my right hand. 'Starbreeze,' I called. 'Break off.'

Starbreeze tore herself away from Thirteen. Her form was tattered, mist leaking from her wounds. She shot me one terrified look and fled. Thirteen didn't pursue, instead turning back to me, her primary target. She'd shed the last of the glitterdust and as she moved she faded into invisibility again.

Thirteen was the greater threat; I should eliminate her first. I turned my back on her and looked to the other side of the room. 'Onyx!'

Onyx had crippled Rachel, sending her limping into the darkness of the pillars; now he turned to me. 'Rules changed, Chosen,' I told him. I kept walking, placing myself between the two killers. 'Surrender or die.'

Onyx didn't waste time answering. A whirlwind of razor-edged discs of force flashed towards me.

I sidestepped and the attack hit Thirteen just as she swept in at me from behind. She flashed into visibility as the force blades chewed her to pieces. Her mouth opened in surprise, and she looked at me with wide eyes, and for a moment I thought she was going to speak. Then she was nothing but wisps of drifting air.

I looked back to see Onyx staring at me in shock. That attack should have hit me; I knew it, and he knew it. 'Last chance,' I said.

Onyx threw a lance of force at me, followed by a spinning sawblade that could have cut me in half. Next was a series of hammer blows, then a force wave, then he just blasted the entire area in a thirty-foot radius.

He might as well have saved his strength.

The power the fateweaver gave me was beautifully simple. My divination magic let me see what might happen; the fateweaver let me pick what *would* happen. Together, they were invincible. Fighting Onyx was like a chess match where I got to play both sides of the board. Each attack had a hole, a flaw; I lined up each flaw with my own movement so that it would miss. I didn't even move fast enough to break a sweat.

'What the fuck!' Onyx screamed as I walked through the blast, bits of stone chipping and bouncing around me.

I kept advancing, and Onyx backed away. 'Your aim really is terrible, you know that?'

Onyx threw an entire wall of force at me. He was panicking now, and that made it even easier; I found a flaw in the wall, enlarged it, and chose the future where the flaw was aligned with my course. I had to dip my head slightly as the wall ruffled my hair, then I straightened up and kept walking. 'What the *fuck*!' Onyx screamed again. 'I hit you! I *know* I hit you!'

I sprang at him.

Onyx struck with everything he had, but my attack had been a feint and I slipped away as Onyx filled the air around him with missiles. Onyx's strikes were frantic, uncontrolled, and it was easy to curve one of the bolts of force around to strike him in the back. The impact threw him from his feet, blood spattering the stone.

Onyx struggled to rise, gasping, until the sound of my footsteps made him look up. I was walking towards him, and as I did I slid my knife from its sheath, letting its blade glint in the dusk. 'Should have listened when you had the chance,' I told Onyx, and I was smiling as I said it.

Onyx looked up at me, and for the first time I saw fear in his eyes. I knew Onyx was no coward. He could face battle without flinching, but this was something beyond his understanding, and the magic that had been a sword and a shield since childhood had betrayed him. To Onyx it must have seemed as though his world had turned upside down. He made his decision and acted in the same instant, and his body vanished in a mote of darkness as he teleported away. All that was left were drops of blood on the stone.

I came to halt with an annoyed *tch*. If I'd been paying more attention, I could have anticipated Onyx's flight and prevented it. Still, not bad for a first try, I suppose.

'Alex?'

I looked around to see that Luna was the only one still moving. She was still kneeling, chained to the pedestal, staring at me with wide eyes. 'He got away,' I said, unable to keep the irritation out of my voice. 'Stay there.' I began a circuit of the room, checking for survivors.

Griff, needless to say, was very dead. After being shredded, incinerated and disintegrated all at once, what was left of his body could fit in a pencil case. Anyone planning to give him a burial would need a mop and a vacuum cleaner. Thirteen was gone as well, though with her I wasn't sure how permanent it would be. The trouble with incorporeal creatures is that it's always so hard to tell if they're really dead.

The big surprise was that Cinder was still breathing. The back of his head was a mess, and he was carrying a few broken bones, but he was still alive, for the moment at least. I searched his body, then glanced up as I sensed movement.

Rachel was standing a few pillars away. Her mask had been torn away in the battle, and for the second time that day she was Rachel rather than Deleo again. She didn't move. 'Rachel,' I said with a smile, rising to my feet. I lifted the fateweaver and raised my eyebrows. 'Want to try and take it?'

Rachel didn't answer and I walked towards her. 'Don't tell me you're not thinking about it,' I said. 'You're wondering if you can succeed where Onyx failed.' I reached Rachel and began to walk slowly around her. 'Do you think you can?'

Rachel swivelled to stay facing me, limping slightly as she did. Her hair was disarrayed, matted in one place with blood, but her eyes followed me unblinkingly. 'Well?' I said.

Rachel shook her head slowly, not taking her eyes off me.

'Why not?' I leant in and suddenly I was right behind Rachel, whispering into her ear. I could smell her scent, blood and sweat and dust . . . and something else, as well, something that made my nerves quicken. 'You like to kill by touch, don't you? You're close enough. Show me what you've learned.'

Rachel shook her head again. 'Why not?' I said again, softly into her ear.

Rachel was silent for a long moment. 'You'd win,' she said at last, her voice as soft as mine.

'Yes,' I said. 'You were always good at knowing when you were outmatched, weren't you? Not like Shireen.'

Rachel held very still. I withdrew, pulling away from her. 'Now,' I said coldly. 'Why should I let you live?'

'We had a deal—'

I laughed, then, my voice suddenly cruel, and Rachel stopped. 'Did you think I was that stupid?'

There was fear in Rachel's eyes, but there was something else too: she was looking at me with respect for the first time, and I found I liked it. 'Still,' I said. 'You might be some use. But payment is only put off. I'll be calling on you. Understand?'

Rachel nodded carefully. 'I understand.' She stepped away, backing towards Cinder.

I lifted an eyebrow. 'You want him as well?'

'He's all I have,' Rachel said. She spoke simply, and I had the odd feeling that for once she was being honest.

I shrugged. 'He can share your obligation. Go.'

Rachel nodded again, then opened a gateway and started to pull Cinder through it. Her movements as she pulled the big man were oddly tender. Then the gate closed behind them and I was walking back towards Luna.

'I don't understand,' Luna said as I reached the dais. She'd gotten to her feet, and was standing with her arm cradled awkwardly, staring at me. 'How did you do that?'

'Back off two steps,' I said. Luna did, causing the chains to rattle and draw out. As the links stretched I identified the weakest points, created a pair of hairline flaws, then shattered them with two stamp kicks. I turned towards the wall. 'This way.'

'But—' Luna said, then found she was talking to my retreating back. She hurried after me, the broken chains rattling. 'Where's Starbreeze?'

'She'll be fine.' I stopped in front of a featureless section of wall, then spoke a command word. It darkened, then faded away, and I stepped inside. 'Come on, unless you want to stay.'

Luna started, then followed me in. I touched a control crystal on the wall and with a shudder the room sealed itself and began to move.

'Alex?' Luna asked. 'What does that thing do?'

I smiled. 'Oh, Luna, I wish you could feel it. It's like being able to see where you were blind. Watch.' I stepped forward.

Luna flinched. 'Don't!'

I laughed. 'Your curse? That can't hurt me now.' I could see the silvery mist drifting around me, never quite reaching. Occasionally a strand would touch me, but I simply grounded it in the floor, along with the remnants I'd picked up from earlier. It was just as well I'd found the fateweaver when I had; I'd gotten altogether too close to Luna over the past few days. I pointed at Luna's broken arm, and as she flinched I translated her movement into resetting the bone, aligning the fragments into their proper place. Luna gave a yelp of pain, then stopped suddenly, staring down at her arm. 'It doesn't hurt.'

'I did some encouraging of your body's healing system. Once we find a healer I'll have it fixed before you know it.' I raised my eyebrows. 'And what do you say to having your curse lifted?'

' . . . What?'

I laughed again. 'Anything that's possible, I can make

real.' The room came to a sudden halt and one side opened. 'Our stop.'

The journey out didn't take long. Luna trailed along behind me, shell-shocked, as I strode along the corridors, eagerly laying plans for everything I was going to do once I got outside. Before anything else, I'd visit Morden. I was going to enjoy our next meeting, though I didn't think he would. After that, I had a score or two to settle with Levistus. Then there were the others . . .

I was so absorbed I hardly noticed once we reached the exit. 'Hold up the cube,' I told Luna.

Luna hesitated, looked around. We were in a small, featureless room. 'This isn't the way we came in.'

I felt a flash of annoyance that I had to explain things to her, then smoothed it over. 'This is the back door. It'll take us into the countryside.'

Luna hesitated a moment longer, then obeyed, speaking the command words I ordered her to use. The cube lit up and a gateway opened in the wall, carrying with it a breeze that smelt of leaves and grass and cool night air. I stepped before the portal, next to Luna, and looked upwards. For a moment I could see nothing, then I started to make out pinpoints of white light. Gradually the stars took shape before me, and as my eyes adjusted I could see the shape of a hillside, trees silhouetted against the night sky. I stood there for a long moment, drinking in the starlight, basking in the rush of triumph. I'd done it. I'd won.

'Let's go, Luna,' I said. 'We've got a world waiting for us.'

Then suddenly there was a whirlwind in front of me, pushing me away. I jumped back with a curse, bumping into Luna and making her cry out. The whirlwind solidified, taking the form of a waif-like girl with spiky hair. 'Don't!' Starbreeze said urgently.

'Starbreeze?' I recovered my balance. 'What the hell are you doing?'

'Wrong! Don't go!'

'You're in the way.' I tried to walk forward and again found myself in the middle of a whirlwind of air, driving me back. I came to a stop and looked angrily at her. 'Starbreeze!'

Starbreeze didn't move. 'Can't go!'

Luna looked at me in puzzlement. 'What's going on?'

'I have no idea,' I said in exasperation. Starbreeze wasn't intending any harm, else my precognition would have sensed her, but she wasn't budging either. 'You can't go,' Starbreeze insisted. 'Wrong!'

'Maybe it's dangerous?' Luna asked doubtfully.

'Luna, there's nothing out there within a hundred miles that's a danger to me,' I said impatiently. 'Starbreeze, get out of the way!'

Starbreeze shook her head again. 'Wrong.'

I took a threatening step forward. 'You stupid little—'

'Wait!' Luna said urgently, looking between us. She was close enough to Starbreeze to be dangerous, but Starbreeze was focused so desperately on me she didn't even notice. '*What's* wrong?' Luna asked Starbreeze. 'Isn't this the way out?'

Starbreeze shook her head again. 'Can't go.' She stared at me anxiously. 'He's wrong.'

'This is the way out,' I said. 'Starbreeze, move or I'll make you move.'

'Wait,' Luna said. 'What does she mean?'

'Who cares?'

'Wrong,' Starbreeze said again, insistent.

'She keeps saying that . . .'

'*Who cares?*' I wanted to get out of this place, walk outside the boundaries of the tomb and taste the night air, wanted it so badly I could taste it. Starbreeze was stopping me, and that was making me angry.

Luna hesitated. 'Shouldn't we listen to her?'

'No!' I said in frustration. 'There's nothing for us to go back for. We are *done* with this place!'

As I spoke, Luna started. 'Wait!'

I was almost ready to kill Luna. 'NOW what?'

'There *is* someone we need to go back for. Sonder!'

I stared at her for a second. 'Who?'

'*Sonder!* Alex, you saw him, Griff hurt him, don't you remember? He must be back in those corridors.'

'He's probably dead.'

Luna started as if I'd slapped her. 'He's not! He was breathing when Griff took me away. He could still be alive!'

I started to answer and suddenly came to a halt. Luna was right. When I'd last seen Sonder he'd been alive. Griff hadn't killed the younger mage, he'd only stunned him. So why had I been so sure he was dead?

Luna was looking at me as if waiting for something. 'What?' I said at last.

'Aren't you going to . . .?' Luna said. When I didn't respond she trailed off.

'We'll go back for him later.' I didn't want to think about Sonder. I just wanted to get out.

'He might be dead by then!'

'Plenty more where he came from.'

Luna started again, her eyes going wide. 'Why do we

have to deal with this now?' I said in irritation. 'Let's get out of here.'

'I can't believe you're saying this! Alex, you were the one who told him to stay with us!' Luna was staring at me in shock. 'What about what you told me? You said that you shouldn't let someone die if you could help it. I *believed* you.'

'When did I . . .?' I trailed off as I remembered telling Luna that. It had been after we'd helped Cinder and Rachel. Except I didn't really believe it, it had just been something to say to—

No, it hadn't just been something to say. I had believed it. I *did* believe it. Luna was right. I couldn't just leave Sonder back there; I needed to go back and help him.

No, Sonder didn't matter. What I needed was to get out.

Wait, that was wrong. Leaving Sonder in the middle of that maze would be like killing him.

But I didn't care about that.

Yes, I did.

I made a noise and turned away, holding a hand to my forehead. I was getting a headache; it felt like there were two voices in my head at once. I paced back and forth between the walls of the tunnel. 'I don't know,' I muttered. 'Let's just get out of here.' I felt I'd be able to think clearly if I only got outside.

'*No*,' Starbreeze said urgently to Luna. 'Wrong.'

'Shut up,' I snapped. Their voices were making the headache worse. 'I don't—' I turned and saw that both Starbreeze and Luna were looking at me now, and both had the same strange look on their face. 'What are you staring at?'

'Back in the chamber,' Luna said slowly. 'You were ready to kill them.'

'Of course I was!'

'I'm not sorry about Griff,' Luna said. Her left hand moved unconsciously to her crippled right side, but she seemed to have forgotten about her broken arm. She was staring at me intently. 'But I've never seen you like that, not until—' Luna stopped, and something changed in her eyes.

For some reason I felt a sudden stab of fear. I wanted to push past, make a run for the exit, but Luna and Starbreeze were blocking my way now, staring at me. 'What?'

'Alex?' Luna asked, and all of a sudden her voice was very careful. 'What happened when you picked up that thing?' She gestured to the wand in my hand.

I opened my mouth to reply, and suddenly everything was silent and I was standing outside my body again. Luna and Starbreeze were looking at where I stood, but I couldn't hear them any more.

I rolled my eyes. 'Not you *again*.'

'Are you going to stand around all day?' Abithriax demanded, striding into view. He'd appeared right next to me in his red robes, and he looked seriously pissed off.

'Shut up,' I muttered. As soon as Abithriax had reappeared, my headache had gotten worse, bad enough that it felt like someone taking a hammer to my skull. Just talking was making me nauseous.

'Listen, Verus,' Abithriax said. His voice was on edge, tense. 'I've been sitting listening to this conversation and I'm thoroughly bored with it. Just get us outside and I'll teach you to help this Sonder boy however you want.'

'Leave me alone,' I said through clenched teeth. If only

my head would stop hurting. 'Why do you care about getting outside anyway?'

Something flickered in Abithriax's eyes and I stopped. I'd only wanted to shut him up, but that look made me pay attention. I'd stumbled on something Abithriax didn't want me to know. More than one thing. I shook my head. If only I could think straight.

'Look,' Abithriax said carefully. He'd calmed down again and his voice was calm, reasonable. 'I've got nothing against the boy. It just wouldn't be sensible to go back now. If we can get to somewhere with more facilities, then we can . . .'

Abithriax kept talking, but I wasn't listening. I was looking up through the portal at the stars shining down from the night sky. Starlight. What did that remind me of?

'. . . more safely,' Abithriax was saying. 'In any case—'

'The greater power for the lesser,' I said absently.

'What was that?'

'Abithriax?' I said. All of a sudden my headache was gone. I could think clearly again, and all of my attention was focused on the man in front of me. 'How do you know my name?'

'I'm sorry?'

'My name,' I said pleasantly, and I didn't take my eyes off him.

'Well – your friend.'

I shook my head slowly. 'Luna calls me Alex. Not Verus.'

'One of the others, then.'

'Which one?'

Abithriax hesitated. Just for a second his eyes shifted, and I saw something behind them, something calculating and cold.

No, it had always been there, I just hadn't been looking

for it. '*I'll open my mind to you, my knowledge and skill will be yours . . .*' Stupid, stupid, stupid. If I could look into his mind, he could look into mine. Why hadn't I asked how someone who'd been sealed away two thousand years could speak perfect English?

'Why do you want to get out of here so badly, Abithriax?' I kept my voice friendly, but inwardly I was tensing. When I'd merged with Abithriax last time, I'd touched him. He might be a ghost to everyone else, but if I could get close . . .

Abithriax stood still for a long moment, then straightened. 'All right.'

I tried to move, but Abithriax was faster. All of a sudden I was paralysed, frozen. There was no spell or gesture: one moment I was talking, the next rooted to the spot. All I could move was my eyes.

Abithriax walked forward. As he did he seemed to grow in presence, become larger, more *there*, as if until now he'd been holding himself back. The red streaks in his hair and beard stood out brightly, and all of a sudden they made me think of blood. 'You just had to make this difficult, didn't you?'

I couldn't answer. Behind Abithriax, I could see Luna and Starbreeze. They were talking, speaking to my frozen body, but I couldn't hear what they were saying. 'Still, I suppose I should be impressed,' Abithriax said. 'Normally my wielders never even notice. The name was careless of me . . . lack of practice, I suppose, it's been such a long time . . .' He glanced at me. 'You asked how I did it. I suppose it's only fair. I was a mind mage. That was how I was able to imbue myself into my fateweaver. But I always hesitated to make that final jump . . . until the alternative was death. But once I'd adjusted to my new form, learning to control a bearer was quite straightforward . . .'

Luna was standing next to my body, now. She was trying to pull the fateweaver out of my hands, struggling with her one good arm. Starbreeze had joined her, heedless of the pain, and Luna was shouting silently, her face frantic. 'Interesting,' Abithriax said. 'She's worked it out. I think I'll keep her, if she doesn't make too much trouble . . . Where was I? Oh yes. First I took revenge on my betrayers in the Light Council. It took them quite some time to realise what was happening. They'd kill my wielder, but then they'd take the fateweaver for themselves, and of course I'd just start all over again.' Abithriax shook his head. 'And yet even when the last few figured it out, they couldn't bear to destroy me. All that power, you see. So they built me this tomb and sealed me away, hoping to find a way to take my power for themselves. And eventually they stopped coming and I was left to wait out the years, alone in the dark.'

I was struggling to move, but couldn't. I wasn't panicking yet, but things were looking bad. Abithriax was talking to me the way you do to someone who's not going to be around long enough for it to matter.

'And then *you* came,' Abithriax said. 'I hadn't expected it to be this easy. But perhaps I shouldn't be surprised. It may have been two thousand years, but mages haven't changed. Power, power, power.' Abithriax took a final glance back at Luna and Starbreeze, and nodded to himself. 'Well, we'd better get on with it.'

Abithriax placed his hand flat against my chest. For a moment nothing happened, then I felt a draining sensation, as if the strength was flowing out of me and into the man – the ghost – in front of me. I fought against it, trying to pull it back. 'There's no point resisting,' Abithriax said calmly. 'Each time you used my powers you granted me more of a hold. If you'd fought me from the instant you picked me up you might have had a chance, but it's far too late now.'

Starbreeze was still trying to pull the fateweaver away, with no success. Luna was standing in front of me, and I could see she was crying. I could make out the silver mist of her curse clearly, its tendrils soaking into Starbreeze, but curling away from my body. 'There's no need to be afraid, Verus.' Abithriax's voice was reassuring. 'I looked into your memories, and isn't this what you always wanted? To be powerful enough that you needn't be afraid any more? Soon you'll be the most powerful mage in the world. Well, it won't exactly be *you*. But you'll still be in there, watching everything that happens.' Abithriax paused. 'At least, I think so.'

Abithriax's voice was getting stronger, and I realised it was starting to sound like mine. He was taking over my mind, and soon he'd have the rest of me as well. My strength had been drained so far now that if I hadn't been paralysed, I wouldn't even have been able to stand. All I could do was look at Luna and taste despair. *Oh Luna, I'm sorry. All this way, and this is how it ends. I don't want to think about what this man's going to do with you once I'm gone, but I can't stop him. He's going to win, and there's nothing I can do . . .*

The light seemed to be fading, but I knew it wasn't the light that was going, it was my vision. Because of that, it took me a moment to notice what was different about Luna and, when I did, I would have blinked if I could. The silvery mist around her was changing to gold. She was standing close to me, head down as if praying.

'Goodbye, Verus,' Abithriax said, and he was smiling. 'I've never known exactly what this feels like, but I don't think it'll hurt.' *But I don't very much care if it does,* his eyes added.

Behind Abithriax's back, Luna placed her good hand on my body's shoulder, pulled herself up on tiptoes, and kissed me.

The golden light around Luna seemed to flash, then jumped into my body. To me, it felt like being struck with a bolt of energy. I felt Abithriax's hold on me slip, and all of a sudden I was free, my strength rushing back. I staggered, and Abithriax jerked in surprise, staring at me. For a moment he hesitated.

I didn't. Before Abithriax could react I'd caught his wrist, twisted, and come in behind him, my arm locked around his throat. Abithriax choked. 'Surprise,' I snarled into his ear.

'What—?' Abithriax gasped. 'How did—?'

'That was an interesting talk, Abithriax,' I said, my voice shaking with anger. 'I was paying *very* close attention. You said I might have a chance if I'd fought you from the beginning? Let's find out.'

Abithriax was struggling desperately, but I was stronger and better trained. I brought up my other arm, changing my grip to a hammerlock, and I felt Abithriax struggle wildly as I cut off his air and blood supply. 'You'll kill us,' Abithriax managed to gasp. 'If I die – you—'

I tightened my grip and Abithriax's voice trailed off in a gurgle. 'Oh, I don't think so,' I said. 'I learn fast, you notice that? I think you're lying again, and this time you're not getting any more chances.'

Abithriax couldn't speak any more. The side of his face that I could see was red, turning purple. He clawed at my arms, but I only tightened my grip further. Around me, the world was starting to blur, the corridor and Luna and Starbreeze going in and out of focus. 'Goodbye, Abithriax,' I snarled into his ear. 'I don't know if this'll hurt, but I *really* hope it does.'

Abithriax made a last desperate attempt to get free, then went limp. All around me, reality seemed to unravel and fade to black.

When I woke up, I felt as though I'd just taken a long, relaxing nap. I would have liked to stay sleeping, but someone was calling my name and I had the feeling I ought to answer. I shifted slightly and let myself come awake.

'Alex? *Alex!*'

I opened my eyes to see Luna's face. 'Oh,' I said agreeably. 'Hey.'

'Alex!' Luna looked like she'd been crying, and her face was drawn and pale, but she was desperately hopeful now. 'It's you?'

I yawned and looked up. 'Hey, Starbreeze. You stuck around too?'

Starbreeze was floating a little way off, her face anxious. Luna looked back at her happily, then froze. She looked back at me, suddenly watchful. 'Wait. How do we know it's you?'

I smiled. 'Good girl.'

Luna let out a breath and slumped back against the corridor wall. 'It's him.'

I looked to my right. The fateweaver was lying on the floor, an inert wand of ivory. Experimentally I tried to manipulate the futures ahead of me, and found I couldn't. The power had gone with Abithriax. 'By the way, what happened?'

'What *happened*?' Luna demanded. 'I couldn't move you,

and Starbreeze couldn't either, and she kept saying that it wasn't you, and I didn't know what was going to happen, and— *You* tell *us* what happened!'

I closed my eyes and couldn't help but smile. 'Let's just say it's good to have friends.'

We rested a little longer before I pulled myself to my feet. I reached down and picked up the fateweaver between thumb and forefinger. 'Wait!' Luna said in alarm.

'Don't worry,' I said. The fateweaver was a wand of ivory again . . . for now. 'I just think we should put things back where we found them.'

Starbreeze looked at me closely, then nodded in satisfaction. 'Sleeping.' She looked through the portal at the piece of night sky, hopefully. 'Go?'

'Soon,' I said. I took a look up at the stars, then turned back. 'Well, then.' I gave Luna a grin. 'I think we've got someone we need to go back for.'

Luna scrambled to her feet. It must have hurt her, but she was smiling. 'You wait here,' I said.

Luna shook her head, still smiling. 'I think I'll go back with you.'

'Find someone?' Starbreeze asked in interest.

I looked between the two of them, then laughed. I turned and started walking back down the corridor, and both Luna and Starbreeze followed. The power from the fateweaver had gone, but my magic hadn't, and I could still tell where to find Sonder. I didn't think it would take long.

## 15

It didn't.

We found Sonder back in the central room, searching for us amidst the traces of the battle. I think he was under the impression that *we* were the ones who needed rescuing by *him*. I would have laughed, except I was actually pretty impressed he'd been able to follow us at all.

I put the fateweaver back on its pedestal and Luna relocked the force barrier with the cube. It's sat there for two thousand years, and as far as I'm concerned, that's where it can stay.

Luna and I were nearly dead on our feet by the time we stepped out under the night sky of England. A call on the communicator brought Talisid running, who took one look at us and fetched a healer. Luna went out like a light as soon as she was treated. The life mage who mended her arm told me afterwards she was surprised Luna had been able to stay conscious, much less walk.

Starbreeze followed us part of the way back, then got distracted and flew off somewhere. I didn't mind.

The official Council report was released a week later. It stated that a group of renegade mages had launched an unprovoked attack upon a Council research team studying an archaeological find. A volunteer force had mobilised to protect the researchers, and a battle was fought. Although there had been numerous casualties, the only mage to die was Griff Blackstone, the leader of the research team, who had been tragically killed while protecting the mages under his care. The attack appeared to have been random and unmotivated, with no organisation behind it. Several prominent Dark and Light mages were quoted as condemning the attack, and stating that it demonstrated the need for greater integration. The report finished by stating that since the item had been damaged beyond repair, it would henceforth be placed in stasis.

Probably the biggest surprise from my point of view was that no one tried to blame me. In fact, the report singled me out for praise for my 'heroic efforts to protect non-combatants'. I was invited to a ceremony where I was publicly congratulated by a low-ranking Council representative. Before and after the ceremony, I was taken aside by several less public and considerably higher ranking Council representatives and told to keep my mouth shut, or else. I did as I was told. I was fairly sure I'd made enough enemies without going out of my way to look for more.

With the crisis over, the ones who'd been in hiding emerged again. Helikaon returned to his country house, and Arachne came back to her lair.

And I went home.


And that's how it is.

I still run my shop in my quiet little side-street in Camden. Most of the time it's still clueless kids, but I get a lot more mages now. Ever since the affair at the museum, quite a few people seem interested in talking to me. Sonder drops by from time to time, and sometimes he brings friends.

I haven't heard anything from Levistus or Morden, or

from their servants. With the fateweaver out of play, I'm not important to them any more. I've taken precautions though, and it'll be a long time before I forget again to scan ahead for danger when I travel somewhere.

Rachel and Cinder disappeared off everyone's radar and I haven't seen them since. No surprise.

For a week or so after returning I was dogged by bad luck — tripping over, hitting myself, little things going wrong at the worst possible moment — all after-effects of Luna's curse. I didn't complain; it was cheap at the price.

Speaking of Luna, she visits every couple of days now. She still brings me items, but that's not her reason for coming, not any more. Instead we go to Arachne's lair. After all, apprentices need a place to train.

She's started to learn how to control it, you see. That was how she was able to help me against Abithriax; she took the protection her curse gives to her and lent it to me, just for a little while. Since then, she's begun to control the negative sides: keeping it away from people she doesn't want to hurt, directing it where it's safe. She can't do it reliably yet, and her touch is still almost as deadly as ever, but for the first time she can hope that one day that might change.

And as for me? I left something behind in Abithriax's chamber, something that had been following me a long time. And I took away something in exchange, something harder to name. Maybe a sense of purpose, maybe simply knowing who my friends are. The memories are still there, and I still don't fit into either world, but that's okay. There are worse things than not fitting in, worse things than having to watch your back. Rachel taught me that.

My nightmares have stopped too. Mostly.

I think sometimes about Abithriax's claim that he could cure Luna of her curse, and I remember what it felt like to wield that power . . . and I think about the fateweaver, resting on that pedestal within that bubble, locked away to all but those of us who know the secret. I wonder whether I killed Abithriax, or whether he's still there, trapped in the artifact that's become his prison, waiting for the next mage to pick him up. But then I shake it off, and go back to what I was doing.

My world's still not a safe place to be. The proposal to appoint Dark mages to the Council was dropped, but the Dark mages are still out there, still doing what they do in their mansions, behind soundproofed walls. Not all of them stay in their mansions, either. There are things that come out after nightfall that you'd do well to stay away from.

But in my little corner of the city, things aren't so bad. So if there's something you need help with, drop by the Arcana Emporium. It's easy enough to find if you try. You probably won't take it seriously at first, but that's okay.

Seeing is believing, after all.

# extras

# about the author

**Benedict Jacka** became a writer almost by accident, when at nineteen he sat in his school library and started a story in the back of an exercise book. Since then he has studied philosophy at Cambridge, lived in China and worked as everything from civil servant to bouncer to teacher before returning to London to take up law.

Find out more about Benedict Jacka and other Orbit authors by registering for the free monthly newsletter at www.orbitbooks.net

# interview

*Fated* is a fabulous read, a real urban fantasy romp – what is it that drew you to write in this particular genre?

I've always loved urban fantasy – something about the combination of the magical and everyday life appeals to me. I like stories that take fantastical themes and go 'Okay, what would this be like if it was actually around in the modern world?'

You've previously written YA novels, but *Fated* is your first novel for an older audience – what issues did you face, if any, in this transition, and did you find it easier or more difficult writing for adults?

Easier, definitely! My previous novels were quite dark by YA standards, and I'd have editors asking me to lighten the story or cut bits out that they thought were too ruthless. I've always tended to write quite 'serious' stories, so the transition was easier than I'd thought it would be.

Alex Verus's London – particularly Camden – comes to life in *Fated*, almost as a character in its own right as he and Luna fly from landmark to landmark to solve the mystery of the fateweaver. What do you think it is about this city that is so attractive to writers of speculative fiction?

I think it's the sense of history. London's very old and

every bit of the city has so many stories behind it – you have layers built on layers. It's a great setting for fantasy because there's so much material out there waiting to be used.

**As a seer, Alex's enviable ability to view potential outcomes comes into its own in *Fated* when he finds himself in increasing danger from various mage factions. If you had a superpower, what would it be and why?**
Difficult question! Alex's power is incredibly useful, but I think it might be as much of a burden as anything else. Something like flight would be more fun.

**Did you always want to be a writer? What sort of professions were you involved in before you turned to writing?**
I wrote stories as a child, but I honestly never had any intention of becoming a writer until one day I started writing a story and it just kept going and going until it turned into a book. I kept writing through university and after – I've done it full-time for a couple years, but most of the time I've had some kind of other job to support myself. I worked in the Civil Service for almost a year, spent a while travelling as an EFL teacher, and I've been a bouncer too.

**Do you have a particular writing routine, or do you write as and when the muse strikes? And do you have any bizarre or unusual writing-related rituals?**
Back when I was writing full-time, I used to have a routine where I'd write for six hours every day – 12.00 p.m. to

3.00 p.m. and 12.00 a.m. to 3.00 a.m. I got a lot of work done, but I ended up sleeping at pretty weird hours!

**It's fantastic to see that genre fiction of all sorts is finding more and more mainstream readers these days. What do you think is so appealing about fantasy in particular?**
I think it's a combination of things – the fantastic elements, the idea of imagining how something so different would work, the danger and excitement and the focus on good and evil. I loved fantasy and especially urban fantasy when I was younger, so it's really satisfying to me to see it become so popular now.

**Finally, when you aren't busy working on your own novels, what kind of books do you like to read?**
Lots of things! *Watership Down* and *The Lord of the Rings* were my favourites when I was younger, and I also love Agatha Christie – I've read pretty much every book she wrote. Other authors I really like are Jack Vance, Jim Butcher, Paul O. Williams and Orson Scott Card.

if you enjoyed
FATED

look out for

# A MADNESS OF
# ANGELS

by

Kate Griffin

Not how it should have been.

Too long, this awakening, floor warm beneath my fingers, itchy carpet, thick, a prickling across my skin, turning rapidly into the red-hot feeling of burrowing ants; too long without sensation, everything weak, like the legs of a baby. I said twitch, and my toes twitched, and the rest of my body shuddered at the effort. I said blink, and my eyes were two half-sucked toffees, uneven, sticky, heavy, pushing back against the passage of my eyelids like I was trying to lift weights before a marathon.

All this, I felt, would pass. As the static blue shock of my wakening, if that is the word, passed, little worms of it digging away into the floor or crawling along the ceiling back into the telephone lines, the hot blanket of their protection faded from my body. The cold intruded like a great hungry worm into every joint and inch of skin, my bones suddenly too long for my flesh, my muscles suddenly too tense in their relaxed form to tense ever again, every part starting to quiver as the full shock of sensation returned.

I lay on the floor naked as a shedding snake, and we contemplated our situation.

*runrunrunrunrun*RUNRUNRUNRUN! hissed the panicked voice inside me, the one that saw the bed legs an inch from my nose as the feet of an ogre, heard the odd swish of traffic through the rain outside as the spitting of venom down a forked tongue, felt the thin neon light drifting through the familiar dirty window pane as hot as noonday glare through a hole in the ozone layer.

I tried moving my leg and found the action oddly giddying, as if this was the ultimate achievement for which my life so far had been spent in training, the fulfilment of all ambition. Or perhaps it was simply that we had pins and needles and, not entirely knowing how to deal with pain, we laughed through it, turning my head to stick my nose into the dust of the carpet to muffle my own inane giggling as I brought my knee up towards my chin, and tears dribbled around the edge of my mouth. We tasted them, curious, and found the saltiness pleasurable, like the first, tongue-clenching, moisture-eating bite of hot, crispy bacon. At that moment finding a plate of crispy bacon became my one guiding motivation in life, the thing that overwhelmed all others, and so, with a mighty heave and this light to guide me, I pulled myself up, crawling across the end of the bed and leaning against the chest of drawers while waiting for the world to decide which way down would be for the duration.

It wasn't quite my room, this place I found myself in. The inaccuracies were gentle, superficial. It was still my paint on the wall, a pale, inoffensive yellow; it was still my window with its view out onto the little parade of shops on the other side of the road, unmistakable: the newsagent, the off-licence, the cobbler and all-round domestic supplier, the launderette, and, red lantern still burning cheerfully in the window, Mrs Lee Po's famous Chinese takeaway. My window, my view; not my room. The bed was new, an ugly, polished thing trying to pretend to be part of a medieval bridal chamber for a princess in a pointy hat. The mattress, when I sat on it, was so hard I ached within a minute from being in contact with it; on the wall hung a huge, gold-framed mirror in which I could picture Marie Antoinette having her curls perfected; in the corner there were two wardrobes, not one. I waddled across to them, and leant against the nearest to recover my breath from the epic distance covered. Seeing by the light seeping under the door, and the neon glow from outside, I opened the first one and surveyed jackets of rough tweed, long dresses in silk, white and cream-coloured shirts distinctively tailored, pointed black leather shoes, high-heeled sandals composed almost entirely of straps and no real protective substance, and a handbag the size of a feather pillow, suspended with a heavy, thick gold chain. I opened the handbag and rifled through the contents. A purse, containing £50, which I took, a couple of credit cards, a library membership to the local Dulwich Portakabin, and a small but orderly handful of thick white business cards. I pulled one out and in the dull light read the name – 'Laura Linbard, Business Associate, KSP'. I put it on the bed and opened the other wardrobe.

This one contained trousers, shirts, jackets and, to my surprise, a large pair of thick yellow fisherman's oils and sailing boots. There was a small, important-looking box at the bottom of the wardrobe. I opened it and found a stethoscope, a small first-aid kit, a thermometer and several special and painful-looking metal tools whose nature I dared not speculate on. I pulled a white cotton shirt off its hanger and a pair of grey trousers. In a drawer I found underpants which didn't quite fit comfortably, and a pair of thick black socks. Dressing, I felt cautiously around my left shoulder and ribcage, probing for damage, and finding that every bone was properly set, every inch of skin correctly healed, not even a scar, not a trace of dry blood.

The shirt cuff reached roughly to the point where my thumb joint aligned with the rest of my hand; the trousers dangled around the balls of my feet. The socks fitted perfectly, as always seems the way. The shoes were several sizes too small; that perplexed me. How is it possible for someone to have such long arms and legs, and yet wear shoes for feet that you'd think would have to have been bound? Feeling I might regret it later, I left the shoes.

I put the business card and the £50 in my trouser pockets and headed for the door. On the way out, we caught sight of our reflection in the big mirror and stopped, stared, fascinated. Was this now us? Dark brown hair heading for the disreputable side of uncared for – not long enough to be a bohemian statement, not short enough to be stylish. Pale face that freckled in the sun, slightly over-large nose for the compact features that surrounded it, head plonked as if by accident on top of a body made all the more stick-like by the ridiculous oversized clothes it wore. It was not the flesh we would have chosen, but I had long since given up dreams of resembling anyone from the movies and, with the pragmatism of the perfectly average, come to realise that this was me and that was fine.

And this was me, looking back out of the mirror.

Not quite me.

I leant in, turning my head this way and that, running my fingers through my hair – greasy and unwashed – in search of blood, bumps, splits. Turning my face this way and that, searching for bruises and scars. An almost perfect wakening, but there was still something wrong with this picture.

I leant right in close until my breath condensed in a little grey puff on the glass, and stared deep into my own eyes. As a teenager it had bothered me how round my eyes had been, somehow always imagining that small eyes = great intelligence, until one day at school the thirteen-year-old Max Borton had pointed out that round dark eyes were a great way to get the girls. I blinked and the reflection in the mirror blinked back, the bright irises reflecting cat-like the orange glow of the washed-out street lamps. My eyes, which, when I had last had cause to look at them, had been brown. Now they were the pale, brilliant albino blue of the cloudless winter sky, and I was no longer the only creature that watched from behind their lens.

*runrunrunrunrunrun*RUNRUNRUNRUNRUNRUN-RUNRUN!

I put my head against the cold glass of the mirror, fighting the sudden terror that threatened to knock us back to the floor. The trick was to keep breathing, to keep moving. Nothing else mattered. Run long and hard enough, and perhaps while you're running you might actually come up with a plan. But nothing mattered if you were already dead.

My legs thought better than my brain, walked me out of the room. My fingers eased back the door and I blinked in the shocking light of the hundred-watt bulb in the corridor outside. The carpet here was thick and new, the banisters polished, but it was a painting on the wall, a print of a Picasso I'd picked up for a fiver – too many years ago – all colour and strange, scattered proportions – which stole our attention. It still hung exactly where I'd left it. I felt almost offended. We were fascinated: an explosion of visual wonder right there for the same price as a cheap Thai meal, in full glory. Was everything like this? I found it hard to remember. I licked my lips and tasted blood, dry and old. Thoughts and memories were still too tangled to make clear sense of them. All that mattered was moving, staying alive long enough to get a plan together, find some answers.

From downstairs I heard laughter, voices, the chink of glasses, and a door being opened. Footsteps on the tiles that led from living room to kitchen, a *clink* where they still hadn't cemented in the loose white one in the centre of the diamond pattern; the sound of plates; the roar of the oven fan as it pumped out hot air.

I started walking down. The voices grew louder, a sound of polite gossipy chit-chat, dominated by one woman with a penetrating voice and a laugh that started at the back of her nose before travelling down to the lungs and back up again, and who I instinctively disliked. I glanced down the corridor to the kitchen and saw a man's back turned to me, bent over something that steamed and smelt of pie. The urge to eat anything, everything, briefly drowned out the taste of blood in my mouth. Like a bewildered ghost who can't understand that it has died, I walked past the kitchen and pushed at the half-open door to the living room.

There were three of them, with a fourth place set for the absent cook, drinking wine over the remnants of a salad, around a table whose top was made of frosted glass. As I came in, nobody seemed to notice me, all attention on the one woman there with the tone and look of someone in the middle of a witty address. But when she turned in my direction with 'George, the pie!' already half-escaped from her lips, the sound of her dropped wineglass shattering on the table quickly redirected the others' attention.

They stared at me, I stared at them. There was an embarrassed silence that only the English can do so well, and that probably lasted less than a second, but felt like a dozen ticks of the clock. Then, as she had to, as things probably must be, one of the women screamed.

The sound sent a shudder down my spine, smashed through the horror and incomprehension in my brain, and at last let me understand, let me finally realise that this was no longer my house, that I had been gone too long, and that to these people I was the intruder, they the rightful owners. The scream slammed into my brain like a train hitting the buffers and tore a path through my consciousness that let everything else begin to flood in: the true realisation that if my house was not mine, my job, my friends, my old life would not be mine, nor my possessions, my money, my debts, my clothes, my shoes, my films, my music; all gone in a second, things I had owned since a scrawny teenager, the electric toothbrush my father had given me in a fit of concern for my health, the photos of my friends and the places I'd been, the copy of *Calvin and Hobbes* my first girl-friend had given me as a sign of enduring friendship the Christmas after we'd split up, my favourite pair of slippers, the holiday I was planning to the mountains of northern Spain, all, everything I had worked for, everything I had owned and wanted to achieve, vanished in that scream.

I ran. We didn't run from the sound, that wasn't what frightened us. I ran to become lost, and wished I had never woken in the first place, but stayed drifting in the blue.

Once upon a time, a not-so-long time ago, I had sat with my mad old gran on a bench beside a patch of cigarette-butt grass that the local council had designated 'community green area', watching the distant flashes of the planes overhead, and the turning of the orange-stained clouds across a sullen yellow moon. She'd worn a duffel coat, a faded blue nightdress and big pink slippers. I'd worn my school uniform and my dad's big blue jacket, that Mum had unearthed one day from a cardboard box and had been about to burn. I'd cried, an eleven-year-old kid not sure why I cared, until she'd saved it for me.

We'd sat together, my gran and me, and the pigeons had clustered in the gutters and on the walls, hopped around my gran's slippered feet, wobbled on half a torn-off leg, flapped with broken, torn-feathered wings, peered with round orange unblinking eyes, like glass sockets in their tiny heads, unafraid. I had maths homework which I had no intention of doing, and a belly full of frozen peas and tomato ketchup. Winter was coming, but tonight the air was a clean, dry cold, sharp, not heavy, and the lights were on in all the houses of the estate. I was a secret spy, a boy sitting in the darkness of the bench, watching Mr Paswalah in number 27 ironing his shirts, Jessica and Al in number 32 rowing over the cleaning, old Mrs Gregory in 21 flicking through 300 TV channels in search of something loud and violent that when her husband had been alive she had felt too ashamed to watch, it not being correct for a lady raised in the 1940s to enjoy the *Die Hard* films.

So I sat, my gran by my side, as we sat many nights on this bench; just her, me, the pigeons and our stolen world of secret windows.

My gran was silent a long while. Sitting here on this bench, with the pigeons, was almost the only time she seemed content. Then she turned to me, looked me straight in the eye and said, 'Boy?'

'Yes, Gran?' I mumbled.

Her lips were folded in over her bright pink gums, her false teeth inside the house beside her little single bed.

She chewed on the inward turn of them a long while, head turning to the sky, then back to the ground, and then slowly round to me. 'You sing beautiful in the choir, boy?'

'Yes, Gran,' I lied. I may have cried to save my father's coat, but I had enough teenage self-respect to not be caught dead singing in the school choir.

'Boy?'

'Yes, Gran?'

'You cheat at tests?'

'Yes, Gran.'

'I told 'em, I told 'em, but the old ladies all said . . . Angelina has a problem with her left ear, you know? You cheat at tests, boy?'

'No, Gran.'

'Always gotta keep your pencils sharp before the ink runs dry!'

'Yes, Gran.'

Silence a long, long while. I remember staring at my gran's legs, where they stuck out beneath the nightdress. They were grey, riddled with bright blue veins, large and splayed, like some sort of squashed rotting cheese grown from the mould inside a pair of slippers.

'Boy?' she said at last.

'Yes, Gran?'

'The shadow's coming, boy,' she sighed, fumbling at her jacket pockets for a tissue to wipe her running nose. 'The shadow's coming. Not here yet. Not for a while. But it's coming. It's going to eat you up, boy.'

'Yes, Gran.'

She hit me around the ear then, a quick slap like being hit with a thin slice of uncooked meat. 'You listen!' she snapped. 'The pigeons seen it! They seen it all! The shadow's coming. Young people never listen. He's coming for you, boy. Not yet, not yet . . . you'll have to sing like the angels to keep him away.'

'Yes, Gran.'

I looked into her fading, thick-covered eyes then, and saw, to my surprise, that tears were building up in them. I took her hand in sudden, real concern, and said, 'Gran? You all right?'

'I ain't mad,' she mumbled, wiping her nose and eyes on a great length of snot-stained sleeve. 'I ain't crazy. They seen it coming. The pigeons know best. They seen it coming.' Then she grinned, all gum spiked with the tiny remains of hanging flesh where teeth had once been. She stood up, wobbling on her feet a moment, the pigeons scattering from around her. She pulled me up, my hands in hers, and started to dance, pushing me ungainly back and forth as, with the grace and ease of a drunken camel, we waltzed beneath the sodium light of the city. All the time she sang in a little tuneless, weedy voice, 'We be light, we be life, we be fire, te-dum, te-dum! We sing electric flame tedum, we rumble under-ground wind te-dum, we dance heaven! Come be we and be free . . .'

Then she stopped, so suddenly that I bounced into her, sinking into the great roll of her curved shoulders. 'Too early to sing,' she sighed, staring into my eyes. 'You ain't ready yet, boy. Not yet. A while. Then you'll sing like an angel. The pigeons don't have the brains to lie.'

And then she kept right on dancing, a hunched singing sprite in the night, until Mum called us in for bed.

Looking back, I realise now that the problem wasn't that my gran knew more than she was saying. The truth of the matter was, she said exactly and honestly what it was she knew, and I just didn't have the brains to see it.

I stopped running when my feet began to bleed. I didn't know where I was, nor what route I'd taken to get there. I knew only what I saw: the edge of a common or a small public park, a dark night in what felt like early spring or late autumn. Leaves falling from the giant plane trees round the edge of the green – autumn, then. It was drizzling, that strange London drizzle that is at once cold and wet, yet somehow imperceptible against the background of the pink-orange street lights, more of a heavy fog drifting through the air than an actual rain. I couldn't think in coherent words; it was too early for that. Instead, as my brain registered all my losses, panic immersed it like the splashing of a hot shower, preventing any reasoning of where I might go next or what I might do.

I found a dim, neon-lit passage leading under a railway line, that no beggar or homeless wanderer had colonised for that night, and sank down against the cold, dry paving with my knees against my chin. For a long while I did no more, but shivered and cowered and tried to seize control of my own thoughts. The taste of blood in my mouth was maddening, like the lingering dryness of cough medicine that couldn't be washed away. I played again the bright blue eyes of a stranger reflected in my reflection, tried to put those eyes in my face. The memories didn't bring physical pain; the mind is good at forgetting what it doesn't want to recall. But each thought brought with it the fear of pain, a recollection of things that had been and which I would move to some uninhabited rock away from all sodium lamps and men to escape again.

For a brief moment, I contemplated this idea, telling myself that the loss of everything was in fact a liberation in disguise. What would the Buddha do? Walk barefoot through the mud of an unploughed field and rejoice at rebirth, probably. I thought of worms between my toes, fat wriggling pink-grey bodies, cold as the rain that fed them, and we changed our mind. We would run; but not so far.

Instinctively, as it had always been when afraid, I let my senses drift. It was an automatic reflex, imparted as almost the first lesson of my training, the first time my teacher had . . .

. . . my teacher had . . .

*Give me life!*

*. . . a shadow is coming . . .*

*runrunrunrunrun*RUNRUNRUNRUNRUNRUN-RUNRUN

Breathing was strength, the wall was safety. I pressed my spine into it, my head against it. Fingers would not grow out of the wall, claws would not sprout from the shadows. The more of me was in contact with something solid, the fewer places there were for the darkness to crawl, the better it would be. I imagined a great barking dog, all teeth and slobber, squatting by my side to keep me safe, a loyal pet to stand guard when I grew too tired. There were things which could be done, almost as good as a guard dog; but I didn't know if they would attract too much attention.

And so, again, as my breathing slowed, my senses wandered, gathering information. Smell of electricity from the railway overhead, of urine being washed away by the rain, of spilt beer and dry mortar dust. Sound of the distant clatter of a late-night commuter train, carrying sleepy one-a-row passengers to the suburbs and beyond. A bus splashing through a puddle swollen around a blocked drain, somewhere in the distance. A door slamming in the night. The distant wail of a police siren. As a child, the sound of sirens had comforted me. I had thought of them as proof that we were being protected, by guardians all in blue out to keep us safe from the night. I had never made the connection between protection and something we had to be protected *from*. Now the sirens sang again, and I wondered if they sang for me.

My clothes were too thin for the night. The drizzle made them soggy, clinging, itchy and cold to my skin. I could feel damp goose bumps up the length of my arms. We were fascinated by them, rolling up our sleeve to stare at the distortion of our flesh, and the little hairs standing to attention as if they were stiff with static. Even the cold interested us, how disproportionate it made our senses, our freezing feet too large for the space they inhabited, our numbed fingers huge pumpkin splatters across our thoughts; and it occurred to us that the human body was a very unreliable tool indeed.

Crispy bacon.

The smell of pie.

Taste of blood.

Memories of . . .

. . . *of* . . .

Half-close your eyes and it'll be there, all yellow teeth and blue eyes, looking down at you; press your eyes shut all the way and the blood will roll once again over your skin, pool and crackle across your back and sides, tickle against the sole of your foot, thicken in the lining of your socks.

You really want to remember all that?

Didn't think so.

Don't close your eyes.

I rolled my sleeve back down, tucked my chin deeper into my knees, wrapped my hands around myself, folded my feet one on top of the other.

There were other senses waiting to report in.

A little look, a quick gander, where was the harm? No one would ever know; breathe it in and maybe it will be all right, despite the shadows?

I inhaled, let the air of the place wash deep into my lungs, play its revelations through my blood and brain. Here it comes . . .

The feel of that place where I huddled like a child had a sharp, biting quality, thin on the ground, not so heavy as in other places where life moves more often and more densely, but carrying traces of other areas drifting in the air, snatched across the city in tendrils that clung to the commuter trains rattling overhead. What power and texture I could feel had a strong smell, but a slippery touch, retreating from too firm a command like a frightened bird. It gave me comfort, and a little warmth.

I pulled myself up and looked at the white-painted walls, examining the graffiti on them. Most of it was the usual stuff – "*J IS GAY*!" or "*P & N FOR EVER*" – but there was across one wall an orange swish of paint, all loops and sudden turns, that I recognised. It felt warm when I pressed my fingers to it, and tingled to the touch like slow-moving sand. A beggar's mark, delineating the edge of a clan's territory. It was good to find my senses still sensitive to such things – or even, I had to wonder, more sensitive than they'd been before?

Though we could see the advantages, the thought did not comfort me.

I staggered down the tunnel, examining now in careful detail each splash of paint and scratch across the white-washed walls. Messages like:

**DON'T LET THE SYSTEM GET YOU DOWN**

or:

⊠⊠ULTRAS⊠⊠

or:

*Don't lick the brushes*

melted into each other over the cemented, painted surface of the bricks.

One splash of paint at the far end of the tunnel caught my attention, and held it. It had none of the usual trappings of protection that most who understood such things used to defend their territory, but was written in crude capital letters across the wall in simple black spray-paint. It said: 'MAK ME SHADOW ON DA WAL'.

It made me uneasy, but other things that evening were taking priority on my list of concerns, so I ignored it. I had no paint, but dribbled my fingers in the sharp sense of that place and, in the middle of the tunnel, started to draw my own mark on the wall, feeling even that slight movement give me comfort as I made the long shape of the protection symbol, my own ward against evil and harm. Not quite a guard dog; but close enough.